"Well-drawn supporting characters and logistical details or running a prosperous household complement the intricate plot. *Downton Abbey* fans will be delighted."

—*Publishers Weekly*

"Fans will enjoy the continuing exploits of the clever cook, who gets to solve two complex mysteries."   —*Kirkus Reviews*

"The Kat Holloway mysteries are extraordinarily well-written and enjoyable visits to Victorian England, full of detail of lives both 'Upstairs' and 'Down.' The characters are vivid with all the virtues and defects of human beings in any age. I highly recommend the series and am looking forward to the next one."

—*Mystery & Suspense Magazine*

"As always, Jennifer Ashley writes a well-written and page-turning novel."   —Fresh Fiction

"The style is pitch perfect, with varying and authentically voiced dialog combined with well-balanced description and consistent perspective. Ashley's fans will be pleased, but it's also highly recommended to new readers fond of Victorian settings and multilayered mystery." —*Historical Novels Review*

"Jennifer Ashley definitely has a fan in me, and I can't wait to read more in this series."   —Robin Loves Reading

"A top-notch new series that deftly demonstrates Ashley's mastery of historical mysteries by delivering an impeccably researched setting, a fascinating protagonist with an intriguing past, and lively writing seasoned with just the right measure of dry wit." —*Booklist*

"A smart and suspenseful read, *Death Below Stairs* is a fun series launch that will leave you wanting more." —Bustle

"This mood piece by Ashley is not just a simple murder mystery. There is a sinister plot against the crown, and the race is on to save the queen. The characters are a lively, diverse group, which bodes well for future Below Stairs Mysteries, and the thoroughly entertaining cast will keep readers interested until the next escapade. The first installment is a well-crafted Victorian adventure." —RT Book Reviews

"A fun, intriguing mystery with twists and turns makes for a promising new series." —Red Carpet Crash

"What a likeable couple our sleuths Kat Holloway and Daniel McAdam make—after you've enjoyed *Death Below Stairs*, make room on your reading calendar for *Scandal Above Stairs*." —Criminal Element

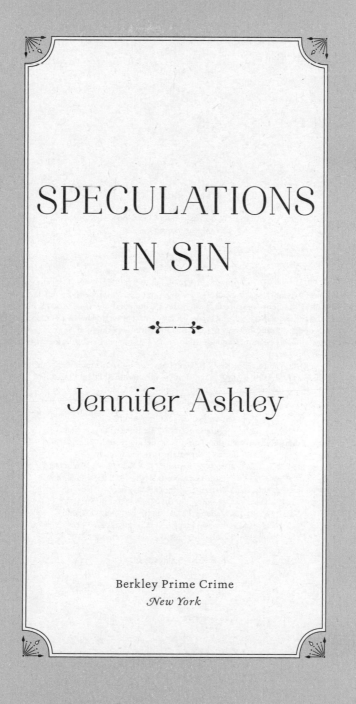

SPECULATIONS
IN SIN

Jennifer Ashley

Berkley Prime Crime
New York

BERKLEY PRIME CRIME
Published by Berkley
An imprint of Penguin Random House LLC
penguinrandomhouse.com

Library of Congress Cataloging-in-Publication Data

Names: Ashley, Jennifer, author.
Title: Speculations in sin / Jennifer Ashley.
Description: First edition. | New York: Berkley Prime Crime, 2024. |
Series: Below stairs mysteries; 7
Identifiers: LCCN 2023037758 (print) | LCCN 2023037759 (ebook) |
ISBN 9780593549919 (trade paperback) | ISBN 9780593549926 (ebook)
Subjects: LCGFT: Detective and mystery fiction. | Novels.
Classification: LCC PS3601.S547 S64 2024 (print) |
LCC PS3601.S547 (ebook) | DDC 813/.6—dc23/eng/20230829
LC record available at https://lccn.loc.gov/2023037758
LC ebook record available at https://lccn.loc.gov/2023037759

First Edition: March 2024

Printed in the United States of America
1st Printing

Book design by Laura K. Corless

I would like to dedicate this novel to my mother, who passed away as I was writing its first chapters. When I was ten, she gifted me a hardback copy of the Writer's Market *and never ceased believing that I'd one day become a published author. She was proud of me to her last day.*

1

January 1883

I was finishing a pleasant visit on my day out with Joanna Millburn, the friend of my youthful days who looked after my daughter, when I detected that something was very wrong.

The windows of Joanna's cozy sitting room were already dark, the blustery winter day at an end. The time was nearing when I must reluctantly take my leave and return to Mount Street, where I was a cook in a fine Mayfair household.

Setting down my teacup, I sent Grace from the parlor with the excuse that I wanted a recipe for tea cakes from Joanna's hardworking cook. Grace eagerly dashed away, closing the door behind her, as she'd been taught, to keep out drafts.

Once we were alone—the four Millburn children were in their father's study, attending to their books—I turned a severe eye on Joanna. "Tell me quickly, before Grace returns. What is troubling you?"

Joanna started so forcefully that the dregs of her tea splashed from the cup. She wiped the droplets from her wrist with agitated fingers.

"Whatever do you mean?" She tried valiantly to sound surprised, but her voice trembled.

"My dear, I have been your friend since we were tykes in pigtails. I know when something is the matter. You had better tell me at once. Grace will only be a moment."

Joanna continued to stare at me as though she could not imagine why I thought all was not well in her idyllic world. I continued with my persistent gaze, until at long last, she wilted.

"Kat, I don't know what I am to do." Joanna set down her cup and balled her hands in her lap. "Samuel's firm has threatened to sack him. We eke out a living as it is—if he loses this post, we'll be destitute."

My own cup clattered to its saucer. "Oh, darling, no." I reached for her tight hands and clasped them hard.

Such a situation would be dire. Sam and Joanna had four children of their own. The oldest, Matthew, was a bright boy, and they'd hoped to find a tutor for him so that he might have a chance to attend university in a few years. They also had to pay the rent on this modest home in a lane off Cheapside, an area so much better than the rookeries they'd likely inhabit without Sam's clerk's job at a private international bank.

There was another obvious consequence of Sam out of a job, one I knew Joanna did not want to voice. Without Sam's income, they would no longer be able to take care of Grace.

I sent Joanna as much money as I could for her upkeep, but the Millburns paid quite a bit out of their own pocket. Five children to feed took a hefty toll, and if Sam was dismissed, gone would be the hopes for Matthew's education. I would have to ease their burden and house Grace elsewhere, but at this moment, I had no idea where that would be.

"Why would they sack him?" I demanded. "I should think Samuel Millburn is a model clerk."

"They have accused him of embezzling funds." Tears filmed Joanna's eyes. "They haven't stated this outright as yet, but the hints are there. They are trying to shame him into confessing or leaving on his own. But Sam has done nothing wrong. I know it."

I knew it too. Samuel Millburn would no more embezzle than he would grow wings and fly. I'd known Sam since he'd come to woo Joanna fifteen years ago, when she'd still been living in Bow Lane next door to me and my mum. He'd fallen madly in love with her and devoted himself to her, and nothing much had changed since. I'd been a bridesmaid at their wedding in Bow Bells church, so happy for my friend and yet lonely for losing her.

But I'd never found anything objectionable in Sam. Through the years, he'd proved to be a good friend to me as well. In his professional life, he was respectable, punctual, capable, and dogged, all the qualities any employer would wish.

I read stark fear in Joanna's eyes. She loved her husband, believed in him, but I saw her flash of doubt, and the misery that engendered.

"Joanna, I will tell you right now that this is absurd," I said firmly. "Samuel would never do such a dishonest deed. I know it, and so do you."

"He has been working so hard, and with so little acknowl-edgment." The words were faint, ones Joanna must have been repeating to herself, afraid to state them out loud.

"I assure you, it is nonsense. If Sam were annoyed, he'd simply take things up with his head clerk. It would never occur to him to sneak money from his accounts. There are few honest men in the world, but Sam Millburn is one of them."

"I believe him." Joanna sent me the look of someone begging to have their fears proved wrong. "I am his wife. Of course I do."

"It has nothing to do with being his wife," I said sternly. "Whether he is married to you or not, he would never steal from his employer."

Joanna slid her hands from mine and rested them on her brown wool skirt. "You are right, Kat. I know you are. But that niggling voice inside me asks: What if I am wrong?"

"You are not. Samuel would never embezzle, and we both know it."

"But what are we to do?" Joanna's question held despair.

What indeed? I unfortunately had witnessed such situations a time or two in my life. An important person committed a crime, and the blame was shoved off onto someone deemed not so important. The insignificant man—or woman—was arrested and made to pay, thus preserving the reputations of the lofty. The scapegoat was inconsequential—except to his wife and children who would be destitute and share his shame and ruin.

I could not let that happen to Joanna and her sons and daughters.

"I will look into it," I said with assurance. "Never worry, dear Joanna. I will find out who has truly done the embezzlement and clear Sam's name."

Did Joanna clasp her hands, gaze at me in adoration, and thank me profusely? No, indeed. Her face fixed in tired lines, fear exhausting her.

"How can you, Kat? I know you have helped the police before, but these are men of the City. Wealthy men, from prominent families. They have power, influence, and a long reach. They care nothing for the likes of Sam Millburn." The tears in her brown eyes spilled to her cheeks.

I leaned to her and rested my hand on her knee. "I cannot tell lords and dukes what to do, no. But I know people who can—honest men and women who have influence. I promise you, my friend, I will leave no stone unturned until I prove that Sam is innocent."

Again, Joanna did not hug me to her bosom and weep with relief. I saw a flicker of hope in her eyes, but it was quickly suppressed.

"It is kind of you, Kat."

I held up my hand before she could try to tell me why I shouldn't bother. "You leave it to me. I will be discreet—do not worry."

Joanna opened her mouth to argue further, but the door swung open, and Grace danced inside, a folded paper in her hand. Joanna lifted her teacup again, while I took the recipe from Grace and praised her for writing it out so neatly.

The time had come when I must leave my daughter for the reality of my drudgery. I pushed the thought aside and hugged Grace, memorizing the feeling of my daughter in my arms. That memory would have to sustain me until I could visit again.

I tried to give Joanna a reassuring smile as I departed, but I left a woman dejected. Grace began to tell Joanna of the sights she and I had seen on our walk today, and Joanna tried to brighten. She'd never let her troubles upset the children.

I stepped out of the house into the cold winter air, the lane that led to Cheapside already dark. I adjusted my hat and trudged toward the main street, in search of an omnibus to take me back to Mayfair.

The lack of light went with my mood. I had vowed to make everything right for Joanna, but she spoke the truth. The powerful and wealthy would throw Sam to the wolves to save themselves, and I, a woman and a domestic servant, had even less influence in the world than Sam did.

I pondered the problem as the crowded omnibus bumped across the Holborn Viaduct and along to Oxford Street. I descended at Duke Street to continue on foot south through Grosvenor Square to South Audley Street and so to Mount Street. A hansom could take me home faster, but Mrs. Bywater, the mistress of the house, would have much to say about a cook who got above herself being dropped off in a hansom at her doorstep.

As I walked through the cold, flakes of snow settling on my coat, I confessed to myself that I had little idea how to begin on Joanna's troubles. The few men I counted as my friends concerned themselves with science or police matters, not finance.

Mr. Bywater, nominally the head of the household that employed me, worked in the City, but I had no idea what he did. I'd never been much interested in his day besides knowing what he liked on his dinner table by the time he returned home.

I could not openly seek Mr. Bywater's help, because I'd have to explain who Joanna was. Such information might inadvertently reveal that I had a daughter—a fatherless one, at that—whom I was supporting in secret.

Nothing for it, but I would have to turn to the one person I did not want to be obligated to, for reasons I did not quite understand. Daniel McAdam had been nothing but good to me, but I supposed I feared to be under the power of a man ever again. Grace's father had ensnared me, lied to me, and then left me destitute. I'd believed myself married to him, but that had turned out to be false.

Daniel would never do such things to me, I understood. He would help, for Grace's sake, if nothing else. He'd become quite fond of Grace, and Grace of him.

For Joanna, I decided, I'd seek Daniel's aid. Daniel was familiar with all sorts of crimes, from brutal murder to clever fraud to forgeries to treason. I wouldn't be surprised if he already knew, or knew something about, all parties involved in the embezzlement at Sam's bank.

I'd reached Mount Street by the time I finished my musing and descended the outside stairs to the warmth of the house. I had to pass through the scullery, and greeted Elsie, the scullery maid, who was elbow deep in water, scrubbing pots.

"Did ye have a nice day out, Mrs. Holloway?" she asked over the clanking in the sink.

"It was quite pleasant, thank you, Elsie," I replied absently as I moved past her to hang up my coat. I unpinned my hat but would carry that upstairs to put away safely when I changed my clothes. "Is all well here?"

"Think so. Mr. Davis has gone out and not come back, and isn't Mrs. Redfern annoyed about that?"

This information penetrated the haze of my thoughts. Mr. Davis, our butler, rarely took a day out. That he'd chosen to depart on a Thursday, which everyone knew was my full day off, was curious.

"I'm certain he will return in time for supper." I continued into the kitchen, where Tess, my assistant, bent over the work table, slicing potatoes like a mad thing. "Good afternoon, Tess."

Tess ceased banging her knife and glanced up at me without her usually cheery expression. "I'm that glad to see you, Mrs. H. Mrs. Redfern is in a right state."

From the loudness of this proclamation, I gathered that Mrs. Redfern, the housekeeper, must be above stairs where she could not hear us.

"I'm certain everything will be well, Tess. Do carry on."

Tess's knife began thumping away again, so much so that I feared for the condition of the potatoes. Telling myself that Tess had things in hand, I slipped out and along the slate-tiled corridor to the back stairs.

The door to the butler's pantry was shut, and no light flickered under the crack beneath it. On impulse, I tried the handle, but the door was locked.

I reasoned, as I mounted the stairs, that Mr. Davis's affairs when he was not in the house were his own. His outing must have been important, and I had no doubt he'd soon return. He'd never let the footmen attend supper without his eagle-eyed supervision, especially when Mr. and Mrs. Bywater had guests, as they did this evening.

Upstairs, I swiftly changed into my gray work dress. I shook out and brushed my good brown frock, before hanging it in the wardrobe. The hat went into its box on the wardrobe's top.

I'd been able to acquire a few more pieces of furniture for my small room: a bureau that held my washbasin and undergarments, and this wardrobe. I didn't have many gowns—two besides my work frocks—but Lady Cynthia, the Bywaters' niece, had insisted Mrs. Bywater put some cast-off pieces of furniture in my room. Mrs. Bywater, who didn't want the bother of hiring someone to lug the unused furniture away, allowed Cynthia this indulgence.

I'd done perfectly well without all these furnishings, but

Cynthia was trying to be kind. I admitted it was nice to have a place to keep my best and second-best gowns free of dust.

After washing the soot of London's coal smoke from my face and hands, I descended to the kitchen again. I needed to pay attention to the meal, I decided as I began to help Tess chop vegetables at the table—we'd have ten at dinner tonight—but my mind strayed back to Joanna and her troubles.

Poor Sam. He worked hard to provide for Joanna and his four children, and uncomplainingly had taken in my daughter when I'd turned up on their doorstep with her nearly thirteen years ago. I'd been a wretched and terrified woman, sobbing in their parlor, my babe in my arms. Grace, always sensitive to atmosphere, had been crying as well.

Joanna, my dearest friend since we'd been tiny girls, had pulled me into her embrace and promised she'd do anything in the world for me and Grace. Sam had sat down with us and assured me that we could devise a way to keep Grace safe while I sought a position in a kitchen.

Their compassion brought tears to my eyes now, blurring the leeks I was slicing for a soup à la julienne.

"Mrs. H.?" Tess's voice shook me from my thoughts. "How many slices of these potatoes do ye want? I've done about a thousand, I think."

She exaggerated, but she did have a heaping pile of creamy white potatoes on the cutting board.

I brought myself back to the present. I needed to cook, not woolgather.

"That should be sufficient," I said, trying to be my usual brisk self. "Now, I see you have some water simmering. Excellent." I had instructed her that a pot of hot water must always be available on the stove, as it took too long to heat the water every time one wished to cook a vegetable. "We will boil those and then put them in a pan with butter, parsley, and a bit of leftover velouté sauce. Then we'll heat that in the oven, season with lemon juice, and send it up with the roast."

"Mmm." Tess closed her eyes, savoring the dish in her mind. "What's that called, then?"

"Potatoes à la maître d'hôtel," I informed her. I'd also tear up winter greens for a salad and finish the meal with both a gâteau with orange liqueur sauce and a lemon tart. It was the season for citrus, which both ripened in hothouses and was brought in by ship from the world over.

"That's a funny name," Tess said about the potatoes. "What's it got to do with a hotel?"

Usually, I had a lecture prepared to explain the origin of dishes, but today I hadn't the fortitude. My worry about Sam was increasing as the kitchen filled with the sounds and scents of our cooking. I could stoutly proclaim Sam would never dream of stooping to theft, but the lofty men who ran his bank could make him take the blame no matter what.

What happened to Sam if he was shut up in a prison? What happened to Joanna and her children? To Grace?

"You all right, Mrs. H.?" Tess once more jerked me from my doleful contemplation.

"Yes, I am perfectly fine," I said. There was no use in giving way. I'd have a good night's sleep and make a start on the problem in the morning.

"It's just that you've torn that lettuce into teeny little bits. No one will be able to lift that on a fork, try as they might."

I looked down and saw that yes, my hands had shredded the pieces of dark green and red lettuce until they were nearly minced. I gathered them up and dropped them into the bowl of carrots Tess had already cut into matchsticks, following those with the leeks I'd chopped.

"I'll put all this into the soup. A bit of lettuce gives it body. Now, cease gawping at me and put those potatoes on. They won't cook themselves."

Tess sent me an aggrieved look, not happy being admonished when she'd done nothing wrong. I tamped down on my anxiousness and tried to get on with the meal.

We made good headway, though I had to fold my lips to keep from snapping when Tess dropped a potato slice and spilled the salt. Not her fault my dearest friend's world was crumbling and possibly taking mine with it.

Finally, the meal was finished, the platters loaded onto the dumbwaiter, which Tess cranked upward to the footmen in the dining room. The dishes weren't much different from what I'd do for a family supper, though there was a larger quantity in each. Mrs. Bywater had invited several of her friends and their husbands to dine tonight. Lady Cynthia had been coerced into attending, which she'd promised to grit her teeth and bear.

Just before eight o'clock, when supper was to be served, Mrs. Redfern hastened into the kitchen, her heeled boots clicking in an agitated fashion.

"Mr. Davis still has not returned," she announced. "The footmen are milling about in disorder and the wine hasn't been opened or decanted. The master is not best pleased. Whatever are we to do, Mrs. Holloway?"

2

M rs. Redfern's distress grated on my already raw nerves. "What on earth *can* we do, Mrs. Redfern?" I snapped. "Do you wish me to go above stairs and serve the dishes myself? Open the wine at the sideboard so Mr. Bywater won't be unhappy?"

Mrs. Redfern stared at me in astonishment. I rarely snarled at her or any of the staff, but at the moment, lack of a butler in the dining room was the least of my troubles.

"If Mr. Bywater is upset, he can have all of us dismissed." Mrs. Redfern's crisp tones returned. "Mrs. Bywater's rants can be brushed aside, but *Mr.* Bywater has a bit more authority. When I see Mr. Davis, I will shake him hard."

I half expected Mr. Davis to glide smoothly into the kitchen on her last words, inquiring in his mild tones if she would truly do such a thing.

The doorway remained empty, however, Mr. Davis noticeably absent.

"I apologize, Mrs. Redfern," I made myself say. A household in which the staff was at one another's throats was a miserable one, I well knew. "I have had a trying day, and having to cook a large meal on top of that has made me short-tempered. I will open and decant the wine before it's sent up. You can pour the wine and supervise the footmen—you have the necessary dignity for the dining room."

"I should hope so." Mrs. Redfern's color rose as she strove to check her anger. "Very well, then. Let us pray that Mr. Davis set out the wine for the evening, so we don't blunder and serve the wrong sort."

"I do know something about wine," I said. "What goes with what dish, I mean. I used a bit of what he serves in my cooking."

I wiped off my hands and moved past her on the way to the butler's pantry. I tried to ignore Elsie and Tess, standing together in the scullery doorway, eyeing Mrs. Redfern and me in consternation.

Mrs. Redfern had the keys to unlock the butler's pantry. I did as well, in case I needed a certain wine when Mr. Davis wasn't available, but I let her lead. She opened the pantry and lit the sconce beside the door, its faint yellowish glow soft in the dark room.

Thankfully, Mr. Davis had set out two bottles of Beaujolais and one Viognier on the large table near the silver chest.

I had become skilled at opening bottles and decanting wine. The butler in one house I'd worked for had had the unfortunate tendency to drink half the bottles before they reached the table, so I'd taken over the task of preparing the wine and placing it on the dining room sideboard. I'd let that butler choose the wines, however. He'd had excellent taste and thorough knowledge of viticulture—probably learned by imbibing every sort of wine imaginable.

The white would be served directly from the bottle, but reds gained in flavor from interacting with the air. Decanting the red wines prevented any sediment in the bottom of the bottle from ending up in an unlucky diner's glass.

Under Mrs. Redfern's watchful gaze, I uncorked the Beaujolais and lifted the decanter. Holding the decanter at a slight angle, I let the bloodred wine trickle into it from the bottle. When I spied grit in the bottle's neck, I quickly upended it, halting the flow.

I stoppered the decanter, placed it and the unopened bottle of white wine onto a tray, and presented the whole thing to Mrs. Redfern.

"I can carry it up for you, if you like," I offered, trying to be civil.

"No, thank you. I will manage." Mrs. Redfern all but snatched the tray from me and marched away, her footsteps loud on the board stairs. She navigated the door at the top without hazard, letting it bang shut behind her.

I smothered a sigh and returned the Beaujolais bottles to the table. I started to exit the room, then halted and surveyed it by the steady light of the sconce.

What clues I thought I'd find to Mr. Davis's whereabouts, I didn't know. I saw nothing at all to indicate where he'd gone. His coat and hat were missing, but of course he'd have taken those, as the January day was freezing.

He'd left the corkscrew I'd used near the decanter and bottles, as though he'd meant to return soon and open them. Two more bottles rested on a small table near the door, but I did not know what he'd intended those for.

Nothing in the room indicated that Mr. Davis hadn't planned to be in the house in time for supper.

I left the butler's pantry, locking the door behind me.

In the kitchen once more, I continued clearing up the mess from cooking supper, and began preparations for the next morning. A kitchen never truly rested.

In addition to the water I kept simmering on the stove, I also had a pot of stock on the warming burner. I could quickly add this to soups, use a portion to make gravy, or to boil it down into demi-glace—a rich thickener for sauces.

I moved to this pot to give it a stir, and remained there, the spoon going around and around while I stared at the wall.

"Everything all right, Mrs. Holloway?"

I jumped. Tess stood behind me, a rag in her hand and concern in her eyes. Her freckled face was smudged with flour and grease, her hair straggling from under her cap. Tess had worked very hard while I'd been out. I ought to be praising her, not ignoring her.

"Yes, I am fine." I laid down the spoon. "You did well today, Tess. You will soon be ready to cook meals all on your own."

Instead of flushing in pleasure, Tess's eyes rounded, and her face lost color. "Oh, Lord, Mrs. H. Ye ain't thinking of leaving, are ye? I can't do this without you, and that's a fact. Ye can't go. *Please.*"

Her voice rose through this speech, ending on a near wail.

"Whatever are you talking about?" I asked in bewilderment. "I have no intention of going. What has gotten into your head?"

Tess's lower lip quivered. "Ye said ye had a trying day, you're cross with Mrs. Redfern and me, and you nearly put a handful of salt in that soup. Would have if I hadn't stopped ye."

True, I had thought I'd reached for arrowroot to give the soup a little thickness, but my hand had closed around the salt bowl instead.

"Yes, I know I've been a bit pensive this evening . . ."

"More like not yourself at all," Tess contradicted. She took a step closer, lowering her voice so Elsie in the scullery would not hear. "Anything wrong with your little girl? Is she ill?"

Her concern for Grace touched my heart, and I softened. "No, no, nothing like that. She's well and bonny. No, my friend Joanna has had a bit of trouble, that is all. I am trying to decide how to help her."

Penetrating the world of high finance was nothing like investigating missing paintings from the home of Lady Cynthia's friend or even a murder in this house or next door.

I only ever went to the City to visit my daughter or to find comestibles at special markets like Smithfield or the many shops in Cheapside. I rarely ventured down Poultry, Threadneedle Street, or Cornhill, where the Bank of England, the Royal Exchange, and other houses of high finance lay. That was a closed territory to me. I turned over most of the pay I received to Joanna for Grace's keeping and kept the remainder well hidden in a box in my chamber.

"If there's anything I can do, you say the word," Tess stated.

Her eagerness to assist disarmed me. "Thank you, Tess. That is good of you. I did not exaggerate when I said you did a fine job today. You have a talent for cooking."

Tess did flush now and dropped me a habitual curtsy. "You're that kind to me, Mrs. H."

"It isn't kindness—it is the truth. Cease all your nodding and bobbing and get on with scrubbing the table."

Tess grinned as I spoke in my more usual tones. She skipped back to the work table and plied her rag with vigor.

I thought that would be the end of it, but as I sorted through the remains of today's meals, deciding what to tuck into the larder for later, Lady Cynthia appeared in the kitchen doorway.

She'd dressed in a frock tonight, as she'd attended supper

with her uncle's guests. This gown was a dark blue, with an easy swing to its straight skirt and a close-fitting but not overly tight bodice. No bustle, no multitude of lace, ribbons, and cloth flowers, and no waist cinched into impossible proportions.

Cynthia's artist friend, Miss Judith Townsend, who dressed in a similar fashion, had influenced Cynthia into having these sorts of dresses made up. Cynthia's aunt, Mrs. Bywater, expressed dismay that Cynthia did not bedeck herself in layers of fabric over a creaking cage, fearing she'd never attract a gentleman without them. Mrs. Bywater herself dressed quite plainly, but I suppose she justified that with the fact that she was already married.

Cynthia strode into the kitchen when she saw that only Tess and I were there. She halted in the middle of the flagstone floor and regarded me quizzically.

"What has happened, Mrs. Holloway?"

"Pardon?" I continued separating the leftover food. The beef from the roast would become a cold aspic or be put aside for a quick bite with a bit of bread tomorrow.

"You know exactly what I mean. Davis did not serve at table tonight, which must mean the Second Coming is imminent. And while your meal was good as always, it didn't have your usual flair."

I ceased scooping up leftover potatoes and gazed at her in dismay. "Did the guests complain? Did Mrs. Bywater? Which dish was off?"

"None of them," Cynthia answered with impatience. "The guests raved, and said they never ate so well in their lives. Aunt and Uncle didn't notice either. But you've rather spoiled me, and I can tell the meal wasn't your best. Which means something is wrong. You had better tell me at once, so we can solve the problem, and I can return to the one thing in this house that is worth living for—your food."

Her mixture of flattery and command would amuse me any other time. I shot a look across the passageway to the servants' hall, where the footmen, finishing their own meals, had become loud and unruly. Without Mr. Davis to tame them, they took the opportunity to shout at one another and even pitch hard-crusted rolls across the table. Rolls it took two days to make, the wretches.

"I cannot speak to you here—"

"The housekeeper's parlor, then," Cynthia said. "Mrs. Redfern is upstairs still tending the guests, and we will be private there." She swung out of the kitchen and paused at the servants' hall. "Oi, you lot. Cease your bellowing, or Auntie will be down here demanding you lug things about for her."

The volume receded quickly. "Sorry, your ladyship," one of the footmen muttered. Cynthia moved on down the hallway, expecting me to join her.

"You go on, Mrs. H.," Tess said. "I'll finish up here."

I knew Tess wanted very much to know what troubles I had found on my day out but bravely suppressed her curiosity. She no doubt hoped I'd confide in her later.

I wasn't certain I wished to confide in anyone, as the problem was not my own. Joanna would hardly want it put about that her husband was suspected of embezzlement. So many people were quick to believe what was said about anyone without the first shred of proof.

I removed and rolled up my stained apron, dropping it on a chair before I left the room. My feet ached with the walking I'd done today as well as moving about the hard stone floor of the kitchen.

It was a relief to sink onto one of the soft chairs in the housekeeper's parlor. They were mismatched—castoffs from upstairs—but none the less comfortable for it.

Cynthia closed the door behind us and sat on the horse-hair Belter chair. "Now then, out with it. Is your daughter all right?"

Her voice softened as she spoke. As when Tess had expressed concerned, my barriers crumbled, and tears wet my eyes.

"Grace is well." I blinked quickly. Weeping about this would help nothing. "But Joanna—Mrs. Millburn—my greatest friend. She—"

"Oh dear." Cynthia leaned to me, resting a smooth hand on my knee. "Is she ill?"

I shook my head vigorously, realizing I was already making a mess of explaining. "She is well in body, as are her husband and all her children. But poor Sam. He's been accused of all sorts and might lose his post."

The story came tumbling out. I did not know any more than what Joanna had told me, but I explained what I understood. Telling Cynthia was different from blurting out Joanna's problems to any random person. Cynthia had lived with deception and tragedy and knew how to keep her silence.

She listened with sympathy, then sat back in indignation when I'd finished. "Good Lord. Of course the great merchant lordships will make a humble clerk take all the blame for their difficulties. As though one in a minor position could destroy a lofty bank."

I rubbed my sweating palms against my skirts, my agitation pumped high. "It is gracious of you to believe he is innocent."

"It is not graciousness. You have known Mr. Millburn for many years, and you are a very good judge of character. If you state that he is innocent, then he is. The difficulty is proving someone else has done this embezzling, to preserve Mr. Millburn's reputation. Is that right?"

"Exactly." My gratitude made me even more shaky. "Joanna is most upset. I promised to help, but I know next to nothing about banks. Or even what sort of thing Mr. Millburn does in his job."

"Which bank is it?" Cynthia asked. "Not the Bank of England, is it?"

"No, an international bank. It's called Daalman's Bank, which is a merchant bank, whatever that is. The original owners were from the Netherlands, Joanna once told me."

"Mmm. I've heard of it. They're not a bank a man walks into to withdraw his cash for a holiday in Brighton. Daalman's does investments, speculations, that sort of thing. It's called a bank because it does take some deposits, but it trades with other banks and funds merchant voyages to India and other far-flung places. Been around for ages."

"Do you know much about them?" I asked hopefully.

"Of course not. Most of these grand establishments of the City won't let a lady walk into them—at least not one unaccompanied by her father, uncle, husband, or some other overbearing male member of her household. But Uncle Neville probably knows all about them. I'll ask."

My eyes widened in alarm. "Please, do not involve Mr. Bywater in this—"

"I don't mean I'll tell him about your chum's husband's misfortunes," Cynthia interrupted me. "I will pretend to take an interest in banking and quiz him. Uncle Neville likes when I ask about that sort of thing. He actually does believe a woman should know about finance, to keep from being taken advantage of. Auntie believes a woman's husband should be in charge of all that, but Uncle's job has showed him that many a wife has been duped by an unscrupulous or incompetent husband." She huffed a laugh. "Uncle is not so much forward-thinking as practical."

"What does your uncle do in the City exactly?" I asked, my curiosity swimming through my worry.

Cynthia crossed one leg over the other, her skirts rippling. "From what I understand, he coerces ordinarily sensible people to part with their money, which he gives to others who promise to pay out a token every year for letting them use it. That is my description of a stockbroker, anyway. Apparently, Uncle is rather good at it. He receives a percentage of the money that goes back and forth, so whether an investment is good or bad, he doesn't lose. That is, until every investment goes bad, and then no one trusts him anymore."

"Rather a risky occupation, I'd think."

"It is, indeed. Which is why Uncle takes solace in your excellent meals and the wine my brother-in-law laid in that Davis pours into his glass the instant he arrives home. Where on earth is Davis, by the way?" Cynthia glanced at the door as though she could see through it and across the hall to the butler's pantry.

"That I do not know." My worry about him returned. "He went out while I was gone this afternoon, and no one seems to know where."

"I do hope the man did not have any mishaps," Cynthia said. "Mrs. Redfern is nearly in hysterics—well, hysterics for Mrs. Redfern. Which means she is more brusque than usual. I suppose if Davis does not return, we'll have to summon the police."

"I would prefer to try other means first," I said quickly. I had resources who could hunt through London for him if need be. I knew Mr. Davis would never forgive me if I asked the police to track him down.

"I understand. Davis is a very private man." Cynthia sighed and sat in silence a moment. "Tell you what though. I wager Thanos would know something about this embezzlement business. He might understand how the funds were taken and possibly who did it. He'll probably uncover the whole thing simply by sitting in his office at the Polytechnic and thinking it through. He is a genius at numbers." Her nose wrinkled in a wry smile. "At the same time, he can never remember to have his landlady darn his socks. She finds them, she tells me, with as many holes as Swiss cheese." She chuckled.

I wondered if Cynthia realized that if she and Mr. Thanos someday wed, she'd be expected to do all his darning. From her innocent amusement, I thought perhaps not. I then wondered if Cynthia knew how to darn at all.

"I would welcome Mr. Thanos's opinion," I said.

"Then it's settled." Cynthia brought her hands together in one clap. "I will pretend I am interested in investing and ask Uncle all about Daalman's Bank. On my next outing to the Polytechnic, I'll buttonhole Thanos and have him lecture me."

Cynthia now assisted Mr. Thanos in his position as tutor at the Polytechnic in Cavendish Square. She spoke casually about it, but I knew she looked forward to her afternoons there.

"I'd best be taking myself back above stairs," Cynthia said, rising reluctantly. "Don't want Auntie hunting high and low for me and then blaming you. Never worry, Mrs. H. We'll find out the truth, and your friend will come to no harm."

I knew she was trying to cheer me up, but I would not shun her offer. "Thank you," I said sincerely as I got to my feet.

"Not at all. I have lost count of the number of times you

have assisted me. Good night, Mrs. Holloway. Let's hope old Davis hasn't had himself an accident."

Again, her tone was nonchalant, but Mr. Davis's absence was concerning.

"I will send word the moment he arrives home," I promised.

Cynthia took herself away then, squaring her shoulders to return to her aunt and uncle's company.

I remained in the housekeeper's parlor, pondering things, until I heard Mrs. Redfern returning. At the sound of her footsteps, I snatched one of my cookery books from the shelf and pretended to be consulting it when she swept in.

"When I see Mr. Davis again, I will wring his neck," was Mrs. Redfern's greeting to me. "Waiting at table is *not* what I was meant to do."

"I'm certain he has a reason," I ventured.

"It had better be a good one. Good night, Mrs. Holloway."

Mrs. Redfern did not move, so I interpreted her farewell to mean I should leave her parlor. I replaced the cookery book, bade her have a good evening, and exited.

Tess glanced at me inquiringly when I returned to the kitchen, but I could not tell her the entire tale, as the servants' hall was still busy, and Elsie and another maid chattered in the scullery.

"Tess, do you think Constable Greene might keep an eye out for Mr. Davis?" I asked her as I joined her at the table to mix dough for tomorrow's bread. "Discreetly?"

Caleb Greene walked the beat on Mount Street and nearby roads and had fallen for Tess's good nature and lively eyes. Tess had changed her day out to Saturday because it was also Caleb's day off.

Tess edged closer to me. "Do you believe Mr. Davis got himself murdered?" she asked in a dramatic whisper.

"Certainly not." My response was swift, but I felt a qualm. Robberies happened in London, and Mr. Davis was not the sort to tamely hand over his money. Ruffians could make short work of him and leave him by the side of a road, or push him into the river to be found days later by a boatman trawling for flotsam.

"What, then?" Tess asked.

I pulled my thoughts from their gruesome track. "I meant perhaps Caleb could find out if there have been any reports of incidents involving Mr. Davis. An accident, most like."

"An accident?" Again, the whisper. "He might have been run down by a wagon, you mean?"

"Tess, do not be so theatrical. He might have gone out for a walk and tripped and fallen. Or lost his way somewhere." Mr. Davis had lived in London for many years, so that was unlikely, but one never knew. "I am certain he simply has better things to do than rush home, but just in case, I'd feel better if Caleb had an ask around."

"I'll tell him." Tess tapped the side of her nose, her voice quiet. "You leave it to me."

I hoped I had not erred sharing my worries with her, but I knew Caleb would not instantly report the request to his superiors. He was a sensible young man and would understand our reluctance to involve the police.

"You go on up to bed now," I said. "You did a mountain of work today, and I'm certain you are fatigued. I'd rather have you fresh for tomorrow, not dragging yourself about."

Tess sent me a grateful look. "You're that good to me, Mrs. H. I don't deserve ye."

"Enough of your buttering up. Go on."

I pretended to ignore her and continued mixing the flour, water, salt, and starter, my hands squishing through the dough.

Tess showed how much she'd learned about kitchens by not simply dropping the knife with which she'd been slicing dark green peppers for tomorrow's soup and fleeing upstairs. She carefully put the peppers into a bowl and wiped off the knife, laying it next to my others, which I would wash and sharpen later.

Only then did she dance away. Two years ago, she'd have simply rushed out, leaving everything for me to clear up.

I finished mixing and kneading the dough, wiped my hands, and moved the bowl to the back of the stove to rest. Elsie made room for me in the scullery, where I washed up the knives and then took them to the table to dry and oil them.

Once Elsie and the others had finished their final duties for the night and drifted up to bed, I threw on a coat, took up a basket of food scraps, and hastened out the back door. I always carried unusable leavings from the meal to give to the beggars who crept into Mayfair in search of food, a good excuse to depart the house.

It was freezing cold tonight, and I wished I had blankets or coats to give the poor souls as well. As I distributed the food, I dispensed the advice to seek Mr. Fielding, the vicar at All Saints in Shadwell, who'd arrange for a warm place for them to sleep if need be. A bit of a walk in this weather, of course, but I knew Mr. Fielding would help.

A well-bundled lad slouched next to the gratings and didn't reach for the food.

"It's a bit chilly to be waiting to run an errand, James," I told him.

The tall young man who was Daniel McAdam's son grinned down at me. He'd grown at least a foot since the day I'd met him.

"I never feel it, Mrs. H. What do you need me to do?"

3

Is your father about?" I asked James casually.

Daniel had recently gone to Ireland to do who knew what for Scotland Yard. Upon his return, he'd visited as usual but could not tell me what he'd been about. On my day out closest to Christmas, he'd taken Grace and me to a pantomime, which Grace had adored. After that, he'd become elusive again, which I knew meant he was helping the police solve various crimes.

"He's around somewhere," James answered with his usual bonhomie. "Want me to fetch him?"

"He is not a bushel of potatoes," I said. "I'm not certain he wants to be fetched."

James laughed, eyes dancing. "He won't mind if it's for you."

"Don't be cheeky, young man." I spoke admonishingly, but simply standing near James could lift one's spirits. "If he has the time, I would like to speak with him on a matter."

"Right you are, Mrs. H. I'll find him." Touching his cap, James sprang from the pavement and sprinted down Mount

Street in the direction of Berkeley Square. He was correct that the cold darkness seemed to not affect him in any way.

I suspected he'd be hurrying to the house in Southampton Street, south of Covent Garden, where Daniel took rooms. Daniel also had a small house in Kensington—at least he'd had at one time. He moved where it suited him, and one never knew in which dwelling he'd be found. That is, I never knew—Daniel usually told James where he'd be, thankfully.

"The young's always in a hurry," an older man who'd taken a few of the food scraps said to me. "I remember them days like they was yesterday. Funny fing, missus. I don't feel like I'm more than nineteen in my head, but my body tells me a different tale." He chuckled, his breath wheezing.

I fumbled in my pocket and slipped him a coin. "You get indoors as soon as you can. The vicar in Shadwell is a . . . kind . . . man and will see that you're warm tonight." I stumbled over the word *kind*, but there was no proper adjective to describe Mr. Fielding.

"Thank ye, missus." The man pocketed the coin without awkwardness and showed missing teeth in a smile. "Ye're a good one, no mistake."

He warmed my heart, but I hoped he would not simply use the coin for drink. I did not regret handing it to him, however, no matter what he did with it.

My basket empty, I bade the stragglers good night and returned to my kitchen.

Now, to wait for Daniel.

He never arrived. I stayed up as long as I dared, checking the dough, rearranging the bowls of ingredients for the morning meals, sharpening my knives, and making notes about recipes.

I gave up on Daniel at two in the morning and climbed my quiet way upstairs to my chamber.

I was too tired to wash up and had no desire to do so in water that had long gone cold in the basin. Climbing into bed, I shivered until the covers warmed me enough to let me sleep.

My dreams were of Daniel lounging in his small house in Kensington, his stockinged feet on an ottoman. I was there as well, insisting that his socks, full of holes, needed darning.

The dreams turned hazy, and I woke with the vague notion that I'd been trying to hide Grace, Joanna, and all her children in my tiny bedchamber while Sam languished at Dartmoor.

Not in the best mood, I descended to find the rest of the staff up before me. Mr. Davis had still not returned.

"Most vexing of him," I said as I divided the bread into pans and set them aside for their next rise. My truncated sleep had left me less anxious and more annoyed. "Mrs. Redfern and I will have to cover his duties as well as our own."

Tess was already toasting yesterday's leftover bread on a rack in the oven. She removed the toast rack with tongs just as the bread became golden brown. After slathering the slices with butter from a crock, she stacked the toast into a dripping, warm tower and slid the next batch of bread onto the rack.

"I had a word with Caleb," she told me. "I was up early this morning, since I had such a nice sleep. Nipped out and found him. He said he'd keep an eye out for Mr. Davis or any mention of him in the police reports."

"Thank you."

I tamped down on my churlishness. Mr. Davis was not an irresponsible man, and his absence might signal something dire. Other butlers I'd worked with had waltzed in and out as they pleased, or been found drunk on the floor of the butler's pantry, but never Mr. Davis.

I switched my irritated thoughts to Daniel. He was much more lackadaisical about timekeeping than Mr. Davis, though I supposed I was being unfair. Daniel worked for a man who seemed barely human, and his days were not always his own. I should be more alarmed about what the odd Mr. Monaghan had sent Daniel off to do that had prevented him visiting.

On the other hand, James's behavior last night had indicated that Daniel would be easy to find. Had James simply assumed so, and had something occurred to keep Daniel from coming to me?

Focusing on cooking should help take my mind from worrying about so many people, I reasoned, but thoughts niggled away in the background.

Breakfast went up without mishap, and Tess and I snatched a few minutes to enjoy the buttery toast along with some poached eggs. Then we were cleaning up and preparing for the next meal.

Out came the peppers Tess had chopped last night, along with onions and carrots. I ladled broth into a large pot to begin soup, adding all that we'd chopped. The soup burbled away, lending a fragrant warmth to the kitchen.

It began to rain, the fine, needlelike, cold rain of winter. Now, I brooded about Caleb walking along the streets in this freezing weather and hoped he was keeping his feet dry.

Lady Cynthia came to find me in the hour before luncheon, a broad smile on her face.

"Do you have time to speak to me, Mrs. Holloway?" she asked. "There's only Auntie and me for luncheon, so no need to fuss."

She brimmed with eagerness, so I stepped with her into the

passageway to the housekeeper's parlor. Mrs. Redfern was above stairs, keeping her watchful eye on the maids as they swept, dusted, and cleaned, so we would be undisturbed.

"Mr. Davis still isn't home?" Cynthia asked worriedly as we passed the butler's pantry.

My misgivings, which I'd managed to submerge while I concentrated on cooking, resurfaced. "No."

"Dear heavens, we really might have to send for the police." Cynthia closed the door to the parlor after we entered. "Even if he'll be enraged that we did."

"Constable Greene has been informed," I said. "He can report to his sergeant, if need be."

"The constable is a bright boy." Cynthia plopped onto the Belter chair. She wore a similar frock as last evening, this one in a deep maroon color. "He'll keep his mouth closed until necessary. Maybe McAdam could also have a search round for him."

"I sent for Dan—I mean, Mr. McAdam—last night." I seated myself, but my gaze strayed to the cookery book I'd taken from the shelf the previous evening. A recipe had caught my eye, and I intended to copy it out. "But I have not seen him either."

One thing I'd meant to ask Daniel was whether he could check the morgue, in case Mr. Davis lay in it. Death swirled around foggy London, especially on its coldest days, and Mr. Davis might well have met with misfortune.

I realized as the thoughts formed that I knew nothing of Mr. Davis's family or even friends who would have to be informed of his passing.

"McAdam will turn up." Cynthia spoke confidently. "He always does."

"Like a bad penny," I tried to jest. Cynthia smiled, but more to bolster my spirits than in agreement.

"I had a good chin-wag with my uncle at breakfast this morning," Cynthia said. "Auntie decided to be a delicate lady of the house and eat in her bedchamber, so I had Uncle all to myself."

I slipped out the notebook I always carried in my apron pocket and turned it to a clean page. I'd recently acquired a new pencil, nicely sharp, which I held at the ready.

"Very efficient," Cynthia said approvingly. "I hope I learned something worthy of noting." She stretched out her feet, crossing her practical lace-up boots. "I let Uncle believe that I thought of investing the small trust my grandmother left me in an international banking venture. I suggested I'd heard fine things about Daalman's Bank. I expected him to steer me from it, given what you've told me, but instead he brightened and said it would be a wise place to deposit my funds."

"Did he?" I asked in surprise. From Joanna's concern, I'd envisioned a place of vile corruption run by sinister men.

"Indeed. I thought he'd encourage me to give my money to his stockbroking firm, but he seemed pleased I'd decided upon Daalman's. Apparently, it is an old and respected bank, which stretches back to the days of the Hanseatic League."

I hadn't heard of this league, but Cynthia appeared to be impressed. "What does that mean, exactly?" I asked, pencil poised.

Cynthia laced her fingers together. "The Hanseatic League was a loose collection of bankers and merchants who traded all over the coasts of Europe—the Baltic and North Seas mostly. German and Dutch traders were particularly powerful, and a fellow called Jurgen Daalman started a bank in Amsterdam to fund merchants and take advantage of all the money floating around. Uncle is very taken with Daalman's Bank."

"Highly respectable, then?" I asked unhappily.

"One of the most respected institutions in the City, according to Uncle. The Daalman family can trace their ancestry back to the 1400s or so, when the bank first opened. They set up a branch in London about a hundred years later, so Dutch traders in London would have a place to quickly borrow cash or stash the mountains of money they made selling goods. The merchants' fortunes rose and fell, but the bank always seemed to be in profit."

"What do they *do*, exactly?" I wasn't prepared to understand high finance, but I needed at least the basic idea of this bank's business.

"Hmm." Cynthia pondered a moment. "Say you want to begin a business shipping cloth you churn out of your factory using the best British wool. You want to pay the people who are raising and shearing the sheep and keep running your factory of spinners and weavers. You also want to sell this wonderful wool to people all over the Continent and into Asia and the Americas—to those climates where people need woolen shirts, that is. You toddle to Daalman's and say, 'Hey-ho, I need to buy some ships and the crew to run them.' They essentially buy those ships for you, and you promise them a share in your profits in return. If the ships go down, they bear the brunt, but if your business is successful, they make a nice amount from investing in you."

I paused in my writing. "I thought you said you would invest your money in this bank. I doubt you'll convince them you want to ship woolens to China."

"Giving merchants loans and insuring their ships is only part of what they do," Cynthia said easily. "The other thing they do is take money from those who have it to help fund these ventures. I basically would be buying a share of this ship spreading woolly cloth all over the world, and then I am paid a percentage of any profit. After the bank takes its large fee, that is."

I scribbled all this down, hoping it would make more sense when I thought it through.

"They must have made wise choices about which merchants to help," I said when I raised my head again. "Since this bank has lasted for centuries and won the respect of your uncle."

Cynthia chuckled. "It appears so. They assess the risk, of course, says Uncle, and choose whether it is worth their while to fund or not. Some ventures are riskier, but those can be more profitable. Uncle advised me to tell them I wanted only moderate risk even if I'd earn only a modest return. After all, how much money can a lady need?"

She finished with humor, but I saw a glint of frustration in her eyes. If Cynthia had had a great deal of money, she could be more independent, like Miss Townsend. Miss Townsend's wealth, inherited in trusts from female relatives, let her live on her own terms. Cynthia greatly envied her.

"What did your uncle tell you to invest in?" I asked.

Cynthia waved an airy hand. "He told me to leave it up to the bankers and not fret my head about it. But I will consult Thanos. He can calculate profit margin, risk, loss, and all those other things in his head. Then I will march to Daalman's Bank and tell them exactly what to do with my little funds. Uncle agreed to write to them and fix an appointment for me."

My eyes widened. "My dear Cynthia, you do not have to actually go to the bank and give them your money."

"Why not? I do have some funds from my father's mum who wisely did not trust my father with them. Not much, but I am intrigued. I will ask Thanos for his opinion on the best venture and tell the banker I meet with to put it all on that. Like betting on the fastest horse in the Derby, isn't it? While there, I can quiz the banker and find out whatever I can about your friend's dilemma."

"Gracious, I cannot let you do that." I snapped my notebook closed. "You should not endanger your own money in a place that is prone to embezzlement. Did your uncle know anything about that?"

"Not at all." Cynthia's mirth fled with her frown. "He was surprised I'd heard such a rumor and told me I must be mistaken. Which means that whatever troubles Daalman's Bank is having, they are keeping them very quiet."

I rolled my pencil uneasily between my fingers. "I imagine they know it has to come out soon, and have already decided that Sam will be their scapegoat. He has no high standing in society or family to protect him. They are whispering rumors all over the bank, so that when the scandal comes to light, and Sam is either dismissed or arrested, no one will question his guilt."

"And once they rid themselves of the supposed culprit, the bank reassures their clients, and everything goes back to normal. Or at least they pretend it does." Cynthia banged one fist on the arm of the chair. "It's dastardly."

My anxiousness mounted. "The bank goes on without a stain, but Samuel's life is ruined, as are those of his wife and children. They'll put him in prison." I'd already imagined him breaking rocks in Dartmoor, surrounded by hardened men. "I cannot let that happen."

"We will not." Cynthia's voice rang with determination. "I will interrogate my uncle further. He said that the family who owns the bank is very interesting, but Mrs. Redfern entered at that moment, and my uncle ceased speaking and rushed off to the City. He is quite delighted with me for taking an interest in finance. I have no doubt he'll write for the appointment as I asked."

"You should not go," I said quickly. "Questioning your uncle is enough."

"Nonsense. My money is sitting in an account doing nothing at all. The only assistance the account gives me is that my father has no access to it." She barked a laugh. "Uncle has always thought I should do more with it, but he feared it wasn't his place to advise me." Cynthia leaned to me and lowered her voice. "He means he doesn't want my mother to get wind of the fact that he is of more help to me than my own father. Mother is a bit protective of my pa, bless his boots."

Cynthia's father, the Earl of Clifford, had once been a confidence trickster of some skill. Lady Clifford, Mr. Bywater's sister, would not hear a bad word said of him, however. Cynthia's mother and father were still dreamily in love with each other and quite defensive against outsiders, which sometimes included Cynthia.

They'd had their share of tragedy, I reminded myself, losing both a son and another daughter. I was always torn between pity and anger at them for not treasuring the daughter they had instead of wishing they could exchange her for the others.

I suspected I would not talk Cynthia out of going through with her appointment at the bank, so I simply nodded.

"Now, we must return to the topic of Davis," Cynthia said abruptly. "I don't know anything about his family, or anyone who he might have gone to visit. My sister hired him years ago, and he's rarely left the house since. Perhaps he has no

family or close friends, and so sees no reason to go out. Or—"
She warmed to the topic. "Maybe he had a wife and lost her in
tragic circumstances. Uses his work to forget."

The Mr. Davis I knew would never be that melodramatic.
Also, the mention of husbands and wives, living or deceased,
arises in casual conversation when one works with someone
for a long while. I'd been asked quite often if there was a Mr.
Holloway. I'd evaded the answer by explaining that cooks are
called "Mrs." out of respect and that Mr. Holloway was my
long-departed father.

Mr. Davis had said not one word about a wife, current or
past, nor any brothers, sisters, uncles, cousins, or close friends.
I recalled how the housekeeper before Mrs. Redfern had
hinted that he had taken male lovers in the past, and Mr. Davis had laughed at her. *That old chestnut,* he'd scoffed.

I'd taken his words to mean he'd been accused of such at
one time. Whether true or not, he'd be in a precarious position
if the rumors resurfaced. The police, I believed, could not arrest a person for such things without witnesses and proof, but
if Mrs. Bywater got wind of it, she might turn out Mr. Davis
without a reference.

Much better for me to find out where he was and what had
happened before we brought the police into it.

"Perhaps if I could enter his bedchamber, I might find some
clue as to where he's gone," I mused.

"An excellent idea. Shall I lead you up?"

I started. "I did not mean this instant. And I ought to do
such a thing alone." The staff had little to themselves as it was.
Mr. Davis would certainly not be happy if he knew Lady Cynthia had gone through his things.

"Ah yes." Cynthia tapped the arms of the chair, one foot
kicking out as she uncrossed her legs. "I think I see what you

mean. But I had better go up with you anyway, in case Auntie or Mrs. Redfern tries to intercept you. I can draw their fire."

What excuse she'd give for hurrying upstairs with me, I did not know, but I decided not to argue with her. This was Cynthia's home, and she could do as she pleased here.

Cynthia was impatient to begin. I left with her, setting my cookery book on a table near the door so I could reach it easily later.

The main floor was quiet when we emerged to it from the back stairs. I heard Mrs. Redfern's voice floating down from the upper floors as she ordered the maids about, but there was no sign of Mrs. Bywater. Either she had gone out on her morning errands or was still in her bedchamber. I guessed the errands, as Mrs. Bywater was of a robust constitution and disliked sitting about for too long.

Sometime in the past, this house had been two narrow town houses, before an enterprising owner had purchased both and knocked them into one. It made the house quite large and had also given it mismatched back staircases. The one to the kitchen ended at the ground floor, which meant the servants had to cross briefly through the downstairs hall to another concealed staircase that took one to the upper floors and attics.

Cynthia confidently opened the door of the second staircase and ushered me inside. When we reached the second floor, she pushed open the panel that led to the family side and stepped out. I was a bit breathless, but she'd moved briskly without breaking stride.

"You go on," Cynthia said in a rather loud whisper. "Let me know what you discover."

She saluted me, turning away with a merry greeting for Sara, the upstairs maid. Sara was clearly puzzled about why Cynthia was popping out of the back stairs, but I saw her shrug and decide there was no accounting for Cynthia's eccentric ways.

I continued the climb to the attics, which were abysmally cold this morning. I was lucky to have a chimney rising through my chamber, which lent a modicum of warmth, but the maids and footmen were not so fortunate. They slept two to a bed, which at least helped, but we would all be glad when summer came.

The attics were divided into rooms for the male and the female servants, a door in the short hall separating the two. I cautiously peered into the men's side, but no one was about. The footmen were busily working, fearing Mrs. Redfern's sharp tongue even more than they did Mr. Davis's.

Mr. Davis's room shared the thick chimney with me—the brick wall dividing our rooms had once been the end wall of the separate houses. His chamber was a bit larger than mine or Mrs. Redfern's, but he did hold the superior position of all the staff in the house.

His room was painfully neat, I noted as I stepped inside and closed the door. I opened the wardrobe to find his suits hung in an orderly line. Two pairs of boots, polished until they shone, stood in a perfect row beneath the suits.

The bed had not been slept in, the pillow and coverlets without a crease. I found no sign that Mr. Davis had hastened away in agitation, no evidence that he'd packed his things and fled the house for good. A valise rested on top of the wardrobe but by the wilted look of it, was empty.

Nothing lay on his bedside table, no book or Bible, no candle to light his way. I doubted he dressed and undressed in the dark, so he must have taken any candlestick downstairs with him yesterday morning. Mr. Davis sometimes rose earlier than I did.

The drawer in the bedside table was likewise empty, and the wardrobe held nothing but his suits, boots, and in a drawer at the bottom, his shirts and unmentionables. Nowhere did I find personal possessions of any kind, or any trace of ones he might have taken away. Absent knickknacks would leave a clear spot in the thin film of dust on the night table; a book's cover might leave a smudge in a drawer.

Not even monks lived this austerely, I reflected as I scanned the chamber. Or perhaps Mr. Davis simply hid his things well. I did not leave my letters, my one photo of Grace, and my hoard of cash on top of my bureau for all to find.

I sank to my hands and knees and lifted the hanging coverlet to peer under the bed. Mr. Davis must sweep here—or had a footman do it—because no snarls of dust greeted me. I saw only smooth boards, nothing to indicate any were loose, providing a convenient hidden cavity.

I was about to give up, when a bit of paper sticking out from under a slat that supported the mattress caught my eye. My heart beating faster, I thrust my hand under the slat and closed it around a stack of what felt like letters. I pried them out, careful not to drop any, and seated myself on the floor to study them.

There were a dozen in all, each directed to *Mr. Emery Davis*, either care of his agency or this house in Mount Street. I was loath to open and read Mr. Davis's post unless it became absolutely necessary, but I did note the return addresses scratched on some of the envelopes.

Most came from Bury St. Edmunds, Suffolk, the address written in a clear, slanting hand. No personal name accompanied the direction, but the house was called Medford Cottage.

The remaining letters either came from his agency or had no return address at all. I could speak with his agency, I supposed, and ask if they had heard from him, but I was reluctant to do so. They might scratch Mr. Davis from their books if they thought him unreliable.

I stacked the letters together in the same order I'd found them and returned them to their hiding place, leaving the tiny corner peeping out as before. I climbed to my feet and brushed off my frock, feeling defeated.

The chamber had no other papers, no photographs or souvenirs. I knew Mr. Davis did not like clutter, but the bareness of his chamber was depressing. Then again, he might tuck anything personal into a cupboard or drawer in the butler's pantry, which was where he spent most of his days. That would be the next place I thoroughly searched.

Finished here, I turned for the door.

The handle was yanked out of my hand even as I touched it. The door wrenched open before I could puzzle out what was happening, and Mr. Davis himself paused on the threshold.

His usually affable face went slack with shock before he drew himself up into his butler's icy hauteur.

"Mrs. Holloway," he demanded in fury. "What in the name of all that is holy are you doing here?"

4

Shame rolled over me, making my face hot and my mouth dry. I must have worn the same expression as the footman I'd caught the other day nicking a bite of pie out of the larder.

"Mr. Davis," I managed to say.

"That is my name, not an explanation."

His tone froze me to the bone, and I strove to retain my dignity.

"I do apologize," I said. "You are right. I have no business here, except that I was terribly worried about you and trying to decide where you had gone."

Mr. Davis stepped into the passageway, motioning me out as he would an unwanted guest from the house.

"Where I have been is my own affair. I took a day out, is all, and had difficulty returning before now. Had I meant to stay away longer, I would have sent word."

I scuttled past him but turned back in the passageway, his high dudgeon beginning to vex me.

"If you had told Mrs. Redfern you would be away for all this time, we wouldn't have imagined you'd been run down by a coach or a train. None of us knew what to think."

"I told the master. *He* had no need to question me or to search my chamber. I was visiting a friend who was ill, if you must know. Good day, Mrs. Holloway. I will see you in the kitchen."

My ire now moved to Mr. Bywater. He might have mentioned Mr. Davis's planned absence and saved us some grief. I could be charitable and assume Mr. Bywater thought Mr. Davis would tell us himself, but I was embarrassed and unnerved and did not feel at all charitable at this moment.

"Next time, at least tell *me*," I stated. "I would have kept your business private from the others had you asked me. You had no call to plunge us into such worry, Mr. Davis. I thought we were friends."

For a moment, surprise flickered in his eyes, then the frost descended once more.

"I never inquire where *you* go haring off to on your days out, especially with Daniel McAdam, of all people. I do not approve of him, but I do not stop you, nor do I search your bedchamber for indication of what you get up to. I would think a *friend* above such things."

I lifted my chin. "Friends do look out for one another. I apologize for disturbing you. It will not happen again."

I marched off, my back straight, and slammed the door of the partition behind me. Once on the women's side, I leaned against the wall, breathing in gulps of cold air.

Mr. Davis had the right of it—I had no business snooping into his personal life, and none at all to go through the pile of letters he'd clearly hidden from everyone in the house.

But I had the right of it as well, I insisted to myself. He oughtn't to have simply disappeared, leaving Mrs. Redfern and me to manage his duties. Mr. Bywater ought to have told Mrs. Redfern, or at least his wife or Cynthia. That neither Mr. Bywater nor Mr. Davis had bothered made me grind my teeth.

"Men," I muttered.

Heaving a sigh, I pushed myself from the wall and began the journey downstairs to inform the rest of the staff that Mr. Davis had returned.

Another man I was annoyed with also returned that afternoon. Daniel McAdam made his noisy way down the outside stairs and slung sacks of flour I had not ordered onto the clean kitchen floor.

"There you are, missus," he said to me.

He flashed me his warmest grin, just as he had the day he'd entered my kitchen at Mrs. Pauling's, four years ago now, winking at me like the impudent man he was. I'd struggled to be stern with him, telling him he'd better have wiped his feet, but I'd been quivering inside. Daniel's smile could melt one.

I kept up the pretense that his presence did not affect me in any way. "I do hope this is from the finest miller," I said coolly. "One who does not add chalk to fill out the bag."

"Best in London," Daniel assured me. He flashed another smile at Tess and Elsie—Elsie leaned on the doorframe to stare dreamily at him.

"Back to work," I commanded both young women. "You cannot cease your labors whenever a handsome man walks in the door. Where would you be then?"

"She says I am handsome," Daniel informed the room. "Mrs. Holloway, you are too kind to me."

"Oh, get on with you." I resumed chopping onions at the table, forcing my knife to be steady.

Daniel lifted a bag onto his shoulders once more and hauled it down the hall to the larder. He was allowed to do things like that in this house, and I appreciated the help.

I could not hope to speak to him alone, because the staff came out of the woodwork whenever Daniel arrived. He cheerily greeted the footmen who suddenly had things to do below stairs and waved at the maids, who'd likewise appeared to gaze at him.

Only Mr. Davis, who'd emerged from his butler's pantry at the noise, sent Daniel a disparaging look.

"I've got more provisions in the cart," Daniel said when he returned from depositing the first bag. I watched his muscles work as he hefted the second bag, the onion pieces under my knife growing smaller and smaller. "Perhaps you want a look at them? I'm earning an extra bob or two on the side selling to kitchens on my route."

I took the hint. As Daniel trundled the second bag to the larder, I handed Tess my knife to continue with the onions and prepared to accompany Daniel outside.

Mr. Davis grew still colder as he watched from the doorway of the servants' hall. *You see?* his expression seemed to say.

I silently slid on my coat and followed Daniel, when he returned from the larder, through the scullery and up the outside stairs.

The sun shone today, but the wind was brisk. I huddled into my coat, wishing for a warm hat.

"My apologies for not turning up last night," Daniel said as soon as we were up on the busy street and a few yards along from the house.

Daniel's wagon, harnessed to a large and patient horse, was indeed full of boxes of vegetables and greens. Dark red beetroots, creamy white parsnips, and deep green spinach tempted my eyes, as well as bright oranges that poked round flesh above the crate.

"I assumed you were well into some intrigue," I replied, brushing a finger across a fragrant orange.

Daniel huffed a laugh. "Not so much intriguing as tedious. I sat most of the night in front of a building in Mile End Road, waiting for two thieves to come out of it. They'd been robbing their way through every goods depot in the East End, stashing their take in a derelict warehouse."

"Did you catch them?" I asked. Daniel's blue eyes were darker than the sky, and I found myself standing as close to him as I dared.

"I did indeed, with the help of seven constables who resented being assigned such a cold, dismal vigil. The thieves are now comfortably in cells awaiting the magistrate, with the constables being congratulated on a job well done."

"Why were you there?" I asked in some indignation. "If the constables did the arresting and received the praise?"

"Because the thieves didn't act alone." Daniel rested his arm on the side of the wagon. His coat was worn and patched, but I knew he layered plenty of solid clothes beneath it. He played the down-at-the-heels deliveryman well, but he had no intention of freezing. "They could never have done all that burglary on their own. It was my governor's hope that they'd beat a path to their leader, but that did not happen."

"Your governor," I repeated. "You mean Mr. Monaghan, who sent you out to sit in the icy darkness because he could."

"Of course he did." Daniel shrugged. "He is not wrong about the gang's leader—a criminal responsible for thousands of pounds' worth of silver plate and costly furnishings being

stolen out from under the nose of the railroads. Their lordships in Mayfair are not receiving the finery they ordered, and
they are leaning on Scotland Yard to stop the man."

He glanced at the tall houses around us as he spoke, whose
tenants were the very men pressuring Mr. Monaghan to send
Daniel out to the East End on a January night.

"Still, there are plenty of other policemen who could have
performed the task," I said. "How long will he punish you?"

"As long as he can," Daniel answered with good humor. "I
vowed to him I'd do one last big job, but he is holding off on
that."

"Sending you on many small ones in the meantime," I said
in disapproval.

"This is so." Daniel's smile was genuine, as though he found
Monaghan's machinations amusing.

I did not. Mr. Monaghan, a high-ranking official of some
kind at Scotland Yard, blamed Daniel for the death of one of
his men. He'd been making Daniel pay that debt for years
now, by sending him into highly dangerous situations.

According to Daniel, Mr. Monaghan had once been a very
bad man—Daniel was vague about what he'd actually done in
the past—but had turned coat to help the police. This did not
mean he'd become a good man, I often reminded Daniel. Mr.
Monaghan, in my opinion, was unnecessarily cruel.

Daniel broke my thoughts. "My dear Kat, I did not come
here to debate what my governor should or should not have
me do. You sent for me, but you didn't tell James what for."

My umbrage at Mr. Monaghan receded as my troubles came
back to me. "It is Joanna."

As it had when I'd confided in Cynthia, the entire tale flooded
out. I ended up face-to-face with Daniel, my shoulder against

the wagon's side, as I spoke. He listened with sympathy, with flashes of anger on Sam's behalf.

"Daalman's Bank," Daniel said when I'd finished. "A bastion of success and respectability. The London branch was opened by a daughter and son-in-law of the family who controlled the business in Amsterdam. That was about four hundred years ago. Their descendants are now very British, but interestingly, the business in England has been handed down mostly through the female line, with the daughters and nieces marrying men who step in and run things."

"Gentlemen must vie to marry these ladies, then," I said.

"Wealthy heiresses all," Daniel agreed. "A few lordships have wormed their way into the business, but the gentlemen who hold the reins are firmly of the City. No one who doesn't wish to work his fingers to the bone need enter their ranks."

"Who runs the bank now?"

"At the top, the matriarch of the English branch of the Daalman family. A no-nonsense woman who has her fingers firmly entrenched in the enterprise. Her son and daughter, and the daughter's husband, are on the board, along with a few other family members of one sort or the other. A head banker, who shows up at the office every day, is the second cousin of the matriarch."

"This is what Sam is up against," I said with a qualm.

"I'm afraid so. Poor beggar."

"What can we do? Sam is no embezzler."

"Of course he isn't." Daniel's belief in Sam warmed me. "If an outsider of no consequence is responsible for any of the bank's troubles—if these troubles are even reported—the investors won't demand all their money back at once."

"Which would collapse the bank," I finished.

"It certainly would. I doubt they could cover everything that has been put into it. They are supposed to be able to, but four hundred years' worth of investments and dividends probably has muddied the pool."

I regarded Daniel glumly. "So, they are scrambling for a solution. I wonder if they've been embezzled at all, or if they are trying to invent a reason that they are short of funds."

"You could have hit upon it." Daniel's hand rested very near mine. "I know you are fond of the Millburns, Kat. I will do everything I can to help you, and them."

"More than fond of them. Joanna is my dearest friend, a second mother to my daughter." I let out a breath, which fogged in the January air. "What on earth am I to do if she can no longer care for Grace? I cannot hide Grace in my attic room." I laughed feebly, but my heart was like lead.

Daniel rested his rough glove on my cold fingers, his strength a comfort. "Grace will be looked after. I promise you this."

My heart thumped. I wanted so much to believe him, but the chill of reality told me I could not assume all would be well.

"I might have to send her out of London," I continued, my voice shaking. "I'm not quite certain what I will do if I can't see her even the small amount I do."

"London is full of smoke and danger." Daniel gestured to the miasma that hung in the air. "Grace would have places to run in a village, fresh air, no fear when she walks out to the shops. Perhaps that would be better for her."

He was trying to find a bright spot in the gloom. "All you say is true." I tilted my head to study him. "But answer me this: If country life is so excellent for children, why have you had James live all this time in London with you?"

Daniel's grin flashed, and he lifted his hand from mine. "Would you believe me if I said he refuses to go?"

"A bit. James has a mind of his own. But you could have made him go, and you know it."

Daniel's smile turned to a chuckle. "You've caught me. I like having the lad underfoot. He is my son, and I'd move the moon for him. But I'd much rather have him next to me."

"That is it, exactly." I folded my arms against the cold. "I feel very selfish to hope Sam does not lose his post for Grace's sake. The day Joanna told me she'd happily look after Grace while I sought work was the day I ceased falling. I'd imagined myself with Grace in a workhouse or giving her to the Foundling Hospital." I shivered, which had nothing to do with the winter day.

Daniel did not reach for me, but his voice held surety. "That will never happen. I know enough good people that if Grace needs a home to live in, she will have one."

"That I would pay for," I added quickly. I refused to be on another's charity.

"Of course. It would be a similar arrangement to what you have now."

The certainty in Daniel's eyes told me that he understood. He usually did, which was why I'd grown so fond of him, blast the man.

"I ought to go back inside," I said with reluctance. "It is cold, and I have much work to do."

"I will come when I can." Daniel's voice held promise, and I tried not to be pulled to it.

"As you like." I hoped my nonchalance rang true.

Daniel started to bend to me, then stiffened and stepped away, taking his stance as the affable deliveryman once more. I glanced at what had caught his attention and saw Mr. Davis at the top of the outside stairs to the house, radiating disapproval at us.

"He is very angry with me," I explained. I quickly told Daniel how Mr. Davis had caught me searching his room and why I had done so in the first place.

"Interesting." Daniel sent Mr. Davis a lazy salute. "Bury St. Edmunds, you say?"

"A place called Medford Cottage." I spoke in a whisper, though the rumble of wheels between us and Mr. Davis would muffle my words. "There is no reason to investigate the man. If he says he went to an ill friend, then he did."

"I have no doubt." Daniel's eyes twinkled with humor, but I saw the same curiosity in him that I felt. "I won't pry if it's not necessary."

"You have worked for the police too long," I chided him. "You want to investigate everything."

"I know." Daniel's mirth evaporated. "I've seen too many bad things while trying to do good. It's tiring, Kat."

I wanted to give him a comforting caress, but with Mr. Davis staring, I could do no such thing.

"Hug James for me, if he will allow it," I said. "I will be grateful for any help you can give me with Joanna's plight. Sometimes we have to plow through bad things to find the good things once more."

Daniel's expression cleared, and his sunny smile returned. "Such a wise woman you are, Mrs. Holloway. Wisdom and beauty in one wonderful lady."

I warmed under his flattery but made myself roll my eyes. "Now you sound like your reprobate brother. Save your charm for those who will succumb to it. Good day, Mr. McAdam," I said loudly. "I will take a crate of those oranges. Put them in the larder, please."

I turned my back on Daniel and strode to the house. "I am

well, Mr. Davis," I said as I started past him down the stairs. "I can pore over fruit and vegetables without danger. No need to look out for me."

"I was not." Mr. Davis's tones were as cold as the winter air. "I need to ask you what has become of the Beaujolais I'd reserved for Mr. Bywater's guests this evening. He has invited his colleagues from the City for wine and discussion."

I glanced back at him. "Do you mean the bottles I decanted for last night's meal? You left them out in your pantry, I assumed for supper. And the Viognier. They went well with my roast."

Mr. Davis's sigh rattled the air. "No, those were for tonight. The bottle of Côtes du Rhône and the sweet white set on a table right next to the door were for last night."

I recalled seeing those bottles as I'd scanned the butler's pantry for any clue as to where Mr. Davis might have gone.

"Well, as you'd left the corkscrew near the Beaujolais and no further instruction, I cannot be to blame." I did not fault him for being angry at me for entering his private chamber, but I would not accept responsibility for every other mistake in the house. "There might be something left in the decanters."

"I will begin leaving lengthy documents of all I intend for the meals, if it will help," Mr. Davis said in biting tones. "I was called away unexpectedly. I had no time to explain."

I halted in the open space at the bottom of the stairs. At the top, Daniel began climbing down, the crate of oranges in his strong arms.

"Let us not argue," I said when Mr. Davis reached me. "I apologize for being a busybody, but I acted out of concern for your well-being. I understand why you dashed off, and I am sorry for your friend. Let us continue as we were, please."

"I have heard your explanation and comprehend it," Mr. Davis said loftily. "Your solicitude is appreciated, but I have not yet decided whether to forgive you."

His words stung, but I had to tell myself I'd feel the same if I'd come across him going through *my* things. We all had secrets we did not want exposed.

"While you are deciding, please make clear which wines should be served with the meals," I said, entering the scullery. "And I shall leave you in peace."

"I am pleased to hear it, Mrs. Holloway. Be careful with that, you."

Mr. Davis addressed the last words to Daniel, who'd landed at the door while we'd gone through it, a corner of the crate nearly hitting Mr. Davis in the back.

"Sorry, guv," Daniel said in his good-natured way. "Stairs are slippery."

Mr. Davis made a noise of exasperation and strode through the scullery to the kitchen and out, making his way to the sanctuary of his pantry.

"Those look ever so nice." Tess set aside the peas she'd been shelling and came forward to peep at the oranges Daniel set on the dresser. "Did you pick 'em yourself?"

"Too cold here to grow them, except in a hothouse." Daniel rested one arm on the side of the crate, as though settling in for a chat. "I know a chap who has an orangery—which is like a very large hothouse. Sells to us lackeys sometimes. When I lived in the south of France, I could walk outside my doorstep and harvest my breakfast from the orange and lemon trees there."

I'd returned to my onions and gave him a frown, but I wondered if his tale was true. Daniel had lived in Paris for a time, where he'd helped stop assassins, he'd told me. He might have also sojourned in Marseille or Nice or another town on the south shore of that country. In what guise? I wondered. For his own pleasure, or had he been tracking some nefarious criminal?

"I wish I could go to the south of France," Tess said dreamily.

"One day, maybe you will," Daniel said, dispensing optimism as usual.

Tess laughed. "Don't speak no French, do I? Except for what Mrs. Holloway teaches me, and that's only about food." She resumed her stool and peas, gazing longingly at the vivid oranges that peeked from the drab crate. They brightened the room. "What will you do with all those, Mrs. H.?"

"A number of things," I answered. "An orange-flavored almond cake. Some sorbet, perhaps served in cups cut from the oranges themselves. We can trim them into pretty shapes."

"Mmm." Daniel closed his eyes, enraptured. "You'll be sure to save some of that for your hardworking Mr. McAdam, won't you?"

"Oranges are expensive," I said. "I imagine there won't be any leavings. Those are supposed to go into the larder, you know." I gestured at the crate with my knife as Daniel opened his eyes again.

"Ah, Mrs. H., you are cruel. Can a man not rest his feet a moment?"

"You've had plenty of rest since you arrived here, nattering on about all sorts." I pretended to be severe. "Add the price of the oranges and flour to our account. Mrs. Redfern will pay up as usual."

My scolding only made Daniel's eyes sparkle. He hoisted the crate and tramped out with it, making for the larder. He was back very quickly.

"Always a joy to see you, Mrs. Holloway," he said as he skimmed through on the way to the back door. "Keep yourself on the straight and narrow, Tess. Remember, your beau is a policeman." Daniel winked at her, and Tess flushed.

"Cheeky," she said, but did not look offended.

Daniel waved at us, said a good-bye to Elsie in the scullery, and was gone.

Tess sighed. "Always feels dimmer in here when Mr. Mc-Adam's gone, don't it? A breath of fresh air he is."

"A whirlwind, more like," I said, keeping up my no-nonsense briskness. "Now cease your chatter and get on with things. We have much to do."

The next day was Saturday, Tess's day out. Without her assistance, I was run off my feet in the kitchen. I did make the almond-orange cake, which turned out light as a feather, every piece devoured in the dining room. I'd wait to begin the sorbet until I had Tess here, as I'd need much help juicing the oranges, then cutting the rinds into shapes.

Cynthia came downstairs that afternoon to tell me that her uncle had fixed an appointment with her at Daalman's Bank for Monday afternoon.

"You can come with me," she announced. "As my chaperone."

5

———✦—✦———

I regarded Cynthia in surprise as she beamed at me across my work table. "Why would your uncle not take you?" I asked. "I thought Daalman's wouldn't let you darken the door if he was not with you."

"Because Uncle is far too busy, of course," Cynthia answered without rancor. "He believes that once I am in the hands of the competent bankers, they will relieve me of my cash to make me richer. I have only to sit demurely and let them make all the decisions. Then Uncle will come round later and sign all the forms for me, or they'll send them to him, or something. He has arranged for me to be seen by the top banker, who has decided it is all right if I have a lady companion with me to guard my virtue. Uncle approved of my choice of you as that companion. You are quite respectable in his eyes."

Her light tone and good-humored smile overlaid Cynthia's bitterness that she could not be trusted to invest her own money. However, she'd used her dependency on the males in her life to arrange for me to see the bank and its inhabitants for myself.

"Thank you," I told her. "This will be very helpful. I only hope your aunt will not forbid me to accompany you."

"I did not plan to inform her," Cynthia said, her smile broadening. "If Uncle mentions it, I will invent some explanation. But what you get up to on your day out is your business, I say."

Not every mistress agreed with this idea. Maids or footmen who disgraced themselves during their day out reflected badly on the household that employed them—or so it had been stressed to me since I'd begun life in service. Such servants were usually dismissed and removed from their agency's books.

I agreed to the plan, since it was clear Cynthia would not hear of my disagreeing. I did want to see the bank and the people who were accusing Sam of stealing from them, and afterward, it would be a short walk to Joanna's house and Grace.

Cynthia sailed out, happy with her plans. I wasn't certain whether she'd yet had time to consult Mr. Thanos, but I assumed she'd tell me what he'd advised.

The rest of Saturday was taken up with much cookery. Though Mrs. Bywater went out to the theater with friends that evening, and Cynthia had plans to attend a soiree at Miss Townsend's home on Upper Brook Street, I did plenty of preparation for Sunday's dinner and more for Monday when I'd be out. I did not like to leave Tess obligated to concoct meals from nothing.

I heard no word from Joanna that day nor did I on Sunday. Sam would be home enjoying his own Sunday roast, the bank shut. Almost all businesses took a day of rest on Sunday. "Only the domestics worked as hard as usual," I muttered sourly to myself.

Tess and I juiced a good bit of the oranges on Sunday, putting the juice aside in the larder, and started carving the orange rinds into pleasing shapes. I showed Tess how to fashion them into a tulip-like cup or make an undulating rim to look like a pretty bowl. The cut oranges would keep in the larder, which was quite cold these days, until we were ready to make the sorbet itself. That I'd do on Tuesday, serving it at a supper Mrs. Bywater had planned on Wednesday. There would be enough left over for treats for the staff the rest of the week.

Mr. Davis spoke little to the rest of us throughout the week's end. He was stiff lipped around me, very cool to Mrs. Redfern, and snapped at the footmen if they weren't instantly obedient.

I missed the friendly Mr. Davis who would spread his newspaper across my table during quiet hours in the house and read out interesting bits to me. I wondered if Daalman's Bank had ever featured in any stories he'd perused, but in this present state of affairs, I could not approach him to ask.

On Monday, I helped Tess set up the luncheon for both upstairs and down, then I changed into my best frock and hat. Giving final instructions to Tess, who shood me off in some exasperation, I departed.

I was tempted to announce loudly to Mr. Davis that I was leaving, and what time to expect me back, but I decided to keep my silence. Such a thing would not help mend our fences.

Clouds had lowered, and the wind blustered as I walked to Berkeley Square. There, as I'd requested, Lady Cynthia was to await me in a coach she'd borrowed from Miss Townsend for the errand. While Mr. Bywater had approved of me accompanying Cynthia, I preferred that her aunt, who disliked my friendship with her niece, did not watch us rolling off in a fine carriage together.

The sleek coach with liveried coachman lingered in Berkeley Square on the corner closest to Mount Street. A fascinated street boy held the horses while the coachman—his name was

Dunstan, if I remembered correctly—assisted me inside as though I were a titled lady.

"Afternoon, Mrs. H.," Cynthia greeted me with enthusiasm. "Off we go."

Dunstan slammed the door, and the coach listed as he climbed to his place. The carriage eased back a few inches and then jolted forward as Dunstan steered us through Berkeley Square and south toward Piccadilly.

Cynthia had chosen to wear a blue gown trimmed with pink piping along the lapels, collar, and cuffs. Blue silk-covered buttons that held the bodice closed matched the blue of her woolen coat. Pink ruffles on the skirt's hem gathered to a point, over which drooped a pink cloth rose.

She'd paired the ensemble with a green velvet hat with a high crown covered with ribbons and flowers. Where she'd obtained such headgear, I had no idea. Cynthia's hats were usually small, quiet affairs that went well with her sensible gowns.

"Fine feathers, aren't they?" Cynthia moved her head so the flowers would jiggle. "I wanted to appear a frivolous lady needing guidance with her funds. Gents will tell one more if they feel superior, won't they?"

"Possibly," I said. The banker might be distracted by a slim figure and fine blue eyes and not notice the gown's frivolity, but I agreed that the guise might work.

"Thanos appeared at Miss Townsend's do last night," Cynthia went on. "We had a lively discussion about investment and Daalman's. After a long explanation of bonds, market risks, bear market attacks, and the lessons France's struggling Central American canal company can teach us, he advised me not to let Daalman's invest my money."

My brows rose. "Did he tell you why?"

"After another long explanation, most of which was beyond me, he said that they have a history of placating their large investors at the expense of their small investors. Robbing Peter to pay Paul, in other words."

That adage I understood. I'd often had to resort to paying what I could and making promises to others when I'd been first left on my own.

"In that case, best not make any promises to them," I said.

"I will not. Thanos is interested. He's itching to look at Daalman's books to see where the money is going, but I told him that I couldn't put their books under my arm and walk out with them. He looked disappointed, the silly man."

She laughed, but I saw the softening in her eyes that she had whenever we spoke of Elgin Thanos.

As we conversed, the coach bumped around Regent Circus and past Leicester Square into St. Martin's Lane. The pretty church of St. Martin-in-the-Fields slid past, and we entered Trafalgar Square, with the solemn bulk of the National Gallery on our right. From there, Dunstan moved to the Strand and along that crowded thoroughfare to Fleet Street and so into the City.

The grandeur of St. Paul's soon filled my vision. To me, its dome would always mean that we were nearing the house where my daughter lived.

The coach jostled past the passageway called Clover Lane that led from Cheapside to Joanna's home, and I turned my head to keep it in view as long as I could. Dunstan continued through Poultry and past the edifice that was the Bank of England on Threadneedle Street.

Not far beyond the Royal Exchange in Cornhill, Dunstan turned the carriage down a smaller street, which had barely enough room for the carriage, and halted before a tall stone house. Another enterprising lad sprang out of nowhere to hold the horse. They were everywhere, these boys who loved horses. They knew coachmen might throw them a ha'penny for their assistance and so were ready to pounce whenever one stopped.

Dunstan helped me alight. The triangular pediments over the house's windows frowned their disapproval as I descended.

Cynthia emerged next, clinging to Dunstan's hand as though she'd never walk upright on her own. She settled her skirts and hat, lifted her chin, and led me haughtily up a short flight of steps to the front door.

The house, while imposing, did not possess the weight of the Bank of England, which announced its importance from every column. This might have been a private residence, except for the discreet plaque beside the door that more or less whispered the name *Daalman's*.

A doorman in livery opened the door for Cynthia before she could ring the bell and ushered her inside. He bent a cool eye on me as I slid in behind her, then dismissed me as either her maid or an unimportant lady's companion.

The interior could also have been that of a private house, and I wondered if the building had once been home to the Daalman family itself. A wide hall ran from the front door into dim recesses, with the hint of a staircase at the end. Demilune tables graced the walls, each holding an elegant statuette or bust of some pompous-looking gentleman on its marble top.

The doorman snapped his fingers, and a youth, also in livery, darted from a tiny room off the vestibule and reached for Cynthia's coat and then, to my consternation, mine. I never felt right turning over my wraps to a stranger. If I never saw them again, I'd be hard-pressed to replace them.

A young gentleman dressed in a suit similar to the sort Mr. Bywater habitually wore emerged from a room not far along the hall. He approached Cynthia as though he was expecting her.

"Welcome, your ladyship." He gave her a bow and bade us to follow him.

The young man led us to the rear of the shadowy hall, no candles or lamps to cut the gloom. We reached the stairs, which were of polished marble, and ascended into a corridor that held a little more light from wide windows on either end of it.

I heard voices now and footsteps behind the doors to the left and right of the grand corridor. The mundane noises were a relief—human beings actually inhabited this lofty and rather cold edifice. I'd never pictured this as the place where the cheerful Sam Millburn spent his days, but perhaps the rooms on the other side of these carved and polished doors were more cozy.

I wondered if his room was on this floor and what would happen if he spotted me here. I hadn't sent word to Sam and Joanna that I'd venture into his bank today, as I hadn't wanted Sam to forbid it. Not that he could forbid me doing as I pleased, but I did not wish him to be angry at Joanna for confessing all to me.

The voices behind one door I passed held some agitation, though their words were muffled. I slowed, trying to hear specifically what the men worried about, but our guide moved at a rapid pace, and I had to rush after him and Cynthia.

The young man led us to the very end of the hall, which put us at the front of the house once more. He tapped diffidently on the last door in the corridor, then opened it at a muted, "Enter."

Cynthia and I were ushered into a massive office that held several of the large, scowling windows I'd observed from the outside. The windows looked ordinary from this side and admitted plenty of light. Thick draperies, tied open, lent each window an elegant air.

The office's high ceiling was decorated with dark and polished wooden corbels. An ivory-and-gold-colored carpet filled the room end to end, ensuring that its inhabitants' feet never had to touch bare floor. A desk sat in the exact center of the room, within the middle circle of the carpet's design, its dark wood contrasting with the light colors of the rug. Two chairs reposed on our side of the desk with a small round table between them.

The man who rose at our entrance wore a black suit whose cut told me it had been immaculately tailored for him. He had light brown hair, pomaded slickly back from his forehead, a trimmed beard of the same color, a narrow face, and a thin nose.

Brown eyes assessed us, instantly noting that of the pair of us, Cynthia was the aristocrat. He dismissed me from that moment, his attention all for Lady Cynthia.

"Welcome, your ladyship. Please, sit. I will send for tea or whatever refreshment you would like."

"Tea would be lovely." Cynthia settled onto the chair with a flip of her skirt and gazed about the office with lively curiosity.

I sat on the second chair, my handbag in my lap, quietly and demurely fading into the background as a lady's companion should. Or so it appeared. While trying to keep my countenance blank, I studied the room, the man, the desk, and anything I could discreetly put my gaze on for any clue that would help Sam.

The chamber, despite its size, held very little furniture. I'd expected bookshelves filled with tomes on banking or investing, or glass-fronted shelves holding documents or some such. Instead, the desk, the graceful chairs, and two side tables between the windows, each holding a vase of hothouse flowers, made up the room's entire contents.

"I am Mr. Harmon Zachary, one of the head bankers," the man said smoothly. "Your uncle, Mr. Bywater, wrote a fine letter on your behalf."

Daniel had told me that one of the head bankers was second cousin to the owners, and I wondered if this was he.

Cynthia ducked her head demurely. "How kind of him."

Mr. Zachary did not answer. Before his silence could puzzle me, a door on the wall behind the desk opened to admit a maid pushing a tea trolley. Maid and cart were followed by a tall, willowy woman in a slim-fitting gown. They'd been waiting in the wings for their cue, I decided.

The maid, who wore a crisp black frock and pristine white pinafore, parked the tea trolley near the desk. She bobbed a perfect curtsy meant for all of us and glided out with just the right amount of deference.

The tall woman remained. Her dark hair was dressed in neat but fashionable coils, unembellished by any ornament. Her gown was likewise unassuming, with a jacket-like bodice and a small bustle to fill out her skirt in the back. The entire costume proclaimed that she followed fashion but allowed no ostentation.

"This is Miss Swann," Mr. Zachary said.

No indication of who Miss Swann was. An assistant? A lady clerk? A family relation? Another cousin, perhaps? She appeared to be near the same age as Mr. Zachary, who must be in his forties.

He did not give Miss Swann our names, because presumably, she already knew them.

"Good afternoon," Miss Swann said as she moved to the tea trolley.

She lifted the large porcelain pot, which my experienced eye told me was fine bone china, and poured tea into equally exquisite cups. Without asking our preferences, she spilled a small dollop of cream into each cup, followed by exactly two lumps of sugar. "Your ladyship. Madam."

She carried the cups in saucers to us, handing the first to Cynthia and then one to me. Her tip of head to me was no less courteous than what she had given Cynthia.

Once our cups were safely delivered, Miss Swann poured tea for Mr. Zachary. She returned to the trolley once more to lift petits fours—one white with cream icing, the other pale pink with deeper pink icing—onto plates with minute silver tongs.

Cynthia graciously accepted the petits fours and set them on the table beside her. I nibbled the pink one, always curious to try baked goods. It was far too dry, in my opinion, the berry flavor the cake's color indicated barely noticeable. The petits fours had been sliced with exactness, every layer the same size, the icing neither too thick nor too thin. But the baker, whoever he or she was, had sacrificed taste for appearance.

I finished the petit four to be polite but set its fellow aside and resumed my tea. This was good at least, the best oolong Twinings sold.

Her tea duties finished, Miss Swann lifted a notebook and slim pencil from Mr. Zachary's desk and positioned herself three feet to his left, ready to take notes.

Mr. Zachary, having drunk a bit of tea but without touching the cakes, smoothed a paper in front of him.

"Your uncle indicates you have a small legacy from your grandmother that you would like to invest," he said with approval. "I commend him for suggesting that we at Daalman's can help you. You can put your full trust in us, your ladyship."

Miss Swann nodded, her small smile telling us that Mr. Zachary spoke with wisdom.

"Excellent," Cynthia said. "What will my money be invested in? Something exciting, like silk, or diamonds? I do like both of those."

She tittered like an empty-headed debutante. I sipped tea and kept my face straight.

"Excitement is not what one wishes when one invests, your ladyship," Mr. Zachary said, his tone indulgent. "But we will put your money into accounts that will please you, I think."

He spoke as a wise adviser should, with the right amount of encouragement tempered with warnings of prudence. Miss Swann completely agreed with him without saying a word. I wondered if she were here to reassure Cynthia, another woman showing that Lady Cynthia could have full confidence in Mr. Zachary.

And yet, beneath this play of perfect financial advice, I sensed uneasiness. I saw it in the flick of Mr. Zachary's fingers on the paper and Miss Swann's shift of weight. Her feet might ache in her narrow shoes, but there was more to it than that, I wagered.

"You will be paid a dividend at the end of every year," Mr. Zachary continued. "We will set up an account for those dividends and send a letter to your uncle when they are available. I recommend leaving them in place to be reinvested, but you can always have a little pin money out of the proceeds. Your uncle indicated he was to be the correspondent, but if you prefer your father, his lordship, to assist you, I am certain Mr. Bywater would understand."

Cynthia hid a wince at the suggestion of her father anywhere near her money and beamed Mr. Zachary a large smile. "My father is rarely in London, and my uncle is so very good at finance. I am lucky to have such fine male relations to look out for me."

I wanted to surreptitiously kick her to warn her not to overdo it, but I was too far from her. I held myself still and sipped more tea.

Mr. Zachary took Cynthia's words at face value, and Miss Swann made a note. Mr. Zachary did nothing so unprofessional as smile, but his eyes tried to tell Cynthia she should let him do whatever he liked with her money.

Cynthia opened her lips to either ask another question or gush more about her uncle, when shouting erupted in the corridor. Doors banged, and then came the sound of quickly tramping feet. More shouting, including a loud and very inappropriate curse.

"Gracious," Cynthia said cranking around to stare at the door. "Whatever is the matter?"

Miss Swann and Mr. Zachary exchanged a nervous glance.

"Nothing at all to worry you," Mr. Zachary said quickly. "Now, I will send your uncle a prospectus of the sorts of investments we'll make for you. He knows much about stock, and he can tell you whether—"

The shouting grew louder, then a thick Cockney rose above the rest of the voices. "Now then, you. Don't be giving us no trouble."

Mr. Zachary and Miss Swann exchanged another glance.

"I did nothing." A man's voice shouted his answer. "I swear to you. Nothing!"

I was on my feet, my legs propelling me upward against my will. I knew that voice, had heard it rumbling through Joanna's house for many years. Usually, it was welcoming and friendly to me, fond and loving to Joanna and the children.

Today, Sam's voice shook with incredulity and fear. They were arresting him.

Fortunately, the two in the office thought I'd risen in general alarm at the commotion. Miss Swann turned a smile on me that was supposed to be reassuring, but it wavered.

"A tramp must have gotten into the building," Miss Swann offered. "The constables will see it right."

The blatant lie grated on my nerves. Sam was being hauled away unjustly, and these people had the audacity to pretend nothing was wrong.

Lady Cynthia sprang up, slamming her teacup to the table. "I suggest you tell us exactly what has happened," she said in her most commanding tones. "At once."

Mr. Zachary instantly rose—no gentleman remained seated when a lady stood. The fact that he'd stayed planted in his chair when I'd left mine told me exactly where he placed me in his world.

"I assure you, your ladyship—" he began.

"I suppose it will be in all the newspapers tomorrow," Miss Swann interrupted him with resignation. "No sense in trying to hide things."

Mr. Zachary made a gesture of defeat with his thin hand, but it was Miss Swann who explained.

"I am afraid, your ladyship, that a man was killed here this morning."

Cynthia's eyes widened, but the floor teetered under my feet. I grasped the back of the chair before I could collapse.

The others didn't note me—they were focused on Cynthia, much more concerned about her reaction.

"Do not worry." Miss Swann held up her hands as though to

prevent Cynthia from racing out in a panic. "The murderer has already been caught. The police are taking him away now. It was a quarrel between two men in the clerks' room, nothing to do with anyone else. There is absolutely no danger to you."

The shouting now sounded outside in the lane. Unnoticed, I hurried to one of the windows and pulled back its lace undercurtain to peer out.

Three constables had burst from the doorway below me, dragging the struggling form of Sam Millburn between them. His customary pleasant tones deserted him as they shoved him at the waiting black police wagon, the South London cant he'd spoken as a youth returning.

"Take your hands off me, bloody peelers. I ain't done nothing."

A man in a dark suit, with a shock of blond hair and a thick mustache of the same color, stepped out of the bank's door and slapped his hat onto his head with a satisfied air.

There was no reason this man should choose that moment to look up at the wide window in which I stood. Glittering eyes locked onto me, and the confidence the detective inspector had displayed suddenly evaporated.

Inspector McGregor sent me a scowl that would have singed a lesser woman to the bone. As it was, I simply gazed back at him.

Turning abruptly from me, Inspector McGregor gestured to the constables with the snap of his hand, then strode past the wagon, every step betraying irritation.

The slam of the wagon's iron door echoed up and down the lane. The horses started, jostling Sam away to the nearest nick.

6

I swung back from the window to find Cynthia regarding me with worry, Miss Swann and Mr. Zachary in indignation.

"Who was killed?" I asked them.

"Really, madam." Miss Swann's tones could freeze the tea in all our cups. "It is hardly a seemly thing to discuss."

"But possibly important," Cynthia returned. "After all, I'm asking your bank to take care of my funds."

"As Miss Swann said, there was an argument between two clerks that became unruly," Mr. Zachary said. "Nothing more, I assure you. The head clerk should not have hired Mr. Millburn at all. He has an unsavory background, as it turns out, but he managed to hide it from all of us. He has been rooted out and will trouble us no more." Mr. Zachary spoke as one washing his hands of all responsibility.

My temper flared, but I knew it would do no good for me to rail at him. I balled my hands and settled for pinning Mr. Zachary with a grim stare that made him turn to avoid it.

Poor Joanna. I wondered if Inspector McGregor or anyone from the City police would bother sending word to her that Sam had been arrested. Sam would be taken to the City lockup, as this road lay within the square mile of London. What Inspector McGregor from the Metropolitan Police had been doing here, I wasn't certain. The two forces never mixed except in very special circumstances.

"What was this quarrel about?" Cynthia asked, continuing in her guise as worried investor. "Anything to do with the shareholders' funds? Or was it personal?"

Miss Swann broke in. "The problem had nothing to do with shares. I assure you, your money will be quite safe here."

"Mr. Stockley did not even work on the same floor as Mr. Millburn," Mr. Zachary put in.

He flushed as Miss Swann turned a harsh gaze on him—he'd blundered and given us names instead of deflecting our attention from the situation.

"And all will be well?" Cynthia widened her light blue eyes in a childlike expression.

"Indeed." Miss Swann exuded relief that she finally understood. "The bad man has been taken away, and tranquility will resume."

As if her words were a command, the hall outside the office quieted. Footsteps retreated, and doors closed firmly, rendering the house silent once more.

"I am certain the matter is settled," Cynthia said. "Do send the prospectus to my uncle, Mr. Zachary. He will instruct me on how to proceed."

"Delighted to, your ladyship." Mr. Zachary's relief matched Miss Swann's. "You may be assured your funds will be in safe hands."

He came around the desk, primly upright. He did not do anything so familiar as to offer to shake Cynthia's hand, but he gave her a shallow bow.

Miss Swann, once more cued, opened the door and ushered us out. She did no bowing or curtsying apart from a deferential nod to Cynthia. Miss Swann did not look at me at all as I scurried past her, but she made clear her disapprobation that I'd asked questions without the permission of my betters.

The young man who'd herded us upstairs waited restlessly halfway down the hall. Miss Swann relinquished us to him and disappeared back into the office. She'd successfully handed us off to the next player in the chain, and her part was done.

"I apologize for the disturbance, your ladyship," the young man said as we joined him. "A slight problem with the lower staff."

"A man was murdered," Cynthia said as she strode past him, making him jog to keep up with her. "That sounds like more than a slight problem."

I slowed, letting them go ahead of me. Cynthia and our guide reached the stairs at the same time, and the young man spluttered as Cynthia charged down the staircase without waiting for him to lead.

Neither noticed they'd left me behind. Once the hall was deserted and silent, I grasped the handle of the door from which agitated voices leaked and peeked inside.

I found a large room crammed with standing desks in face-to-face pairs, a narrow corridor of space between the rows. The bookcases I'd expected to find in Mr. Zachary's office lined the walls, filled with books and stacks of papers that threatened to tumble down in any draft. Each desk held cubbyholes stuffed with more papers. How anyone found the exact sheet they sought was beyond me.

The clerks—or whoever they were—were not working industriously behind their desks. Instead, they gathered in the center of the room in argument. One man declared stoutly that Sam Millburn would never do all the things he'd been accused of, especially not murder.

My heart warmed, then chilled again when the others chorused that the speaker was a fool—Millburn had done this all right. That's what came of letting those no better than factory workers into a respectable bank like Daalman's.

The man who'd spoken up for Sam clamped his mouth shut, but his sullenness told me he wasn't convinced of Sam's guilt. He was about the same age as Sam—early thirties—his brown eyes matching his hair, which like Mr. Zachary's glistened with pomade.

He caught sight of me hovering in the doorway, and his scowl turned to a frown of puzzlement. One of the others noted his gaze and turned to see what he stared at.

"Yes?" The clerk who'd proclaimed Sam was little more than a factory worker addressed me, barely forcing politeness into the word. "Can we help you, madam?"

I wanted to demand they tell me everything. But I knew the dozen or so men in this room would never obey an unknown woman who'd blundered into their midst.

"I lost my way, I am afraid." Still shaken from Sam's arrest, I sounded feeble without trying very hard. "Could one of you show me out?"

The man who'd spoken to me showed contempt at my ignorance. "Stairs at the end of this hall. Will take you down to the ground floor. The front door will be obvious."

None of the others offered any advice. They wanted me gone.

The clerk who'd stood up for Sam pushed his way through them. "I'll take you, madam."

I backed into the hall as he came out the door. The man gave his fellow employees a glance of disgust before he slammed the portal behind him.

"My apologies for my colleagues' rudeness," he said. "We've had a bit of an upset today."

Unlike Miss Swann and Mr. Zachary, he did not rush to reassure me that all was well.

As he led me through the echoing corridor, I took a chance. "I saw Sam be arrested," I whispered.

The man halted so abruptly, I nearly ran into him. He swung around and stared at me in shock.

"You know Sam—Mr. Millburn?"

"Very well, yes."

He continued to stare, trying to decide who I was. I'd used Sam's Christian name, a highly improper thing for a woman to do, unless she was a relation or on other intimate terms. I did think of Joanna as my sister, and Sam, by extension, as my brother. In their home, we addressed one another by our given names, as did Grace, she appending "Aunt" and "Uncle" to them.

"His wife is my dearest friend," I supplied.

"Ah." He cleared his throat, his face softening, as though he'd met the warmhearted Joanna. "I'm Mr. Kearny. Roderick Kearny. I've known Sam for years and am his closest friend here." He glanced around as though worried about listening ears. "Probably his only friend," he muttered.

"Then I am glad to make your acquaintance, Mr. Kearny. I am Mrs. Holloway. I have known the Millburns for years myself." I lowered my voice. "Why on earth did they accuse him of murder?"

"To quiet things down as quickly as possible." Mr. Kearny's

disgust shone forth. "Easier to throw Millburn to the dogs and declare everything solved than have a proper investigation. That would bring around the police and journalists, and this bank prides itself on discretion."

"It was a Mr. Stockley who was killed, correct?" I asked. "Who was he, exactly?"

"Who told you that?" Mr. Kearny demanded.

I folded my lips and looked wise.

Mr. Kearny sighed. "I suppose everyone will know soon." He echoed Miss Swann's declaration. "Mr. Stockley is a senior clerk. Upstairs." Mr. Kearny pointed straight upward. "He often clashed with Mr. Millburn, who is a junior clerk. Mr. Stockley was the sort who thought he was right about everything."

I had met plenty of people like that in my life. "Is that what you are, a senior clerk? Or a junior?"

"Neither. I am one of the bankers. Trusted with the funds of the great and good." He sent me a self-deprecating smile. "It was hard work that took me up the ranks, not genius. Luck as well." Mr. Kearny's mouth pinched. "It was on *my* recommendation that Millburn obtained his post at all. I'm certain blame will be laid on me for that." He frowned in puzzlement. "Millburn has never mentioned me?"

"He does not speak of his office work at home," I said. "Sam's attention is all for his wife and his children then. Granted, I am not there much when he is home."

Mr. Kearny nodded as though my glib explanation soothed his feelings. "Poor Mrs. Millburn. Perhaps I ought to—"

"I will see Joanna today," I assured him. Mr. Kearny's softening expression when he spoke Joanna's name made me suspect he was sweet on her. She'd neither need nor welcome his awkward attempt at comfort. "I have no doubt this will be cleared up soon. After all, the police will need evidence that Mr. Millburn actually committed the crime. Not just the wishes of his superiors."

"I don't have much faith in the peelers, Mrs. Holloway," Mr. Kearny said darkly. "Or the law. They decide who to bang up, and that's it. Small comfort when the judge is proved wrong long after a bloke's been hanged."

My spirits plummeted at the thought of Sam facing the gallows. I could not let that happen, but truth to tell, I didn't have much faith in the law myself. I'd been arrested for murder once upon a time, and only Daniel, with the assistance of Mr. Monaghan, had been able to get me released.

Miss Swann abruptly opened the door to Mr. Zachary's office, sending a draft down the hall to flutter my skirts. I hastily made for the stairs and began to descend, with Mr. Kearny clattering after me in a hurry.

"Who is she?" I asked him when we reached the ground floor. Miss Swann banged her way into another room and did not follow us—hopefully, she hadn't noticed me lingering.

"Miss Swann?" Mr. Kearny's brows climbed. "She's Mr. Zachary's guardian angel. He'll do nothing without her by his side. There's nothing romantic, mind you." He sounded amused. "She is a cousin of the Daalman family and knows more about this bank than anyone. Raised in it. Mr. Zachary trusts her completely."

Miss Swann had made a show of being the perfect factotum, serving us tea and backing away to write in her notebook while Mr. Zachary spoke. But as soon as the unexpected intruded, she'd taken over.

I had assumed that Mr. Zachary was the cousin, based on Daniel's information, but I now had to rearrange my ideas.

Daniel hadn't indicated whether the cousin was a man or a woman.

Mr. Kearny escorted me along the hall and gestured toward the front door, where the liveried doorman stood at attention.

"Good day to you, Mrs. Holloway," Mr. Kearny said. "Please greet Mrs. Millburn for me. Tell her that if I can help her in any way, she has but to ask." His eagerness would have been comical at any other time, but I could not indulge in his obvious fancy for Joanna now.

"Do you think it would be possible for me to speak to you again?" I asked him. "If need be, to convince the police Sam is innocent?"

Mr. Kearny appeared doubtful. "Don't know what good we can do, Mrs. Holloway. It's in the hands of Providence now, I suppose."

Abandoning all effort to the Lord was in my opinion a weak-willed evasion of a problem.

"Even so." I adjusted my hat and hoped I could find the coat that had been taken from me. "I will try my best to see that Sam is freed."

Mr. Kearny regarded me in confusion, obviously wondering what a smallish, plump young woman in an outdated brown frock could do in the face of the police and the rulers of Daalman's Bank.

"Good day, Mr. Kearny," I said firmly. "And thank you."

"Good day, Mrs. Holloway." His farewell was more hesitant.

With no more to say, I marched toward the vestibule and the imposing door to the outside world. The youth who'd taken my coat darted into the cubicle and fetched it for me, to my relief.

I donned my wrap, then sailed out of the unnervingly quiet

bank. A brisk wind blew down the narrow lane as I stepped into it, as though trying to scour away the secrets of London's financial world.

The coach waited for me at the end of the lane, with Cynthia already inside it. The boy who'd held the horses handed me up, and I landed in the seat beside Cynthia. I was too agitated to search my bag for a tip for the lad, but Cynthia tossed him a penny, which he expertly caught.

"Ta, miss," the boy called, and then disappeared into the heavy traffic of Leadenhall Street.

The lane to the bank emerged opposite the Leadenhall Market, an enclosed building teeming with shoppers for produce and all sorts of goods at this hour. It would normally have beckoned me, but I barely noted it as the coach inched past.

"Well, they were cold fish, weren't they?" Cynthia said decidedly. "Don't worry, Mrs. Holloway. They'll release Mr. Millburn right away, when they see he had nothing to do with it."

She was trying to be kind. I knew full well that people like Sam—of no consequence in the world's eyes—were blamed for whatever crime needed a culprit. My only hope lay in the fact of Inspector McGregor's interest, and that Daniel would move the earth to help.

For the moment, Sam was off to a lockup, and Joanna would be alone.

Cynthia did not remark upon the fact that I'd sunk down onto the seat next to her, instead of taking the rearward-facing seat as I ought. Another kindness.

"Can I be let down in Cheapside?" I asked. "I must see to Joanna."

"I have already instructed Dunstan to do so. Would you like me to come with you?" Cynthia added. "To break the news?"

She spoke without hesitation, ready to lend her compassion to my friend in need. Her continued generosity had me in danger of becoming a melted wreck.

"No," I said quickly. Joanna would be upset enough without the strain of having an earl's daughter in the house—Joanna would feel the need to cater to her. "It is good of you, but . . ."

"I quite understand. We'll spare her the fuss of me." Cynthia spoke the words glibly, but I heard an undercurrent of exasperation, not at me or Joanna, but for the social rules she could not avoid.

"Thank you. If you could perhaps send word to Mr. McAdam of what has happened? Though I will be surprised if he does not know already." Daniel not only had many connections with the police, but also an uncanny ability to know exactly what transpired in connection with me.

"I would be happy to, Mrs. H.," Cynthia said at once. "I have to wonder though. Why the devil did Mr. Zachary or his Miss Swann not cancel my appointment? Afraid of losing the custom of the Earl of Clifford's daughter, I suppose." She answered her own question. *"Let us cover up something as embarrassing as a murder so her ladyship will flood our bank with money and good repute."* She huffed. "I will tell Uncle Neville that I prefer to invest my little funds elsewhere. If anywhere at all. Are any of these institutions safe?"

Cynthia waved a hand at the massive buildings rolling past, each one large and solid, their countenances somber. But inside these edifices were people who lived, loved, worried, made mistakes, stole, and apparently killed one other.

My thoughts continued in this muddle as we rode the short way to Cheapside. At the end of that road nearest St. Paul's,

Dunstan halted the coach. I was too distressed to wait for him or any ambitious boy to help me descend, and climbed to the ground myself the moment we stopped.

"Anything she needs, you have but to ask," Cynthia called to me.

Her concern truly touched me, but I could only throw her a distracted thanks and farewell before I hurried up Clover Lane to the little house in the middle of the row.

Usually, my heart was light when I approached this narrow brick edifice with its white painted windows and black shutters. Behind the door with its brass knocker, my daughter would be waiting.

Today, lead weighted my chest and my feet felt numb as I approached the house.

The front step was scrubbed clean, the short iron balustrade polished and shining. Joanna and Sam didn't have much but scraped together enough to pay a man and woman of all work to help keep the place tidy, as well as a cook to feed the five children who lived here.

The door opened before I reached it, Grace bouncing on the balls of her feet on the doorstep. I ran the last few yards and caught her to me in a hard embrace.

Her warmth and the feeling of her arms around me calmed my agitation, but at the same time ramped up my worry about what would become of her. Of us both.

"What is it, Mum?" Grace asked, always sensing when I was unhappy. "Has something happened?"

I released Grace, smoothing her hair and cupping her face. "I need to speak to Aunt Joanna, love. By myself, at first."

Grace nodded, puzzlement but also understanding in her eyes.

She was so beautiful, my daughter at twelve, who teetered

on the brink of becoming a young woman. Her face had lost
its child's plumpness and was now slim and curved, holding a
comeliness that only increased my fears. Her young beauty
could catapult her into so much danger. I longed to wrap her
in my arms and keep her close until we were both too old and
gray for the world to bother about.

Grace's hand in mine broke my thoughts. She guided me
inside and toward the sitting room, where I could hear Joanna
admonishing one of her sons for some minor transgression.

I knocked on the door, but I could not find my voice to announce myself. It was Grace who said, "Aunt Joanna, Mum has
come."

Joanna broke off as Grace opened the door, her beaming
smile as she rose from the sofa breaking my heart. Her younger
son, Mark, shamefaced about whatever he'd done, brightened
at my entrance.

"Aunt Kat, I'm that glad to see you," he said happily.

He meant that his mother would cease scolding him now,
the young scamp. Grace held out her hand to him.

"Come along, Mark. Let's see what Cook is making for tea.
I'll wager something fine, now that Mum's here."

Mark, his scolding forgotten, raced out past Grace, pound-
ing toward the back stairs. Grace sent him an indulgent glance,
then carefully shut the door on her way out.

Her consideration wanted to make me burst into tears, but
I forced myself to remain quiet.

"He's a devil, that one," Joanna was saying as she resumed
her seat. "Tried to trick his sisters into giving him their share
of bread and butter this morning. Had all sorts of arguments
why they should. I had to have a chat with him . . ." She trailed
off, her smile fading as she noted my dismal expression and

the fact that I'd not yet shucked my coat and hat. "Why, Kat, whatever is the matter?"

"Oh, Joanna." I sat down next to her and squeezed her hands, my calm deserting me. I could not think of a gentle way to break the news, so I simply plunged in. "They've taken Sam away. My darling, I am so sorry, but I could not stop them."

7

Joanna's expression shifted from consternation to stark fear. "Took him away? What do you mean? Took him where?"

"I'm not sure yet, but they've arrested him. They'll take him to a City nick, but—"

"Arrested him for embezzlement?" Joanna's voice rose in rage. "This is nonsense."

"No, my dearest." I firmed my grip on her hands. "For murder. One of the senior clerks—"

"What?" Joanna's face drained of color, and her chest rose with a shocked breath. "Murder? No, no. They have made it up. No one has been murdered."

"I am afraid someone has been. One of Sam's friends at the bank, a Mr. Kearny, told me what happened. Mr. Stockley, a clerk who works upstairs from him, had been arguing with Sam. Now he's dead, and they are blaming Sam."

"One of Sam's friends at the bank?" Joanna gazed at me as

though I'd slapped her. "How did you speak to him? Were you there, at Daalman's? Why were you?"

"Trying to find out why they were accusing Sam," I said. "Don't be angry with me, my love. Just listen."

Joanna opened her mouth to blurt out more questions but closed it as I rapidly told her the tale of Sam's arrest and what Mr. Kearny had told me. She stared at me dully as I began, then wilted as the tale went on. Finally, she was in my arms, the always-tranquil Joanna weeping heavily into my shoulder.

"My Sam. My poor, sweet Sam," she sobbed. "What will I do without him?"

I held her, trying to soothe her. "I will not let Sam be convicted for this crime, I promise you. *We* will not. Daniel and I will make certain he comes home."

Joanna lifted her head, her face wet, eyes red. "How can you know? The police do as they please. We can't afford a good barrister to speak for him in court. He'll be hanged."

"No." I put firm hands on Joanna's shoulders and made her meet my gaze. "We will find proof. Daniel will speak to the police, and even if the case comes to court, I and my friends will make certain Sam has the best advocate we can find."

"Will any barrister want to take the case?" Joanna asked bitterly. "Even solicitors are expensive, and they'll have to persuade a barrister that he can win, or at the least, give Sam a gentler sentence."

I had no answer for her. In the trial system in Britain, as I understood it, only the barristers who roamed the Inns of Court could stand up in the Old Bailey and other criminal courts of the land and make the case either for the prosecution or the defense.

The accused had to appeal to the barrister through a solicitor, and the fees for both could be quite high. The more sought-after barristers could pick and choose their cases. The ones Sam and Joanna could afford might be worse than having no advocate at all.

"What will become of my children?" Joanna's hands fell to either side of her as though she no longer had strength to hold them up. "They'll take them from me when they know I can't cope without Sam. And what of Grace?" She looked at me, stricken, as though ashamed of just now having thought of her.

I caught Joanna's hands again, trying to spill my warmth into them. "My dearest friend, do you think I'd let anything happen to your children, when you have taken such care of mine? No matter the outcome, they will always be cared for. I will see to it."

As when I'd promised Sam's acquittal, Joanna's eyes filled with both hope and skepticism.

"We are only women, Kat, of the working classes, no less. Sam might have found a soft job, but he came from nothing, and everyone knows it. Less than nothing—when the judges find out what sort of company he kept before I met him, they'll build the scaffold before the judge dons his black cap."

"What sort of company?" I'd met Sam when Joanna had introduced him to me years ago. After weeks of hinting to me, her face rosy with blushes, that she was walking out with a fine young man, she arranged an outing so he could meet me. He'd been friendly, cheerful, and polite to me. He'd obviously doted on Joanna, which had gained him my approval.

Now that I thought it through, I realized I knew little of who Sam had been before he'd appeared in Joanna's life. He'd grown up south of the river—which to some in my neighborhood might have been another country. However, he'd never done anything that indicated he'd been less than sober and honest. I'd assumed he'd come from a poor but respectable family in a poor but respectable neighborhood.

Joanna slid from my grasp and wiped her eyes with the heel of her hand. I slid a handkerchief from my pocket and held it out to her.

"I met some of his old pals once," Joanna said, taking the handkerchief with shaking fingers. "Sam did not mean for me to—they happened upon us several years ago, when we'd gone to a music hall. They were the same sort of brutes who used to roam Bow Lane, ones we learned to stay far away from. They told Sam not to be so proud of what he'd accomplished, and to remember where he came from. And I did not like the way they looked at *me*."

I listened, startled. "What did Sam say to that?"

"He told them to keep a civil tongue around his wife, and the ruffians turned a bit more respectable. As though they knew better than to cross him."

"Did they?" I asked in some surprise. "Sam is the gentlest of souls."

"Of course he is, especially with me and the children. But he looked at them so sternly, and they backed down. Then they said if he ever had need of them, they'd be around. Sam told me we'd leave, and we walked home rather quickly."

"Did he explain who they were?" I asked.

Joanna's shoulders drooped. "He would not say anything at first, until I pointed out that if those men would be a danger to our children, I wanted to know. Then he told me all sorts of terrible things." Her voice caught on a sob. "Sam had grown up with street toughs and became one of them. But he'd wanted a better life—he saw what happened to most of the boys, who either got themselves killed, or carted off to Dartmoor or worse places. A vicar of his parish helped him, found him books and tutored him, and Sam proved himself to be good at numbers. He worked very, very hard, and met and became friends with a young gentleman who eventually got Sam his position at the bank."

"You mean Mr. Kearny?" I asked.

"I still do not know why you thought you needed to go to Daalman's today, but I am bloody glad you were there." Joanna, I recalled, had been able to swear quite vehemently when we'd been children, though she'd become most genteel since then. "Yes, Mr. Kearny. He and Sam got along splendidly—enjoyed many of the same books and things. They were from different walks of life, but this did not seem to matter to either of them."

"Perhaps Mr. Kearny will speak for him," I said, trying to sound confident. "If they are such friends. A gentleman's word will count for much."

"Possibly." Joanna was not convinced. "But when an Old Bailey judge gets wind of what Sam got up to as a lad, he'll instruct the jury to convict."

Judges and magistrates were supposed to be impartial, in theory. However, I had enough experience to know that when a judge took against the prisoner at the bar, he did his best to thwart the barrister defending him and tell the jury exactly what verdict he wanted to see returned.

"I will *not* let that happen," I said. "I know you are in despair at the moment, Joanna, but I promise you, we will do everything in our power to bring Sam home again."

Joanna tried to nod assuredly, but her lip trembled. "Do you think I can see him?"

"I am not certain," I had to say. The City's police headquarters was in a lane called Old Jewry, off Gresham Street, which

was not far from here. A magistrate would conduct a preliminary hearing in the morning, and more than likely transfer
Sam to another, more secure prison to await his trial.

"Why not? I'm his wife." Tears slid once more from her eyes.
"I should be able to speak to him."

"I don't think you should go there, Joanna. Sam will not want
you to see him like that. You stay here with your children. They
will need you."

"They'll send him to Newgate." Joanna crushed the handkerchief to her face. "That horrible place."

"I know." I'd once landed in the common room of that notorious prison myself, an experience I did not wish to recall.
"As I continue to state—we will get him released, free of this
charge, and brought home. Again, think of your children. You
will have to be strong for them."

Joanna nodded, crumpled handkerchief at her nose. Joanna
was quite strong, but just at this moment, she needed to weep.

"There is nowhere I can send my little lads and lasses," Joanna said. "You know I have no one. None but you."

"If I can contrive to stay here with you tonight, believe me,
I will." I wanted to with all my heart. Joanna should not be left
alone for this ordeal.

I thought of Mr. Davis, who'd vanished for nearly two days
to tend an ill friend, or so he'd claimed. Mr. Bywater had looked
the other way—would he and Mrs. Bywater extend the same
courtesy to me?

If not, I would have to think of someone who could look in
on Joanna, or at the very least, prowl the street outside to make
certain she was safe.

Joanna drew a long breath and attempted a smile, which
trembled. "No, no. I won't put this burden on you, my friend.
You have enough to concern you. I will be all right on my own."

"You will not be," I stated flatly. "Let me speak to my mistress and spend the night here if I can. As long as I cook her evening meal today and breakfast tomorrow, it should not matter where I sleep in between."

I spoke confidently, but I had my misgivings. Mrs. Bywater was not the most understanding of women. She spent much of her time raising funds for charities and at the same time doing little that was of practical help to anyone.

"You are kind, Kat." Joanna held on to her wavering smile. "I will be brave as soon as I can be. And you are right. My children will need me. I include Grace in that statement."

I wanted to give her more words of comfort, but at the moment, I could not dredge them up. I pulled Joanna into my arms instead, and we rocked together on the sofa, our future uncertain.

At last Joanna released me, blowing her nose delicately into the handkerchief. "Thank you, Kat," she said. "Thank you for telling me before the police could. I imagine they'll be coming here to make our lives miserable."

"Another reason I will try to return here tonight." I wound my hands in my lap, realizing I still wore my gloves. "I will have to explain to Grace. Do you want me to break the news to your children as well?"

"No." Joanna gave her eyes one last wipe. "No, I will tell them. They need to understand. To be prepared."

Prepared for when their father's name was destroyed, and his body hanged for a crime he'd not committed.

"Assure them Daniel and I will do everything in our power to bring him home," I said quickly. "Very soon."

"Yes." Joanna's word died away. She was still in shock and unconvinced that her happy life had not been abruptly and irreversibly taken away.

"Joanna." I pulled her to face me. "He will come home."

Joanna's tears threatened to flow again, but she gave me a brave nod. "It will be as you say."

She did not believe me, but at least she sat more calmly now.

I left her to warm herself by the fire while I descended to the kitchen and told the cook to brew Joanna a large pot of tea and prepare her a hearty slice of meat pie, warmed up. Joanna might not have an appetite, but even a few bites of the steaming pie dripping with gravy would do her good.

Joanna would have to begin economizing, no matter what happened, I speculated as I glanced around the kitchen. The bank would no doubt suspend Sam's pay packet, and I had no idea if he had any savings. Once Sam was freed, he'd likely have to—and want to—seek other employment.

I pictured the lump of money hidden in my wardrobe. I'd gladly dip into that to assist Joanna until all this was settled.

I did not tell the cook or Carrie, the maid of all work, what had transpired. I told them only that Joanna was low and would need help today. They'd learn of the troubles soon enough.

When the tea and pie were ready, I carried the tray upstairs myself and sat next to Joanna until she ate a bit. There was no sign of the children—I imagined Grace was keeping them out of the way. She was a perceptive young lady.

Once Joanna was drinking tea and a little quieter, I went in search of Grace.

I found her at the back of the house in the room Sam had set aside for himself as a study. His sons and daughters used this chamber as a schoolroom during the day, with Joanna as their teacher. When I peeked in, Grace and the two boys and two girls were playing a game that involved drawing numbers on sheets of paper. I beckoned to Grace, and she happily left them to it and joined me in the small dining room.

"Now, my dear," I said, once we'd seated ourselves on the worn wooden dining chairs. "I need to tell you something, and I do not want you to be afraid."

Grace's eyes rounded. "Is Aunt Joanna ill, Mum? Is this what the fuss is about?"

It was not an unreasonable question. So many, even in these times, suffered from deadly ailments that such an occurrence was unfortunately commonplace.

"No, indeed," I said. "Joanna is in robust health, as am I. It concerns Sam." I explained to her, patiently and clearly, what had happened. Grace's face lost color as she, who'd never been a fool, understood every implication of Sam's arrest. "Daniel will never let him stay in prison," I finished, trying to sound reassuring. "He will be home soon, mark my words."

"I will pray for him," Grace said, her face serious.

"You do that. Say a prayer on my behalf as well." I smoothed her hair, which was growing thick and luxuriant. "Give Joanna your strength and your help. She will need it, poor lamb."

"Uncle Samuel is a good man," Grace said without hesitation. "Whatever he is accused of, it is a mistake."

"I agree with you, but now, we must make the magistrates believe that." I sighed. "I will not hide from you that it will be a difficult task."

"Because Uncle knew bad men growing up," Grace said in her frank way. "He's told me stories about when he was a boy, I think to teach me what kinds of people not to trust. But he reformed himself into a fine man. I hope I can marry someone like him."

Hearing twelve-year-old Grace speak so matter-of-factly about marriage made my heart constrict. I was certainly not ready for *that* yet.

"No matter what happens, I will always take care of you," I told her. "Never doubt that for a moment."

"I don't." Grace's smile flashed. "You cook so I can live here instead of in a workhouse or orphanage. I've told you, when I grow up, you will be able to put up your feet, and I'll look after *you*."

If she had a husband and children of her own to take up her time, she might not have much left for her old mum. But perhaps I could have a corner where I could sit and play with my grandchildren. An idyllic scene.

"Or you will marry Daniel, and we'll all live in his little house in Kensington."

I jolted from my misty visions back to the plain dining room, cold rain falling outside the window. "Now, do not start with that again. Mr. McAdam is at the mercy of his job. When he's done with that, what if he doesn't have two coins to rub together? Where would we be then?"

"Together," Grace said.

The simple word made me stop.

I'd been avoiding thinking about the hint Daniel had given me that he'd like what we had to grow into something more permanent. I'd panicked, uncertain what to do. While Daniel was far more honorable than the man who'd tricked me into a bigamous marriage had ever dreamt of being, I had not been in a position to encourage Daniel at that time.

Since then, Daniel had spoken nothing of our connection. He came around to the kitchen several nights a week when he was in London and took Grace and me when he could to sights on my Thursdays out. He and Grace had become closer, but he'd ceased terrifying me by telling me he considered me his young lady. We'd studiously not mentioned the subject.

Together. Me, Grace, Daniel, and James. A family. As it should be.

"Let us not put the cart before the horse," I said, pulling myself back to the present. "Let us help Joanna through her time of trouble, and then we will see what the future brings."

"Yes, Mum." Grace's answer was obedient, but her eyes held wisdom.

I remained at the house until after darkness fell—night began quite early in January. I sat with Joanna while she explained to her sons and daughters why their father wasn't coming home that evening.

To their credit, they bore it well. Matthew, the oldest and a couple of years older than Grace, declared that his mother needn't worry, he was perfectly capable of being the man of the house for a night or two. Jane, Grace's age, said she was up to supervising the supper and closing up the house if Joanna wished to rest.

Joanna was in tears again, this time in gratitude for her family. The younger children were understandably anxious, but they held in their worries under the older ones' gazes.

Grace stepped out the front door into the cold evening with me as I departed. "We'll take care of Aunt Joanna, Mum," she said. "You needn't worry."

"I will still try to return here tonight, even if I have to sleep on the sitting room sofa," I promised. The bulky thing was rather uncomfortable, but there were no beds to spare in this tiny house. "It will be a pleasure to spend the night with you."

Grace's face lit, and I wished I could spend every night with her, and every day besides. However, I would not punish myself for doing the best I could manage. That way led to despair, and despair never solved anything.

I pulled Grace into a tight embrace. We held each other on the doorstep, Grace clinging to me with a need she usually pretended to be too strong for.

At last, we released each other and said our good nights, me repeating that I'd try to be back. Grace slipped inside the house, surreptitiously wiping tears from her eyes.

I turned from the doorstep and found Inspector McGregor standing in the shadows a few yards from the house. His eyes glittered in the light of the lane's single gas lamp, and his expression told me he'd been standing there for quite some time.

8

$\textreferencemark$

"I nspector," I said when I found my breath. I tried to sound nonchalant, but my voice cracked. "What are you doing here? This is the City, not your patch."

Inspector McGregor did not answer. I realized that standing and staring at him would accomplish nothing, and started off to Cheapside, as though his appearance hadn't shaken me to the bone.

He fell into step with me, droplets of the icy rain shining on his greatcoat.

"City sometimes asks for the Met to help them, especially in a thorny case like this one," Inspector McGregor said as he tramped along beside me, rain dripping from his hat. "Too many prominent men of business involved, too many connections to the titled and wealthy. I'm here to observe and assist, but the arrest and conviction is theirs."

"And Scotland Yard sent you?" I could not hide my surprise. Inspector McGregor was a clever man, in spite of his surly demeanor, but those at the Metropolitan Police office did not always see that.

"They did." His answer was dry. "No other detective inspector wants to risk his job on this one."

"You had no choice, then."

"None whatsoever." His hazel gaze cut through the darkness at me. "Your daughter lives with the family?"

I disguised my nervous start by adjusting my coat. He'd have deduced Grace was my daughter by the way I'd embraced her, even without her distinct *Good night, Mum* before she'd disappeared into the house. Inspector McGregor would not have to be a detective to understand the relationship.

"She does. Not much room for her in my kitchen." I tried to keep my voice light. We'd reached Cheapside, and I halted at the corner, turning to him. "I would appreciate very much, Inspector, if you mentioned nothing of this to anyone at the Mount Street house."

"They don't know?" Inspector McGregor's thick mustache moved, but I could not tell if with indignation, amusement, or commiseration.

"The fact that I have a child might cost me my post," I said. "A post I can ill afford to lose."

"You are lying to them, then?" His shrewd eyes pinned me.

I lifted my chin. "I am a widow." This was more or less true. "But many mistresses prefer their servants to be unattached. I am not ashamed of Grace, but my employers might not be so understanding. So yes, I lied to them."

"Mmph," was his enlightening reply.

"If you must know all, Joanna Millburn is my greatest friend and looks after Grace as though she were her own. I assume you have come here to tell her about Sam?"

"Of Millburn's arrest, yes." Inspector McGregor glanced out

into the busy street of Cheapside, its lamps barely penetrating the rainy gloom. Coach lights sliced into the darkness, the carriages of the wealthy lit inside as well.

"And to question her about him, I am certain," I said. "I will ask you, Inspector, to leave Joanna be tonight. This has been a great shock."

"Learning that your husband is an embezzler and murderer?" The mustache moved again. "Yes, I imagine it must be."

"Put that out of your head right now, please. Samuel Millburn never killed that clerk, nor did he steal from the bank. I know this."

"That's not what witnesses tell me."

"Did anyone see him strike the man down? Or whatever happened to him?"

"No," Inspector McGregor had to admit. "The clerk was found in a strong room on the third floor of the bank, struck on the back of the head. Base of the skull. Probably with a paperweight or something similar, sometime in the early morning hours. It's a little-used strong room, which needs keys to open, so no one found him until later in the day. Millburn was known to have been seen near the bank early this morning but arrived for work half an hour late, nervous and ill at ease, according to his colleagues."

"Which does not make him a murderer," I said.

Inspector McGregor shifted uncomfortably. "His prior arrest sheet conveys he's familiar with violent crime. I grant you, that arrest sheet is twenty years old."

"He has reformed from his youthful escapades and made himself a better man," I said firmly. "Sam did not do any of this. I can guarantee it."

"I never said I agreed with those accusing him," Inspector

McGregor said without looking at me. "I am here to investigate, not send the first man thrust in front of me to Newgate."

"Well, I am grateful to hear it." I was truly grateful, my knees going weak with it. I was also grateful to him for giving me the details of the death, which he did not have to. Though I rather suspected he'd told me to keep me from turning up at Scotland Yard to pester him about it.

"On the other hand, I have no other suspects." His declaration made me grow even more shaky. "Mr. Millburn will have to do for now."

"Nonsense, Inspector." I drew a breath. "There is an entire building full of possibilities for both the murder and the embezzlement."

Inspector McGregor turned to me in exasperation. "You are not a detective, Mrs. Holloway."

"That does not mean I cannot see things that are right in front of me. I would question Mr. Zachary, who seems to be high up in the company, and Miss Swann, who surreptitiously tells him what to do. She is related to the bank's owners, by the way. Also, speak to a junior banker called Mr. Kearny, who knows Sam well. Anyone in the clerks' rooms, upstairs or downstairs, could have killed Mr. Stockley. I'd say the only ones who could not have done the murder are the doorman and his assistant, as they'd be unlikely to know much about the building beyond their posts or have keys to a third-floor strong room. Although I suppose one of them could have managed it somehow."

Inspector McGregor's exasperation became near outrage. "Has Millburn's wife been filling your ears?"

"Joanna knows absolutely nothing about what goes on at Daalman's Bank," I said. "Sam spoke little of it at home. You will not interrogate that poor woman about this, and especially not tonight. As I said, leave her be."

"You are certain," Inspector McGregor snapped.

"Very certain. Let Joanna at least have time to absorb what has happened. Question her tomorrow, or the day after, in the daylight. Preferably with me next to her to reassure her."

Inspector McGregor made a sound like a growl. He straightened his hat, which sent an additional fall of water cascading from its brim.

"I understand your concern for her," he said tightly. "Very well, I'll let her alone—for now. If she legs it in the night with all the money her husband has stolen, I will hold *you* accountable."

"I have no qualms about that," I said. "Joanna is certainly not going to pack up all her children and flee to the Continent. Best you turn your attention to others at the bank and leave Joanna in peace."

Inspector McGregor glanced briefly skyward. "I will return when I please. Then I will question her, whether you are present or not."

He touched his hat brim one more time, letting down another trickle of water, then turned his back on me and marched down Cheapside in the direction of Fleet Street.

I let out a long breath of relief. I knew if that Inspector McGregor had truly believed Joanna would run off in the night, he'd never have walked away. He had his doubts about Sam's guilt, mercifully.

I hastened back down the lane to Joanna's front door and told Carrie that Inspector McGregor might return in the morning. I planned to return myself tonight and be there if Inspector McGregor arrived, but I wanted to warn Joanna, just in case.

Thoroughly soaked now, I hastened back to Cheapside and sacrificed a few coins for a hansom to take me to Mayfair.

* * *

Below stairs at the Mount Street house, where Tess sautéed chops on the stove, Elsie washed pots and pans, and Mr. Davis chivied footmen in the servants' hall, seemed so normal I wondered if the previous hours had been a bad dream. I unbuttoned my coat with numb fingers and slid it from my arms. No one had greeted me, so absorbed in their tasks they hadn't noted my return.

In the back of my mind this cheered me—evidence that the kitchen would not collapse without me. I could leave for a time without incident.

Tess was the first to spy me, having turned to snatch a bowl of dried herbs from the dresser. She ought to have had all the things next to her to prepare the dish, but I decided not to admonish her for it.

"There you are, Mrs. H.," she sang. "Did you have a fine half day?"

I had no words to describe my afternoon, so I simply nodded as I moved through the hall to the stairs. I'd need to change to my work frock if I was to help get supper, but on the way, I would also approach Mrs. Bywater to obtain leave to stay with Joanna.

Mr. Davis had stormed back into the butler's pantry and was decanting wine by the time I reached his door. He refused to look up, even when I bade him a good evening. I gave up and ascended the back stairs, which were shadowy dark.

Mrs. Redfern opened the door at the top just as I reached it. "Mrs. Holloway." She cordially stepped back into the main floor to let me pass. "Did you have a good afternoon out?"

I usually was happy to answer the question, but not tonight.

"Mrs. Redfern, will you tell Mrs. Bywater that I would like to speak with her about something?"

Mrs. Redfern's welcoming smile died on her lips. "Is anything the matter?"

"It is nothing that will interfere with my cooking, I assure you," I said. "Please tell her the same."

"Very well." Mrs. Redfern's chain of keys jingled as she strode along the main floor toward the rear of the house.

I scurried to the next set of back stairs and continued my climb to my chamber. Once there, I removed my good dress and hat, brushed them as clean of rain and mud as I could, and put them carefully away. Before I closed the wardrobe, I dug out the cloth that wrapped my savings and carried it to the bed.

The collection of coins and banknotes looked pitifully small in the candlelight. I didn't have much by Mayfair standards, but I was only a cook looking to retire. I'd not be able to buy the shop I envisioned with this, but I could help Joanna with what she needed.

I wrapped up the money again and hid the bundle under the loose board at the bottom of the wardrobe. My two spare pairs of boots went firmly atop the hiding place.

In front of my tiny mirror, I smoothed my hair and pinned on my cap, a cook once more. Descending through the house, I paused in the main hall to await Mrs. Bywater.

Mr. Davis shot through the green baize door with the decanters as I reached the main floor, sending me a disapproving look as he skimmed into the dining room.

Mrs. Bywater strode out of the back sitting room at the same time Mr. Davis entered the dining room, she as annoyed as Mr. Davis at the sight of me above stairs.

"Mrs. Holloway." Mrs. Bywater stopped before me, the two of us standing in the exact center of the hall. Mrs. Bywater was an angular woman who wore plain, narrow-skirted gowns that did not disguise her thinness. Her hair, as usual, was dressed in a simple knot. She eschewed any sort of primping and made certain everyone knew her views on overly ornate ensembles. "You should have waited for me in the kitchen."

I hadn't wanted to announce my business to the rest of the staff, which was why I'd wished to speak to her in private upstairs. At least here we were away from the rushing maids and footmen, but Mr. Davis and Mrs. Redfern, who'd moved into the sitting room, were well within earshot.

"I would like to stay with a friend tonight, ma'am," I explained. "After supper is finished, of course. I will return in time to prepare breakfast in the morning."

"With a friend?" Mrs. Bywater stressed the last word, as though amazed I actually had a friend.

"Yes, ma'am." I kept my tone deferential. "She is poorly, and I would like to make certain she is all right tonight."

"I see." Mrs. Bywater's skepticism rang out. "I am sorry, Mrs. Holloway, but not every member of staff can suddenly have ill friends. My husband told me Mr. Davis went off to tend one, and now your friend is ill as well."

I sensed Mr. Davis listening as he pretended to straighten things on the dining room's sideboard. Likewise, Mrs. Redfern hovered near the sitting room's open doorway.

My ire rose. "I assure you, ma'am, that this is not a ruse. She needs me."

"I am certain any number of friends need you," Mrs. Bywater said crisply. "That does not mean you can rush about London in the night to visit them all. Your place is here, and here is where you will stay."

"The supper and breakfast will be on the table on time," I tried.

Mrs. Bywater raised a thin hand. "Do not presume to argue with me, Mrs. Holloway. That is my decision. If all the staff rushed off to their sick friends, where would we be?"

Her pale hazel eyes held no sympathy, and the stubborn set to her lips told me I'd waste time trying to win her to my side. I could only drop a curtsy and quiet my voice.

"Yes, ma'am."

I bowed my head and moved sedately to the door to the back stairs, though I was seething with anger and frustration.

Mr. Davis studiously did not look at me as I passed the dining room. I heard Mrs. Redfern's keys as she bustled about the sitting room as though she had great need to tidy things there.

Mrs. Bywater made a huff of finality and mounted the stairs, feet thumping on the carpet as though punctuating her annoyance.

I sped through the door to the back stairs and just stopped myself slamming it behind me. I did, however, let myself curse between my teeth as I stomped down the stairs.

Joanna needed help tonight. I would send word to Daniel through James—if I could lay my hands on James—to keep an eye on her house, though she needed comfort and reassurance as well as protection. I fumed as I gained the lower floor and made my angry way along the hall.

"Mrs. Holloway."

Mr. Davis's voice had me turning back on the threshold of the kitchen.

"Yes, Mr. Davis?" I tried to keep my voice even, but the bite of irritation came through. "I do not have time to listen to your lectures. I have a supper to cook."

I continued into the kitchen, ready to continue preparations for the meal, though I couldn't for the life of me remember what I'd planned to make. Tess turned from her sauté pan, questions in her eyes, but I had no answers.

I wanted to throw down my apron, fetch my things, and walk out of this house, never to return. Only my habitual caution, born of fear and self-preservation, did not let me. A cook who quit her post without giving notice would be hard-pressed to find another. I made myself walk to the work table and take up a carrot. What I'd do with it, I had no idea.

"Is your friend truly unwell?" Mr. Davis asked me. His voice was stiff, holding the coldness it had since he'd caught me snooping in his bedchamber.

I turned, carrot in my tight hand. "She is most distraught, yes."

Tess dropped her fork onto the floor with a clatter. "Oh no. Do you mean—" She cut herself off before she said Grace's name and amended the question. "Who is unwell, Mrs. H.?"

"Mrs. Millburn," I said to both Tess and Mr. Davis. "A close friend."

"Oh, poor lady. Is she very ill?" Tess had met Joanna at Christmas, when Joanna had dared visit the kitchen to bring us gifts she and her children had made. Tess had been quite taken with the motherly Joanna.

"I dislike leaving her alone, but there is nothing for it." I forced my tone to be brisk. "I will ask someone else to look in on her."

Mr. Davis came to me, lowering his voice. "Go."

I started, the carrot's green top swaying. "I beg your pardon, Mr. Davis? Go where?"

"To your friend. I don't mean this instant. Wait until after service, then instead of retiring to bed, go to her. I'll make certain the mistress believes you are in your chamber."

Tess's eyes widened, and I stared at Mr. Davis in astonishment.

"Why would you do such a thing?" I asked.

Chill annoyance settled over him again. "I am still unhappy with you, Mrs. Holloway, but I know what it is like to have a friend who needs you. Your Mrs. Millburn should not suffer because of our mistress's pique."

"Oh." I realized I was gaping, and popped my mouth closed. "That is very good of you. Yes, I will stay with her and be home before breakfast."

"Your comings and goings are your business, not mine." Mr. Davis emphasized the last words. "I will make certain the mistress does not seek you until you have returned to the house."

"What if she goes to Mrs. Holloway's bedchamber?" Tess asked in a dramatic whisper. "And finds her not there?"

"I will prevent that," Mr. Davis's voice became strained. "I told you."

I quickly turned to the table, taking up my knife to whack the top from the carrot. "Thank you kindly, Mr. Davis. We will say no more about it."

He made a noise of relief, pivoted on his heel, and marched out of the room.

"He's in a temper," Tess said.

"Never mind him," I said. "Put that fork in the scullery and fetch another one before those chops burn to a crisp. We must get on with supper—the hour is late."

Cynthia had not yet returned from our outing, I heard from Mrs. Redfern as Tess and I finished up the meal. She had instead sent word she'd visit Miss Townsend and would return late.

I wondered if Cynthia had decided to confide Sam's difficulties to Miss Townsend, and I hoped so. Judith Townsend came from a powerful family, and perhaps she could put words in the right ears on Sam's behalf.

After we sent up the meal, we prepared the staff's supper and consumed ours in the kitchen. I quietly explained to Tess what had happened to Sam, and why I truly wished to visit Joanna. Tess made noises of distress, but I bade her keep the story to herself.

"I'll never say a word, Mrs. H. But if you'd like Caleb to keep an ear open about it, he will. He's only a beat constable though. The tecs don't always talk about their cases where he can hear."

Caleb had been quite a mine of information in the past, and I could not push aside such an offer.

"He should only tell us what he can learn legitimately," I said. "I have no wish to have Constable Greene lose his post."

"He gets into plenty of trouble on his own, don't he?" Tess grinned. "He's very inquisitive, but that's a good thing in a policeman, innit?"

Not always. Those higher in the organization, from what I'd seen, preferred constables to stay in their places and not interfere.

I lingered as the staff ate their meals and continued their duties. Never had it taken so long for the kitchen to be cleaned, the next morning's preparations made, or the other servants to clatter off to bed. Elsie was the last to leave, bidding us a friendly good night behind her yawns.

Tess offered to stay behind to make sure I got out all right, but I told her firmly to go to bed. I could not trust that she'd not make up some long rigmarole about where I was if she encountered Mrs. Bywater.

Once Tess was gone, I quietly fetched my coat and gloves. I left my apron and cap behind but did not change out of my work dress.

When I peeked from the kitchen into the passageway, I saw Mr. Davis at the doorway of his butler's pantry. He stood like a sentry, the last of the staff to remain downstairs.

I gave him a faint wave, which he acknowledged with a nod. His stiff back told me he still hadn't forgiven me, but I would not throw away the opportunity he handed me.

I would owe Mr. Davis quite a few favors, I mused as I ducked back into the kitchen. I buttoned my coat, slid on my gloves, and climbed the outside stairs into the cold Mayfair night.

9

London in the late hours was a frightening place. It was one thing to travel across the City in the early evening, quite another nearing midnight.

The aristocrats and wealthy had barely begun their revelries, and carriages swarmed Mayfair, taking their inhabitants to soirees and suppers or across the metropolis to operas and the theater. The Season was a few months from its height, but already the hostesses were vying with one another to create the most talked-about parties of the year.

The activity did not make it safer for me, a lone woman hurrying through the dark. Pickpockets and worse roamed the night, including men who would drag their victims into lonely lanes and beat them senseless for the few shillings in their pockets.

At the moment, my greatest concern was that one of the neighbors, rolling by in a splendid carriage, would remark that she saw Mrs. Bywater's cook hurrying through Berkeley Square in the dead of night.

I followed a lane from Berkeley Square across New Bond Street, then turned down Conduit Street to Regent Street. Here, I searched for a cab, not wishing to plunge into the theater district and beyond on foot.

Hooves clopped loudly behind me as a hansom came out of Conduit Street on my heels. I ducked aside and pressed myself against the wall of the nearest house to let it by, assuming it was already engaged. Empty cabs waited at a stand down the street.

"Take you somewhere, missus?"

A voice I recognized called down to me. The cabbie was Lewis, a hansom driver who was Daniel's friend. I exhaled in relief and lost no time climbing into the low-slung vehicle and pulling its half doors closed.

"Happened to be passing, were you?" I demanded to Lewis's back as we joined the crush of traffic on Regent Street.

"McAdam told me to keep an eye out for you, love," Lewis said over his shoulder, his beaky nose silhouetted against the night. "I spied you sprinting out of your house, your collar around your ears, and decided you needed a way out of the neighborhood."

"Well, thank you, even if Mr. McAdam is presumptuous. Cheapside, please."

Lewis chuckled. "Right you are, missus."

He sped us alarmingly close to the larger carriages as we skimmed along Regent Street toward Piccadilly. Lewis was competent at the reins, but I shrank into the seat, hoping I made it to Joanna's unscathed.

Lewis conveyed me there without mishap and saluted me sunnily when I descended.

"A shilling, is it?" I asked, reaching into my pocket.

"McAdam already gave me the fare," Lewis informed me as he turned the cab. His horse, a large, patient bay, rotated the front of his body around his nearly motionless back legs until the cab faced the way we'd come.

"Mr. McAdam does not pay my way," I informed Lewis. I thrust out the shilling, but Lewis slapped the reins to the horse and rolled away, ignoring me completely.

Burying my irritation, I hastened to Joanna's house, letting the anticipation of sleeping in the same house as Grace flood me instead.

Carrie opened the door a crack and peered out cautiously when I knocked, then heaved a breath of relief. "Oh, it's you, missus. Thank the good Lord."

She stood aside so I could enter, then shut the door quickly and slammed the bolt across it.

"Have the police been bothering you?" I asked as I shed my coat and hung it on the hall tree. My gloves landed on the hall tree's bench, and I straightened my hair in its mirror. "I shall have to have another word with Inspector McGregor."

"No, ma'am." Carrie's worn face was blotchy with tears and worry. "No police have come. It's the other blokes that I don't like the look of."

I paused to stare at her. "What other blokes?"

"The ones what—"

Carrie's explanation was cut short as footsteps sounded on the stairs, and Grace came off them, flinging herself at me. I caught her, holding her warm body against mine. She was in her nightdress without a wrapper, though at least she'd thrust slippers on her feet.

"I knew you'd come," Grace announced into my shoulder.

I made myself release her. "What are you doing out of bed,

young lady? And without a dressing gown? You'll catch your death. Upstairs with you."

Grace grinned happily, knowing my scolding was hollow. I took her up the stairs myself, and she scampered ahead of me.

I longed for this, I realized with a pang in my heart. I wanted to be Grace's mother in truth, chiding her for being up too late, cooking meals for her, and hugging her whenever I wished.

For now, I eased my yearning by steering her to the bed-chamber she shared with Joanna's daughters, Jane and Mabel.

Two bedsteads filled the small room—Jane and Grace shared one, while Mabel slept on a smaller bed in the corner. Both girls were sitting up, candles lit on their bedside tables.

"All you scamps are awake, are you?" I said, trying to be stern. "I'll take care of your mum, don't you worry. But you have to sleep. You won't help her if you're crosspatches in the morning, will you?"

"Are you really staying?" Grace hopped up on the thick mattress beside Jane, who moved the covers aside for her.

"For tonight." I shook out the blankets as Grace lay down and settled them over both girls. "You go to sleep now." I bent and kissed Grace's cheek.

I wanted to burst into tears as I did so. I should be doing this every night, soothing her fears, admonishing her to rest, perhaps sitting on a chair at her bedside and reading out from a book. Mothers were supposed to do that.

I quickly moved to give Jane a peck on the forehead and then Mabel, as she too snuggled down. My eyes blurred, and I had to take a moment to blink them clear.

"Good night, Mum." Grace, ever cheerful, enjoyed the moment.

I could not resist kissing her again, smoothing her hair before I made myself snuff out both candles and leave the room.

I closed the door and then stood in the hall until I could breathe properly again.

I peeked into the room across the hall, where the boys, Matthew and Mark, likewise were not asleep, but sitting in the middle of their bed, murmuring to each other. I could not blame the children for their restlessness, but I was right in saying that they would do no one any good if they took sick from wakefulness and worry.

I told the two lads to lie down and cease talking. They obeyed me without hesitation, though I suspected they'd simply wait until I was abed before they continued their conversation.

Joanna was in the chamber she shared with Sam, though she was not in the bed. She sat listlessly in an armchair, her gaze wandering to the shuttered window, which rain had begun to batter. Joanna did not rise when I entered, though she must have heard me puttering about her children's bedrooms.

She'd undressed but had wrapped herself in a worn flannel dressing gown of faded maroon. A man's dressing gown, I saw—Sam's.

A fire had been built on the hearth sometime today, but it had died to a smolder, the room chilled. Many houses in London now had stoves rather than open fireplaces, but this modest home, standing in this lane for more than a hundred years, had no such amenities. Sam's salary went to a decent cookstove in the kitchen, but no further.

I poked the coals until flames flickered again, then pulled a chair next to Joanna's.

"Who are these blokes Carrie says have come here?" I asked without preliminary. "Journalists? Or men from the bank?"

Joanna started at my abruptness, then let out a bitter laugh. "Nothing so easily dealt with. A few gents from Sam's old life turned up, offering to help me. I knew what they meant."

They could have meant many things, from them lending her money to offering to marry her if Sam was convicted. "Tell me exactly what they said," I instructed.

Joanna flushed. "Nothing I wish to speak about."

"I must know everything if I am to help you. It might be very important. This is me, your dearest friend. You can tell me anything."

Joanna slumped into the chair. "What is the use? All Sam's shame will come out when he's in the dock, with a clever prosecutor dredging up his past. His old mates offered to break Sam from Newgate, spirit him to safety, and give him a different life. Kind of them, isn't it?"

My brows shot up. "They could promise that?"

"Oh yes. These are some of the hardest men in South London. They weren't afraid to come around these parts, which is saying much."

Indeed. London's neighborhoods, especially its eastern quarters, were divided into territories that had nothing to do with parish borders or the police beats, no matter how fondly the government and police believed they controlled the areas. South London toughs did not interfere with those of Cheapside or Bow Lane, who in turn did not venture into Whitechapel or Shadwell. One knew the periphery of one's domain.

The fact that these men swaggered to Joanna's home without worrying about what the Cheapside lads would do to them meant their South London leaders would see that nothing untoward happened to them.

"What do they want in return?" I asked. No one in these gangs did things out of the kindness of their hearts.

"Money. Me." Joanna's mouth twisted, then a fierce light entered her eyes. "My daughters. They considerately said they'd wait until they were older."

"Bloody devils." My anger rose at the same time as my fear. "We won't let them touch them."

"Too right, we won't."

We shared a look that took us back to our girlhood days. The only way to deal with the bullies of Bow Lane had been to dig in our heels and not back down. My mother coming after them with a broom hadn't hurt either. She'd only have to pretend to reach for it to make the youths flee. Joanna and I had made a formidable team.

"Daniel will help," I promised. "He can have men posted here to watch over you while Sam is . . . away."

"Police constables?" Joanna scoffed with the experience of one born in London's dark lanes. "I'm not sure boys in helmets will be any match for Sam's old mates."

"Police, and others. Daniel knows many sorts."

Joanna frowned. "I don't want to be obligated to them as well."

"Never. Daniel is a good man. You know him."

"Yes, and I recognize a former villain when I see one." She softened the words with a shaky smile. "Doesn't matter how charming he is. Mr. McAdam is from South London, isn't he?"

"I believe so, yes."

I spoke the words uncertainly. Daniel could sound like a man who'd never been north of the river in his life, but then he could also mimic an upper-crust accent so well that those of the upper crust accepted him in their midst. Any questions they had about his family and connections he neatly sidestepped.

I knew he'd spent some of his boyhood years in Bethnal Green with a man called Mr. Carter, until that man had been killed by villains worse than himself. But where exactly Daniel had come from in South London, I had no idea. He flitted from pillar to post, and there was no telling where he'd originated.

"He might know these men from Sam's past," Joanna said.

"Possibly. It has been a long time, though, since Daniel lived on the streets. He's beyond that now. Mostly."

The intense anger faded from Joanna's eyes, though the concern did not. "My poor Kat. You do not know what to make of him, do you?"

"Not really," I had to say.

"I was the same with Sam. He sat me down and told me where he'd come from, and how he wanted to leave that life behind. I believed in him. I was willing to marry him and help him."

"And he did it," I said. "Sam has made himself so thoroughly respectable I never suspected for a moment he hadn't always been."

"He must not have been very important to his old gang," Joanna reflected. "They let him go easily. Except for the chance encounter at the music hall, we've never heard a peep from them, until now."

"That is interesting." I thrust my hands at the fire to warm them, the coldness of the room finally ebbing. "I wonder why they've come forward. Do they believe Sam did rob the bank of that money and they might obtain it from him or from you? Or are they worried about what Sam might say to the police? Secrets coming out?"

I imagined the sharp-witted Inspector McGregor visiting Sam in jail, noting anything he said about a South London gang, and then rounding up officers to hunt them down. That is, if Sam said anything at all. We learned early that it was always best to stay silent in front of the law.

"I don't know, but they unnerved me," Joanna said. "If they do manage to help him escape, the police will hunt Sam down. I'll never see him again, no matter what."

Her face crumpled, and the tears she'd bravely sought to

contain returned. I gathered Joanna to me, and she sat like a child against me while I tried to comfort her.

I had not much comfort to offer. I would rally every force I could—Daniel, Lady Cynthia, Miss Townsend, and, if necessary, Daniel's underworld connections—to keep Joanna's family safe. It would be a monumental task to bring Sam home, but I determined to do it.

At the moment, I could only hold my friend like I would my daughter, my heart heavy for her plight.

I shared Joanna's bed that night, not wanting her to sleep alone. She did sleep, thanks to the chamomile tea laced with milk I made her drink, though she was restless.

My natural inclination to wake early had me up before dawn. I dressed hastily, hugged Grace, who'd come into the hall when she heard me, and sent her back to bed while I descended. I left Joanna sleeping, but I knew she'd understand I had to hurry back to my employment.

The maid was already up, sweeping the front step when I departed. Her eyes were red-rimmed, and her concern for the family heartened me. Some servants would simply abandon a household caught in scandal and try their luck elsewhere. That Carrie and her husband and the cook remained loyal to Joanna was reassuring.

"Let no one in," I told Carrie. "Only me or Mr. McAdam. If Inspector McGregor arrives, tell him Mrs. Millburn can't rise from her bed. I do not want him interviewing her without me near, and I can't stay this morning."

"Not letting anyone in," Carrie said, her worn face set in determination. "My man and me will look out for her, never you worry."

"Make sure she eats something," I admonished her, and Carrie nodded readily.

"You can count on me, Mrs. Holloway." Her resolve ebbed a moment. "Will Mr. Millburn be all right? He never did that man over, did he?"

"No, indeed." I settled my gloves. "Mr. Millburn is innocent, and he will be freed. Let us never forget that."

Carrie nodded, if glumly. I made myself turn and go, knowing I had to get myself home before I was missed. I'd meant to be here when Inspector McGregor called, but the mistress forbidding me to go had put paid to that idea.

A cab rolled to a halt in front of me when I reached Cheapside. I recognized the large bay horse and Lewis the cabbie driving it.

Daniel had certainly instructed him to be at the ready for me. It was good of him, I decided as I climbed aboard. A friend looking out for a friend, not a man trying to tie me to him with obligation.

Still, a woman had to be careful what sort of man she owed favors to. Some called in their debts in sinister ways, as Sam's old friends were trying to do with Joanna.

I wondered who these men were exactly, and why they were coming around now. Sam had been gone from their territory for twenty years—even Inspector McGregor had admitted that. What had Sam done to make them hunt up his family the minute they were vulnerable? I recalled Joanna saying he'd made a few of them back down when they'd accosted her and Sam at the music hall. Perhaps Sam had been higher in the ranks than Joanna was assuming.

Joanna had given me the name of one of them as I'd put her to bed, though she'd done so reluctantly. I'd had to reassure her I would not seek out the man myself. I would mention him to Daniel and see what he knew of him, or what he could find out. Such a man was likely well known to the Metropolitan Police.

I dozed in the cab as we rattled our way to Mayfair. I snapped awake once or twice, then concluded I should let myself sleep. I wouldn't get much more rest today than this.

Lewis woke me when he halted in Oxford Street near Grosvenor Square, where I'd instructed him to let me out. Again, he refused payment, pretending to be engrossed in turning the hansom—which the horse knew exactly how to do, I could see—when I tried to hand him coins.

I called after him to tell Daniel I wished to see him. Lewis raised a hand as he headed east on Oxford Street, but whether he'd heard me or would pass on the message remained to be seen.

I popped into a greengrocers I liked, finding the grocer just setting out his wares. The best time to shop for produce was early, as canny servants and housewives would pick the finest bits, leaving wilted, browning specimens to those who shopped later. I assuaged my worries by filling a basket I borrowed from the grocer's wife with crisp heads of lettuce, bright orange carrots, and onions that would roast up sweet.

From there I hurried through Grosvenor Square and down South Audley Street to Mount Street, clattering breathlessly down the stairs to the kitchen.

I swept indoors in time to hear Mrs. Bywater say sternly, "Good morning, Mrs. Holloway. You've been outdoors, have you?"

10

❖———❖

I strove for a nonchalant expression as I faced Mrs. Bywater.
I must look a fright, with my hair windblown, my face
ruddy from the cold. I'd borrowed a brush from Joanna and
repinned my hair this morning, but the brisk January breeze
had tugged tendrils free. Mrs. Bywater, by contrast, was neat
and trim, a cameo brooch, her one adornment, set precisely in
the middle of her collar.

"I have indeed, ma'am." I clutched the basket of produce in
both hands, my greens and vegetables piled in it. "One must
go to the greengrocers early or be unlucky."

Under Mrs. Bywater's pinched face and hard stare, I strolled
to the table and plunked the basket onto it. Tess, who'd turned
from the stove in relief when she heard me enter, set down her
spoon and hurried to begin sorting my purchases.

Mrs. Bywater watched closely as I unbuttoned my coat, as

though she expected to see me bedecked in an indecent frock for my nighttime frolic. When only my work dress appeared, she sniffed.

"Well, get on with your duties." She moved to the kitchen door, then paused. "I do hope your friend mends, Mrs. Holloway. However, I find that when a person has a good constitution, she will recover whether there are friends hovering over her bedside or not."

Giving me a decided jerk of her head, she strode away. Tess opened her mouth, but I held up a finger, warning her to silence until we heard the mistress climb the stairs and slam the door at the top behind her.

"A daft thing to say." Tess scowled into the passageway. "She means that if the friend has a *weak* constitution, us being at their side won't help them either."

"Mrs. Bywater is a bit shortsighted," I agreed. "But remember, Tess, we must never disparage our employers."

"Not where they can hear, anyway." Tess returned to sorting the greens, her temper not soothed.

I sensed rather than heard Mr. Davis glide in. I moved to the small mirror near the coatrack and tucked up my straggling hair.

"She came down very early," Mr. Davis explained. "I had a job keeping her out of the kitchen, I must say."

"Thank you, Mr. Davis." I tied my apron's strings as I turned to him. "I meant to return before anyone rose, but it is a long way to Cheapside, and I truly did stop to buy the produce."

"A mercy you did." Mr. Davis lingered a moment, as though he wished to say more, then he simply nodded and slid back into the hall, making for the butler's pantry.

Deflecting Mrs. Bywater was his way of indicating he wanted

us to continue as friends, I supposed. Well, I would not complain because he hadn't thawed all the way yet. He hadn't been wrong to be angry with me in the first place.

"Let us get on," I said to Tess.

She was full of questions, I could see, but I said nothing as I tiredly helped her pile the bacon and toast on platters, as well as egg cups with the master's favorite boiled eggs.

I wanted answers myself. Sam would be up before a magistrate this morning, in a court in the City, who would decide whether there was enough evidence to try him. I longed to be there, to shout his innocence, though I knew that would do no good.

Would Inspector McGregor respect my wish to be present when he interviewed Joanna? Or grow impatient and interrogate her and her household anyway? Inspector McGregor at least was always adamant to arrest the correct person for a crime, not the most convenient one, but what if he decided the evidence against Sam was too strong?

I could only keep my head down over my work and pray that those Sam faced would see reason. I went through my routine of preparing breakfast for both the household above stairs and the staff below, though I didn't have much appetite for the pile of eggs and toast Tess shoved at me.

My cook's mind hummed away beneath my troubles, surfacing now and then to remind me of my duties. I had pitchers of orange juice and cut rinds waiting for me to make them into sorbet for Mrs. Bywater's supper tomorrow night. They would need at least a day to become solid enough to serve.

I also had the fresh produce I'd purchased this morning to wash, sort, and prepare for dishes I'd make this evening. A kitchen never ceased. No matter what disasters happened in the world, people still needed to eat.

I bade Tess fetch the oranges, juice, and rinds and made my way down the hall to the butler's pantry.

"Mr. Davis—"

"Say nothing, Mrs. Holloway." Mr. Davis did not look up from the silver he polished on his table. He wore gloves, and dipped a cloth in a foul-smelling muck he made himself. His silver polish, he swore, was far superior to anything sold in shops these days. "Do not ruin our truce."

"I came to ask if you'd mind sharing the newspaper today. When the master is done with it, of course."

Mr. Bywater read through three newspapers as he took his breakfast, then tossed them to Mr. Davis to dispose of. Mr. Davis carried them downstairs, smoothed them out, and read them cover to cover himself.

"Any particular bit of news you are looking for?"

My face went hot. "Perhaps. It is of no matter, Mr. Davis. Never mind."

"I ask because Mr. Bywater reads two financial newspapers as well as the *London Times*. Not because it is my business what sort of news you seek. Which newspaper did you want?"

"All of them, I suppose."

A sensational murder would more likely be reported in a newspaper covering the general news of London, but a financial paper might mention troubles at Daalman's Bank. I needed to understand that institution and the people who worked there if I were to decide who was to blame. It was too bad Mr. Bywater did not take a paper like the *Police Gazette*, which was sold to the public at newspaper stands, but he was far more interested in finance than crime.

Mr. Davis's brows rose the slightest bit. He was curious, I could see, but was holding to his self-righteous vow to not pry into anyone's affairs.

"Very well. I shall bring them to the kitchen when the master is finished."

"Thank you." I paused in the doorway. "I am truly sorry about mixing up the wines. I was in a hurry and should have been paying more attention."

Mr. Davis lifted a cloth-laden hand. The polish on it was a strange gray-green, but the silver always shone. "Stop, Mrs. Holloway. As I said, do not spoil it."

"No, indeed, Mr. Davis." I resumed my usual tones and left him to it without a farewell.

Tess had piled the orange ingredients on the table. "Quite a lot of them," she said as I entered.

"They'll be eaten up quickly." Everyone loved a bright, sweet orange ice, like a taste of summer in the midst of winter.

"Is Mrs. Millburn all right?" Tess asked me in a low voice as we began to set out the cut orange rinds. "Her kiddies and Grace too?"

"She is upset, naturally, but she will rally." I spoke with the confidence I did not feel. "Her children will need her to be strong, and she understands that."

"Still, it must be hard for her." Tess's mouth drooped in commiseration. "I know what I go through when people try to take my brother away. As though locking him into an asylum will do him any good."

Tess's brother was a simple lad, and part of her wages went to look after him.

"Sam will be released." I sloshed sugar into a bowl. "He has to be."

I'd take Joanna and our families somewhere far away if Sam was hanged for this murder. We could move to the country, to a little village in the north perhaps. I'm certain that people who lived in Carlisle and thereabouts might be thankful for a good cook seeking a post.

The fact that I'd be leaving everything I'd known all my life and all my friends here, I pushed aside. No use fretting over something that hadn't happened yet.

I added plain, clean water to the sugar, making certain I had exactly the same proportions of water and sugar. This I put in a pot on the stove, and had Tess watch it carefully. The sugar should dissolve, and the liquid should just boil, making a light syrup. If I'd wanted caramel, I'd have let it continue to boil until it was golden and formed a little ball on the tines of my fork. An amazing array of syrups could be made from the simple mixture of sugar and water.

To a good helping of orange juice, I added some grated orange zest, a tiny bit of salt, and a dollop of vanilla. I had made the extract myself, adding leftover vanilla bean pods to a bottle of spirits and letting it sit for months on a warm shelf.

Once Tess announced the syrup was boiling, I carefully poured it into a clean bowl and set it aside to cool. We turned our attention to juicing more of the oranges, then when the syrup was ready, I added it to the juice and vanilla mixture.

"Why's it called *sor-bay*?" Tess asked as I gently stirred. "Looks like a tasty orange drink to me."

"It's a French pronunciation of sherbet, which is a Turkish cool drink. I believe," I amended. I was going by what a chef had told me, but I'd never seen this explanation in a cookbook. "Sorbet is essentially a flavored ice, but with a fancy name. We will put this in the larder until it is nice and solid."

I headed for the larder now with the bowl, Tess following with the pans I instructed her to bring. The back corner, the coolest part of the room, contained a cupboard built into the wall. A block of ice could be put into its top shelf, and I often broke up more to put in a zinc tub to use as an ice bath.

While Tess hovered with a towel to catch spills, I poured the orange mixture into a long metal pan and set this into the tub to chill. The ice cradled it and would have it solid enough in some hours.

Ice was a commodity I'd had to battle with Mrs. Bywater to continue. She found it a frivolous expense. Ice had to be delivered regularly by a man who picked it up from a so-called ice well near King's Cross Station—really an underground storage tank for ice carted there from frozen ponds in England and abroad.

The expense was necessary, I'd argued, if she wanted sorbets and ices for her supper parties. Because the ice did not actually go into the sorbet itself, Mrs. Bywater thought I could make it simply by putting the mixture on a cold windowsill or setting it outside.

I had to point out that such a thing would attract every cat, bird, and rat in Mayfair, as well as become coated with soot. Mr. Bywater had ended the argument by saying he'd write to Lord Rankin—who owned the house—and ask if he'd mind paying for ice.

Lord Rankin, by now exasperated by his deceased wife's aunt and uncle, had told Mrs. Bywater to spare no expense in the kitchen; he would cover it all.

I'd never approved of Lord Rankin, who had been accustomed to having his way with a maid when the fancy struck him, but I was thankful for his support against Mrs. Bywater. Then again, I knew many of Lord Rankin's secrets, and those of his wife and her family. He likely believed he had to placate me to keep my silence.

Whatever Lord Rankin's reasons, I now had ice delivered regularly to help keep food cold and fresh.

I returned to the kitchen to turn more of the orange juice into orange creams, which was essentially the same as the sorbet but with an addition of cream and some isinglass to make it firm. The rest I'd make into marmalade and also to flavor an almond gâteau.

Throughout all this preparation, I received no word from Daniel, Joanna, or Inspector McGregor about Sam and what had happened to him. I knew I'd not be the first person contacted—Joanna would—but as the hours dragged on, my nerves were grated as raw as the onion that would go into the pork pies.

I went in search of James to send for Daniel, but I did not see the lad. I'd have to hope that Lewis the cabbie had heard me ask him to send Daniel to see me.

Caleb passed by on the street on his usual beat that afternoon, and Tess hurried up to speak to him. She came down looking as anxious as she had ascended.

"He's heard nothing," she said in a loud whisper as she rejoined me at the stove. "Word of the arrest at the bank came through, but it was noted and put aside. It's a City crime, so it's left to them. Caleb only saw Sam's name and the fact that he'd been taken to the City lockup, but that's all."

"I could not expect much more," I said. "I can't have Constable Greene ask Inspector McGregor, because Inspector McGregor knows Constable Greene will tell me." The inspector was not happy I'd recruited Caleb to be my spy.

The only person with any news was Lady Cynthia. Mrs. Redfern brought me word at the last minute before luncheon that Cynthia and Mrs. Bywater were entertaining a guest for the meal. This annoyed me, as I had to make the meal for three instead of two when it was already finished, until Mrs. Redfern said that the guest was "that polite Miss Townsend."

I quickly added a salad with orange slices and another chop to the platters that went upstairs, and I saw Mr. Davis dive into the closet that was the wine cellar to pull out a good bottle. The staff liked Miss Townsend, who was well-spoken and courteous.

After the meal, I heard cultured voices in the hallway, and then Lady Cynthia led Miss Townsend into the kitchen.

"A delightful luncheon, Mrs. Holloway," Miss Townsend said. She wore her usual ensemble of elegant simplicity, her dark hair in neat curls that framed her face. "I apologize for the inconvenience of my addition. I hadn't meant to arrive just as a meal was ready. But I'd never turn down the chance to enjoy your food."

"Thank you." I bent my knees in a curtsy. "It was no inconvenience at all."

The twinkle in Miss Townsend's eyes told me she knew I told a polite lie. "The almond-orange cake was delightful. Almost as good as your lemon one." The twinkle deepened.

I'd been known to bribe Miss Townsend and her lady friend Lady Roberta Perry—Bobby as she was called—with lemon cake for their help in sticky problems.

Cynthia sat down at the kitchen table, getting flour all over the elbows of her nice frock. She glanced around to see who might be listening, but Elsie made plenty of noise in the scullery and the other staff were busy upstairs.

"Told Judith all about this bank business last night," Cynthia said. "She's dismayed that your Mr. Millburn was arrested—she knows what he and his wife do for you."

"That is kind of you." My words were perhaps not as filled

with gratitude as they could be, but my lack of knowledge chafed me.

"I came to tell you I have recruited a barrister who will speak for Mr. Millburn, if it comes to it," Miss Townsend said.

"I do not know if he'll be sent to trial," I said. "I've had no word about his plight at all. I am assuming that if he'd been released, Joanna would have sent a message." That she'd remained silent worried me.

"I can possibly find that out for you as well," Miss Townsend said. She remained standing a few feet from the table and out of range of the stove, her shoes planted on the cleanest tile in the kitchen. "There are people I can ask . . ."

"I shouldn't like to draw attention," I said quickly. As much as I wished to know what had happened to Sam this morning, I did not want every magistrate wondering why he was so interesting.

"The advantage of being an eccentric, Mrs. Holloway." Miss Townsend bathed me in her serene smile. "My male relations look upon me as an oddity who is curious about all sorts."

"It's kind of you," I said with sincerity. "And for the barrister, though I doubt Sam will be able to afford a very lofty one."

"Nonsense, the fellow owes me a favor and so will waive his fee. He's a silk, and arrogant about it, but quite good. If there is one chink in the evidence against Mr. Millburn, my friend will find it and render the chink a chasm."

"I do hope Sam can be proved to be completely innocent," I said. "Not let off on a technicality."

"I'd take the offer, Mrs. H.," Cynthia said. "It might be the best anyone can do."

"Forgive me—I do not mean to sound ungrateful." I rested my hands wearily on the table. "Any help is most welcome, and

I'm certain Joanna will agree, eventually. I worry that Mr. Millburn will be disgraced, even if he is acquitted, and he and Joanna will have to scratch for their living."

"We will do everything in our power to prevent that," Miss Townsend said.

She had a way of speaking that made all believe in what she told them. I saw, however, a tiny flicker of doubt in her eyes. Perfectly innocent people who were absolved of a crime could still be tainted by the accusation. The seed was planted in others' heads and wasn't easily erased. I'd seen it happen time and again throughout my life.

"In any case, he'd have wanted to look for more work soon," Cynthia said. "Thanos says the bank is on shaky ground. Talked to him at length last night about it. Bobby too. She says her brother has pulled out of investments there."

"Oh?" I asked. "Is that common knowledge?"

"Both Thanos and Bobby say no. Bobby says her brother is cagey, not because he's heard anything definite, but he's jumpy when his dividends go down by a penny. Thanos knows a chap who keeps his finger on the pulse of economic ups and downs, and that chap knows what banks are on sound footing and what are taking too many risks. Daalman's is in the second category."

"Yet Mr. Zachary sounded so confident when he talked about investing your money," I said.

"Very practiced," Cynthia agreed. "Doubtless he's perfected the act over the years. Like my father. Though I think all bankers are swindlers."

"Not quite, darling," Miss Townsend said.

"Judith has lived a blameless life among honest people," Cynthia said with a grin. "She is not convinced that those who work in finance most want to steal it."

"Not quite true either," Miss Townsend said with good humor. "Perhaps we should leave Mrs. Holloway in peace. She cannot make her wonderful concoctions with us hovering."

"I do appreciate your kindness," I said.

"It is not kindness. It is gratitude." Judith came to me and took my hands, as though I were a friend, though mine were covered with grease and flour. "You have a been a boon to Cynthia, and through her, to me. If there is anything I can do for you, you have but to ask."

I wasn't certain if her words were simply polite, but her eyes, as her gaze held mine, were earnest.

"Well," I said, taking a chance. "Is there any way one of you can look in on Joanna? I worry that the police will badger her. I have tried to get word to Mr. McAdam, but—"

"He is elusive, as always?" Cynthia finished. "Never fear, Mrs. H. We'll make certain your friend is all right."

I had no idea what Joanna would make of Miss Townsend or Cynthia descending on her, but I could not go myself until Thursday. I doubted Mr. Davis would be convinced to cover for me every night.

I gave them Joanna's exact address, then scribbled a note to Joanna on a page torn from my notebook. Cynthia pocketed the folded paper as she rose from the table, the arms of her frock now well dusted with flour.

"I will make certain she doesn't fuss over us," Cynthia promised. "She and her little ones will be the ones fussed over."

Miss Townsend sent me a reassuring glance as she ushered Cynthia out, brushing off the backs of Cynthia's arms as they went.

Tess, who'd faded into the background, in awe of Miss Townsend, returned to the table. "Must be ever so nice to be rich and beautiful, mustn't it, Mrs. H.?"

"You are quite comely, Tess," I said, taking up a rag to scrub off the table. "And if you work very, very hard, you might become rich. It happens."

Tess burst into laughter. "Now you are teasing me, Mrs. H. I'll come down to work tomorrow in a tiara, shall I?"

I'd spoken the truth as I saw it, but I was glad, in my low spirits, that one of us could laugh.

I heard nothing from anybody until after I'd sent up supper and began preparations for breakfast.

Mr. Davis, as he'd promised, had brought me the newspapers after Mr. Bywater, and then Mr. Davis, had read them through. As much as I'd scoured them, however, I'd found only one tiny mention of the murder, and that in a back page of the *Times*.

A kerfuffle in the City, in which one jealous clerk beat another over the head, the short article read. *A shame and a tragedy for the dead man. Police have arrested the culprit, who will soon go to his just reward.*

No names, no mention of Daalman's Bank. The financial papers spoke of Daalman's, but only in passing, as a firm who were underwriting an overseas venture of a shipping company beginning next month.

Odd, because journalists in London were very good at flinging all kinds of dirt at everyone, risking libel in doing so. The fact that they'd said very little of this murder, in the middle of a highly respected bank, was amazing. I imagined Miss Swann turning away the reporters with her quiet coolness, them slinking off into the fog.

I returned the papers to Mr. Davis with thanks, and he offered to bring me more tomorrow. I could see he was curious as to what I was looking for, and if things did not resolve themselves soon, I would recruit his assistance.

I was in the middle of mixing up the bread dough for tomorrow when Elsie left her sink and approached me.

"Bloke asking for ya, Mrs. Holloway," she told me. "Said he'd wait for you upstairs." She poked her finger upward.

Since the man had presumably come to the back door, I knew she meant he'd be on the street, not in a ground-floor sitting room. He wasn't Daniel or James, because Elsie would have said so if it were either of them.

"What bloke? Did he give you a name?"

"No, ma'am." Elsie stepped closer to me. "I didn't like the look of him, truth to tell."

I'd thought perhaps it was Lewis come with a message, but Lewis, while rough about the edges, was friendly enough.

"Well, I'd best go see what he wants." I hung up my apron, pulled on my coat, and took up my basket of scraps. I'd be going upstairs to distribute them about this time anyway.

The person leaning back on the railing, his elbows resting insolently on top of it, was unknown to me. He was thin, but I sensed wiry strength under his thick wool coat. He was only a few inches taller than me, with light-colored hair combed neatly under his cap, and blue eyes that held plenty of ice.

Like Joanna, I recognized a villain when I saw one. Clutching my basket before me like shield, I approached him.

"Who are you?" I demanded.

His eyes flickered, as though he'd expected me to approach fearfully, asking in a timid voice if he was the one who wanted to see me. I'd give him none of that.

"Name's Jarrett," the man said. "Ben Jarrett. Sam Millburn is me best mate. And you, love, are going to help me extricate him."

11

I took a step back. Jarrett was the name Joanna had given me, telling me I was under no circumstance to speak to him.

I drew a breath and glared at Mr. Jarrett with scorn. "I'm going to help *you*, am I? There's nothing to say Mr. Millburn will be in any place from which he'll need to be extricated. At least not permanently."

Jarrett snorted a laugh. "You are funny, missus. Millburn's already in Newgate. Magistrate at Old Jewry took one look at him this morning and sent him off."

My heart sank. I'd hoped against hope that the magistrate would wait for more evidence or send Sam home for lack of it. But I'd known deep inside that Sam would be held over. The bank wouldn't stand for him being released. Undoubtedly, someone from Daalman's had had a word with the magistrate, or the police, or both.

"Still, he is only awaiting trial," I said with a confidence I did not feel. "Once that happens, he will be acquitted, because Mr. Millburn never killed that clerk."

Jarrett shrugged his lanky shoulders. "Maybe he did, maybe he didn't. Won't matter. The likes of Millburn won't be let off, even if he's innocent as a newborn babe."

I did not like to agree with this specimen, but he had a point. "That may be true, but I will not be assisting you in 'extricating' him. I will work to find out the truth."

Jarrett's snicker made me flush with anger. "I heard you was a droll one, missus. Feisty too. I like that."

I already knew several things about this man. He liked to reach for vocabulary he never learned on the streets as a lad, he did not know what to do with women who talked back to him and so mocked them instead, and I did not like him.

"What do you mean, you heard I was a droll?" I asked sharply. "Heard from who?"

"Oh, your reputation precedes you, love. The underworld of London knows all about *you*."

His continued laughter indicated he was not going to tell me who was bandying my name about but could also mean he knew less about me than he claimed. It was a bully's tactic, to imply they had information you did not and only your subservience would reveal it.

"I am certain they do," I replied. "What do you really want, Mr. Jarrett? It is highly unlikely I can break Sam out of Newgate, or Dartmoor, or wherever they send him, so what is it?"

"No?" He left the railing and advanced on me, one small step at a time. "But you can take him fine cakes like what you've got in your little basket. Slip him a lockpick or something baked in your bread."

My scorn increased. "First of all, bread and fine cakes are

two entirely different things. Second, I wouldn't ruin a batch of either by baking things into it. I am certain his jailers would check that sort of thing anyway."

Jarrett's soft laughter made my blood cold. He had too much arrogance to be a simple street thief, stealing what he could to feed himself and his family or to give to a gang leader. He was a higher-up, I wagered, a lieutenant to a powerful group or maybe even its leader.

"Jailers are just blokes," Jarrett said. "Easy to sway to your side, especially for a pretty thing like you."

"Now you have entered into the realm of nonsense. Were you bothering Mrs. Millburn yesterday? Or one of your men? I must tell you to cease."

"I went round, yeah." Jarrett shrugged. "She's alone now, inn't she? She'll need help. We're happy to provide it."

"You told a vulnerable woman you'd assist her if she gave you her favors and those of her daughters. You are disgusting."

Jarrett quickly lifted his hands. "That weren't me. That were a bloke what didn't understand what we was offering. He got my fist in his teeth for it, believe me. I don't want no harm to come to Millburn's wife or his little 'uns."

The fact that this man or any of his blokes had gone anywhere near Joanna and her children made me furious.

"You will stay away from Mrs. Millburn and her family," I stated. "Far away."

"Don't throw away a chance for her to come out well from this," Jarrett said, his amusement gone. "The other little girl there. Your daughter? The likeness is amazing."

I couldn't see anything after that. I went at Jarrett, ready to shove him somewhere, anywhere. If he shot out into the street to be struck by a passing carriage . . .

A man appeared out of nowhere to stand like a bulwark between me and Jarrett. He faced Jarrett, however. Once the mists cleared from my eyes, I saw that he had Jarrett against the railing, not with his hands, but simply with his stare.

"Bit far from your patch, aren't you?" Daniel asked him. "This is Mayfair, where they don't want the likes of you."

"Toffy bastards." Jarrett spit, but not, I noticed, where that spittle would reach Daniel.

"Why are you bothering Mrs. Holloway?" Daniel's tone was conversational, but Jarrett was trying to shrink as far from him as possible without betraying that he was.

"Told her."

"I heard what you told her," Daniel answered. "The idea that you were recruiting her help is a lie. If you wanted Millburn out of Newgate, you'd find your own way without involving Mrs. Holloway. So, what is it?"

"Things you need to know." Jarrett's arrogance had dimmed a notch, but it was still there. "Sam Millburn didn't just happen to trot out of South London and become respectable. He left a shambles in his wake, things the peelers are still trying to fit him up for. That's the sort of man what's looking after your daughter."

The mention of my daughter almost made me have a go at him again, but I restrained myself with effort. He wanted to get a rise out of me. Another tactic of a bully.

I recalled Inspector McGregor saying Sam had once had a long arrest sheet, but twenty years ago. "That was a long while back," I said.

"True, but them magistrates are going to churn up the muck, and they'll find the sorts of things Millburn once did. Had others do for him." Jarrett sniffled and wiped his nose with one finger. "But with your assistance, and his wife's, all that can go away."

"You mean if she pays you." Daniel's tone became more steely. "You think Millburn took that money, don't you? And gave it to his wife for safekeeping." He leaned closer to Mr. Jarrett. "Even if he did, why should she give it to *you*?"

"To keep him from being buried in the deepest hole the beaks can shovel him into, if they don't hang him on the spot."

"You can prevent this fate how?" Daniel asked.

My heart hammered, my mouth dry even thinking of such a thing happening to Sam. But I was wise enough to stand motionless and let Daniel question the man without interfering.

"Let's just say we've got people in our pockets that can either make things bad for our Sammy, or good for him. Could go either way."

"Unless Mrs. Millburn pays you a vast sum she doesn't have, is that it?"

"She has it." Jarrett nodded sagely. "Mark my words, old Sam has squirreled away that cash, has done so for years. Time for him to pay his dues."

"He has not," I said vehemently, unable to stop myself. "He shucked you and your mates a long time ago, and never looked back. Only a dishonorable man can't recognize honor when he sees it."

Daniel shifted a little to his left, which blocked me from Jarrett, and Jarrett from me, if the man decided to take a swing at me for my insult. Jarrett's eyes narrowed, but he was prudent enough not to come at me.

"You didn't know Millburn in the old days." Jarrett clicked his tongue against his teeth. "What he wouldn't get up to. I'll leave ye be now that you have your tough to fight for you, but we'll be back, you mark my words."

The basket's handle was scraping my hands raw, I held it so tightly. "It will do you no good to accost me again."

Daniel's words slid through mine. "If you come near Mrs. Holloway or Mrs. Millburn, I'll make sure you regret it. For the rest of your life, I imagine."

"That a fact?" Jarrett turned his sneer on Daniel. "You know who I am?"

"I do." Daniel faced him comfortably. "You have a nice gang of toughs that terrorize South London, and now you're trying your luck here. You're out of your depth, Jarrett. Go home and stay there."

Jarrett came off the railing, his jabbed pride giving him courage. "So, you do know who I am. I'm not prepared to take orders from a deliveryman who's plied his trade in Mayfair so long he thinks he's a toff."

"Do you know a man called Bernard Compton? Of South London? Or of him—I believe he's deceased now."

"He is, and good riddance to bad rubbish." Jarrett rubbed his lower lip as though preventing himself from spitting again. "What of him? We took over his patch once he was gone."

"I know you did. Mr. Compton had the keeping of me from an early age. He taught me many things." Daniel let that seep into Jarrett's thoughts. "One more thing you should know. *I got away from him.*"

Jarrett's eyes widened before he remembered to show no fear. But Daniel's words impressed him.

"Yeah, well." Jarrett straightened his jacket and then his hat, as though hoping the actions would give him time to find words. "Tell Millburn's wife I'm sorry for her. But she can send for me if she wants. Her choice."

Daniel only regarded him steadily. Jarrett finally turned way, jamming his hands into his pockets before he slouched off down the street. He never said a word to me.

I didn't relax my grip on the basket until Jarrett had disappeared into the shadows beyond South Audley Street in the direction of Hyde Park. If any constables on Park Lane saw him, the man would have to scarper. The police there didn't like any insalubrious characters near the homes of the wealthiest in London. They'd chase Jarrett away if they didn't arrest him outright.

Daniel's warm hand landed on my arm, and he relieved me of the heavy basket. "I am sorry I didn't reach you sooner. But I didn't think someone like Jarrett would approach you, here in Mayfair."

"He is arrogant." My voice shook, I pretended with cold. The night was frigid. "Has been unchallenged too long."

"He won't go nigh Mrs. Millburn, I promise you." Daniel's words rang with determination. "I have men stationed around Clover Lane, watching who goes in and out. They won't be afraid to stop Jarrett."

"Which means they are just as bad as him."

"Worse." Daniel gave a short laugh. "You remember Grimes?"

Zachariah Grimes had been a childhood friend of Daniel's. He was a congenial man but big and tough. I relaxed a bit. He'd guard Joanna well.

"Thank you," I said.

"I told you I'd help." Daniel flashed me his smile. "I know I didn't send word to you today, but I've been running all over London. I take it you know Millburn was sent to Newgate pending his trial?"

"So Mr. Jarrett told me. No one else did."

"I'm sorry." Daniel became more apologetic. "I told Lewis to convey the news, but he must not have had the chance. James has been kept hopping as well. I'm trying to find a good solicitor for Millburn, but the ones I approached won't touch the case."

"Miss Townsend already offered a barrister," I said. "I suppose she will seek a solicitor as well." Solicitors had to approach the barrister on the client's behalf. I suppose it was gauche for barristers to actually speak to a client without a go-between.

"Did she? Excellent news. I imagine anyone she suggests will be clever and impeccable."

"It is likely." My teeth began to chatter, truly with cold now. My coat only kept out so much, and I had no hat or gloves.

"My dearest, let us get you inside." Daniel took me by the elbow and began leading me to the stairs only a yard away.

I shook him off and reached for the basket. "I haven't handed out the food yet. There are those less fortunate than me waiting for the only meal they might have today."

Daniel didn't relinquish the basket to me. "I'll help you. I enjoy doing good deeds. Here you are, sir." He turned to a man who'd approached. "Finest food in London."

It was the older man I'd sent off to Mr. Fielding on Thursday—he was back, accepting from Daniel the cloth-wrapped left-over chops and bit of bread in his threadbare-gloved hands. If I was handy at knitting, I'd make him another pair.

"It is that," the man agreed. "Always a queue for the queen of Mayfair."

Daniel laughed, his breath fogging. "An apt name for her."

I shook my head at the both of them as Daniel moved on to the next person. "What absolute nonsense."

The older man touched my arm as Daniel moved down the line, dispensing the contents of my basket with a jovial word for each recipient. I heard chuckles and laughter warming the January air.

"A word to the wise, missus," the man said. "Be careful around that bloke. He's a bad 'un. Everyone south of the river knows *him*."

"I realized he was a complete villain," I assured him. "That's why Mr. McAdam sent him off. Do not worry—he'll not be back in these parts."

"No, not *'im*. 'E's nothing." The man dismissed Mr. Jarrett with a wave. He ducked his head closer to mine, his breath sour with the remnants of gin. "*That* one." He jerked a thumb at Daniel. "The one you call McAdam. Not the name 'e used in my day. Have a care of 'im, missus. There, I've warned ye."

"What do you mean? What name did—?"

My words cut off as the man slid into darkness, beating a hasty retreat toward Berkeley Square. At the same time, Daniel swung back to me, eyes glittering under the gas lamps.

"All done," he announced. "Now, we go inside out of this weather. No argument."

Daniel seized my arm and led me downstairs, my questions dying on my lips.

12

My shock at the man's proclamation didn't leave me, though I was grateful for the kitchen's warm embrace. I woodenly hung up my coat and turned to the table, where Daniel was greeting Tess.

Tess took the basket from him to return to its place beside the dresser, beaming happily. "Always brighten the place, you do, Mr. McAdam."

"At least someone is welcoming tonight." Daniel sent his teasing glance to me. "Mrs. Holloway has forgotten how to speak."

"I am cold, is all." I moved to the stove and held my hands over it, my fingers tingling with returning circulation. "I suppose you've come for nourishment," I said to Daniel.

"Of all kinds."

Words like that should make me flush with heat, but I still reeled from the declaration the man outside had given me.

Daniel had mentioned the name Bernard Compton, which had worried Jarrett, but then said he'd been very young when he'd been with him.

I knew Daniel had still been a small lad when he'd gone to live with an East End leader called Carter. I refused to believe Daniel had terrorized South London as a tiny tot.

Unless he'd gone back there after Carter's death ...

Mr. Fielding, Daniel's foster brother, had told me that after Mr. Carter had been killed, Daniel had become quite remorseless. Had done things worse than Mr. Fielding had ever contemplated, he'd said. Mr. Fielding was an accomplished liar, it was true, and I wasn't certain what to believe.

Daniel had seated himself, thanking Tess, who slid a plate of meat pie in front of him. Elsie gazed at him admiringly around the scullery doorway, and footmen hailed him from the passageway. Mr. Davis, exiting the servants' hall, raised his brows at Daniel's presence, then walked on without a word.

I could not interrogate Daniel while so many passed in and out of the kitchen, all happy to greet him, so I rinsed my hands in the sink and continued with my preparations for the next morning.

Daniel regaled his audience with tales of interesting people he'd seen on the streets during his deliveries. He described a woman in Covent Garden market chasing off a would-be thief with a bundle of celery, wielding it like a club, and a dog who defended his master, a thin old man, from toughs who ran off in a fright.

The footmen and Tess and Elsie laughed about the woman and cheered for the dog, encouraging Daniel to tell even more. stories.

I listened, wondering which were true things he'd seen today, and which were ones he'd stored up to cover for where he'd really been.

Daniel managed to shovel in the entire large slice of meat pie as he spoke, and a hunk of almond cake Tess produced for him as well. Daniel at last wiped his mouth with a handkerchief and heaved a contented sigh.

"The best food in London," he proclaimed. "I am not wrong. The queen of Mayfair is a good name for you."

"And you are the king of absurdity," I admonished. "I also notice you turn up here whenever there's extra food to be had."

"Always happy to help eat it before it goes bad." Daniel patted his stomach. "A chap needs to keep up his strength."

"The excuse of many a glutton," I said, but I kept my tone light. Daniel was always strong and agile, no matter how much he ate. I did wonder sometimes if he took any food other than the leftovers I fed him.

Daniel continued his banter with those in the kitchen, and I could see he was waiting for them to depart before he spoke to me. They did finally go, two of the footmen mimicking the lady chasing off the thief with celery. I had to relieve one of an actual stalk of celery he'd picked up from my produce box on the dresser.

Elsie finished wiping up her sink, then she and Tess went up together. Their laughter made me soften to Daniel again—he knew how to cheer up even the gloomiest of people.

Mr. Davis was still shut in his butler's pantry, but Mrs. Redfern had gone to bed, and Daniel and I were quite alone in the kitchen. I'd washed and put away the dishes he'd used, and now I seated myself at my scrubbed-off table. I opened my notebook, ready for us to share our information.

"Again, my apologies to you," Daniel began. "I've been trying to persuade anyone who will speak to me about it to release Millburn, but none will budge. Monaghan informed me bluntly that I'd used up all my favors in that regard," he finished glumly.

I knew what he meant. Three years ago, Daniel had promised Mr. Monaghan I knew not what to have me released from Newgate when I'd been put there for a crime I'd not committed. Monaghan had that sort of leverage, but presumably he was tired of using it to liberate Daniel's friends.

"Well, we shall have to prove indisputably that Sam is innocent," I said.

Daniel regarded me with an unreadable expression. "I think that is what I admire most about you--your unshakable confidence."

"Easy to have it when I know I am right," I said, my pencil poised to write.

Daniel's face softened with his smile. "There are other things I admire about you equally, but you'll return the word *nonsense* if I tell you."

The pencil shook in my hand. "If you are going to go on in this way, we'll never accomplish anything."

The smile became a grin. "As always you bring me back to earth. I will have to compliment you profusely another time. And you are quite right. Millburn is in danger—I can't pretend to you that all is well. His prior villainy is not helping him with the magistrates, no matter that he has been a model of goodness these past twenty years. Those at Daalman's chose their scapegoat well."

"We can't let them succeed," I stated. The confidence he attributed to me was waning. "I can't let this happen to Joanna. It is not simply that she and Sam look after Grace. I love Joanna dearly. I cannot let her happy life be taken from her.

And she is right—she might lose her children if Sam is convicted."

"I know." Daniel moved his hand as though to reach for mine, but he returned it to the tea mug Tess had given him before she'd gone upstairs. "But I will remind you that we have succeeded in saving the queen, and we will succeed in saving a banker's clerk."

He was trying to reassure me—which I appreciated—but at the moment, I was less than hopeful.

"I suppose Ben Jarrett could have something to do with all this," I said, writing his name in my notebook. "Why else would he suddenly pop up after leaving Sam alone all these years? At the very least, he's been watching Sam, because he pounced the moment something went wrong."

"True." Daniel sat back, cradling his tea mug. "Jarrett's network hears that Millburn has been suspected by his employers of embezzling. He hopes he can exploit that to gain a hold over Millburn—for whatever reason Jarrett wants that. Revenge over some past slight, probably. When Daalman's is slow to have him arrested, Jarrett decides a greater crime will have to occur. He targets the senior clerk, Stockley. Perhaps he has seen Millburn and Stockley arguing as they exit the bank or some such. Jarrett and his crew wait until Stockley works late one night, creep in, and kill him."

"This all sounds highly unlikely," I said, my pencil still.

"I agree, but we must start somewhere."

"Inspector McGregor said Stockley was killed in a little-used strong room on the third floor," I pointed out. "Jarrett would never know where that was, and he'd likely need a key—unless one of his men obtained a job there and scouted the building. But Sam would realize this, I should think. It is doubtful

Stockley would let himself be lured into the strong room by a ruffian. And if the murder was done to make Sam look guilty, surely Stockley would be found in front of Sam's desk, with something belonging to Sam as the murder weapon."

Daniel made a conceding gesture. "As you say, highly unlikely."

"But we must discover why Jarrett has turned up. He has been beastly to Joanna, so thank you for sending Mr. Grimes to watch for him. Mr. Grimes is sufficiently large and frightening."

"He is that," Daniel said in amusement.

"I need to know exactly when the murder occurred, and where," I said, my pencil moving again on the page. "I mean, where this strong room is precisely, why Mr. Stockley went into it, what time he died, and who would have access to the building at the time." I paused. "Mr. Kearny might know all this. I'd like to speak to him again."

"Mr. Kearny, one of the bankers? Millburn's mate?"

That Daniel knew about him didn't surprise me. "He spoke to me when I was there. Sam obtained his post at Daalman's at Mr. Kearny's recommendation. I'd think Mr. Kearny would be eager to prove that his endorsement of Sam wasn't wrong."

"Then we will speak to Mr. Kearny. I can get word to him." Daniel spoke with assurance.

"I also need to know what the police have investigated. Inspector McGregor had not arrived when I had to leave this morning, and I hope he has not pestered Joanna too much. Lady Cynthia and Miss Townsend said they'd check in on her and make certain she was all right." I sighed with some emotion. "I am grateful I have such friends."

"You attract honorable people," Daniel said. "They will intimidate McGregor if nothing else, but I know he hasn't been to question Mrs. Millburn. Not yet. The City police have been persuaded to leave her be for a bit as well."

"Persuaded?" My eyes narrowed.

"That is my word for it." Daniel betrayed no shame. "McGregor knows Mrs. Millburn has nothing to do with any of this and, in his own way, has some sympathy. I also mentioned to him that the investigation should focus on Daalman's Bank as a whole instead of a junior clerk with spurious origins. He agreed with me, if peevishly."

I'd told Inspector McGregor the same thing. I imagined his exasperation when Daniel repeated the advice.

I warmed to Daniel's understanding. The elderly man's pronouncement about Daniel might be true, but equally true was that Daniel, like Sam, had been working for years to absolve himself of old sins.

"And the City police?" I asked. "Why have they eased off?"

"Because McGregor told them to. Not that the City chaps are obligated to listen. McGregor is on the case at their invitation as an observer and adviser, but you know how McGregor is."

Short-tempered, growling, and utterly sure of himself. He gave orders and people followed them without quite knowing why.

"It won't last," Daniel said. "They'll have to speak to Joanna eventually, looking for evidence to support their case at trial. You say Miss Townsend and Lady Cynthia have agreed to look in on her, but I imagine McGregor will choose his moment when they are not there. Please do not worry, Kat." He held up his hand before I could speak. "I'll make certain she is not alone. I've told Errol to watch out for her and arrive just as the police do."

"Mr. Fielding?" I checked my surprise by realizing that yes, he'd do very well as a chaperone. The police, and even McGregor, would be more respectful to Joanna with a vicar next to her in the parlor. "Why would he agree to do this?" I asked. "I'd think Mr. Fielding would prefer to be as far from the police as possible."

Daniel had begun a sip of tea, and he coughed. "Not at all." He set down the cup and wiped his lips. "Performing as the dithering, zealous vicar before the unsuspecting peelers is something Errol will enjoy. I only hope he doesn't overdo it."

"I believe he's wise enough to know how far to go," I said. "And he'll be on Joanna's side. Please thank him for me."

Daniel winced. "Not sure I should. If he knows you're happy with him, he'll take advantage."

"He won't," I said with confidence. Mr. Fielding and I had reached an understanding. He knew I did not approve of his swindling leanings, and he reined those in around me and my acquaintances. "He'll appreciate a cake or tart in gratitude, I think."

"You are a wise woman, Kat Holloway. As I always say."

"Flattering words. Yes, you always say them." I sent him a smile to show him my speech was not all that disapproving.

"Because they are true. All my compliments to you are." Daniel reached for my hand, pried the pencil from it, and laid it aside. His fingers were warm from the tea mug. "When I told you that Grace would always be taken care of, I meant it. She'll never have to fear, or rely on strangers. I know plenty of good, kind people she can stay with if absolutely necessary, but she'll never be taken from you. I promise you that."

I squeezed his hand, a lump in my throat. "I slept at Joanna's last night. I got up in the dark to check on Grace, smoothed her blankets, watched her sleep." I blinked stinging eyes. "I want to do that always, Daniel. I want my daughter."

"I know."

He said nothing more, though I read in his expression that he wished he could move heaven and earth to make it happen.

"The world isn't an easy place, is it?" I said. "The life one wants doesn't come from wishing. One has to work hard and plan, and be clever and brave—all those things I do not feel at the moment."

"You have done that, been that, for years now." Daniel lifted my work-worn hand and pressed a kiss to it. My fingers tingled anew, but this time not from cold. "Your work will be rewarded. I will make certain of it."

I wanted to believe him. I knew that Daniel was in a dangerous position and had come from a dangerous past. I also knew he was a good man in his heart, which he'd proved time and again.

"My life is not up to you." I softened my voice. "But I think the two of us, in time, can put things right. For the both of us."

Daniel went very still, his face losing its habitual good humor. Even his wild hair didn't move.

"Do I understand you aright, Kat?" He spoke as though reluctant to say the words. "Do I dare let myself?"

"You do understand." I tightened my grip. "And you should dare."

Daniel studied me gravely, the cheery man who teased me and whose kind interest won him many friends absent from his eyes. I saw a vast emptiness in him, a loneliness, a yearning, one I'd never had to feel myself. I'd lost my mother at a fairly young age and had been betrayed by a husband, but I'd retained close friends and made more, and had a daughter I loved beyond reason, who loved me in return.

Daniel had made his way alone, from childhood. He loved James fiercely, but had missed most of James's young years, not realizing he even had a child until James was a tall youth.

I wanted Daniel to know that now he had me. As much as I waffled over whether I could trust a man with my heart again, or worried what his job would lead him into, I knew that I wanted Daniel in my life. Likewise, I wanted to be in his.

Daniel's throat worked. "The coming years could be a very bright place, then."

"I'd like them to be," I said.

We shared another look, each fearing to say too much, to spoil what hovered between us. But I knew I did not want to let go of him, though the way ahead was precarious.

"We have much to do," I reminded us both. "I will not worry about Grace going to strangers, because we will prove Sam's innocence and win him free. He will come home, and we will go on as before."

Daniel released me, relaxing into his warmth again. "Your determination is contagious, my dear Kat. You are right. We will win this, which means we must cease being maudlin and work."

"Who is Bernard Compton?" I asked.

Daniel froze in the act of lifting his mug. He quickly set it down again. "Damnation, Kat, you ought to warn a man when you're going to spring on him."

"The name frightened Mr. Jarrett. He had no idea what sort of man you were until you said it. Who is he? Or was? You said he was deceased."

"He is, thank the Lord." Daniel drew a long breath. "Very well, since I know you will badger me for years to come if I do not tell you now, I will not be coy. He led a gang of thieves, housebreakers, and murderers in South London for years. Always eluded the police, no matter how many of his followers were caught and arrested. Not much different from Naismith or Carter for that matter. A man doesn't get to be a general without strategy and winning battles."

Naismith was the man suspected of murdering Mr. Carter, whom Daniel had looked upon as a father. Naismith was still a king in the East End, and one of Daniel's many goals was to bring him down however he could.

"I don't badger," I said. "I am insistent, rather, when the information is important. This Compton recruited you? As Mr. Carter did?"

"No." Daniel again became somber, darkness returning to his eyes. "He took me. I was a mite—could not have been more than three years old. One day I was living in comfort, the next, I slept in a cold hovel working like a slave for Compton. He was training me up, he said. He took children from the workhouses or orphanages, one or two at a time, and raised them to be part of his army. Loyalty couldn't be bought, he knew, but it could be ingrained."

I stared at him in horror. "He abducted you?"

"He did indeed. Do not ask me from where, because I don't remember. He erased those memories, or perhaps I buried them, to keep from despair. As well, don't ask me what sorts of things he had me do, because I want to bury those memories as well. Suffice it to say that Compton made monsters out of perfectly ordinary boys, and the streets feared us. They feared his older ruffians more, and Compton conferred a special terror even on hardened villains, like Jarrett. He was merciless if opposed. The tortures of the Inquisition were nothing to what he could put a man through."

My heart thudded in sickening beats. "You got away from him."

"I did. I took what I'd learned about housebreaking and

lock picking, as well as trickery and coercion, to get myself out of his house and run like the hounds of hell pursued me. Which they did. Again, my teachings and a natural bent for deceit aided me. I fled to Bethnal Green, a place I knew even Compton's boys would hesitate to enter, and lived by my wits until Carter found me. Needless to say, I did not trust Carter for a long while, no matter how genial he was. Anyone, for that matter."

"Daniel." The bleakness I'd seen inside him from time to time became understandable. It wasn't only losing Carter that had hurt him, but what had come before. The idea that he as a lad had finally found someone he could trust, and that person had been taken from him, was unbearable.

I rose and went to Daniel's side of the table, slid the mug aside, and wound my arms around him.

"My love, I am so sorry."

Daniel started, then he pulled me down to him, burying his face in my shoulder. I found myself sitting on his lap, we entwined in each other, Daniel's shuddering breath warm on my neck.

"It was a long time ago," he whispered.

True, but some scars ran deep. Well I knew this.

I raised my head, liking being so near him, and smoothed his hair from his forehead. "The gent outside warned me of you," I said. "He couldn't have meant because you were a frightening boy."

"Mmm." Daniel avoided my gaze. "He might have been referring to the interval after Carter was killed and before I decided to hunt villains for the police. I took myself back to South London to see what was what. Many of Compton's lads were either dead or imprisoned by that time. Compton was still alive, though, and not pleased to see me, once he understood who I was."

"Oh." I did not like the direction the conversation was going. "You did not kill him, did you?"

"No." The grim word only slightly reassured me. "I did not kill him, though I might have sped his demise. I was not gentle with him, but I wanted information, not vengeance."

"Information?"

A ghost of Daniel's smile crossed his lips. "Ever curious, aren't you, Kat? I wanted to know where he'd taken me from. I remember comfort and contentedness, as I said, and workhouses and orphanages, in my experience, have neither."

"What did he say?" I asked anxiously. Daniel was right, my curiosity was a besetting sin, but I could not contain myself.

"The damnable man could not remember." Daniel's bitterness returned. "He'd seen me, a sturdy lad with a fearless air, and knew I'd do well for him. So, he nabbed me." Daniel brushed light fingers across my cheek. "And that is why, Kat, when you ask what my name was when I was born, long before I became Daniel McAdam, I don't tell you. It is because I don't know."

13

I had no words to answer Daniel. I could only lay my head on his shoulder and hold on to him.

My father had died when I'd been tiny, and I had no memory of him, but my mother had been a bulwark in my life, guarding me and teaching me, loving me. Her death had left a gaping hole.

But to not know of either parent, to have none of that . . . A terrible thought. Daniel must have had that love, and then been taken from it forcibly. It wasn't right.

Did his parents never try to search for him? I didn't have the heart to ask him. Perhaps they had, diligently, and then slowly given up. Children were lost all the time in London, either gone to early deaths by accident or taken by evil men and women who exploited them. Those children either died from their labors or grew up to be as evil as those who'd abducted them.

No wonder Daniel had walked the line between good and

bad all his life. He struggled to be the best he could be in spite of his harsh existence.

"You love James so much," I said after a long silence. "It is clear. You are a good father. They didn't turn you evil."

"But it has been a close-run thing." Daniel's answer was quiet. "When I saw James, and knew what could have happened to him, and I'd not been there to prevent it . . , I couldn't walk away from him. No matter how much he wanted me to."

"He loves you in return." I raised my head to look at Daniel. "That is clear, as well."

"Not at first, he didn't." Daniel vibrated with laughter. "It took him a long while to trust me. You too." His amusement faded. "Every time you begin to have faith in me, something happens to change that."

"That is my fault," I said generously. "I find it difficult to trust, and you can be very secretive."

"Only about things I'm duty bound not to tell . . . or what I am ashamed of. I want you to think me the perfect man, my Kat."

Daniel's lopsided grin returned, the one I'd fallen for years ago. "Being taken from your family and raised by one villain after another is not your fault. You've turned out remarkably well under the circumstances."

"I live for your flattery, you do know." The sparkle returned to Daniel's eyes, which relieved me. I did not like to see him so morose.

"You did not let them break you," I continued. "I know it is a popular notion that if a person is born angelic no situation can change that, but I have seen too much of the world to believe that is true. You persevered through the darkness and remained yourself."

"Are you saying I was born angelic?" Daniel's merriment

surfaced. "I might have to argue with you there. I remember being perfectly happy to be a devil."

"I said you remained *yourself*. You have plenty of wickedness in you, Daniel, do not worry."

"I am happy all my wickedness has not driven you away." Daniel's arms tightened around me. "I do need you in my life."

"I am pleased to hear this, as I prefer you to stay in my life as well," I said softly.

We sat still a moment, absorbing these revelations, and simply enjoying holding each other.

Daniel released me to touch my lower lip with one finger. "That is as close to a declaration that you're fond of me as I can hope for. I will not shun it."

I slid from his lap, praying that no one had peeked into the kitchen to see us in so intimate a position, and shook out my skirts. "Of course I am fond of you, Daniel. I'd hardly leave food back for you if I was not."

Daniel burst out laughing, which lightened my spirits. His past life had been cruel, but it had not broken him. And perhaps one day, with my help, he could find out where he'd truly come from.

"You take food to those who live on the streets, so I imagine you are fond of them too." Daniel's grin made the kitchen brighter.

"You are very silly. I feel sorry for *them*. But for you—compassion, yes, pity, no."

Daniel leaned back in his chair while I moved to the stove to pour hot water from the kettle into the now-empty teapot. I carried the teapot to the table, setting it aside to steep, and resumed my seat and my notebook.

"I am pleased I have your compassion," Daniel said, more seriously.

"Why would you not? Now, we must pool all our resources to help poor Sam, whom I do pity at present. Do you think I could speak to him? I'd like to hear his side of the story."

"As would I, and I think we might be the only ones to listen to it. I will see what I can do." Daniel turned his mug around, impatient for tea to be brewed enough to drink. "If Miss Townsend has found him a solicitor in addition to the barrister, we might be able to sit in on that conference with him."

"I'd rather speak to him alone, friend to friend. A solicitor is supposed to help him, but Sam might be reticent in front of one."

"I take your point. I will do my best to procure an appointment."

I skimmed through the notes I'd made, a sudden shyness coming over me. I'd learned more about Daniel tonight but also more about myself and my feelings for him. Me spontaneously launching myself at him unnerved me a bit. We'd shared plenty of kisses by now, but I'd never simply leapt into his arms. That he had caught me made me flush with heat.

Daniel watched me with his usual verve—there was never anything shy about Daniel.

I poured tea when sufficient time had passed, and I banished my shyness to go over what we knew and what we could do. Daniel restated that he'd get word to Mr. Kearny that I wanted to meet and to the governors at Newgate to find a way in to see Sam. He also promised to keep an eye on Inspector McGregor and find out what he knew as soon as the inspector knew it.

Finally, Daniel drained his mug and heaved himself regretfully to his feet. "As always, I hate to say good night to you, but I am not selfish enough to keep you from sleep." He stepped closer to me as I rose, his breath touching my face. "Also, I do not want to shock Mrs. Redfern, or Davis, or heaven forbid,

Mrs. Bywater, by being here with you when they enter in the morning." He laughed softly. "What might we have been getting up to, eh?"

My blush must have been obvious, because the laughter increased. I stepped away from him.

"You are quite right, Mr. McAdam. I'd be out a place if that happened. Good night to you."

Daniel wasn't the least bit contrite. He shrugged on the coat he'd hung up and pulled on gloves, squashing his flat cap in his hands. I walked with him to the door, mostly to make certain he actually left, but also to lock up after him.

Before he slid out the door I opened for him, Daniel closed his hand around the lapel of my work dress, gently pulled me to him, and kissed my mouth.

The cold scullery, the wintry draft coming through the open door, and the dark loneliness evaporated like dew in the sunshine. I savored the kiss, the world narrowing to only Daniel and me, understanding each other and enjoying the warmth.

Daniel eased from the kiss, touched my cheek, then gave me a brazen wink before he slapped his cap to his head and swept out the door. I heard his bootsteps on the stairs as he faded into the darkness, then his cheerful whistling.

I let out a breath, shut the door and bolted it, and turned around to find Mr. Davis standing in the kitchen doorway.

He had been there long enough to see the kiss, I knew from his stillness. I braced myself for admonishment, a lecture that Daniel McAdam was a man from the gutter and that I could do so much better. He'd told me such things before.

Mr. Davis said nothing. His expression remained neutral, neither condemning nor forgiving.

"Mr. McAdam and I have been walking out together, as you know." I attempted to keep the nervous quaver from my voice.

"Nothing untoward, I assure you. I doubt very much it will be more than that."

Mr. Davis entered the kitchen, saying nothing until he was closer to me. In the dim light, I saw that he'd left off his hairpiece. He was not entirely bald, but had a receding hairline that left the crown of his head bare. He did not look unattractive without the fussy hairpiece, but men are vain about such things.

"Your daughter?" he said, as though asking me to confirm her existence. "How old is she?"

I swallowed hard. Mr. Davis knew I'd been widowed, or at least married in the past, but he'd held his tongue about it. He never gossiped about his fellow servants, I was pleased to note.

But he must have overheard Daniel and me discussing Grace tonight, then waited until Daniel had gone to confront me about it.

"She is twelve," I answered in a whisper.

Mr. Davis's tight shoulders relaxed. "Then she is not McAdam's?"

I blinked. "Gracious, no. I've only known Mr. McAdam for the last four or so years. Grace's father is deceased."

"I see." Mr. Davis continued to gaze at me as though he'd ask something more, but pressed his mouth closed.

"She lives with a friend," I said. "That friend was who I visited last night."

"You do not have to explain, Mrs. Holloway. We all have a past." Mr. Davis cleared his throat and reached up as though to straighten his hairpiece, remembering at the last moment that he'd removed it. "I was concerned that the little girl was the person unwell."

"No, she is right as rain, thank the Lord," I said. "My friend, though, has had a bit of trouble."

"I am sorry to hear this. Can I be of any assistance?"

Though Mr. Davis's tone was as stiff as it had been since he'd caught me in his chamber, I read genuine concern in him.

"That is very kind," I said. I dithered asking for specific help but in the end decided to risk it. Mr. Davis's information had been key in solving cases in the past. "If you could keep a lookout for any newspaper stories—or any mention at all—about a bank called Daalman's, that would be of aid."

Mr. Davis's brows went up. "Daalman's? Favored of millionaires throughout the world? Reputed to have invested heavily in the French canal in Colombia? That Daalman's?"

"Yes, indeed. What do you know of it?" I asked eagerly.

"I was footman many years back to a man who had sunk his entire fortune into Daalman's and its investments. Lost half that fortune and sacked most of the staff, though he did gain his funds back quickly. He was too wary to hire more servants, so those who remained, like me, did all the work—in a bloody large house too. I've seen Daalman's shares rise and fall over the years. Too much vacillation for me. I bank at a small institution in Regent Street whose interest has been exactly the same for decades. I believe you have to have rather a lot of cash to invest at Daalman's, in any case. I don't recommend you bank with them, Mrs. Holloway."

"No fear of that," I said fervently. The funereal atmosphere that hid scandal plus the mean-spirited blaming of innocents made me never want my money to touch that bank as long as I lived.

"A building society might be more to your taste," Mr. Davis went on. "To help you save to purchase a cottage or something when you retire."

I hadn't thought of that. Perhaps a building society, which pooled money to assist its members to purchase homes, might help with the tea shop I dreamed of. Then again, they might want me to be married to a man who would handle this money and shop purchasing for me.

"I will consider it," I said. "Thank you."

Mr. Davis paused before he spoke again, as though choosing his words. "I hope your friend does well. If there comes a time where you need someone to look after your daughter, I know a woman of kindly disposition who might be willing. She was housekeeper in the home I worked in before this."

"She's in London?" I asked with some hope.

"Bury St. Edmunds," Mr. Davis answered. "Not far by train."

No, but far enough. I might have to sacrifice my feelings, though, to make certain Grace was taken care of.

Bury St. Edmunds had been the address on the letters sent to Mr. Davis I'd found in his room. Was this lady looking after his sickly friend? Or was she someone else entirely, a lady from Mr. Davis's past?

As intrigued as I was, I knew prying would only annoy him. "I do hope *your* friend is well. Have you had any word?"

Mr. Davis shook his head. "He is gravely ill. I'm afraid it is only a matter of time."

The grief in his voice was obvious. I softened mine in sympathy. "I am so very sorry. Is there anything I can do for *you*?"

"When the time comes, I might have to leave abruptly. I will make certain the correct wines for each meal are marked," he finished with a whiff of humor.

"I will cover your duties to the best of my ability," I promised. "Mrs. Redfern will as well. We do not mind in the least."

Mr. Davis's expression betrayed skepticism that Mrs. Redfern would be happy to assist. "Thank you, Mrs. Holloway. I appreciate your understanding. Now I will say good night."

"Good night," I answered. When he turned to go, I added, "I am glad we are friends again."

He swung back to me, a hint of his steel returning. "As long as you stay out of my chamber, Mrs. Holloway."

I sent him a warm smile. "I wouldn't dream of entering it again, Mr. Davis."

I had a bit of a headache in the morning, the result of rushing outside into the winter cold without a hat. A drink of chamomile tea helped, but I was out of sorts. I longed to run to Newgate and hammer at the gates until they let Sam out, then move the entire Millburn family, including Grace, far from London and the evil men at Daalman's.

I also wanted to return to Daalman's and shake each and every employee until one confessed to the murder. Any of the wretches could have done it—at least, any who could enter the building early enough in the morning. I supposed the coroner who'd examined the body knew Mr. Stockley had been killed early—it had been kind of Inspector McGregor to give me that detail.

Did Mr. Stockley have a key to the building? Perhaps he'd arranged to meet one of the other employees before working hours and let them both in. Or he and his killer had been at the bank overnight, for whatever reason, with the murder happening after a quarrel.

In either case, I was back to anyone who worked at the bank, including whatever charwomen cleaned at night, having opportunity to kill Mr. Stockley.

I penciled the word *Keys* in my notebook, reminding me to inquire whether Mr. Stockley had had his own. If not, then that narrowed the possibilities. He'd have had to be let into the building early in the morning, possibly by his killer.

Our speculation that Mr. Jarrett had killed him to put Sam in the frame was a wash. If the doorman had stumbled over Mr. Stockley lying in a pool of blood on the bank's doorstep or even in the foyer, then Jarrett would be a good suspect. The fact that the police hadn't rounded up vagrants in the area and coerced a confession from one showed that they believed someone from the inside had killed the man. I wondered if Inspector McGregor's sensible advice was making the City police work a bit harder to find a culprit.

I could imagine the coolly efficient Miss Swann telling Inspector McGregor that no one in her bank could possibly have committed murder. Except Sam, of course. He'd been handed over on a silver platter.

Blast the lot of them. I wanted to rush across London and knock heads together until someone told the truth.

As it was, I had to calmly continue my duties and prepare for Mrs. Bywater's supper party that evening. My only consolation was that tomorrow was Thursday, my full day out. I'd be able to not only hold my daughter close but do the rushing about to discover the truth. The fact that someone at Daalman's was robbing me of the precious time with Grace angered me further.

Tess, sensing my mood, was subdued that morning, but worked steadily.

Today we retrieved the now-frozen sorbet from the icebox, and I broke it from its pan with a clean ice pick. Working in the larder rather than the hot kitchen, I dumped the chunks of sorbet into a bowl, then Tess and I mashed and whipped the mixture until it was fluffy but still chilled. We quickly scooped the concoction into the prepared orange rind cups, which I set back into the ice tray to remain cold until ready to serve them.

"They look ever so pretty," Tess said longingly, as she studied the shaped cups heaped with light orange ice.

"I'll save a few back for us," I promised. "Now, we will take some of the leftover orange peel and shape it into roses for more decoration. I'll show you."

"Fancy carving food like you would a sculpture," Tess said as we moved back to the kitchen.

"There are those who carve ice itself into structures," I told her. "Dragons and beasts, and all sorts."

"Truly?" Tess sent me a look of amazement. "You'd have to have a cold dining room, wouldn't you? Or it would melt and be all over."

I had to smile, in spite of my gloom. "That is true. Sugar sculptures are much safer. Unless someone knocks them over or spills hot liquid on them, of course."

Tess stopped in the middle of the floor. "There are sculptures made of *sugar*? Well, I never. Waste of perfectly good sugar, if you ask me."

I had to agree—those whose bellies were never empty thought nothing of turning food into inedible artwork. My little sorbet cups and orange roses at least were made of the part of the orange that wouldn't be eaten.

We worked on the rest of the meal—lemon sole and a medley of parsnips and potatoes, along with salads of the greens I'd bought yesterday morning. Dried fruits and walnuts would be served alongside the sorbet for a light dessert.

Amid this activity, James arrived. His youthful buoyancy reminded me of Daniel's story last night, of how Daniel had been taken from who knew where to be used by an unscrupulous criminal. I imagined Daniel's alarm when he'd discovered he had a son, fearing that James might have gone through a similar experience.

James was quite robust, no darkness in him at all. Daniel had found him in time to save him.

"Message for you, Mrs. H.," James said, oblivious of my contemplations. He handed me a folded piece of paper.

I opened the letter with trepidation, but it was a note from Joanna.

Men from the City police arrived to thoroughly search Sam's study and all his things. What they hoped to find, I cannot say. They remained respectful, however, thanks to the kind vicar Mr. McAdam sent to sit with me. Please thank Mr. McAdam for his foresight.

Lady Cynthia's friend, Miss Townsend, sent me a letter explaining she'd found a solicitor and barrister to take Sam's case. The solicitor, Mr. Crowe, went to confer with Sam this morning, she said, but I have not spoken to him yet. How we will afford the fees, I do not know, but at this moment, I will do anything to help my Sam.

Grace and I count the minutes until we can see you again.

Your loving friend,
Joanna

"Thank heavens for Mr. Fielding," I said with some relief as I folded the paper again. "Though I admit when I first met him, my sentiments about him were somewhat different."

"Uncle Errol's all right," James pronounced. "As long as you don't trust him too much. Any answering word, Mrs. H.?"

I had much to say but no time for a written reply. "Tell Mrs. Millburn I will see her tomorrow and assure her of my affection. All of her family as well."

I did not name Grace out loud, as the kitchen and downstairs were much too busy. I believed I could count on Mr. Davis's discretion, but no more of the staff needed to know of my private life.

"Right you are." James prepared to dash away with his usual speed, but I stopped him and handed him a cruller leftover from this morning.

He thanked me warmly, cramming the thing in his mouth as he raced out the door.

"Everything all right?" Tess asked me anxiously.

"Not really, but no new calamities," I answered. "Just the police ransacking Joanna's house looking for evidence, as Daniel predicted. He sent Mr. Fielding to safeguard her."

I wondered if Joanna had seen through Mr. Fielding's guise as the ingenuous vicar. She'd claimed she knew a former villain when she saw one. Perhaps she had known but had chosen to say nothing.

I was impatient to find out what the police had taken away, if anything, but for the moment, I had to be a cook. A good domestic did her work without fuss and pushed any personal concern aside. Or so I'd been told.

Tess and I worked ever more furiously to prepare supper for twelve, the fish waiting to be cooked at the very last minute.

My restlessness was appeased somewhat when Mr. Fielding himself arrived, just as the sole was going into the pan, and asked to see me.

14

I could hardly leave the kitchen at this critical moment to speak to Mr. Fielding, but when I nearly dropped the filets on the floor, Tess grabbed the pan from me and shooed me out.

Mr. Fielding, who stood inside the back door watching our frantic preparations in some amusement, accepted my invitation to speak in the housekeeper's parlor. Mrs. Redfern was upstairs, and I wanted to be within earshot in case Tess needed me. Mr. Fielding hung up his greatcoat and carefully set his short-crowned hat on a clean space of the dresser before following me down the hall.

As we passed the butler's pantry, whose door stood open, Mr. Davis peered out, brightening when he saw Mr. Fielding.

"Good evening, Vicar," Mr. Davis said warmly. "I have a nice port in, or perhaps a lighter white wine is more to your taste."

"How kind." Mr. Fielding, a slender man with trim dark hair

and beard and lively eyes, oozed obsequiousness. "The port, if you don't mind. God bless our neighbors on the Douro, eh?"

"Indeed, Mr. Fielding," Mr. Davis said. "The reason Lord Wellington raced to Portugal in the war against Napoleon was to safeguard our stock of fine port. I will pour a glass."

He did not offer any of this fine port to me—which I would have refused anyway, as I found fortified wine a little too strong—and disappeared into the recesses of his pantry. I opened the housekeeper's parlor and ushered Mr. Fielding inside.

"If the pair of you were any more fawning, I'd be ill," I told him as he gallantly gestured me to a seat.

Mr. Fielding took the Belter chair once I'd sat down, and settled his frock coat. His subdued dark suit that was well tailored for his frame and the ecclesiastical collar around his throat made him appear to be a sober, well-mannered man of the cloth.

I knew better. Mr. Fielding truly was a vicar—he had a divinity degree from Oxford and the living of Shadwell's parish, and was now suffragan bishop for much of the East End. But he'd in his life been a thief and a swindler, and he had not left his trickster ways behind him.

"Mr. Davis enjoys it," Mr. Fielding answered. "We are both playing roles."

I wasn't certain Mr. Davis would like that idea, but I supposed Mr. Fielding had a point.

"Regardless, I am grateful to you for staying with Mrs. Millburn today when the police came. She informed me that they were more civil to her because of your presence."

"I made certain of it." Mr. Fielding erased his rather vacant smile. "I had to be unctuous to the searching constables, and

I suppose I haven't dropped the habit of being the oh-so-anxious-to-please vicar today. My apologies for my fawning, as you put it."

Before I could respond, Mr. Davis carried in a tray with glasses, and Mr. Fielding came out of his slouch, pasting on his ingratiating expression once more.

"Thank you, Mr. Davis," he said. "You are a godsend."

Mr. Davis acknowledged his praise with dignity. "A light red wine for you, Mrs. Holloway." Mr. Davis presented me the tray first, and I took the glass with gratitude.

I drank little, except to taste wine to make certain it was right for my sauces, but this wine's nose was good, and I accepted it readily. Mr. Fielding took the deep ruby port with sincere thanks, and Mr. Davis departed, pleased we approved of his choices.

Mr. Fielding lifted his glass to me. "As I know you will object to me toasting you and your abilities, I will say, here is to a satisfactory end to this problem with the correct criminals paying their dues."

"A toast I can favor." I lifted my glass as well, then sipped the wine. The savory red rolled over my tongue, and I instantly thought of a game dish I could use it in.

"Mrs. Millburn is a courageous woman," Mr. Fielding said once he'd drunk. "I commend her. I can see why you are such friends."

"She is very courageous," I agreed. "Did the constables find anything? Or believe they did?"

"I kept a sharp eye on them." Mr. Fielding took another sip of port and made a satisfied noise. "This really is quite good. I am honored. I sat with Mrs. Millburn a bit, patting her hand, until she was fed up with me, then I trotted after the constables, anxious to help. They went through Millburn's desk in his study, even searched for secret drawers. Pulled out all his books and went through those. I did my best to restore order."

"The children do their schoolwork in there," I said in dismay. "If the constables pestered them in any way . . ."

"They did not. Mrs. Millburn sent all five downstairs to stay with the cook and have an early luncheon while the police roamed the upstairs. I prevented them tearing apart cushions and breaking open cabinets. Mrs. Millburn relinquished her keys to me, and I used them on any boxes that were locked—not many. In this way, the helpful vicar could prevent destruction and understand exactly what they were looking for."

"And what were they looking for?" I asked, tightly clutching my wineglass.

"Balance sheets and other information that could have been taken from the bank. He had a few boxes of papers from Daalman's, unfortunately, hidden in a bookshelf behind some dusty tomes. I offered the explanation that he might have been trying to work out for himself where the missing money from Daalman's had gone, but the sergeant in charge took them away with glee."

"Oh," I said in consternation. "On the other hand, if someone from the police goes through these papers, they will see that Sam had nothing to do with the embezzlement."

"I admire your optimism, Mrs. Holloway." Mr. Fielding raised his glass to me again. "If someone who understands finance sifts through them, you are right, they will realize his innocence." He grimaced. "Unfortunately, they might simply shove them onto the busy prosecutor for the Crown who will use them as evidence Millburn had something to hide."

"Then we must at once inform the barrister and solicitor

Miss Townsend is providing that they should make certain the books are scrutinized," I declared.

"Mrs. Millburn mentioned that Miss Townsend has offered this help. The lovely Miss Townsend." Mr. Fielding pressed a hand to his heart. "Would that she had a liking for gentlemen instead of ladies—what a fine vicar's wife she'd make. But alas."

He could at least make me laugh, even in troubled times. "Miss Townsend is far too lofty to be a vicar's wife," I said. "I believe she enjoys her independence."

"She does, more's the pity. But good for her for finding a legal mind—a silk, no less—to assist. I imagine this barrister will be the most brilliant in the land."

"Miss Townsend only said the barrister owed her a favor," I said. "The solicitor must be one this barrister works with frequently."

"She's a sharp one." Mr. Fielding's admiration continued. "To have a silk willing to add to his no doubt heavy load to defend a banker's clerk. Makes me wonder who else Miss Townsend has in her pocket."

"I have not speculated," I said. "I am simply grateful. Did the police find anything besides the papers?"

"Not that I could see. They were very happy with those. I wish Millburn hadn't tried to hide them. Harder now to make the case that he was a diligent clerk who even worked at night at home."

"Yes, I can see why they'd consider that suspicious. I am guessing Sam did not want anyone from the bank who happened to call to see him with them."

"A good explanation," Mr. Fielding conceded. "Perhaps you should tell that to the solicitor as well. A conscientious man working his fingers to the bone looking after his wife and many children."

"I would rather they acquit him because he did no wrong than from pity. Though I suppose we should take what we can." I let out a sigh. "Joanna simply wants him home."

"She is worried, and right to be." Mr. Fielding became somber. "I comforted her the best I could. False hope won't help her, but despair will not either."

"Thank you," I said. "Daniel was wise to send you to her."

Mr. Fielding's obnoxious smile returned. "She approves of me," he said to the air. "I am crushed with the honor."

I wondered if he'd learned this silly way of talking from Daniel, or if Daniel had from Mr. Fielding.

"Cease your ridiculousness," I said. "Besides the police, did anyone else come to annoy Joanna? Sam's old mates from South London, perhaps? Do you know a man called Ben Jarrett?"

Mr. Fielding paused with the glass of port at his lips and lowered it without drinking. "I have heard of him, but I don't know him. Mrs. Millburn mentioned him as well. Apparently, Millburn wasn't pure as the driven snow in his youth, was he?"

"He left that life behind," I said firmly. "Mr. Jarrett found me and said he and his mates would break Sam free and make certain he could live unhindered. I explained to him that this would not do."

Mr. Fielding gave a short laugh. "I am sorry I missed that conversation. But Jarrett has a bad reputation even among street toughs. I'll put word out to keep him from you and Mrs. Millburn."

"Daniel has already done so. He warned Jarrett off as well."

"Of course he did." Mr. Fielding took a hearty swig of the port. "But in this case, I can't be sorry he got to Jarrett first. There are certain men in this city who should be banged up in Newgate simply for walking about."

I could not disagree, having met many of the sort of men Mr. Fielding meant in my day.

Mr. Fielding continued, "Jarret's upbringing is no excuse, though many people today claim that it is. I was a thorough reprobate, but I have reformed. If I can, anyone can."

In happier times, I'd have burst out laughing. "Do not pretend you are virtuous, Mr. Fielding. I know you too well now."

"Dear lady, you wound me." Mr. Fielding winked. "My statement stands. I did reform—I am a help to those around me instead of preying on them for all I can get. Well, a help to the wretches who deserve it, I mean. I will continue to vex people like Jarrett as much as possible."

"What about Bernard Compton?" I asked. "Have you heard of him? Is he the sort you'd vex?"

I asked because I was curious how much Mr. Fielding knew about the man, or if Daniel had told him his history with him.

Mr. Fielding's levity fled. He stared at me with hard eyes, the affable vicar and the good-natured confidence trickster both gone in a moment.

"That is a name you should never speak," he said severely. "Who told you it? Jarrett? I might have guessed he was made by such a villain."

"No, Mr. Jarrett was frightened by mention of him." I set down the wine. "He is deceased, is he not?"

"Yes, dead, and all the world rejoiced when he went. Still, his reach is long. The lieutenants he trained even now strike terror all over South London. A battle over who will replace him has been waging for some years." Mr. Fielding drained his glass, then sent me a shrewd look. "If Jarrett didn't mention Compton, who did?"

"Daniel," I said.

"Why?"

The word was harsh. I realized I'd blundered—I'd thought Mr. Fielding would know all about Mr. Compton and Daniel's past with him, but apparently not. The fact that Daniel had never told Mr. Fielding meant he did not wish Mr. Fielding to know.

"To frighten Mr. Jarrett," I extemporized. "Compton was from South London, and so is Jarrett. It was effective."

Mr. Fielding, no fool, held my gaze. "As a competent liar, Mrs. Holloway, I know a lie when I hear it. What has my erstwhile brother to do with Compton?"

I closed my hands in my lap. "What I was told was in confidence. I ought to have reined in my curiosity and held my tongue."

"Kat." Mr. Fielding leaned to me, all pretense at being the respectable vicar gone. "Whatever Daniel told you might be very important. This is dangerous knowledge—to Daniel, I mean."

He alarmed me, but I knew that Mr. Fielding always played his own game, no matter how helpful he made himself to me or my friends. Behind the face he showed to the world lay a mind that constantly sought an advantage to himself.

"I am sorry, Mr. Fielding," I said, keeping my voice gentle. "You will have to ask Daniel. I should not have spoken."

"I am certain Daniel will plant a facer on me rather than answer the question," Mr. Fielding said. "But I note you will not waver. The problem, you see, is that now I will have to find out on my own. I might kick over a rock that needs to be left grimy side down."

"Please do not needle me into betraying Daniel's confidence," I said with a bit more heat. "Your threat to reveal it on your own does not move me. If you ask him, and he does not wish to tell you, then you should leave it at that."

"Ever you admonish me." Mr. Fielding's lighter tone returned, but his watchfulness remained. "In most instances, I would agree with you, my dear Mrs. Holloway. In this one, it is beyond your depth. You are a good woman, and you cannot understand evil. But no fear. I will ask Daniel, and if he bloodies my nose for the question, I will return and weep on your shoulder. Now, I must bid you good day." He waited for me to rise, as though I were a lady, before he leapt to his feet. "I am on this side of the metropolis for more reasons than the delight of visiting you, unfortunately. Working for the diocesan bishop means I have so many more duties to perform. I hardly have an hour to call my own."

"I know you are pleased with yourself for your post, so I will not feel sorry for you. Good day, Mr. Fielding." I stuck out my hand. "I do thank you for looking after Joanna."

"A pleasure, my lady." Mr. Fielding pumped my hand in a way he must have practiced to ingratiate himself with his congregation. He grew serious once more. "Never discuss Compton with anyone but Daniel or me. Not even your police detective, Inspector McGregor, or the constable who walks out with your kitchen assistant. An association with Compton—or even knowing an associate of Compton—could land you in a world of trouble."

Even if the man had died years ago? I wondered. I wanted to ply Mr. Fielding with many more questions, though I conceded that he had much more experience of the criminal underworld than I did.

"I asked you only because of your relationship with Daniel," I said. "I will keep silent."

"Good. Compton can reach out of hell, where he surely is roasting merrily, to torment us living beings." Mr. Fielding let out a breath. "Please thank your butler for the port. It was the best I've ever tasted."

He pressed my hand again, then he opened the door, his own thanks springing from his lips as he spied Mr. Davis across the hall. In the space of a second, Mr. Fielding once more became the vacuous and toadying gentleman that I well knew he was not.

M r. Fielding had given me much to ponder. Tess and I finished the supper preparations as Mrs. Bywater's guests arrived—I saw hurrying feet in fine though not frivolous shoes descend from carriages and flow into the house. Mr. Bywater had taken himself to his club for the evening, leaving the way clear for Mrs. Bywater and her female friends.

Cynthia had absented herself as well. I wondered if she were with Miss Townsend and Bobby or looking in on Joanna. I longed for the day to be over and Thursday to dawn so I could fly to Joanna myself.

The sorbet cups went up on a tray by themselves, accompanied with small bowls of walnuts and dried fruit. I came out of my distraction to be pleased that the orange rinds came back down scraped clean. Mr. Davis also stuck his head in the kitchen doorway to tell me the entire meal had been a success.

Tess waltzed about the kitchen by herself in celebration before she whirled beside me to help me clean and prepare for tomorrow.

I hoped Daniel would return once everyone had gone to bed, but he did not. I didn't linger to wait for him, wanting to be up early and gone tomorrow before anyone could invent a reason for me to stay.

Daniel appeared as I was leaving the house at first light, Tess already up and yawning to prepare the household's breakfast.

"Can you spare some time before you visit Grace and Joanna?" he asked as he fell into step beside me along Mount Street. I almost snapped at him that no, I could not, but Daniel quickly continued. "I've managed to convince the governor of Newgate to let us in to speak to Millburn."

15

Daniel led me, once I'd eagerly agreed, to the corner of
Mount and Davies Streets where Lewis and his placid
bay horse waited with his hansom. Lewis bade me a cheerful
good morning, which I answered hurriedly as Daniel handed
me into the cab.

It was bitterly cold, but sitting against Daniel under the lap
robe he pulled over us soon warmed me. Either that or I no
longer noticed the chill.

My feelings for Daniel were beginning to worry me. I'd
vowed never to allow a man to come between me and my common sense again, but now I snuggled into him, happy to let his
nearness and warmth ease my troubles. If I came to depend on
him for that ease every day, where would I be?

Happy, something whispered inside me.

I pushed the voice aside, letting the noise of carts and horses,
and the stink of them too, focus me on the reality of the day.

Lewis took us east by way of Oxford Street. Newgate Jail lay

at the end of the Holborn Viaduct, which passed over Farringdon Street and railroad tracks before it slid back down to
the corner of Newgate Street and Old Bailey.

The road called Old Bailey had, in colloquial speech, given
its name to the Central Criminal Court building, which stood
just beyond Newgate. A tunnel connected the prison with the
courthouse, so that the prisoners could be guided through to
their trials without worry that they'd leg it off into the streets
of London.

Newgate was notorious for a reason. It was full of prisoners
waiting in appalling conditions to learn their fate in the Old
Bailey dock. Once their sentence was handed down by the
long-wigged judge, the prisoner was taken in chains either to
their new home in Dartmoor or another hard-labor prison, or
back to Newgate to wait for their hanging at the beginning of
the week. The judge would then retire home to his brandy and
warm supper, feeling he'd done a good day's work.

Jailers treated prisoners according to their rank and wealth.
A rich man—if he somehow couldn't avoid arrest entirely—
would have a private room with as many comforts as his family could bring to him. Some had their valets with them to
make certain they were dressed, shaved, and well-fed in the
mornings.

The working-class men and women and ladies and gentlemen of the streets were stuck into a common room, where
quarrels and fighting were common, with one bucket for the
relief of several dozen people. If one's family couldn't afford to
feed one, one went hungry.

I'd been in this prison once before, when I'd been accused
of murdering my employer. As I approached the building, all
the fear and despair of that day rushed back at me, and my
knees began to fold under me.

Daniel's strength kept me on my feet. "Steady, lass," he whispered into my ear. "If you'd prefer, I'll have Lewis run you to the Millburns', and I'll speak to Sam on my own."

"No." I clung to Daniel's arm, but steeled myself. Behind the grim and solid gates before me lay desperation and fear, but also a man who needed his friends. "I owe it to Sam and Joanna. I'll be fine."

I would not be, and Daniel knew I would not, but he tightened his grip and guided me forward to speak to the guard.

One would expect a prison guard to be a hard man without humor, but this one grinned and greeted us jovially. He *was* a hard man, I could see, who would not hesitate to beat us down if we attempted to overpower him, or to shoot us with the sidearm he wore.

"Most are anxious to get *out*," the guard joked as he turned the keys. "But if you insist on going *in*, then I will admit you. Give my best to Millburn. He's friendly to us."

That was Sam all over, making friends with the men who'd confine him until he was condemned to death.

The cold of the January morning was hardly cut by the walls of the courtyard, or even by the interior of the prison itself. More guards wandered the open spaces, and one led us down a dark corridor to a door about halfway along.

I breathed a sigh of relief that I wouldn't have to enter the common room, which was on the floor below this, then chastised myself. Sam was enduring it while I slept safely in my bed.

The guard ushered us into a small room, with stone walls whose whitewash had long since worn away. A rickety table sat in the middle of this chamber with two chairs on opposite sides of it. One chair was empty, and the other held Sam, with shackles on his wrists and ankles.

When we entered, Sam half rose with a clank of chains.

"Kat?" He gaped at me, then skewered Daniel with a glare. "This is no place for her, McAdam. Why did you bring her?"

"She insisted." Daniel held out the empty chair for me. The jailers must have assumed Sam would have only one visitor and hadn't bothered with a second. "I've learned not to disregard her insights."

Sam sank back as I took the seat and set my handbag on my lap.

Exhaustion lined Sam's face, which was dark with grime. His mustache, which Joanna always said made him look dashing, was gone, a faint scar where a razor had nicked his upper lip. His very dark hair was dusty, his eyes bloodshot from lack of sleep. The kind, funny man who was Joanna's loving husband lurked in the back of his eyes, but I faced a resigned, unhappy prisoner certain his past had caught up to him.

"Dear Sam." I reached across the table to him, but Sam curled his fingers and pulled away from me.

Daniel closed the door, telling the guard who'd brought us that Sam was in no condition to run away. The guard only shrugged, leaning against the rickety doorframe as Daniel shut him out. He would listen, of course, but since Sam was innocent, there would be nothing untoward for him to hear and report.

"You didn't bring Joanna, did you?" Sam asked me abruptly.

"She is safe at home," Daniel assured him before I could speak. "I agree with you, your wife does not need to be here. Soon, I hope, she'll have no reason to come anyway."

"Because I'll be swinging from the scaffold," Sam said darkly.

"Now, it's no good talking like that," I said. For some reason, his despair rekindled my resolve. "I know you committed no crime, and we will prove it."

"Mr. Crowe, the solicitor, has been to see me." Sam's gloom did not lift. "I want to be proud and refuse the charity your friends are handing me, Kat, but I'm not such a fool as to turn away a competent solicitor and a silk barrister. But Crowe said there's not much chance. The most we can hope for is a softer sentence if we gain the sympathy of the jury for my wife and many children."

"Then Mr. Crowe is talking nonsense," I said. "We will find evidence to free you, and all will be well."

The glance Sam exchanged with Daniel told me Sam had no faith in my declarations.

"Who is the barrister?" Daniel asked.

"Sir Rupert Shepherd," Sam answered without inflection. "Haven't seen him yet."

Daniel whistled. "Heavy artillery. Don't worry, Millburn. With Shepherd on your side, the gentlemen of the jury will be weeping at your tale of woe, bidding their wives knit you socks, and recommending you serve out your sentence in a seaside cottage."

A ghost of a smile passed over Sam's face. "What you mean is, the judge might send me to a place where I walk on a treadmill all day instead of breaking slag in Devonshire."

"Kat is right—you must not give up hope." Daniel feigned hurt feelings. "We'd think you didn't believe in us."

"I mean no offense." Even in his dejection, Sam strove to be polite. "I know you and Kat have handed the police the correct culprits in the past, but this time, we're up against an institution of sterling reputation and long history."

"I've heard that Daalman's is on shaky ground," I said. I did not bother to add that a butler was among those who'd told me this, but Mr. Davis was shrewd and accumulated much useful information. "The institution might be old, but Daalman's is merely a building full of people who are human and make mistakes. I've met some of those people—one of them must be stewing in guilt right now because you're taking the blame for his crimes."

Sam snorted a laugh. "I doubt it. I like my work, and my pay packet is enough for us, but I keep my head bent over my desk. Most of the bankers and clerks are snobbish automatons who can barely bring themselves to speak to me. I'm not one of them, as you know."

"What about Mr. Kearny?" I asked. "He said he recommended you for the post."

Sam's expression softened. "Kearny's all right. I met him years ago, when I was working for a tailor near Smithfield—Kearny has his suits made there. I was taking care of the tailor's accounts. Kearny would chat to me while he was waiting to be fitted, and we became friends. Over a pint at a pub, he wondered if I wouldn't do better in an office instead of a shop, and then he told me of an open post at Daalman's."

"Generous of him," Daniel said. "You didn't find anything suspicious in that?"

"Of course I did," Sam scoffed. "I'm nobody, and didn't have two coins to rub together. I fell in with bad people in South London—no secret now, is it? But I was working to better myself. Kearny understood that. He'd had a leg up himself, and he was passing on the favor, he said. I thought, no harm in going along with him. I had a wife and a child on the way, and the rise in pay attracted me. The head clerk didn't like me on first glance, but Kearny persuaded him to take me on in trial. This was years ago now. If there was something suspicious in Kearny wanting me at Daalman's, he's playing a devil of a long game."

I agreed it was doubtful that Mr. Kearny would wait so

many years if he was setting up Sam for embezzlement and murder.

"Who gave Mr. Kearny the leg up?" I asked. "Out of curiosity."

"Mr. Zachary," Sam answered promptly. "Kearny told me. Zachary was an acquaintance of Kearny's father and heard Kearny was a bright lad. So, like me, he was given a trial period at the bank and then hired on. Worked his way from clerk to banker. Not that they'd ever let me into such a lofty job, and I knew that. Kearny is from a well-educated family in the gentry. They live in a fine home in Harrow, and I was born in the backstreets of Bermondsey. But it was a soft post, and I was good at it. But now . . . Even if you are right and I get off, I'll never be welcomed there again."

"If they are so quick to accuse you, I'd say you had a lucky escape," I said.

"Lucky." Sam laughed bitterly. "You have an odd idea of luck, Kat."

"I stand by the word. The circumstances are not good, but you will be absolved in the eyes of the world. There will be any number of banks or investment firms who want as diligent a worker as you."

Again, Sam and Daniel exchanged the look that said I was daft, but they'd humor me.

I opened my bag and removed the notebook and pencil I'd slipped into it before I'd departed the house. "None of this speculation leads anywhere." I leafed to the pages where I'd begun the notes on Sam's case and readied my pencil. "Let us take things as they happened. You were late the morning of Mr. Stockley's death. Why?"

Sam frowned as though he struggled to recall. "That morning, everything went wrong. The cook announced that she could get no eggs, and we'd eaten all the meat yesterday, and we'd have to make do with bread and butter. I ran out myself to procure the eggs, as no one else could be spared. I had to go a long way to find any, all the way to Leadenhall Market, in fact. Then the children were so unruly while we waited for breakfast that Joanna was at her wits' end. I stayed behind a bit to help her until they were all fed and finally settled down for their studies. Then an omnibus had an accident right at the end of our lane. No one hurt, but there was a mess of carts, horses, people . . . It took me time to squeeze through, and I ran the rest of the way. Miss Swann admonished me as I dashed in not only for being a half hour late but for being disheveled and wet as well. Why she was standing in the ground-floor hallway, I have no idea—to plague me, I suppose."

I imagined the stately Miss Swann looking down her long nose at Sam's rumpled coat and wet hat as he breathlessly hurried inside.

"The children were unruly?" I asked, this statement the most surprising out of all that he'd uttered. "Even Grace? I apologize if she caused any trouble. Though all the children are so well-behaved."

Sam's smile broke through his unhappiness, one so fond it touched my heart. "Of course they are unruly. They are children. On their best behavior when you are there, because they want to please their Aunt Kat. No, Grace was not one of the scoundrels that morning. She was rather impatient with my sons and daughters, wanting to get on with her reading. Grace likes to study." He finished with some awe.

Was it wrong to feel pride that *my* daughter had been good as gold? Then again, Sam might be exaggerating to spare my feelings or keep me from being cross at Grace.

No, I had to believe that Grace had been annoyed at the

other children for vexing Sam and Joanna. She was rather like
me in that respect.

I tried to hide my joy in Grace and continued with my questions. "Excellent. We have witnesses as to the time you came in
and that you ran through the rain—Miss Swann and presumably the doorman and his assistant. And perhaps anyone else
who was inconvenienced by the omnibus crash. What did you
do once you arrived?"

Sam's expression told me he was skeptical about the witnesses. "I went to my desk and started to work. I did ask about
Mr. Stockley, because we'd agreed to meet so I could discuss things with him. But he never sent for me, and I worked
steadily without moving. Others were looking for Stockley,
and I snapped at them that he was likely upstairs, but I was too
busy to think anything of it. Until, that is, the police came to
arrest me. I even ate my luncheon at my desk, because I was
so late. Thank God I did, because the cuisine here is not up to
your cooking, Kat."

"Why did you agree to meet with Mr. Stockley?" I asked,
pretending to ignore his feeble joke about the food. I'd brought
nothing edible with me today because I'd had no time to prepare, but I'd try to send something along. "Mr. Kearny said the
two of you were often at odds."

"We are. Were, I mean." Sam stumbled as he remembered
Stockley was dead. "Stockley was a high-handed prick, if you'll
pardon my language. He was a Cambridge man, from King's
College, he reminded all and sundry. He was a clerk, if at the
top of that heap, but you might have thought he was the lord
chancellor, with all his airs."

I had met such people before. "Was he meeting you to give
you a lecture?" I asked. "The fact that you agreed to see him
sounds more friendly than that."

Sam glanced at the closed door, then leaned across the table to us. "We were meeting because I'd finally convinced him that I was not stealing money from the bank. We were going to discuss the problem in private—he said he had some ideas about who it was and wanted my help in proving them."

16

Sam's words stirred hope in me. The fact that Mr. Stockley thought he might know who the true embezzler was gave that embezzler a strong motive to murder him.

"Did he say who?" I asked eagerly.

Sam shook his head, to my disappointment. "I would have told Mr. Zachary or someone even higher if he had. I truly wanted to squash the rumor that it was me."

"I am amazed anyone could have ever thought so," I said in indignation.

Sam sent me a grateful glance, but shook his head. "Once word went round that I used to be a South London villain, everyone's fingers pointed to me."

"How did someone find out?" I asked. "Presumably you did not confess your past to all and sundry. Even I did not know. I will scold you about that once we have you home, though it scarcely matters now. You have proved yourself an admirable man, in spite of your origins."

"High praise, Millburn." Daniel rested his shoulder against the wall as he stood near us, the guard never having fetched another chair. "I'd accept it."

"I promise I will give you a full dossier on my youthful activities if you want it," Sam said. "As long as you don't tell my sons and daughters. They are a handful enough already—they do not need any more hold over me."

I liked this banter from Sam, because it told me I was making him believe he truly would be freed.

"Let us return to Mr. Stockley," I said. "Where exactly were you to meet?"

"In a file room on the third floor," Sam answered. "I was told he was found in the strong room. Why he went there, I don't know."

"Early in the morning," Daniel supplied. "That is when the coroner says he died. Can we assume your appointment was for later?"

"Stockley said he'd send for me when he had a free moment, and that we'd meet in the file room. Most of the rooms on that floor aren't used anymore, only for storage of records. Several hundred years of records takes up much space."

"The file room, not the strong room?" I asked for clarification. "You are certain?"

Sam sent me an impatient look. "Yes, I am certain. Stockley might have finally believed me, but he wouldn't let a mere junior clerk into a strong room, no matter how ancient its contents. I wouldn't have a key anyway. Two different keys were needed to enter, in any case."

"Mr. Stockley had one?" I asked, scribbling notes.

"Yes, he was rather proud of it." Sam's tone was derisive.

"Who else did?" I prompted. "Who would have the second key needed to enter the room with Mr. Stockley?"

"Oh, I don't know." Sam ran a hand through his uncombed hair. "Mr. Zachary, of course. Any of the senior bankers. The doorman has a multitude of keys he keeps in a cabinet in his little cubbyhole, though I couldn't say what they opened."

"Mr. Kearny?" I wrote his name.

"You speak as though you want to pin this murder on Kearny," Sam said with disapproval. "He is not the sort. He does grow irritated with people, but he relies more on morose sighs and reproachful looks to convey his feelings. He does not fly into a violent rage and bash men to death."

"That you know of," I amended.

Sam made an exasperated noise. "I've been mates with the man for nigh on fifteen years. If he were capable of murder, by now he'd have done in the entire senior clerks' room, Mr. Zachary, and Miss Swann for good measure. He had to fight plenty to reach the position he has. No, he's an upright bloke underneath his fancy suits."

That remained to be seen. I wrote down another name. "What about Miss Swann? Does she have a key to the strong room?"

Sam huffed a laugh. "No, indeed. Zachary would never give a *woman* something so important as keys to rooms in the building she works in."

"Mr. Kearny said that Mr. Zachary did what Miss Swann told him to, not the other way about," I pointed out.

"Zachary relies on her judgment and intelligence, yes," Sam answered. "But to give her anything that amounts to true stature in that company? No."

I recalled the cool hauteur with which Miss Swann regarded Mr. Zachary—and Lady Cynthia and me, for that matter. If she was enraged at Mr. Zachary's distrust of her because of her sex, she had hidden it well.

"Even though she is related to the Daalmans, and Daalman women have passed ownership of the bank through their line for centuries?" I went on.

"Only when there isn't a male heir, so that the bank won't go to anyone outside the family," Sam said. "The ladies sit on the board of directors, and nominally as the chairman, if necessary, but all decisions and daily transactions are in the hands of their male relations and employees."

"Hmph." I kept my head bent over my notebook. "I think Daalman's wouldn't be on the shaky ground it is if the ladies truly ran things."

Sam chuckled, sounding like his old self. "I agree with you, Kat. But I'm not certain things are shaky as you say. I look at the books every day. I copy out contracts and prospectuses, make certain everything is filed into the correct boxes, and copy the transactions the bank makes before sending them on to the senior clerks. There's not much I don't see. Daalman's survived the panic of '73 without a tremor. So many banks people thought were stable did not."

I dimly recalled the furor in England, Europe, and America over banks and stockbrokers who couldn't pay back their depositors or investors and were forced to close, ruining thousands and causing what financiers termed a depression. I'd seen the exclamations in the newspapers, but mostly I'd been cooking twelve hours a day. My money had been safely in a box under my mattress, so I didn't pay much attention.

"But Daalman's had ups and downs before," I persisted.

"Probably." Sam frowned. "Before my time though. We worried in 1873, but we came through. All investments are risky, especially in shipping, so there might have been some losses in the past. However, Daalman's seems to have covered them all without much trouble."

I admitted to myself that journalists liked to sensationalize any weakness in otherwise solid institutions to make people buy the newspapers. The man Mr. Davis had worked for who'd invested in Daalman's might have simply bought risky stock. There were many sides to any story.

I turned a page in my notebook and wrote the word *Embezzlement*. Sam saw it and winced.

"I thought you might want to know about that," he said.

"Why would they accuse *you*?" I asked. "How was the possible embezzlement discovered?"

"Through me," Sam said in resignation. "I told Stockley about it. I'm sorry I ever did."

I wrote Stockley's name under the *Embezzlement* heading. "How exactly did you know money was being taken?"

Sam cast a glance at Daniel as though asking for rescue from my interrogation, but Daniel offered no help.

"As I said, I copy out many contracts, which are agreements between Daalman's and the person or other businesses entrusting money to them," Sam began with reluctance. "Daalman's doesn't let just anyone invest, and so I see the same names cropping up again and again. Not much change over the last decade or so. And then I started noticing new names, odd ones, but which seemed familiar at the same time. I'd see the one contract and then nothing else. I took careful note as I copied them and realized that the payment agreement was strange as well. The investor would make a minimal deposit but earn a quite hefty percentage in dividends, paid every other month. Most of Daalman's contracts are worded so they keep a large part of the money, pay quarterly at most—they strive for annually—and encourage reinvestment of those dividends."

Sam paused for breath and also to let me write all this down. I did not understand the world of high finance, but this lucrative arrangement for the investor sounded fishy to me. I agreed with Sam that banks liked to take money, not give it out.

"Why did you find the names odd and familiar at the same time?" I asked.

"I wasn't certain at first." Sam traced a slow line on the table. "They niggled at me until one night when I started to read to the children before they went to bed." He flushed. "I still read to them—have since they were tiny tots. Grace too. She loves the stories. I realized that the names I'd found were all characters in books."

I eagerly pounced on that interesting fact. "What books? What were you reading to them that night?"

"Not in that particular book—we've been deep into Mr. Verne's *The Mysterious Island*. But it reminded me. When I decided to become a respectable bloke and work in a shop, I started reading every novel I could come across, both to improve my speech and as a window onto the world I wanted to enter. I read a powerful lot of Mr. Dickens. More than most, I'll wager. When I began courting Joanna, we had that to talk about. She likes Mr. Dickens too."

Sam faltered at the mention of Joanna. The longing in his eyes threatened to become despair.

I touched his hand. "Joanna is well, my friend. She is bearing up and is very strong. She knows it's only a matter of time until you leave this place for home."

"You are a good woman, Kat." Sam clasped my hand briefly a moment, his fingertips rough and raw. "You are kind to try to help, you and McAdam both."

"It's not kindness," Daniel rumbled. "Why should you go down for the stiff-necked City hypocrites taking people's money left and right? No, we'll find the right person and let *him* beg for mercy."

Sam's smile flitted across his face. "You're a ruthless cove, McAdam. I am happy you're on my side."

"We are straying from the subject," I reminded them both.

"My heavens, Grace is so like you." Sam turned a full smile on me. "When my boys wander into intense discussions of who knows what, Grace pulls them back to earth. Refuses to let them cut her or my girls out of the conversation."

My heart squeezed with his declaration, and for a moment, the words on my paper blurred. I cleared my throat. "The names, Sam."

Sam chuckled, more relaxed now than when we'd come in. "They were not obvious, or I wouldn't have puzzled over them for so long. Not Martin Chuzzlewit or David Copperfield or anything even the casual reader would recognize. They were names like Edward Dennis—Ned Dennis is a character in *Barnaby Rudge*, an executioner. Anthony Weller—Tony Weller is the father of Sam Weller in *The Pickwick Papers*. Edward Plummer is a character in the Christmas story *The Cricket on the Hearth*, which was very popular in my youth. Allan Woodcourt is a doctor in *Bleak House* who falls in love with and eventually marries the heroine. There were more."

I scribbled all this down, recognizing the titles of the books, especially those that had been made into plays. *The Cricket on the Hearth* had often appeared onstage at Christmas when I was a girl.

"You realized that these were contracts for people who did not exist," I finished.

"Yes, and I took the matter to Stockley. He is the head of the senior clerks' room—I did not report to the head of the junior clerks' room, Mr. Chandler, because I frankly do not think he was intelligent enough to understand the implications or believe me. Stockley at least has read a book in his day. Though I had to bring in the novels in question and show him the names. The first thing he did was accuse me of inventing the contracts to discredit the bank. So, of course, we had a shouting match about that."

"Which whoever is doing this took advantage of," I said.

"Yes." Sam slumped in his chair. "I was trying to do my job, help keep Daalman's from being swindled. This is the thanks I received."

"Honest men always pay," Daniel said. "At least, that's what villains in the past tried to tell me. Though in the end, that is not true."

"Mr. Dickens's books carry that theme much of the time," Sam said wryly. "Most have a happy ending, but only after he puts the heroes and heroines through a hard slog." His grimace said he'd personally rather do without the hard slog.

"How did you convince Mr. Stockley that you were telling the truth?" I asked.

Sam shrugged. "Many discussions and arguments. He told me to bring him any contracts or letters that seemed suspicious to me, so I began trotting them upstairs several times a month. There were only a few at first, but then they began multiplying. I wasn't certain if the dividends were paid to these storybook people, but I started trying to find out."

"Presumably something was paid," I said. "People started whispering that you were embezzling."

"I know. It made me very angry." Sam wore a scowl I'd seldom seen on him. "Stockley might have mentioned he suspected me when I first pointed out the problem, or the true embezzler might have started the rumors to divert suspicion from them."

"Very likely the latter," I said. "The guilty always try to pin their crimes on someone else. Unfortunately, that ploy is sometimes successful."

"As you can see." Sam waved a hand at our surroundings. "The trouble is, anyone could have slid those contracts in with the legitimate ones. Another clerk could have, or one of the bankers, or even Mr. Zachary."

"It would have to be someone who could make sure they were paid out," Daniel said. "Who at Daalman's wouldn't question why someone from *Pickwick Papers* is receiving generous dividends on a miserly investment?"

"Those writing the checks likely have no idea," Sam said. "Unless they were devoted readers of Mr. Dickens, they'd not question the names. Likewise, they might only know the amount to be paid, not the circumstances of the investments."

"Mr. Stockley, though, began to believe in you," I broke in.

"Yes. It took months, but I finally made him see reason. He is—was, I mean—a stubborn chap. Very upright but obtuse. We began meeting in the upstairs file room, where no one went, to discuss things."

"Which brings us to the day of his death." I made another line in my notebook and wrote the date, Monday, 22 January 1883. "He said he would send for you?"

"Yes, he told me this on Saturday—we work half days on Saturday mornings. When I was leaving that day, Stockley took me aside and told me he had thought things over and wanted my help exposing the embezzler. He'd send for me on Monday, and we'd meet in our usual place. He had hold of my coat collar and whispered all this into my ear. I admit his spittle annoyed me and I gave him a little shove to get away from him. Several of the clerks saw that, unfortunately."

Which gave credit to the tale that Sam and Mr. Stockley were at odds.

"I will guess that the embezzler either heard him or already realized that Mr. Stockley was onto him," I said. "He waited for Mr. Stockley near your conferring place, somehow coaxed him into the strong room, and killed him there, locking him in."

"A good possibility," Daniel agreed. "We have to discover how the killer knew Stockley would be in so early and that he'd go to the third floor as soon as he arrived."

"Maybe the killer also arranged to meet him," I suggested. "Said he could explain away why Mr. Stockley thought him an embezzler, perhaps. It sounds as though Mr. Stockley thought himself a superior sort of man and would not hesitate to confront the embezzler, even alone on a quiet floor in a mostly empty building."

"That is his character exactly," Sam said. "Or was, poor chap."

I flipped back to the page where I'd written the word *Keys*. "Was Mr. Stockley's key found on him? In his hand or in his pocket? If two keys were needed to get into the room, then two keys would be needed to lock him inside again. Two keys to open the door again to reveal Mr. Stockley there."

"I will ask," Daniel said. "McGregor would have made note of anything found on the body, and the City chaps will have cataloged it if they are efficient."

"Why did the person who found Mr. Stockley decide to go up to the strong room?" I asked. "Again, they'd need keys, or to take someone with them who had the keys."

"I told them to look there," Sam said, shoulders slumping. "Or at least on the third floor. Stockley was missed, and Miss Swann was vexed. At least, she said Mr. Zachary was vexed, but we knew what she meant. I was busy and harried. When

Chandler, the head of the junior clerks' room, said loudly that Millburn always seemed to know where Stockley was—in the sneering way he has—I growled at them to check the third floor. I didn't intend to give away our conferring place, but as I said, I was rushing to finish copying documents Mr. Zachary had demanded. So up Chandler and Miss Swann went. They seem to have fetched the necessary people to open all the doors up there, they found him, and sent for the constables." Sam let out another defeated breath. "I have helped condemn myself every step of the way."

"A logical person would ask why you'd direct people to find Mr. Stockley's body instead of answering that you had no idea where he was," I said.

"Logical people don't work at Daalman's," Sam answered with a twitch of his lips. "Maybe *you* should be my brief, Kat."

"My dear Sam, if I appeared in court in wig and gown to address the judge and jury, the whole lot of them would faint dead away. Or burst into laughter. The building might fall down as well."

"It would be worth observing," Daniel said, and Sam gave him a feeble laugh.

"When you have finished poking fun at me"—I frowned at the pair of them—"the gist of the matter is this: You found suspicious contracts under fictitious names in the pile of things you were to copy. I will assume other clerks had these sorts of papers in their piles as well but noticed nothing wrong. You approached Mr. Stockley, the head of the senior clerks' room, and persuaded him that something was amiss. He did digging of his own, conferring with you in an unused file room from time to time. On Saturday last, he took you aside and told you to be ready for a meeting with him on Monday. Sometime between Sunday and Monday, Mr. Stockley met his killer on the third floor—either by chance or prearrangement—unlocked the strong room and entered it, unsuspecting. He was killed, the strong room locked again, and the killer departed or went to his own desk to begin work as though nothing had happened. You were late on Monday because of our unruly brood and missing ingredients for breakfast. You then worked hastily to catch up on your work, throwing out the information that Mr. Stockley sometimes went up to the third floor. He was found, police summoned, you arrested."

I finished to find both men staring at me. I sent them a questioning look.

"An excellent summing-up," Daniel said. "Are you certain you won't apply at one of the Inns of Court?"

I rolled my eyes at his impertinence. "Is there anything else you can tell us?" I asked Sam. "Anything at all that could help?"

Sam lifted his slim shoulders. "I can think of nothing. All of this has shocked me until I don't know what I understand anymore." Weariness settled on him. "Please make certain Joanna isn't touched by this. Not her fault I've made a complete mess of our life."

I reached for Sam's hand again and squeezed it. "You have done nothing wrong, Sam Millburn. You remember that. Someone has shoved all their villainy onto you, but we will make them see that was a mistake."

Sam's shaky smile broke through. "You are very certain."

"Of course I am." I tightened my grip, then released him and closed my notebook. "You will be reunited with your family, and everything will end well, just like in one of your favorite books."

"You haven't read much of Mr. Dickens, then," Sam said gloomily. "Wrongly accused men sometimes come to bad ends in them. He knew much of the real world, did Mr. Dickens."

* * *

I was ashamed of how quickly I raced out of the confines of Newgate, drawing a relieved breath once we were through the gates.

"Poor Sam," I said as I took Daniel's offered arm. "Poor, poor Sam."

It was all I could say as we trudged to the corner, where Lewis had promised to wait for us.

Daniel's gloved hand closed over mine. "You were good to bolster his spirits. The unwavering Kat."

I came out of my doldrums to send him an indignant glance. "I did not exaggerate my certainty that we can free him. All we have to do is discover who had keys to that room, who was seen entering the building at the time in question, and who the embezzler was. I wager the killer and embezzler are one and the same."

"That is all we have to do, is it?" Daniel had the audacity to laugh. "You make life sound so simple, my Kat."

"It is simple." As annoyed as I was, I did not withdraw from him. Walking so close to Daniel and his warmth felt nice. "Men always try to make things so much more complicated than they need to be."

To Daniel's renewed laughter, we reached Lewis's cab and Daniel handed me in.

"We'll go to the Millburns' now," I told Lewis.

"Right you are, missus," Lewis said. The cab lurched as the large horse jerked us into traffic.

It was not far from Newgate to the Millburns'—down Old Bailey to Ludgate Hill and from there around St. Paul's to Cheapside. Not long later, I was alighting at the end of Clover Lane.

Daniel climbed down and assisted me out as though I weren't

perfectly capable of descending from the cab on my own. I expected him to take my arm and accompany me to Joanna's, but he released me with regret.

"I have to return to the Yard," he said. "Monaghan is expecting me. But I can confer with Inspector McGregor about this key business. It is the sort of detail he'll pay attention to."

"Thank you," I said with sincerity, "for taking me to see Sam." I shivered with more than January's cold. "We must get him out of there."

"I will do my best. I can bring it up again with Monaghan today. Maybe wear him down, have him put a word in."

"No," I said in alarm. "He made you pay a price for my release. Sam will not thank you for increasing that price for him."

Daniel's expression was unreadable. "Let me worry about Monaghan, Kat. I have his measure."

"And he has yours." I did not trust the bespectacled, ice-cold man, who held who knew what position with the police. I also did not like that it was all so very secret.

"I have learned exactly how far I can goad him, and when to back away." Daniel traced the curve of my cheek with a gloved finger. "Don't waste time worrying about me. Worry about Joanna, and take care of her." He leaned closer, letting a kiss touch my lips. "Give my love to Grace."

With that he backed away, not realizing he'd left me breathless. Daniel doffed his cap and turned back to the cab Lewis held ready, his impudent grin in place.

As soon as Daniel's feet touched the floor of the cab, the horse moved forward. Daniel fell into the seat and waved at me until he was lost behind the carts and cabs that filled Cheapside.

A small laugh escaped my lips as soon as he was gone. Daniel always left me dazzled.

I noted a constable lurking at the end of Clover Lane, trying not to be noticeably watching it. I noted one a little way down Cheapside as well.

I gave both a nod and then hastened down the lane to the house. My steps were light because I'd see Grace, though my heart still ached for Sam.

When I reached the house, the maid, Carrie, pulled open the door for me. "Mrs. Millburn has a visitor," she whispered to me, eyes round.

Fearing the ruffian Mr. Jarrett had bullied his way into the house, I rushed into the sitting room without bothering to shed my hat and coat.

The man who rose at my entrance was not Mr. Jarrett. Joanna looked pained, not fearful, as I gazed upon the rather mournful countenance of Sam's friend Mr. Kearny, the banker who'd been kind to me in the upstairs hall of Daalman's.

17

"Good morning, Mr. Kearny," I said with some surprise.

I relinquished my coat and hat to Carrie, who'd pattered in behind me, and seated myself on the chair Joanna had risen to indicate, as though I were a grand lady caller. Mr. Kearny bowed to me and waited until Joanna and I had settled ourselves before he sat down again.

"I have been meaning to look in on Mrs. Millburn," Mr. Kearny said. "Make certain she is well, and all that."

He spoke like an affable young gentleman, in no different a manner than Mr. Thanos might. But while Mr. Thanos always exuded sincerity, I did not quite know what to make of Mr. Kearny. Sam said he was a friend, and that he was an unlikely murderer, but I was suspicious of everybody. For instance, why, on this Thursday morning, was Mr. Kearny not bent over his desk at Daalman's?

"I had a bit of leave coming," Mr. Kearny said in answer to

my silent question. "I always take a day out now and then, to take care of personal business I don't often have time to do. Send money to my mother, and that sort of thing." He laughed weakly, as though fearing we'd mock him for being kind to his mum.

"Most admirable," I assured him.

While I very much wanted to quiz Mr. Kearny about Daalman's, I also wanted to be alone with Joanna and tell her about my visit with Sam. I noted the children were absent—presumably, Joanna had sent them upstairs when Mr. Kearny arrived. A muffled thump above us confirmed that.

"I will do anything to help old Sam," Mr. Kearny said. "I know in my heart he is *not* a murderer. Magistrate thought nothing of my vouching for him though. The man made me admit I had no idea where Sam was in the small hours of Monday morning."

"Well, *I* know," Joanna said angrily. "He was asleep in his bed. In the morning, he went out, yes, but to purchase eggs from a grocer. I tried to tell the constables this when they ran roughshod all over my house. Everyone here can attest that he brought the eggs home. Quite good ones too."

A vicious prosecutor could make the case that Sam had thrown away all the eggs in the house to invent an excuse to leave on this early errand. He claimed he had to walk all the way to Leadenhall Market to find a vendor, which was why witnesses had seen him near Daalman's early that morning.

"Mr. Millburn does not have a key to the strong room," I pointed out. "After Mr. Stockley was killed, the door was locked again. Sam could not have done that, could he?"

Mr. Kearny flushed. "As it happens, I heard yesterday that the police inspector who came to Daalman's to go through

Millburn's things found both keys to the strong room hidden under his desk. In a sort of cubby under the desktop."

Joanna made a noise of distress. "It is nonsense. Sam would never have stolen those keys."

Mr. Kearny looked unhappy. "I am so sorry, Mrs. Millburn. I didn't mean to spring that upon you."

"Anyone could have put them under his desk," I said. I vowed Sam didn't know anything about them. He certainly hadn't betrayed any guilt about keys this morning. Was bewildered by the whole business, instead. "Quite a number of people work in the junior clerks' room, and more must go in and out."

"That is true." Mr. Kearny seized on my argument in relief. "Everyone enters the junior clerks' room. All the senior clerks, the bankers—me included. Even Mr. Zachary from time to time, though he usually sends an errand boy to pick up or deliver papers for him." He perked up. "One of the boys could have hidden them in his desk."

"Is there anyone you can trust to remember who was near Sam's desk?" I asked. "It would also be very helpful to have a list of who went in and out the day of Mr. Stockley's murder."

"Not certain if any of that lot are *trustworthy*," Mr. Kearny said with good humor, then lost his smile when he caught Joanna's anguished glance. "I beg your pardon. There are one or two gentlemen who are honest and bright. I can ask them."

"Do *you* have a key to the strong room?" I asked. I widened my eyes, as though ready to be awed that he was important enough to possess one.

"I do indeed." Mr. Kearny preened a bit under my gaze. "Here it is." He reached into his waistcoat pocket and pulled out several keys on a chain. "This one."

He lifted the largest key, which was thick and sturdy. I wished

Daniel was here—he could probably tell what sort of lock the key fit and what year it had been installed.

"It looks old," I said.

"It is an old building," Mr. Kearny said. "That particular strong room doesn't hold much of importance anymore. Historical papers and that sort of thing. Anything we need nowadays is in a newer strong room, installed probably ten years ago, on the second floor." He held up a key that looked a bit more modern, its metal still shiny. "This one goes to that."

I let myself look impressed. My point in having Mr. Kearny reveal his keys was to check whether or not *his* key had been slid under Sam's desk to incriminate him. As a friend of Sam's, he could have had more opportunity to get close to the desk.

Keys could be copied, I reminded myself. Mr. Kearny wasn't in the clear yet.

"As a matter of fact, I was one of the fellows who opened the door upstairs and found Mr. Stockley," Mr. Kearny said, his color rising once more. "I'd come in late myself—I live with my family out Harrow way, and I was stuck on a train that wouldn't move for some reason. Miss Swann, when she saw me try to slip in, ordered me upstairs. Chandler, head of the junior clerks' room, was already waiting on the third floor along with another banker, Mr. Kendell, who has a strong room key. Miss Swann bade Kendell and me to unlock the door for her. She was quite angry that she had to ask for our help, but good job she did, seeing as there was Mr. Stockley with his head all bloody, flat on the floor. Begging your pardon, Mrs. Millburn," he added hastily.

Joanna had gone wan, but drew a resolute breath. "It is quite all right, Mr. Kearny. I can weather it."

"The keys are different?" I asked. "Miss Swann needed you and Mr. Kendell both to open the door?"

"Yes, that's right." Mr. Kearny happily returned to the sub-ject. "All the strong rooms are like that—the newer ones that hold the bullion need three. So that one of us doesn't enter in the middle of the night and rob the place down to the ground. If I want to get into the strong rooms, I have to wait until a keeper of the other key is free. A nuisance, but it's wise, I think."

"Who is allowed the keys?" I itched to open my notebook and write, but I thought it better not to in front of Mr. Kearny. He might not be as forthcoming if he knew I'd scribble down all he said.

"Only those well trusted in the firm," Mr. Kearny said, pride in his answer. "Mr. Zachary does not bestow them on just anyone. A man has to be in the firm for years before Mr. Zachary has a key made for him."

"Mr. Zachary must have all the keys, then," I said. "He'd need an original for it to be copied."

"He does. Keeps them in a little box behind a wall panel in his office. I know this because I opened the door too soon once when he called me in to chat, and he was just locking up a cabinet and hiding it with the wall panel. He has a key to the keys." Mr. Kearny chortled.

Interesting. So, Mr. Zachary was the only one in the bank who could have unlocked and locked the strong room door alone. I doubted he'd sacrifice any of his precious keys to slide them under Sam's desk, but he could have had spares made at any time. So, for that matter, could anybody entrusted with one.

The business with the keys showed that the murder of Mr. Stockley was carefully planned. The police might think it a quarrel between Sam and Mr. Stockley, with Sam striking out in rage, but the more I learned, the more likely it was deliber-ate and premeditated.

Whoever had done it had tried their best to throw suspicion

onto Sam. That meant this person had watched Sam and Mr. Stockley interact, had noted where they'd gone, had known what they were conferring about. I supposed that whoever was embezzling from Daalman's had realized he was about to be discovered and had chosen Sam to put his hands up for all of it.

It made me quite furious. I'd find this embezzling, murderous plotter and let Inspector McGregor squash him like a bug.

Mr. Kearny slid his keys back into his pocket and cleared his throat. His glance at Joanna betrayed a flicker of longing he couldn't quite disguise.

I'd reflected once before that he was sweet on her. Joanna was a comely woman, always had been. It did not surprise me that as soon as Sam was locked away, men started to come out of the woodwork to court her. Mr. Jarrett, in his awful way, had done the same as Mr. Kearny.

I gazed at Mr. Kearny as though I expected him to rise and depart at any moment. After all, I'd come to call on my friend, relieving him of the duty of comforting her.

"Oh. Er." Mr. Kearny took the hint and got to his feet. "I should be going, Mrs. Millburn. If you need anything, as I said, you send word to me. I'll be here in a flash."

"That is very kind." Joanna left her chair and began moving to the door, her action encouraging him to go. "Thank you, Mr. Kearny."

"Not at all. Not at all." He dithered until Carrie appeared in the hall behind him, pointedly holding his coat and hat. "Good day, Mrs. Millburn. Mrs. Holloway."

He added my name as an afterthought, then turned and nearly snatched his coat from Carrie's hands.

"Mr. Kearny." I stepped out into the hallway as he struggled to thrust his arms into the sleeves. Carrie watched in amusement instead of reaching to help. "Do you read Mr. Dickens, by chance?" I asked him.

"Eh?" Mr. Kearny turned in a circle, one sleeve eluding him. I caught it so he could slide his arm inside. He sent me a bewildered look at my question. "Why the . . . Dickens . . . do you want to know that?" He guffawed at his joke.

"Mr. Millburn enjoys him," I said. "I thought perhaps you could lend him a book so he can while away the hours while he waits for his trial."

"Been a long time since I read anything," Mr. Kearny said, unconcerned. "But I could pop into a secondhand bookshop and take him something. Poor chap."

"As you like." I backed from him, nonchalant. "Thank you, Mr. Kearny."

"Not at all." Kearny lingered still, and Carrie shoved his hat at him.

He took it, said another round of good days to Joanna in the sitting room doorway, and to me, and finally departed.

"He sprang up out of nowhere," Joanna said as we watched Mr. Kearny amble down the lane. "It was a kindness of him to look me up, I suppose. He was trying to reassure me, rather clumsily, that Sam would be all right."

It wasn't kindness, but I decided not to explain. It was the natural inclination of a man who saw a good woman who might soon be free to look after him. If Mr. Kearny had killed Mr. Stockley and laid the blame on Sam to get to Joanna, I would wring Mr. Kearny's neck myself.

"I've just come from seeing Sam," I said gently as we entered the sitting room, Carrie closing the door behind us. "He sends his love."

Joanna swung to me, stricken. "You should have told me you would go. I want to see him. Let us go back there now."

I put my hands on Joanna's arms to keep her from rushing out of the house, coatless and hatless, to sprint to Newgate.

"I had no idea I'd be visiting him until Daniel intercepted me early this morning. They'll not admit you, my dear. They barely admitted me—I had to go in on Daniel's say-so."

"That is nonsense," Joanna blazed. "Families see prisoners all the time. They feed them."

"Yes, I know. But Sam is being guarded rather closely."

Joanna's panicked eyes began to narrow. "You are lying to me, Kat. He doesn't want to see me, does he?"

"Not like this, no." I caressed her trembling shoulders. "Please understand, Joanna. Sam loves you dearly, and he hates that he's been humiliated and broken. He does not want you to see *him* until he comes back into this house, as the man you admire."

Joanna regarded me fiercely. "That is rot. I love him no matter what. You won't keep me from him. I need to see him before—" She broke off, unable to finish.

"There will be no 'before,'" I said quickly. "Sam will be let off. I and Daniel and this barrister will make certain of it. Daniel referred to Sir Rupert Shepherd as heavy artillery. We will win this, all of us."

"If it were your husband locked away in that filthy prison, you'd not be so sanguine." Joanna glared at me. "Would you? Willing to tamely wait while others decided his fate? You'd be storming the ramparts. What if it was Daniel inside there?"

Her words checked me. I fell silent as I envisioned Daniel in Sam's place, chained and exhausted. Mr. Monaghan could do that to him—invent a charge or dredge up Daniel's old mistakes and punish him for them. Monaghan was quite powerful, and he might succeed in making the charges stick.

Joanna was right. I'd be devastated. I'd round up everyone

I knew and not stop until they'd found a way to rescue Daniel. I'd also be at Newgate every day—to look upon Daniel's face, touch his hand, make certain he was well.

Joanna's gaze sharpened as she observed my distress. "I think you understand," she said.

"I am so sorry," I whispered. "My dearest friend, you have the right of it, and I am a fool."

"Thank you." Joanna continued to watch me, as though diverted from her troubles by a new insight about me. "Will you—"

She clamped her lips closed as Grace opened the sitting room door. "Mum? I saw you arrive. Is Mr. Kearny gone now? Can we have our day out?"

I swung from Joanna and swept Grace into my arms. "We can indeed, darling. We'll have a walk and a fine tea, and talk and talk." I released her, and Grace happily darted off to fetch her coat.

Joanna continued to give me a knowing stare. I was glad that my confused feelings gave her a respite from her own troubles, but her little smile began to vex me. I pointedly closed the door on her and met Grace at the front door, where Carrie was helping the excited girl into her coat.

"How did you know Mr. Kearny's name?" I asked as I took her hand and led her down the lane.

"I recognized him when he came in. We were watching over the stair railing." She grinned at me, guessing correctly I wouldn't admonish her for curiosity. "He's called on the Millburns before. He's Uncle Sam's friend."

Possibly why Mr. Kearny had been certain he'd be welcome. There would be no objection to an old friend making certain Sam's wife was all right.

Was Mr. Kearny guilty of anything but fancying Joanna?

I'd heard him state loudly in the clerks' room, before anyone had seen me, that Sam couldn't be responsible for the murder. He seemed genuinely distressed for Sam, although ready to take advantage of Sam's absence to get in good with Joanna. Hedging his bets, I'd say.

He did not know Joanna very well, I decided. Joanna was thoroughly in love with her Sam and not the sort of woman to eagerly seek another man to take care of her.

Grace's hand tightened on mine. "You'll get Uncle Sam free, Mum. You and Uncle Daniel. I know it."

Her confidence made me want to hug her again. "We will do our best," I said.

"You will." Having made her pronouncement, Grace tugged me onward. "Where shall we go today?"

I did not want to venture far. I settled for one of our usual strolls around St. Paul's, the two of us stepping into its hushed interior to admire the lofty dome and the fine architecture of the late seventeenth century. Both Lord Nelson and the Duke of Wellington, the noble heroes who'd fought Napoleon, lay in the crypt beneath us.

We then walked around the green of the churchyard outside, a quiet space so removed from and yet so close to the bustle of the metropolis.

I realized someone dogged our footsteps as we strolled, which annoyed me. I wanted to take Grace to one of our favorite tea shops, not rush her home to keep her safe. She'd be disappointed as well. Not frightened—Grace was a brave soul.

Daniel sometimes intercepted us on our walks, but I knew it was not Daniel who followed. I'd spent enough time on these streets to know when I was guarded by a friend or stalked by an enemy.

I exited the churchyard to St. Martin's Le Grand, which ran

northward past the large edifice of the post office, hoping to throw our pursuer off the scent. I ducked around the corner at the end of the post office, but heard rushing footsteps in pursuit. I squared my shoulders and swung around to face the approaching menace of Mr. Jarrett.

18

•———•

M r. Jarrett had chosen his ambush point well. This small lane was quiet and empty, the traffic lumbering by on the large street beyond muffling any shout I'd make. The bulk of the post office rose beside me on one side, and a railed-off yard separated the lane from the small brick church of St. Anne and St. Agnes on the other.

However, I too had chosen well. I knew that a quick run would take us around another corner and back to Cheapside. Also, that a second man would step behind Mr. Jarrett as soon as he advanced toward us, and hem him in.

Mr. Jarrett, out of his territory, had followed me into the trap.

"Won't hurt you none, missus," Jarrett said, his swagger too confident.

His short black coat and flat cap were dusty, his light hair greasy beneath it. I doubted he'd been home to bathe and have a change of clothes since I'd last seen him. I wondered where he was staying on this side of the river—friends in the area? Who would dare put him up?

"I know you will not," I said. "There is a policeman nearby."

The constable lingering in Cheapside had kept his eye on me and Grace, and wandered as far as St. Paul's with us, as though he suspected we'd rush to Newgate to try to break Sam from it. The constable *might* have walked up Foster Lane from there toward this little turning, so I did not lie to Jarrett.

Jarret cast a nervous glance past me but retained his belligerence. "This your little 'un?"

His gaze fell upon Grace with interest. Not with lasciviousness, I was relieved to see, but with an air of how he could best use her as a hold over me or Sam and Joanna.

There was a rush of air, and then Mr. Jarrett found himself against the sooty stone wall of the post office, a very large man pinning him there.

I'd glimpsed Mr. Grimes moving among the foot traffic in Cheapside and around St. Paul's Churchyard, his huge bulk difficult to disguise. Mr. Jarrett, on the other hand, had not noticed him, being too arrogant to believe anyone would dog his steps.

Mr. Jarrett hung in Mr. Grimes's very large grip, his arrogance changing to alarm. Mr. Grimes wore a long duster coat and cap that had seen better days, his dark hair as greasy as Jarrett's. His blue eyes, though, bore merriment as he gazed up at Jarrett.

"Now then," Mr. Grimes said. "You're not welcome around here. You pop off home, all right?"

"You're not from around here either." Jarrett tried to hold on to his sneer, but his eyes betrayed his fear. "I know you, don't I?"

"Not well enough," Mr. Grimes answered cheerfully. He

hailed from South London like Mr. Jarrett--they might have crossed paths from time to time. "This lady is my friend, and you have no business with her."

"I do have business." Mr. Jarrett's words were breathy as Mr. Grimes cut off his air. "Have information for her."

"I don't believe ya, but say it and be gone." Mr. Grimes's fingers tightened, and Jarrett's eyes widened.

"Watch out for that man from the bank," Jarrett gasped out. "He's a slippery one."

"Mr. Kearny?" I asked.

"Naw, not the nervous cove who's trying to get his leg over Millburn's lady. The higher-up. Word has it he were skulking around outside the bank on Monday morning, when that bloke got himself offed. What was he doing, eh? Fitting up our Sam, most like."

The higher-up might mean Mr. Zachary. Something worth looking into. "How do you know?"

"Have friends, don't I? They tell me things."

I wondered what sort of friends he had deep in the City. Reliable ones? Or was Mr. Jarrett inventing things to make Sam depend on him again?

"May I speak to these friends?" I asked.

"Can take you to them." Jarrett peered fearfully down at Mr. Grimes. "If you call off your hound."

I was not silly enough to follow Mr. Jarrett through London to a place where he might or might not have mates who might or might not have information. For one, I'd hardly take Grace with me, and for another, it was possible the world would never see me again.

"Perhaps you can tell this to my friend, Inspector McGregor," I suggested.

Jarrett's face screwed up. "Not talking to any bloody peeler. You don't want to know—that's fine by me."

"Let him go, Mr. Grimes," I said. "Mr. Jarrett, please take yourself from Cheapside and its surroundings entirely, and do not return."

Mr. Grimes, never losing his congenial expression, eased Mr. Jarrett to his feet. Jarrett tried to jerk from him as soon as he was standing, but Mr. Grimes kept a firm hold. He spun Mr. Jarrett in place and gave him a hard shove back the way he'd come.

Mr. Jarrett stumbled but quickly gained his balance and hastened toward the larger street of St. Martin's Le Grand, where he vanished into the traffic there.

Mr. Grimes made a show of dusting off his hands. "That's the rubbish gone, then."

"Can you follow him?" I asked. "It would be useful to know where he is staying and who these mates are."

"My orders are to keep an eye on you and your friends, so no. But . . ."

Mr. Grimes stuck his tongue behind his teeth and let out a piercing whistle.

Grace clapped her hands over her ears at the high-pitched sound but looked delighted. I had the feeling she would soon be trying to imitate that whistle.

I heard running footsteps and then several boys burst past me from the other side of the church. Another came belting up from the direction of Cheapside.

"Keep the bloke what I was having a discussion with within your sights," Grimes ordered. "Send word to me where he goes."

The lads, who barely glanced at me and Grace, nodded and charged off in Jarrett's wake. Grubby legs, red with cold, flashed between knickers and boots. Their footsteps soon receded, the boys gone.

"They'll keep him in their sights," Grimes promised. "Danny and me will find out what he's up to."

As would I, I promised silently. It would be good to know exactly where Mr. Zachary, with his prominent set of keys, had been while Mr. Stockley was getting himself murdered. Mr. Zachary, who could go anywhere in the bank he liked, also could easily walk into the junior clerks' room and slide incriminating keys beneath the top of Sam's desk.

"Thank you, Mr. Grimes," I said. "Your intervention was most welcome."

"Danny told me to look after you, didn't he?" Mr. Grimes beamed at me, pulling off his cap, though the wind was cold in this passage. He made a bow to Grace. "Good afternoon, Miss Holloway."

I did not correct the last name—Grace's recorded legal name was Bristow, which I'd given the parish registrant when she was born. I'd believed that Joe Bristow, now deceased, had truly been my husband.

"This is Grace," I said, unable to mask my pride. "My daughter."

"As pretty as your mum," Mr. Grimes said, his smile doting. Unlike when Jarrett had looked at Grace with cunning, Mr. Grimes exuded only friendliness and a fatherly air.

"Thank you, sir," Grace said. "How did you learn to whistle like that?"

Grimes's brows went up, then he grinned. "Years of practice, lass. Tell you what—I'll teach you one day. Well, if your mum allows it."

"I doubt I could stop her, Mr. Grimes," I said with a smile. I turned to Grace. "As long as you don't terrify Joanna with such noises."

"Mum will want to learn as well," Grace said with confidence. She was right, the scamp.

"Where are you off to now, Mrs. Holloway?" Grimes asked. "I'll tramp along with you, if you don't mind, see you there safe. In case the blister or his confederates come at you again."

"That would be welcome, Mr. Grimes. Grace and I are headed to tea."

"Ooh, sounds nice, that does. Shall we, loves?"

"Do you want to come to tea with us, Mr. Grimes?" Grace asked as she fell into step next to the lumbering man. For all his size, Mr. Grimes was a likable fellow and good to Daniel. Grace had sensed that right away.

"Naw, they won't let the likes of me into a fine tea shop. Besides, I just had a luncheon of a large hunk of bread and butter and a nice slice of leftover roast besides. Mrs. Millburn's cook is fair handed with the food."

"She is," Grace said. She skipped along a few steps, then remembered she was a grown-up young lady of twelve and slowed to a more sedate pace.

We walked companionably from St. Anne's Lane to Foster Lane, passing the bulk of Goldsmiths' Hall, which had been the source of much interest this past autumn. Its imposing entrance was even bleaker in midwinter, and I turned from it quickly.

Our favorite tea shop in Cheapside was near the Millburns' home, which was why I'd chosen it today. We'd fill ourselves up with cakes and scones and then have only a short way to walk Grace to the safety of the house.

Outside the tea shop, which exuded good smells when an

exiting patron opened the door, Mr. Grimes halted and tugged off his cap again.

"I'll be about," he promised. "Just wave when ye come out, and I'll walk with you home."

"Thank you, Mr. Grimes," I said with warmth. "You are too kind."

"You're a friend of Danny's, which means you're my friend too. You too, young lady . . . Oi. Look at this." He dove for the ground before I realized what he was doing and straightened again, holding a copper coin. "Someone must have dropped it," Mr. Grimes said. "Ah well. They'll be long gone now, I reckon. It's good luck to find a penny. How about you take it, Miss Holloway? Have some good luck today."

Mr. Grimes held the penny out to Grace. I frowned at him, but I was secretly pleased at his kindness. He'd not found that penny on the ground—any glint of coin would be pounced upon by any street lad for whom a penny was great wealth. But he'd not wanted to hurt Grace's pride by simply giving her a coin.

"Perhaps we should try to find the person who lost it," Grace suggested. Her eyes were on the penny, she not being so angelic that she'd shun it.

Mr. Grimes laughed. "If someone can afford to drop a penny and not scour the ground for it right away, they won't miss it. Besides, it's grimy. Been here for a while, I'd guess." He rubbed away dirt with his gloved hands, revealing a penny far too shiny to have lain on the ground any length of time.

"Then you should keep it," Grace said. "You can buy plenty of rolls for a penny. You found it after all."

"Ain't ye kind, lass." Mr. Grimes's face softened. "But I wouldn't be much of a gentleman if I didn't give all I had to a lady."

His words, in his rough, gravelly voice, made Grace laugh. She must realize she'd hurt his feelings if she didn't take the offered gift, and reached for the coin.

Mr. Grimes relinquished it, then straightened up and sent me a wide smile. "Enjoy your tea, ma'am, miss." He caught the tearoom's door as two ladies left the shop and held it open for us. "Don't forget—look for me when you're finished."

"Thank you, Mr. Grimes," I said again.

He touched his forehead in a salute, then stood back so we could enter.

The inhabitants of the shop were blatantly relieved when Mr. Grimes did not follow us in. The waitress, who was a cold personage, sniffed as we took our place at our usual table. Of course I'd keep that sort of company, I was certain she was thinking.

We settled in and ordered a hot pot of tea and plenty of scones. They arrived soon, accompanied by jam and clotted cream, a feast.

"Aunt Joanna has been crying much of the time," Grace informed me as we dug into the scones. "She pretends not to, but I hear her in her bedchamber at night. We're all worried about Uncle Sam, but I think Aunt Joanna believes she'll never see him again."

"It is her greatest fear," I agreed. "Such a thing is difficult to banish. You and I know that they'll never convict Sam, but she has difficulty believing it."

I spoke with confidence, and Grace nodded, but I read sadness in her eyes.

"I wish I could help," Grace said. "I don't like it when Aunt Joanna cries. It's like seeing *you* cry, Mum."

A thing I had made certain she did not observe very often.

"You can help Joanna by being very, very good and not

upsetting her further," I said. "I know you never would on purpose, but be extra diligent. Perhaps you can also keep the others from troubling her as well."

"I do try. Mark is a bit of a pest—he doesn't like being youngest boy. They pay a bit more attention to Matthew because they want him to go to university and rise in the world. But even Mark has stopped complaining now. He knows his mum is most distraught."

"I spoke to Sam today," I told her. "He so wants to come home."

"Is he all right?" Grace asked instantly. "Do they let him eat?"

I nodded reassuringly. "He has some meals, but I am going to fill a basket and take it to him. I cannot let you come with me." I cut off her request as she drew breath to ask it. "Newgate is no place for a girl. It is no place for me either, but I will risk it to make certain Sam has some decent food."

Grace glanced at her scone slathered with cream and jam, a large crevice in the shape of her front teeth bitten into it. "I feel ashamed to eat this," she said morosely.

"You starving yourself will not help Sam," I stated. "He'd want to know you were enjoying your tea and scones instead of eating dry crusts of bread in his honor. He would be the first to tell you this. Besides, I'll take him plenty of cakes, don't you worry."

"I'm glad," Grace said in relief. She nibbled more, but slowly, as though determined to be mindful of Sam's suffering, which was good of her.

"Sam said he was late to work on Monday because you children were trying him," I said after a time. "He told me you had nothing to do with any of it, but he might have been sparing my feelings." I sent her a mother's stern gaze.

Grace flushed. "He did become quite cross at us—cross for

Uncle, I mean. He never shouts, only becomes rather red in the face and makes spluttering noises. Mark and Mabel were bellowing for their breakfast. We'd been reading about the revolutions in Paris for our schoolwork, and Mark and Mabel were pretending to storm the barricades. They were rather loud. Uncle had to run out and buy eggs himself because cook had run out of them and had forgotten to get more."

I would never let such a thing happen in any house I worked in. The Millburns' cook, while a somewhat talented and a kindly woman, was not always the most efficient of persons.

"And did he come back with the eggs?" Sam had said so, but if Grace and her family could be independent witnesses, it might help his case.

"Oh yes. Carrying a basket like a maid going to market. We all laughed at him, including Aunt Joanna, which seemed to cheer him up. He didn't want to wait for breakfast to be cooked, but Aunt Joanna made him sit down and eat it. She said he'd worked so hard for the bank for so many years they could do without him for half an hour. She's been angry at them since they started saying he was embezzling."

I tried to be surprised Grace knew all about that, but I could not be. The house was small, Grace was inquisitive, and she was not dull-witted.

"I am angry at them too. They are treating Sam shamefully." I returned to her tale. "He ate breakfast and rushed off to work?"

"He did." Grace's eyes filled, and she set down the final bite of scone. "That was the last we saw of him."

"Well, it won't be forever," I said. "Uncle Daniel and I will prove him innocent. You will see."

"I believe you, Mum." Grace sighed and took a fortifying sip of tea. "You are very clever, and so is Uncle Daniel, and

Uncle Daniel has many friends in the police. But it is difficult to wait and worry, isn't it?"

I gave her an understanding nod. "You have the right of it, Grace."

Mr. Grimes was waiting, as promised, when we emerged. He leaned on a wall across the street, arms folded, a formidable bulk. Passersby eyed him warily.

As soon as I signaled him, Mr. Grimes came alive and waved joyously. As he hurried through the traffic to us, beaming at me and Grace, the pedestrians' fearful looks became smiles of indulgence.

Mr. Grimes walked us home as he would old friends, asking Grace what she had for tea, prying out every detail. Soon Grace chatted to him without restraint. Mr. Grimes left us at the end of Clover Lane, again waving and nodding as though sending us off on an important journey.

I was grateful to him not only for watching over us but for cheering up Grace. I'd have to add some tea cakes to my basket for Mr. Grimes when I visited again.

We'd lingered over the tea, and the skies had already darkened by the time we entered the Millburn house. This was a happy home, I reflected as Grace ran upstairs to find Jane and Mabel. Cozy. Sam leased the house, and I hoped the landlords wouldn't force Joanna out once they learned Sam would stand trial for murder.

"Kat." Joanna beckoned me from the doorway of Sam's study. When I hastened to her, she pulled me inside and shut the door. "I meant to tell you this before, but Mr. Kearny was here, and then Grace was so anxious to set off with you."

"Tell me what?" I asked in curiosity.

"When the police were here, they found a few boxes of papers Sam had brought home from work."

"Yes, so Mr. Fielding said."

"Mr. Fielding." Joanna let out a breath. "Please thank Mr. McAdam for lending him to me. I know he is a charlatan, but I was very grateful for his presence. He kept those belligerent young men, who were certain Sam is a vicious murderer, from terrorizing me."

I softened a bit to Mr. Fielding. "Sam had brought the papers home from work? Do you know why?"

"To try to work out where the embezzled money was going. What I want to tell you is the police did not find everything."

Joanna lit a lamp, then moved to the window, which overlooked a small bricked-over yard, and pulled the curtain across it. The window was recessed, with wainscoting over the wall beneath it. Joanna knelt before a panel, nudged it inward, and then pulled off the entire piece of wainscoting, revealing a cavity behind it.

The wainscoting hadn't been crafted to come away, I saw. No secret compartment with clever catches or hinges. The panel had simply loosened with time, and Sam had made use of that fact.

Joanna reached in and pulled out two boxes. Each were about the size of a large book, with a hinged top that revealed neat stacks of paper inside.

"Sam put the other two behind the books in the shelves because there wasn't room for them in here." Joanna thrust the boxes at me. "Please take them. Maybe there is something in them that will absolve my Sam of the charges."

I accepted them readily. "I'll make certain every word is gone over. Several times, if necessary. I might have to take them to Inspector McGregor," I finished hesitantly.

"You claim Inspector McGregor is an honest policeman. If he can help Sam, I am willing to trust him."

I wasn't certain I trusted Inspector McGregor exactly, but he had proved to be very thorough in his job. He did not like wrong convictions. Even if he was only advising on this case, the word of a Scotland Yard inspector held weight.

We bundled up the boxes in an old shawl and placed them at the bottom of a basket. Joanna led me out and down to the kitchen, where we layered a few soft rolls and tea cakes over the boxes. The cook was flattered I wanted some of her cakes, so I did not explain they were only for disguise. The staff at the Mount Street house could enjoy them as a treat.

I departed from Grace and Joanna with many hugs and promises to return as soon as I could on Monday.

Mr. Grimes met me with enthusiasm as I emerged from the lane. I gave him one of the tea cakes, which he accepted with joy, and he stayed by my side until Lewis pulled up in his cab. Lewis had become my personal driver of late—Mr. Grimes explained he'd been requested and paid for by Daniel, who did not want me to risk traveling across the City unguarded.

Kind of Daniel, I decided as I settled in for the ride. Kind of him also to keep watch over Joanna. She'd need income soon—she and Sam had some savings, I knew, but without Sam's regular salary, she'd run through that quickly. She had to pay the lease on the house as well as for food for the family, not to mention the wages of the three who worked in the household.

A woman on her own, who did not have a well-off family at her back or a skilled job she could take up, would soon be destitute.

With these gloomy thoughts, I rode through the dark metropolis to Oxford Street, where I descended and walked south through Mayfair to Mount Street.

I arrived in a kitchen bustling as usual. I unloaded the rest of the tea cakes and rolls, to Tess's and Elsie's delight, and told them to share them among themselves, the maids, and the footmen. The basket I carried upstairs to my room, hiding the boxes of papers under my bed.

After washing my face and hands and changing my frock, I arrived below stairs once more in time to see Mr. Davis, through the half-open door of his butler's pantry, in the act of unfolding a letter.

He skimmed the lines on the paper, then his face lost all color, and he dropped heavily to a chair, his head bowed.

19

⋅◦─────◦⋅

I pushed my way into the butler's pantry, closing the door softly behind me.

"Mr. Davis?" I asked in a gentle tone. "Is it bad news?"

Mr. Davis did not raise his head. He gazed at the letter again as though willing it to tell him something different.

"Mr. Beach has died."

The phrase was so quiet, so flat, that I barely heard it. "Your friend in Bury St. Edmunds?"

I realized as I spoke that Mr. Davis hadn't actually told me that was where his ill friend had been staying, but he didn't seem to notice my blunder.

"I knew when I saw him last there was no hope, but . . ." Mr. Davis heaved a long sigh, folded the letter, and dropped it to the table.

"One always has hope," I said. "We can't help it."

Mr. Davis looked up at me, his eyes red-rimmed and moist. "He was a very dear friend. One I can never replace."

"Of course not." I wasn't certain how to comfort him, but

perhaps simply understanding would help. "You knew him a long time?"

"Since I was a young man." Mr. Davis sank back in his chair, resting his shirt-sleeved arms on the table. He wore black arm guards that would keep polish from marring his pristine white shirt. "We were in service together, when I was a footman. Several years later, we had a falling-out, and we never quite made it up. I didn't see much of him after that."

The regret in his eyes made my throat tight. "You were able to visit him while he was ill," I reminded him. "Did you reconcile then?"

"A bit. So many years had passed though. So many years we can never have back. I'm a stubborn fool. Though so was he." A smile crossed his lips. "Both of us set in our ways. We'd have parted from each other eventually, I suppose."

My curiosity stirred, and I wanted to ask a thousand questions about this gentleman whose death so affected Mr. Davis. Now was not the time, however. The letters I'd found—I wondered if this man had written to him, wanting to make peace between them, or if they'd been from the landlady he'd told me of, keeping Mr. Davis informed on the health of her lodger.

Perhaps one day Mr. Davis would confide in me, but I'd not pry today.

"I am very sorry," I said. "Is there anything I can do to help? Shall I bring you a cup of tea? Something to eat?"

Mr. Davis rose, his smile at me more like his usual one, though his sadness remained. "I've noticed that the first thing you think of when you want to comfort someone is food, Mrs. Holloway. Very endearing, though I suppose you can't help yourself. No, I will be well. The best help would be if you mentioned this to no one. Not the rest of the staff, nor Mrs. Redfern, nor the master and mistress."

"You'll want to attend his funeral," I said quickly. "Perhaps Lady Cynthia can ensure you go."

"Nor Lady Cynthia." Mr. Davis became stern. "I will weather this. There's no need for me to drag myself to the country to stand in a churchyard in a cold rain. I can do nothing for Mr. Beach now."

"You can say good-bye," I reminded him. That was what funerals and wakes and other vigils were for—to say a final farewell to the loved one. Those rituals were for us far more than the deceased.

"I did that," Mr. Davis replied. "When I traveled down last week. Nothing more to be done. Now, I need to get on. Supper will be served soon. That is, if you have time to prepare it."

He sent me a pointed look, and I conceded. "Very well. I will keep this to myself. But if you change your mind, I will happily assist with your duties so that you can go without impediment."

I turned to leave, Mr. Davis impatient for me to be gone.

"Thank you, Mrs. Holloway," he said as I opened the door. "Sincerely."

I sent him a small smile over my shoulder. "Think nothing of it, Mr. Davis."

Supper tonight thankfully was a simple affair, and Tess and I got through it easily. She and the others enjoyed the cakes I'd brought home, though Tess loyally said they were nowhere near as good as mine.

Tess asked me what I'd done today, and I gave her a truncated version of events, ending with my vow to take Sam a basket of food on Monday.

"It's good of you, Mrs. H.," Tess declared. "We'll fix him up proper. But he'll have to hide the things, you know. The other prisoners will try to take them from him."

"Knowing Sam, he will offer them to those who have the least."

Tess nodded. "Poor man. We'll fill the basket to heaping, then."

"Not a word to the others." Mrs. Bywater would object to me taking even scraps to a prisoner in Newgate.

Tess sent me a wink. "You can count on me, Mrs. H."

Mr. Davis reappeared from his pantry in time to supervise the footmen serving at supper. He was his usual cool self, tailcoat brushed and crisp, his hairpiece placed exactly. His sharp commands to the footmen floated down the back stairs as they went up, then the door at the top slammed, cutting him off in mid-admonishment.

After Tess and I sent up the food, I told her to go to bed, as she'd done most of the work today. I tidied up, set out preparations for the morning, then retired myself.

Instead of going straight to bed in my exhaustion, I pulled out the boxes I'd brought from the Millburns' and laid out the papers across my bed. Seating myself on the small wooden chair I'd procured a few months ago, I started reading through them.

It was hard going. I could plainly see words and numbers, but there were so many abbreviations and so much shorthand, it might have been written in another language. I had little knowledge of finance other than making certain my kitchen budget did not go beyond its allotment, and these columns, notes, and rows of numbers meant nothing to me.

There were several sets of handwriting on the papers—one

main hand of whoever had copied it out, which was possibly Sam himself. Others had made notes in the margins or crossed out things on the main body and added corrections. One of the notators embellished their *H*'s and *I*'s with a little uptick at the end of the bottom stroke. The other writings were fairly plain, clear, and easy to read. At least, they'd be easy reading for the man I had in mind who could make sense of it all.

I packed the papers away, hid them with my bundle of money in the bottom of my wardrobe, blew out my candle, and climbed wearily into bed.

In the morning, I bade Sara, the upstairs maid, to ask Lady Cynthia if I could speak to her. Sara returned to the kitchen not long later to say that Cynthia had spent the night out with her friends and had not come home.

I imagined the friends in question were Miss Townsend and Lady Roberta. Though Cynthia had many chums she'd kept from girlhood, whenever she stayed out too late or drank too much wine at a club she and Lady Roberta had crashed, she'd sleep over at Miss Townsend's house or in Lady Roberta's flat. I would simply have to wait for her to return.

Mr. Davis this morning was terse when he spoke at all, so I did not stop him for conversation. He was grieving his friend, I could see, or perhaps grieving for the friendship that could now never be. I hoped he'd change his mind and attend the funeral, and that the Bywaters would be compassionate enough to give him leave to go.

Mrs. Bywater did come down to the kitchen after breakfast, but not to speak to Mr. Davis. She brought a letter to me.

"It is from that so-very-cultured Miss Townsend," Mrs. Bywater said, her sallow face flushed with pleasure. "She wishes you to call upon her—or rather upon her cook, to teach her to make your wonderful orange sorbet. Apparently, she heard some of my friends, as well as Cynthia, raving about it. When my do's are coming to the attention of someone like Miss Townsend, I know I have arrived. A lady like her wouldn't bother being courteous to someone like me otherwise, though I do have connections to the aristocracy."

Mrs. Bywater's connection to the aristocracy was through her husband, whose sister had married an earl—Cynthia's father. Mrs. Bywater was no blood relation to Cynthia or her parents, but she gave herself plenty of airs, as though she had dukes in her immediate family. Mr. Bywater felt no shame in his position as a middle-class gentleman, but Mrs. Bywater yearned for the prestige of the landed nobility.

"I will make a note to visit her on Monday. My half day out," I added, as Mrs. Bywater stared at me as though she had no idea what I was talking about.

"No, no, no, that will never do." Mrs. Bywater waved the letter. "Miss Townsend writes, *at Mrs. Holloway's earliest convenience,* and it will be convenient for you today. We are having no guests this evening, so you won't have much to do."

I bristled that Mrs. Bywater thought producing three meals a day for three family members and nearly a dozen staff wasn't much to do, but I kept my silence. She would not comprehend, and would reprimand me for being impertinent.

"Very well. I will settle things with Tess and go today." I would not throw away the opportunity Miss Townsend had provided. I knew that instructing her cook was a ruse to get me to the house in Upper Brook Street, and I wished very much to know what Miss Townsend had to tell me.

"Do not sound so reluctant," Mrs. Bywater admonished. "Such a prominent lady taking an interest is a compliment to you. And a compliment to *me* for planning such excellent suppers."

Mrs. Bywater hadn't planned the supper beyond telling me she wanted a good meal for fifteen ladies, but again, I said nothing. I'd learned there was no use in speaking my mind to Mrs. Bywater.

Mrs. Bywater took my silence for acceptance, and went away, clutching the letter happily.

I explained to Tess I'd be going out once luncheon was prepared, but I'd try to be back before supper. I told her exactly where I'd be, so she didn't come up with a fantasy of me nipping to the nearest park to spoon with Daniel.

"Go as soon as you like," Tess said as she chopped onions to fry with the luncheon chops. "I used to be frightened when you left for any amount of time, but now I can manage. As long as I don't have to do a party of twenty on me own, I'll be all right."

I thanked her and fetched my coat. I debated changing into a good frock, but if I truly did have to teach Miss Townsend's cook to make sorbet, I wouldn't want to ruin my clothes.

I set off on foot to Upper Brook Street, a short way from Mount Street. I crossed South Audley and turned north on Park Street, reaching Miss Townsend's home at the west end of Upper Brook Street in a matter of minutes.

I watched out for James or Daniel as I went but saw neither of them. Nor did I spy Mr. Jarrett. I hoped that both Daniel and Mr. Grimes had made him fearful of approaching me again.

I pulled the bell at Miss Townsend's tall, elegant house, and the door was opened by the stately butler, Mr. Hubbard.

"Mrs. Holloway," he said without inflection. "How nice to see you. Miss Townsend is waiting for you in the drawing room."

Most days, I was shown up the four flights of stairs to the top of the house, where Miss Townsend had her art studio. She painted much of the time she was home, and I felt privileged to be admitted to that private room. That she had summoned me to her drawing room instead was curious.

Mr. Hubbard hung my coat on an elaborately carved coat-rack, then led me up one flight of stairs to a double-doored chamber in the front of the house. The ceiling was high in this hall, the light from a many-paned window flooding it.

Mr. Hubbard opened one of the doors and ushered me into a grand chamber containing three ladies and a gentleman. The ladies I knew very well, but the gentleman was a stranger.

"Mrs. Holloway," Mr. Hubbard intoned, then withdrew, closing the door with barely a breath of sound.

I stood awkwardly, wishing now I'd changed to my second-best frock, at least. I must make a sorry picture, a young woman with windblown hair and a gray work frock splashed with flour and grease.

Miss Townsend was her usual elegant self in her tasteful gown. Behind her, on a window seat, Lady Roberta lounged in a man's suit with neatly tied cravat and polished boots. Her attire did not seem to surprise the only gentleman in our midst.

Lady Cynthia rose from a sofa at the same time the gentleman climbed to his feet from a Morris chair. He was very tall, his dark suit emphasizing a slimness that was proportional to his height. He was not at all awkward or gangly, but well put together.

He looked upon me politely, neither mocking me for my appearance nor treating me deferentially. I was simply a person standing in the middle of a nicely furnished drawing room.

"Mrs. Holloway, thank you for coming," Miss Townsend began.

Cynthia broke in. "This is Shepherd," she said, waving an

arm at the man. "Sir Rupert as he's called. He very much wanted to meet you."

Sir Rupert Shepherd. The barrister Miss Townsend had talked into representing Sam, who Daniel had termed heavy artillery.

For some reason, I wanted to curtsy, but I restrained myself. "How do you do, sir?" I said politely.

"Very well." Shepherd's voice filled the room with a pleasant rumble. "I have come to ask you many questions about Samuel Millburn. If you sit comfortably while I interrogate you, you'll be able to withstand it better, I think."

He gestured to a wing chair that held several cushions and had an ottoman drawn up to it. If I sat in that, I'd either fall asleep with all the work I'd already done today or become so buried in it the three ladies would have to pull me out again.

I crossed to a balloon-backed chair with beautiful carving, a simple piece but as graceful as Miss Townsend herself. "This will do."

Shepherd's brows went up, but he gazed at me with a modicum more respect.

Bobby, who'd also risen while I'd been introduced to Sir Rupert, grinned at me and resumed her negligent pose on the window seat. Sir Rupert must already know her, as he was not shocked at either her choice of attire or her masculine-like mannerisms.

Cynthia, who wore a gown similar to Miss Townsend's, sat down again, as did Miss Townsend. Sir Rupert, realizing he was the only one standing, plopped onto the edge of the sofa. He rested his long arms on his knees and leaned to me.

The man had very dark hair and very blue eyes. He wasn't all that handsome, having quite a long face and nose, a round chin, and a wide mouth. However, it took some time to realize that. He was arresting, I would say, commanding every eye to linger upon him.

His ability to draw a gaze, along with his rumbling voice, made me understand Daniel's assessment of him. A person would want to listen to whatever he had to say.

"Shouldn't the solicitor be here?" I asked before Sir Rupert could begin. "I thought that was how these things were done."

Sir Rupert waved a wide hand. "If I were speaking to witnesses I wanted to call or to the accused himself, yes. But this is an informal conversation, a chat among friends. I like to do things informally whenever I can."

He might term it informal, but his rich baritone gave even a friendly chat gravitas. I nodded, as though I understood.

"What do you wish to know?" I asked.

"Everything." Sir Rupert made another sweeping gesture. "All you know about Mr. Millburn's childhood, his leap from boy of the streets to respectable man of the City, to meeting his wife, how loving he is as a father, his kindness in looking after a friend's child, his diligence in his job. Anything that will make the gentlemen of the jury bring out their hankies and sob heavily that such a man was falsely accused by enemies trying to bring him down."

By "a friend's child," he meant Grace. I wondered if Sam had mentioned my name in connection with her or preserved my privacy on that matter. Miss Townsend, Bobby, and Cynthia clearly hadn't enlightened him.

"I met Sam when he was courting Joanna," I said. "I don't know what I can tell you about him before that."

"It is a good place to start. How did they meet? Tell me about their courtship, as much as you can."

"Should you not speak to Joanna?" I asked dubiously. "She will obviously know Sam much better than I do."

Sir Rupert shook his head. "Begging your pardon, Mrs. Holloway, but I won't be calling Mrs. Millburn as a witness. Wives are notoriously unreliable in the witness box. Either they are too eager to prove their husband's innocence, or they use it as a chance for vengeance on a hated or cruel husband. Either way, they are prone to lie, even under a Bible oath. You, outside their happy home, will have a more objective view of Mr. Millburn. I need to know everything about him, so I can paint a picture of him that will better his chances of being acquitted."

"I see." I wasn't quite certain I agreed with all Sir Rupert said, but I admitted he had much more experience in criminal trials than I did. "They met at Sir John Soane's Museum. At Lincoln's Inn Fields."

"Yes, I know where it is." Sir Rupert's eyes lit. "A historic museum is good. They went to improve their minds and fell in love."

"I suppose." Joanna had gone because I'd told her about the curiosities collected by Mr. Soane, the architect who'd lived and worked about a hundred years ago. My mother had scrubbed floors in the museum. Sam had chosen to enter, he explained to me years later, because he'd seen Joanna stroll inside. He'd thought her the most beautiful woman he'd ever seen and decided to take a chance and speak to her.

I didn't correct Sir Rupert. Sam happening upon Joanna while seeking to improve his mind made him sound a more upright character than a man who'd simply seen a pretty girl and followed her.

"He eschewed his old life and reformed himself for her, did he?" Sir Rupert went on.

"As you say." This was more or less the truth. Sam had already decided to shuck his former acquaintances and embrace the straight and narrow at that point, but meeting Joanna had set him more firmly on this path.

"They married respectably in a church and settled down to have a family," Sir Rupert went on.

Why he needed my view when he had already decided on the tale, I didn't know. "They did," I said. "Two boys and two girls. Mr. Millburn worked in a shop, and one of the Daalman's bankers was a regular customer. He thought Mr. Millburn trustworthy enough to recommend him for a post at the bank."

"That was Mr. Kearny, wasn't it?" Sir Rupert said. "He might make a decent character witness. Staked his reputation on Millburn, and knew he was a good man through and through."

"Mr. Kearny is of nervous disposition," I said. "He might dither in the witness box."

"I will note that, Mrs. Holloway. Though I think you would face judge and jury without a qualm."

"I'd rather not, if you don't mind," I said quickly. I'd never been on trial at the Old Bailey, but my time against a magistrate at the Bow Street nick had made me never want to enter a courtroom again.

"It might not be necessary," Sir Rupert assured me. "If I can put together a pattern of Millburn's movements that morning, and prove he was far from the bank at the time in question, then the prosecution will be hard-pressed to make a case."

"He went out for eggs." I gave him the tale Sam had told me.

"Hmm." Sir Rupert looked less hopeful. "Well, we will find witnesses to place him every step of the way, including the vendor from whom he purchased the eggs."

"In Leadenhall Market," I said glumly. "Which is around the corner from the bank."

"Ah. Well, he certainly was determined to fit himself up for murder, wasn't he?" Sir Rupert ran a hand through his dark hair. "It is not hopeless, ladies," he added. "Good job Miss Townsend sent for *me*, isn't it?"

He thought much of himself, did Sir Rupert, but as long as he fought for Sam, I wouldn't complain about his arrogance.

"I'm surprised whoever it is decided to try to get Mr. Millburn on murder," Sir Rupert mused. "Always hard to prove, unless the person is seen plunging the knife into the body, and even then, a good barrister can make the witnesses uncertain of what actually happened. Embezzlement is easier to foist on another, especially if the accused is found with coffers of money buried in his cellar and living in a beautiful house with a carriage and four horses, his wife in silks and jewels."

"None of that will be found with Sam," I said. "They are happy they can pay the rent on their small house off Cheapside."

"Then what happened to the money they say he took, eh?" Sir Rupert asked the question to the air, not expecting an answer. "Something for Mr. Crowe, the solicitor, to diligently investigate."

I had some ideas about the money and planned to diligently investigate myself, but I said nothing about that.

"As you can see, Mrs. Holloway, the way we will go at this case is to focus on Millburn's character. A moral man who has wrested himself from his terrible past and now lives a blameless life. Picked out as a scapegoat by whatever villain stole money from this bank and killed a man inside it, precisely because Millburn hails from the laboring classes. Snobbery by the high-and-mighty in the bank. The jury will like that. They probably are tired of haughty bankers looking down their noses at them every time they go to make a withdrawal. Everyone worries about their overdraft."

Another reason I kept my money myself. People teetered on the brink of bankruptcy all the time using funds they didn't have, on the promise that they'd eventually put the money into their accounts. I could not live with that uneasiness.

"I say, Rupes," Cynthia broke in. "Shouldn't we find out who actually committed the murder and the embezzlement? Then Mr. Millburn will be absolved of all wrongdoing."

Sir Rupert sank deeper into the sofa, stretching his arms across its back. "That is the job of the police," he said comfortably. "Oftentimes, a murder is never solved, at least not satisfactorily. My task is to sow enough doubt in the minds of the jury that they return a verdict of Not Guilty. Nothing more."

"Which he will do," Miss Townsend assured me in her quiet tones.

Sir Rupert winced. "When Judith says one must accomplish a thing, one must. And so, I will."

I wondered what sort of favor Sir Rupert owed Miss Townsend. Quite a large one, from the wry resignation with which he viewed her.

I had little doubt that Sir Rupert was a very good barrister. He likely would make certain the jury sympathized with Sam. It depended on the prosecutor as well—a hostile and determined one could turn the tide at any moment. The judges, from what those who had gone through the process had told me, often sided with the prosecutor. The notion that if a man was truly innocent, he'd never be arrested at all was a hard held one in many people's minds.

Sir Rupert had me go over again what a good, kind, loving husband and father was Sam. Only one of his many questions unnerved me.

"He's adopted another little girl, from what I understand," Sir Rupert said. "Daughter of a friend. Can you tell me about her?"

20

My mouth went dry as I tried to formulate my answer. Both Cynthia and Bobby tensed, the two of them exchanging uneasy glances.

Miss Townsend remained her poised self. "The friend will not wish to come forward," she said smoothly. "It is enough that Mr. Millburn, on his small salary, was kind enough to take in yet another child."

Sir Rupert raised his brows at her, realizing that Miss Townsend was leaving out plenty of information. He switched his gaze to me, as though ready to repeat his question, then stilled as he studied my face. I was very hot, so I must have been quite pink with discomfiture. I met his stare without flinching, but it was very difficult to do so.

"I see," Sir Rupert said, his brows rising. "Pity. Such a witness might make all the difference."

"The witness will not want her little girl's name dragged

into a courtroom, or herself sneered upon by righteous gentlemen of the jury," I informed him.

"Hmm." Sir Rupert took in my rigidness, Cynthia and Bobby poised to argue in my defense, and Miss Townsend's quiet but sharp gaze. He let out a sigh. "Ah well. It would have been only one weapon in my arsenal. I have plenty of others." He rubbed his hands together. "A while since I've had such a challenging case."

He did not seem to realize his statement was in any way distressing. What was like sport to him was life and death to Sam and Joanna. I understood why Miss Townsend sent for him, however. He possessed the need to win and would not cease until he did.

Sir Rupert did not have anything else to ask me. He settled himself comfortably on the sofa, as though prepared to relax there for a time.

I rose, and he hopped to his feet as a gentleman should. "I will go," I announced. "I can't leave the kitchen for too many hours."

"Oh, but you must stay a bit longer," Miss Townsend said, rising to advance on me. "I truly do want you to instruct my cook in the sorbet. Cynthia said it was divine."

"And it is," Cynthia answered. "Come on, Mrs. H. I'll take you downstairs and introduce you."

She jumped up to lead me out. Bobby followed us, shutting Miss Townsend in the drawing room with Sir Rupert. I heard Miss Townsend's polished tones float behind us as she engaged him in conversation.

"Old Rupes adores Judith," Bobby informed us as we descended the stairs. "Knows he hasn't a chance, but he'll do anything for her."

"If he manages to have Sam acquitted, I will adore *him*," I said. "Bake him anything he likes."

"Remind me to do you many favors." Bobby chuckled. "But Rupert's all right. A bit oblivious to the concerns of us ordinary folk, but a brilliant orator. My brother went to school with him and says Old Rupes had the world eating out of his hand from a young age."

I believed it, and I hoped so, for Sam's sake.

Bobby ducked ahead of Cynthia to lead the way down the back stairs. Cynthia and I picked our way more slowly along the narrow staircase, the pair of us having to navigate it with skirts.

"Can you get word to Mr. Thanos for me?" I asked Cynthia as we went. "I have papers I'd like him to look at."

"He's buried at the Polytechnic these days," Cynthia answered. "Almost literally, there are so many books in his office. When he has to hunt for a pen it is like an expedition up the Orinoco."

"I take it you find these pens for him?" I asked. Cynthia had become an unofficial assistant to Mr. Thanos, helping him prepare for lectures, writing his formulas on the blackboard, and so forth.

"Indeed, I do." Cynthia's answer held merriment. "For which he is not indifferent. He heaps gratitude on me by the bucketful."

"If he is too busy to meet with me, perhaps you could take the papers to him?" I stepped off the final stair and faced her. "And make certain he doesn't lose them?"

Cynthia hopped from the last step with agility I envied. "I will guard them like a lion. I know exactly how to keep him from losing everything he touches." Her laughter filled the confines of the world below stairs.

She linked arms with me and led me onward to the small kitchen where crates of oranges and a cheerful cook awaited me.

When I returned home a few hours later, Tess blithely greeted me, saying she had everything in hand, but her eyes betrayed her relief at my return. She had done an admirable job locating ingredients for a simple supper for the upstairs as well as the staff, but she relaxed as I tied on my apron and joined her.

Mr. Davis went in and out, bringing me wine for my sauces or commanding a footman to heave himself from his rump and do a bit of work. He was as brisk as ever, but I noted the strain on his face.

My hands were sticky from all the orange juicing I'd done in Miss Townsend's kitchen, but once I'd scrubbed them, I fell into the rhythm of preparing the meal.

Miss Townsend's cook was a bright thing, about ten years older than me and happy to learn a new dish. We'd tasted the sweet juice once we'd mixed it and agreed our work had been good. I'd showed her how to chill it, and envied the large, built-in icebox in Miss Townsend's larder. While Miss Townsend's kitchen was smaller than mine, Miss Townsend had obviously installed the most modern equipment.

The cook had been grateful and sunny, and I knew I had made a friend today.

After supper, Cynthia entered to fetch the papers to take to Mr. Thanos. I'd brought them downstairs during a lull in our preparations, tucking them into a drawer in the kitchen dresser. I did not want Mrs. Bywater catching Cynthia trying to ascend to my bedchamber, or me carrying the papers down to hers.

Cynthia had donned a gentleman's suit rather like the ones

Bobby wore, which meant she was ready to go out on one of her larks. She tucked the boxes under her arm and said she'd take them to Miss Townsend's for Thanos to fetch as soon as he could tear himself from the Polytechnic. Cynthia breezed away, and I returned to cleaning and shutting down the kitchen for the night.

Daniel arrived after everyone but me had gone to bed. He knocked softly on the back door, and I let him in, trying not to be so happy to see him.

I'd saved some of the sorbet for him, which Daniel ate with glee. He didn't speak until the orange cup was empty and he'd licked every drop of sorbet from the spoon.

"I never thought I'd enjoy ice in January," he proclaimed.

"A refreshing treat anytime." I'd brought him a slice of left-over chops while he'd devoured the sorbet along with the last roll Joanna's cook had given me.

While he ate the rest of the meal, I told Daniel how I'd spoken with Mr. Kearny yesterday at Joanna's and then about my meeting with Sir Rupert in Miss Townsend's home this morning. I described the papers Joanna had given me and said I'd sent them on via Cynthia to Mr. Thanos.

Daniel grinned as I described how Joanna had pried out the wainscoting in Sam's study. "A man can hide things from policemen, but not his wife," he said. "Good for Mrs. Millburn for not betraying that the enterprising constables had missed something."

"I don't think Sam hid them from Joanna," I corrected him. "From the wider world and the children, rather. The pair of them share everything."

"An idyllic marriage." Daniel continued eating his chop, mopping the sauce I'd spread over the meat with the roll.

"I've always envied them." I drew my fingertip idly across

the tabletop. "Too much so, I think. I am ashamed of myself sometimes."

"It is perfectly understandable." Daniel's voice gentled. "Bristow put you through a hell of a time, when you wanted a happy home and family. You are glad for Joanna but wish you had some of that happiness for yourself."

"Yes. That is it exactly."

Daniel ceased eating to lay a hand over mine. "You have Grace. The joy of your life. And you have me." His fingers caressed warmth into me. "I will do everything I possibly can to make you happy. Depend upon it."

"Don't say that." I snatched my hand away, uncertain why I did. "Do not give me hope."

"Why not?" Daniel laid his fork across his now-empty plate. "I promised you I would do one last task for Monaghan, and then I plan to court you. Fervently."

"It is as though I'm afraid to let myself be happy." I fumbled for words. "If I let down my guard and find a modicum of peace, it will be snatched away, leaving another hole in my life. What if this task Monaghan sets you on is terribly dangerous? And you perish? Monaghan is not exactly your friend—he might decide to dispose of you in such a fashion. And then here I am. Without you."

My lips quivered as my greatest fears clawed at me. I usually kept them at bay with hard work, exhaustion, and losing myself in moments with Grace, but sometimes the dire possibilities swooped down upon me. Daniel had become very dear to me, and I did not want him gone from my life. I also worried every moment about Grace—if something should happen to her, I would not want to go on.

"I have the same thoughts about you." Daniel regarded me with quiet eyes. "You run gallantly about the City, trying to right wrongs and guard your friends. I know one day you'll run afoul of the worst villain imaginable, and then I will have lost *you*. I'm not certain what I'd do then."

I tried to smile. "How shall we proceed, in that case? Both of us afraid to be happy but both afraid to let go?"

"If I had you always by my side, I would let myself be happy," Daniel said. "And yes, I am always terrified of losing that."

"Which we will one day, whether we like it or not. No one lives forever."

Daniel let out a breath. "Well, aren't we gloomy this evening? Life is sad, yes, but there is also much happiness to be had. I learned that after a youth of nothing but loss, sorrow, and anger so great it nearly destroyed me. There is joy in the little corners of the world—in the brightness of orange sorbet in winter." The corners of his eyes crinkled. "In a lovely woman declaring she doesn't want to lose me. In a greengrocer chasing off thieves with her long stalk of celery. We seize those moments, and we hold on to them."

I nodded, my eyes blurring. I lived for my days with Grace, savoring every second. The friendships I'd formed as I'd struggled—with Tess, Mr. Davis, James, Lady Cynthia, and the one I'd deepened with Joanna—sustained me. Most of all, there was Daniel. Though every layer I uncovered of him only led to more, he'd remained steadfast and kind through it all.

"Let us banish the gloom, then." I wiped my eyes. "And discuss how we are going to get Sam free. Sir Rupert seems competent enough, but there is always the chance he will lose. And I would prefer to wipe all stain from Sam's reputation instead of relying on Sir Rupert's ability to make the jury feel sorry for him."

"'Competent enough'?" Daniel repeated the words with amazement. "Sir Rupert is one of the most celebrated barristers in Britain. Whether prosecuting or defending, he wins almost every time. He'll be a High Court judge one day, and if he's adroit enough, lord chancellor."

"'Almost every time.'" It was my turn to repeat words. "Sam must walk away a free man. I'll not rely on Sir Rupert's silver tongue alone."

I expected Daniel to spout some nonsense about how resolute I was, but he remained somber.

"I must tell you that Monaghan has warned me off this case," he said quietly. "He does not want Daalman's Bank investigated in any way."

My eyes widened in astonishment. "Why the devil not?"

"He did not give me the entire reason, and he won't, no matter how I press him." Daniel opened his hands in a resigned gesture. "But it seems Daalman's has been known to fund traitors to the Crown. Inadvertently, probably, but Monaghan doesn't want a stir created around this bank."

My jaw shook as I tightened it. "So that these traitorous organizations won't be scared off, I imagine."

"You have the right of it. He has his eyes on several financial institutions, like a cat on several mouseholes, waiting for the mice to try for their cheese. He wants us to let Millburn go to trial and carry all the attention away from the bank itself. Whether Millburn is condemned or set free is no matter to Monaghan. He advises me to leave everything in Sir Rupert's hands."

"That vile, bloody . . ." My language became unfortunate—I was a child of Bow Lane after all—and Daniel's brows rose as I went on.

By the time I spluttered to a halt, the amusement had returned to Daniel's expression.

"*I* have to obey Monaghan," Daniel said. "He owns my soul.

But you don't." His smile deepened. "I would like to see him try to tell you what to do. I'd be very entertained."

"Your idea of entertainment is quite strange." My coolness returned. "The entire bank can go hang, for all I care, as long as Sam and Joanna are all right. I'm certain Mr. Monaghan's traitors are careful enough to have already turned to another bank to fund them."

"Unfortunately, that is true." Daniel's eyes darkened. "They are very dangerous people, Kat, and I can't blame Monaghan for wanting to stop them."

"Yes, but I will not sacrifice Sam so that Mr. Monaghan can have the pleasure of arresting conspirators. What would be the point if all the innocents were killed to save the country? There would be no country left, would there?" I was babbling by this time, but my fury and frustration boiled over. "Anarchists have been trying to overthrow the Crown of England for centuries, but they haven't succeeded, have they? Why should they now?"

"There have been a *few* changes in the monarchy," Daniel said. "But I take your point. I haven't said I won't help you. I will not investigate the workings of the bank and their clients directly, but I can certainly assist you in finding the correct murderer to hand to the police."

"Well, I am glad to hear it." I glared at him. "Sir Rupert said he would have the solicitor look into what had happened to the embezzled money, but I thought I should do that myself. Maybe the embezzler is one of Mr. Monaghan's conspirators. Mr. Monaghan would be happy for an excuse to arrest him, would he not?"

"I think the embezzler is more after personal gain than political turmoil," Daniel said. "The conspirators are using the institution to store their money, but we don't think there's a man on the inside. I doubt Daalman's even knows they are being used as such. The board are very careful to be quite loyal to the queen."

"It would be difficult to hide the stolen money, wouldn't it?" I asked.

Daniel considered. "If this embezzler is wise, he'll break up the funds into smaller sums, perhaps spread them through several bank accounts. Or he's made investments here and there at other firms. A large chunk of money in one place would be too obvious."

"People steal money because they want the money," I pointed out. "Perhaps for a virtuous reason, such as paying the crippling debt of a beloved parent, or that sort of thing. But most thieves want it so they can live well without the bother of hard work. Whoever it is must be spending some of it—on natty clothes, or a fine horse, or paintings, or trips to the seaside, or whatever takes their fancy. I think we should look at each of the employees and see who is living beyond their means."

"Every employee of the bank?" Daniel regarded me skeptically. "There are quite a number."

"We can ask Sam how many. And if he can provide all their names and where they live."

Daniel's soft laughter snapped me from my adamancy. "Poor Millburn will probably fall over from exhaustion if we task him with this. But never fear—I have a man at Daalman's. He can give me the list of names and addresses."

I might have known Daniel would already be acquainted with someone at the bank, but I felt a qualm. "Without getting caught?"

"He's a bright chap. No harm in asking him."

My curiosity rose. "Is he investigating the conspirators for you as well?"

"His skills don't run to untangling balance sheets, unfortunately. But this he will do. Then we will run through the names and see which lowly clerk has lace curtains in his windows and employs a high-paid valet from an exclusive agency."

I let myself laugh at his idea of extravagance as I rose to pour Daniel more tea.

He'd said not many moments ago that we needed to find joy in the small corners of life. I decided to savor this moment, of Daniel and me sitting at the table together in the quiet of the night, basking in each other's company. The circle of lamplight shut out the darkness, and the glowing stove pushed aside the cold.

In this slice of time, happiness prevailed, in a warm sanctuary that the howling terrors of the world could not invade.

I woke in the morning telling myself I must be patient. Sir Rupert, Daniel, and Mr. Thanos would need time to do what they could and I would have to wait for the outcome.

Meanwhile, Sam faced another bleak day in the awful common cell in Newgate, Joanna faced another day trying to keep her children's spirits high and herself from despair. I faced a day of cooking for an ungrateful mistress with little time for rest.

On days like these, I longed to throw aside my apron and run to Grace, snatching her up and fleeing with her far from filthy London to carve a life of our own.

Then I'd come to my senses and realize that a destination was reached by the accumulation of small steps. Year after year, I was saving my pay and planning a future. In moments of despair, I'd think my work all for naught, but then I'd see how much my lump of money had grown, and realize that one day, my dream would become real.

I was hard-pressed to cling to this philosophy this morning when Mrs. Bywater demanded I make a mountain of lemon custard that she could take to a charity meeting in Oxford Street that evening. I explained to her that custard did not travel well, and she might be better off with scones. I could make them with lemon zest or dried fruit, very tasty.

No, she must have custard. Why, I could not fathom, but when Mrs. Bywater set her bony shoulders and gave me a steely stare, I had to give in. Custard it was. By the time she reached her destination it would have become watery or fallen apart entirely, and I, the cook, would be blamed.

If I stabilized it with arrowroot and egg whites and packed it in ice, it might survive. I had Tess gather all the cream and eggs in the larder before she went off on her day out and set about creating a vat of lemon custard. I made the scones as well, for good measure. If the custard was a disaster, at least the ladies of her charity organization could praise the scones.

Mr. Davis continued to speak little but went about his duties as though determined to think of nothing else. As this is what I also had to do today, I could not condemn him. We both threw ourselves into work to keep from breaking down. I wished I could comfort him, but at the moment, I had little of that to give.

Mrs. Bywater fussed about using the expensive ice to pack around the tubs of custard, but I assured her they were necessary. I would have to have Cynthia write to Lord Rankin and ask him to have ice delivered a bit more often.

Mrs. Bywater went off, and I scrubbed the kitchen and set about making the leftover lemons into ices and also a buttery lemon cake. Miss Townsend and Bobby raved about my lemon cake, and they'd been kind to me over the Millburns' troubles. I'd find a moment to deliver the cake to them.

Daniel did not arrive that night after service. I hoped Mr. Monaghan hadn't sent him off on some impossible commission, or perhaps on the final, dangerous job he didn't mind if Daniel never came back from. I decided I would inform Mr. Monaghan that if he got Daniel killed, he would have to answer to me. I would not sit by and let him destroy the man I'd come to deeply care for.

On Sunday, Daniel sent word to me through James that he would like me to meet him at Newgate on Monday afternoon, so we could speak to Sam again. Mr. Thanos had run his expert eye over the papers and had much to say about them.

Though I never wished to see the inside of Newgate again, I did want to both bring Sam some comfort and hear what Mr. Thanos and Sam made of the papers. I also wilted in relief that Mr. Monaghan obviously hadn't yet sent Daniel off to his possible death.

I thought I knew why Sam hadn't mentioned the papers to me or explained what was on them. He was the sort who would try to bludgeon through everything himself without bothering anyone until he had answers to give them. Sam was learning the hard way, I supposed, that he had to let others help him. That lesson had been a long time coming to me as well.

I sent James away with the lemon cake to deliver to Miss Townsend, with a few scones for himself. He sprinted off with the energy of youth, cramming an entire scone in his mouth as he went.

Mrs. Redfern came downstairs to tell me Cynthia had said the lemon custard had been a success. Served with the scones, they'd made a perfect repast. Cynthia hadn't been at the do, but she'd heard this from one of her aunt's friends who had attended. I was pleased that the custard had reached Oxford Street intact but grumbled that Mrs. Bywater hadn't bothered to tell me the outcome herself.

I woke Monday with a lighter heart. Today, I would see my daughter and move forward with restoring Joanna's happiness.

After Tess and I sent up the luncheon, I snatched up the basket I'd prepared and walked up the outside stairs to spy Lewis waiting with his cab some way down Mount Street. I hurried to him, passing a scowling gentleman Lewis had just turned away, and sprang into the cab. Daniel hadn't come himself to fetch me, but I was grateful to Lewis for saving my aching feet.

Daniel met me at the gate of the prison. I shivered mightily as we went inside, the same gate guard bidding us a cheery good afternoon.

Sam had been put into the tiny room where we'd met him before. Today, however, the drab space was brightened considerably by the presence of a dark-haired, dark-eyed young man with spectacles, who leapt to his feet when I entered and bathed me in a radiant smile.

21

Elgin Thanos was as sunny-natured in a dreary prison room as he was in a grand parlor. He never noticed or minded his surroundings, just as he never noticed or minded whether his friends were aristocrats or laborers.

"Mrs. Holloway, how lovely to see you." Mr. Thanos advanced on me and seized my hand, though my basket hung awkwardly from my arm. "Come. Sit."

He relieved me of the basket and passed it absentmindedly to Daniel while he led me to the chair he'd vacated. Sam had risen the best he could while still shackled, but I waved him back down as I seated myself.

"Do not be so formal," I told Sam. "Hardly necessary. I've brought you sustenance, which should last until you go home."

Sam shot me a skeptical glance at my optimism, but I noted his gaze strayed longingly to the basket.

I decided to share out some of the treats as we settled around the table. Daniel this time coerced the guard outside to bring in a rickety folding stool for Mr. Thanos, though Daniel remained standing.

Sam lifted the cruller I handed him—a twisted roll fried in butter—and held it to his nose, closing his eyes in rapture. Then he laid it in front of him and waited while I handed a scone to Mr. Thanos, Sam always polite. Mr. Thanos examined his scone as though he'd never seen anything like it.

"They're for eating, not admiring," I said to both of them. "Go on."

Sam obediently bit off a large hunk of the cruller. He inhaled as he chewed, his face relaxing as he took in the buttery, crackling goodness. Mr. Thanos pulled off a smaller bite of his scone but ate with the same sort of thankfulness.

"You are a goddess, Mrs. H.," Thanos said. "How did you know cranberry scones were my favorite?"

"A fortunate guess," I said, but it had been nothing of the sort. Cynthia had described to me how he could easily devour a platter of them.

"You've given me fascinating reading," Mr. Thanos said, as though I'd bestowed a great gift upon him. He swept his arm over the papers laid across the table in unkempt piles. "We've been untangling the puzzle." His eyes had lit, Mr. Thanos never happier than when working through numbers.

"Have you discovered who the embezzler is?" I asked eagerly.

"Well—" Mr. Thanos began, but Sam cut him off.

"Not as such," Sam said. "We've figured out how they did it, but I don't have a name of someone to arrest."

I understood why Sam had interrupted. Mr. Thanos could launch into a long and mostly unintelligible explanation if he wasn't stopped.

"What have you learned?" Daniel asked. "Explain in sentences a layman will understand, please."

"Finish your cruller first," I said kindly.

Sam took another grateful bite, then laid the half-eaten cruller on a napkin I'd brought. He was saving it instead of devouring it in one go. Extending the joy, I realized. I'd brought enough to supplement his meager meals for a week, but perhaps he did not believe he'd leave this place so soon—of his own volition, that is.

"The embezzler has set up many accounts in banks across the City," Sam began. "Small amounts are paid into these accounts, all to different people. No amount very extravagant. Nothing more than most dividends would be. Those who live on the payouts of their investments mostly receive a moderate income. No sudden, vast fortunes. A fortune is what people hope for when they invest, but much of the time, they simply make a steady stream of income that lets them live well but not grandly. None of these payments would raise an eyebrow."

"Taken together, however," Mr. Thanos put in, "a person could live very well indeed. Upward of ten thousand pounds a year."

I stilled in shock. Ten thousand was a princely sum. "Surely, with that sort of money, the embezzler could retire to the seaside and not labor in the bank every day."

"True," Sam said. "But he'd draw attention to himself leaving abruptly. And why go when he can stay and take still more?"

"Your arrest for embezzlement might have cut off his opportunity," I said. "If the trickling of funds continues, Daalman's will have to find a new suspect. Your arrest for murder has drawn the attention away from the embezzlement."

"Are you thinking that is why Mr. Stockley was murdered?" Daniel asked me. "A plausible theory. The embezzler worried

about his income drying up and decided to obfuscate things."
He turned to Sam. "You said Mr. Stockley had an idea who was
the culprit?"

"I think so," Sam said. "He did not give me a name, unfortunately."

"Do these documents give names?" I indicated the piles on
the table. "The same character names from Dickens?"

"No." Sam shook his head. "I think the character names were
only for the contracts. I found the initials of those to be paid,
but they don't match the contracted names. I copied out log-
books of checks made to those initials—here." He pulled out a
long list of numbers and letters written in his careful hand.
"Whoever wrote the checks knew what names the initials stood
for, but that is not unusual. He'd have a key to the names plus
the directions on the investment documents as to how much
to pay. He'd simply write out the checks or send the deposits
to the correct bank."

"Who makes out the checks?" I asked, certain that this person would be involved.

"Most of the senior clerks do—whoever of them has been given
that level of trust. And the bankers can, though they usually
leave that job to the clerks. The clerks are simply writing names
and numbers on checks and putting them into envelopes, or
sending them by locked courier bag to banks for deposit. It's a
fairly tedious job, and those writing the checks don't necessarily have access to the money itself. They only know who is owed
what, and they pay it accordingly."

I deflated. We were back to almost anyone in the bank being able to siphon off the funds.

"The investment document tells the banker who the check
goes to and how much?" I asked, trying to make certain I understood. "How does it?"

Sam selected a paper and turned it to me. "These are the stocks in question and the percentage of return on them, and here is whether those stocks made a profit or loss." He ran a finger across each column. "Then the initials of each investor, how much of the stock they own, what percentage they are paid, and how much that is in pounds, shillings, and pence. What puzzled me was that some of the larger earnings had been broken up into many smaller payments to different investors. That is not unusual if, say, a firm has invested on behalf of employees or clients—they break down the dividends for each person. But those group investors are known to us, and we pay them a lump sum. They take care of dividing the spoils on their end."

"So, Mr. Millburn wondered very much what these payments were," Mr. Thanos broke in, unable to contain himself. "We sorted through it all and came up with a list of initials that occur over and over again. They seem to have invested in quite a number of diverse ventures, all of which have paid handsomely. But no one set of initials gets all the money from each investment. Sometimes one set does get a small payout, and then the next quarter they receive nothing, even if the investment earned money. All very irregular."

"Trying to hide exactly what is going on," Daniel speculated, and Mr. Thanos nodded, as though pleased a pupil had understood his lesson.

"Who did these documents come from?" I asked Sam. "Surely, you'd know who handed them to you to copy. Or whose handwriting this is."

Sam shook his head. "I copy out things for all the bankers, and the papers are brought down to our room by a senior clerk. Then Chandler, the head of our room, doles them out. I usually get documents from the same bankers, but not always. I don't recognize whose hand is what, because I don't necessarily see handwriting other than what's thrust at me. Over time, I've grown to recognize the patterns of certain bankers, but none of *their* papers have ever had irregularities. When I noted the oddities, I started keeping these documents back, a little at a time, after I'd copied them out. I once tried to bring them to the attention of Chandler, and then Mr. Zachary, but I was turned away quite rudely by both of them. Told my job was copying and not troubling myself about the details."

"Hmm." Either Mr. Chandler or Mr. Zachary had something to do with this, or they were simply arrogant men not wanting to bother with a junior clerk's concerns. "Why would the embezzler even risk having these documents copied?" I asked. "I'd think he'd hide them or at least carry them to the check writers himself. Or make certain *he* was the check writer."

"Daalman's keeps painstaking records," Sam explained with some weariness. "Have for centuries, which is why they have rooms upstairs packed with papers. They need to be able to answer to any inquiries, so they have two copies of every piece, sometimes three for very important documents. It would be more noticeable if records were missing than if they were doctored."

"These are originals?" I asked, touching ones that I knew hadn't been written by Sam. I'd seen enough of Sam's penned short greetings in Joanna's letters to me over the years to recognize his writing.

"They are. If it was known I had them, I'd be sacked for not filing them in the appropriate cubbyhole in the appropriate file room." His tone was dry. "Such is the meticulousness of Daalman's."

"And you don't know who made these adjustments?" I

pointed to numbers that had been crossed out, new numbers and initials written alongside them, some with the stylized *H*'s and *I*'s I'd noted before.

"The banker who sent down this document did not make the changes—I do know *his* handwriting," Sam said. "They were inserted after they left his desk, presumably between the bankers' room and the junior clerks' room. Junior clerks are not taught to notice anything, simply to copy and file, and then to pass the information to the senior clerks, who write the checks."

Such arrogance, along with the opportunity to make the changes, pointed to someone like Mr. Zachary. He could intercept papers at any time, or the bankers might have been told that those documents were to come to him first, no matter what. A banker who didn't want to lose his job would obey without question.

"If we discover who made these annotations," I concluded, "we'll find the embezzler?"

"In theory," Daniel said. "A man may disguise his writing if he's up to something and doesn't want to be found out. But a study of all handwriting at Daalman's might help."

"I doubt anyone will let you do that," Sam said. "They'd never even allow you in the door, McAdam. Miss Swann is very particular about who is admitted."

"She might be persuaded." Daniel's eyes sparkled as he doubtless contemplated which guise he'd use to enter the lofty bank. "But I have easier ways of gaining information."

He did not elaborate, but I assumed he meant his man on the inside, whoever that was.

"We are also going to discover whether any of the employees are living more expensively than they should," I told Sam.

Sam did not share my optimism. "Stockley had begun to investigate that. He so far had found no one living extravagantly, except for Mr. Zachary. Zachary purchased a large house near Hampstead Heath and dwells there in high style, but everyone knows this. The bank's owners don't approve. They live in fine but modest homes, pouring most of their earnings back into Daalman's."

I was liking Mr. Zachary more and more as a suspect. He'd been nervous when Cynthia and I had visited, though I admitted that the murder of Mr. Stockley could have accounted for his uneasiness. But his high-handedness, his luxurious home, and the fact that he could doctor any papers he wished made me long to find the man and shake a confession from him.

"We shall see," I said, counseling myself to caution. "For now, Sam, if you and Mr. Thanos can discover anything more in those papers that can help, please send word to Daniel. I will return on Thursday to see if you are well—if that will even be necessary."

I said this last brightly, assuring Sam that he'd be home and free by that time. He did not believe me, but he started to rise, his chains preventing him from standing all the way up.

"I am so very grateful to you, Kat." Sam ignored me waving him back to his seat. "For making sure Joanna is all right and trying your best to help my case. Your friends have been diligent for me, and they don't even know me." He leaned heavily on his hands, his shackles clanking. "At one time in my life, I'd never have believed there was such kindness in the world."

"I would do anything for Joanna," I said without hesitation. "And not only are my friends kind, but they are clever. We will win, Sam. You can depend upon it."

"*I* believe you, Mrs. Holloway," Mr. Thanos said. He'd hopped to his feet, his eyes shining behind his spectacles—which were staying firmly in place today, instead of falling off every time he bent his head. "You can count on her, Mr. Millburn. Mrs.

Holloway is brilliant at these things. Absolutely brilliant. Oh, and so is McAdam."

Daniel laughed as Mr. Thanos added him as an after-thought. "Bear up, Millburn," Daniel said. "Enjoy Kat's cakes. Always a comfort in times of madness."

He was being absurd, but Sam nodded in fervent agreement. "Thank you for that as well," he said to me. "Please tell Joanna…" Sam broke off and sank dejectedly into his chair, his words choked. Mr. Thanos patted his shoulder in sympathy.

"I will tell her you love her desperately," I said. "Though she already knows that. Good afternoon, Sam. Make certain Mr. Thanos leaves some scones for you."

I sent Mr. Thanos a little smile, and he chortled. "I will be sure to, Mrs. H.," he said.

I once again melted in relief when we emerged from New-gate, even with the freezing January wind pouring down the street at us.

"What do we do now?" I asked Daniel. I hunkered into him as we made our way up the street to Lewis's cab. "I'd hoped Mr. Thanos could look at those papers and tell us exactly who had done what, but they were more complex than I thought."

"Even Thanos can't divine the name of the person from scribbles on a page," Daniel said. "But do not worry. We'll smoke him out." He spoke with determination.

"Or her," I said. "Miss Swann could have intercepted the pa-pers and made the changes. Though I'm not certain she could insert false contracts into the works without someone notic-ing. But she seems a competent woman, disdainful of slower-witted men."

"We have her address." Daniel handed me into the cab before he pulled a paper from his pocket as Lewis started off toward the Holborn Viaduct. The page contained a scrawled list of names, streets, and house numbers, presumably obtained from Daniel's man at Daalman's. "Shall we look at Miss Swann's house first? Discover if she has a mansion in Mayfair and a hundred servants at her beck and call?"

"Great Marylebone Street is not Mayfair," I said, peering at the list. "But let us proceed there. Miss Swann might have a gilded carriage or a fortune in artwork—neither of which we will be able to see from passing in the road, I must point out."

Daniel grinned and called the address to Lewis, who nodded and continued along High Holborn. That road became Oxford Street, and from there Lewis turned north into Regent Street. We clopped past the elegant pile of the Langham Hotel and soon reached Great Marylebone Street.

The neighborhood we entered held quiet elegance, but the homes were nothing like Mayfair mansions. The residence the paper guided us to sat on a corner of a smaller lane. Squat and narrow, the house had a door and two windows on the ground floor and three windows on each of the two floors above this. An iron railing separated the stairs that led to the kitchen from the street.

"Very nice," Daniel proclaimed. "But nothing alarming. Miss Swann likely pays her lease from what she earns at the bank. Though she might also have family money from being a Daalman relation."

I toyed with the idea of walking down to the cellar floor and making some excuse to speak to the cook. The cook and maids would know all about any gilded carriages or sumptuous artwork Miss Swann might be hiding. I wasn't certain what excuse

I'd invent—perhaps I could pretend to be starting work in a nearby house and ask the cook to point me to the best market in the area.

Before I could put this plan into motion, the front door of the house opened. The woman who emerged looked so remarkably like Miss Swann that for a moment I thought it was she.

I realized after a moment that this woman was a bit older, her hair holding more gray, her face lined. However, she possessed the same slimness and upright posture of Miss Swann, and wore a simple gown similar to Miss Swann's mode of dress under her unbuttoned plain coat.

An older sister, I guessed, as the resemblance was so close. This woman turned back to assist an even older woman out of the door, one bent with age, who rested her weight unsteadily on a cane. Once the older woman had, with help, navigated the two steps down to the street, Miss Swann's sister twined her arm through the older woman's, and the two set off northward.

At Daniel's quiet command, Lewis started the hansom forward, the horse maintaining a slow pace as we followed the two women.

They continued on foot, ignoring other cabs that rumbled by, in the direction of Regent's Park. The older woman—mother, grandmother, or elderly aunt—limped heavily, but the two plodded on, glancing neither left nor right.

This must be a daily routine, I realized. Both women were neat and respectable, but if Miss Swann had been shunting money home to them, it was not evident in their clothing. Nor did they have a carriage at their disposal, nor did they bother with a paid conveyance, and no servant followed them.

"If she is taking the money, she is hiding it well," Daniel murmured to me.

"From the brief impression I have of Miss Swann, she would know how to hide it," I said. "Perhaps she is saving a nest egg. But I wonder if Miss Swann would embezzle at all. Fraud might seem tawdry to her. Beneath her."

"Even the most respectable of people can commit crimes, in my experience," Daniel said. "We can't rule out Miss Swann. In the meantime, though, let us see if anyone else on the list is living ostentatiously."

The patient Lewis drove us all over north and west London that afternoon, from just above Regent's Park to Oxford Street and along it to Kensington, then back north to Paddington. Many of the bankers and senior clerks lived near one another, I noted, which considerably shortened our time wandering about. Perhaps new employees asked the more experienced where they could find good but affordable lodgings, and so ended up in the same neighborhoods. The Metropolitan Railway let them commute to the City each day relatively cheaply, so they would not necessarily have to live near the bank.

The junior clerks dwelled in smaller homes or in boarding-houses in places like Holborn or within the City, as did Joanna and Sam.

Nowhere did we find imposing mansions, a plethora of servants, lavish gardens, or fine horses in the mews behind the homes. None of the houses were on squares with private parks or even in the most lush part of the particular area in which they were located.

After a few hours of this fruitless search, I asked Lewis to take us to Clover Lane. I did not want to waste any more time of my afternoon out away from Grace.

"I will continue," Daniel offered. "I can make a full report to you tonight."

I leaned tiredly against Daniel as Lewis's horse moved down Farringdon Road toward Fleet Street. I wished we could simply drive together, without investigating or without time ticking behind our enjoyment.

"I thought Mr. Monaghan warned you off," I said.

"He warned me against investigating the *bank*," Daniel replied. "He said nothing about driving past the homes of the people who work there."

"You are being overly literal. He will not see it that way."

"I did not intend to tell him." Daniel's grin told me I'd not win the argument, and in truth, I had no wish to debate the point.

"At least there are only two names outside London," I said as we turned to Ludgate Hill, St. Paul's looming before us. "Mr. Zachary, who as we already know has a sumptuous house at Hampstead Heath. And Mr. Kearny, who lives with his parents at Harrow. Mr. Zachary seems the most likely, I'll admit—"

"Harrow?" Daniel peered at the addresses on the paper, brows rising.

"That's what he told us. As did Sam." My lethargy began to lift. "Why?"

"I have two addresses here for Mr. Kearny."

"Do you?" I peered over his shoulder to where he pointed to Mr. Kearny's name, scribbled a second time near the bottom of the list. "Where did you obtain this information, anyway? Who is your inside man?"

Daniel's smile flashed. "The doorman's assistant. The fellow sees everything and hears everything, even what isn't officially written into the bank's records."

I thought of the young man who'd taken my coat when I'd visited the bank with Cynthia. I'd barely noticed him except to worry about my coat, but I suppose that was the point. He would, unnoted, overhear conversations and gossip, and likely knew much more about the inhabitants of Daalman's than anyone thought. He was exactly the sort of person Daniel would have recruited.

"Wilton Crescent," I read under Mr. Kearny's name. "Where is that?"

Daniel's amusement evaporated. "Belgravia."

"Belgravia?" My brows rose. Belgravia, like Mayfair, held homes of the wealthy. "Perhaps another house of his parents, where they stay for the Season?"

"We will have to find out." Daniel's energy, like mine, returned. "Lewis—turn us around and head for the Strand. We are going to Belgravia."

22

Belgravia lay south of Hyde Park, reached by turning from Knightsbridge to one of the streets that led toward Belgrave Square.

Wilton Crescent, a semicircle filled with a row of town houses, lay beyond a large church called St. Paul's. Near the middle of Wilton Crescent was the house where the doorman's assistant had indicated Mr. Kearny dwelled.

We reached the town house to see several maids carrying a stream of parcels from a landau down the stairs to the kitchen level. Not an unusual sight in a wealthy neighborhood. The lady of the house had obviously been shopping.

I opened the cab and hopped down, approaching a maid who was struggling to hold on to several knobby, brown paper-wrapped packages. Her fellow maids had already disappeared downstairs, and the footman I spied hovering behind the glass-fronted doorway only watched disdainfully. Unloading a landau was beneath him, presumably.

"Let me help you, love." I slid from the careful speech I'd cultivated to the natural tones of my girlhood. "You look all in, and it's a blustery day."

The maid started, but I gave her a warm smile and relieved her of two of the largest parcels.

"Thank ye, miss," she said. "Do I know you?"

"I'm a cook," I said. "At a house in Mayfair. It's me day out, and I was taking a stroll, looking at all the green. Such a lovely place. Wilton Crescent." I paused to dreamily glance about me. "Like a name in a story."

The maid eyed me doubtfully but didn't object to my assistance. I tucked the packages under my arm and followed her down the stairs, still gabbing about how pretty was the neighborhood.

Daniel, across the road, pulled his cap down over his eyes and hunkered into the shadows of the cab. Lewis contrived to look blank-faced and bored as any cabbie would while waiting for his charge to make up his mind. The horse cocked a nonchalant back hoof and shifted his weight with a sigh.

I clattered across the threshold and into the scullery behind the maid and so on into the kitchen.

The cook jerked her head up from the stove where she was basting a whole hen in the oven. Greens and fresh potatoes littered the work table, and several crisp-crusted loaves of bread sat cooling on a rack.

"Who's this, then?" the cook, a red-faced, middle-aged woman, barked. "What's she want?"

"Don't be so cross, Mrs. Gibbons," my maid said. "She's only helping with the parcels. She's a cook, like yourself."

"Oh aye? Who are you, then, love?"

"Mrs. . . . McAdam." I had no idea why that name leapt to my lips. I'd not wanted to give the name "Holloway" in case

Mr. Kearny—or, heaven help me, Mrs. Bywater—learned of my visit. McAdam was the first name that came to me. "I saw this lass struggling and thought I'd help." I set my armload on a bench next to the packages the maid had set down. The other maids had piled theirs onto the bench as well. "Your mistress certainly has done much shopping," I said, observing the heap.

The maid laughed. "Oh, she's a fine one for shopping."

"Mind your impertinence, Jane," the cook snapped. She faced me, butter from the basting brush dripping to the floor. "But she isn't wrong, Mrs. McAdam. Can't go a day without rushing about buying this and that either for the house or to drape on her body. Though I can't complain—I can purchase what I like for the kitchen without argument."

"Your mistress is Mrs. Kearny?" I asked. "I have a friend who is acquainted with Mr. Kearny," I added at their surprised expressions, staying as close to the truth as possible. I left it vague whether I referred to Mrs. Kearny as Mr. Kearny's wife or his mother.

"*Mrs. Kearny.*" The maid, Jane, snorted. Jane might or might not be her true name, as ladies of the house gave their down-stairs maids names they could remember. "That's what the young lady calls herself, innit?"

"They ain't married," the cook admitted. "Shameful it is, but it's a good place." The mistress obviously hadn't engendered loyalty in her servants.

"Oh dear," I said. I did not have to pretend to be shocked—I was.

Mr. Kearny had sat determinedly in Joanna's parlor, gazing at her with barely disguised longing. It was obvious he planned to woo her if Sam was convicted, and all this time, he'd had a lady tucked into a fine house in Belgravia.

Anger quickly replaced my shock. Had Mr. Kearny been

stealing money from Daalman's, allowing Sam to take the blame for it? All the while he'd been bleating about how much he'd help Sam, had *he* been the cause of Sam's misery?

Perhaps this had been Mr. Kearny's plan from the start. To find a post for Sam at the bank, so he could have a scapegoat in place if he needed it.

"How long has she lived here?" I demanded.

The maid and cook started at my abrupt question, but again, they did not tell me to mind my own business. They were eager to gossip.

"Five years now, ain't it?" Jane asked the cook.

Mrs. Gibbons thought a moment, then nodded. "About that. I worked for the family here before Mr. Kearny leased the house. *They* were well-mannered and respectable. Mrs. Wheeler is a gentlewoman, not a tart from the streets, but she's his ladybird all the same."

"Good heavens." I softened my tone into one of idle interest. "Who'd have thought, eh?"

"Those born better than us ain't necessarily respectable, are they?" Mrs. Gibbons continued. "Mrs. Wheeler's well-spoken enough and don't make too many demands of us, but she runs through his money quick."

"I hear them rowing about it," Jane put in. "Sometimes in the middle of the night. He works in the City, makes plenty of coin, but she'll beggar him in the long run, I'll wager."

The cook opened her mouth to continue but was interrupted by a bell clanging across the hall. "That's you, Jane," Mrs. Gibbons announced. "Best get them parcels up to her, right sharpish."

Jane regarded the bundles in dismay and let out a sigh.

"I'll help," I said. "She'll not notice me—she only wants the parcels, I'd guess."

"I won't refuse." Jane lifted several bulky packages under her arms. "Come on, then. And thanks, love."

"Think nothing of it, dear." I seized two parcels and trotted up the back stairs after her, following her all the way to the second floor, where the largest bedchambers would be.

Below stairs had been little different than the kitchen, servants' hall, and scullery at Mount Street—a bit smaller, but similarly fitted out. Upstairs was another matter. The house I worked in was grand, but had been furnished in light, airy colors by Cynthia's sister, the interior harkening back to the simple elegance of a hundred years ago.

This upper hall smote me with a riot of colors. Blue and gold wallpaper adorned the walls above dark and heavily carved wainscoting, and a lavish rose-patterned rug covered the floor. A huge gas chandelier dripping with crystal bugles hung over the main staircase, which opened from the middle of the hall, its wide steps and polished wooden banister spiraling downward to an equally lush hall below.

Double doors to the main bedchamber stood open, revealing a lady who must be Mrs. Wheeler. She was draped in a gown of yellow silk, its skirts drawn back over the bustle, from which a froth of lace cascaded. The skirt's hem was ruffled and trimmed with more lace, the bodice a slim creation fastened with pearl buttons.

The gown was exactly the sort that suited Lady Cynthia's slender build and exactly the sort she hated. *Can't move in the wretched thing*, she'd grumble.

The fresh-faced lady wearing it seemed to be happy to be an adornment. She lifted a string of glittering beads she'd removed from a parcel one of the other maids had already brought up, testing them against her fair hair. Her coiffure, on this day of shopping, was intricately curled and coiled, attesting that her lady's maid was quite good at her duties.

Mrs. Wheeler caught sight of Jane and me lugging in more of the packages. "Just put them there." She waved a hand toward a cushioned bench inside the door, where other packages reposed.

This chamber was a massive suite, with a sitting and dressing room in front and an open door behind Mrs. Wheeler leading to a large bedchamber. A gracefully carved bedstead plumped high with pillows and invitingly draped coverlets waited within the bedroom.

Mrs. Wheeler did not seem to notice that a stranger in a brown gown had joined her black-clad maids. Likely, she assumed I was a delivery woman from one of the shops she'd just enriched.

The lady's maid, glancing up from tidying away gloves she lifted from another parcel, sent me a puzzled look. I curtsied to Mrs. Wheeler in a deferential manner, as though I truly were a shop employee, and beat a hasty retreat.

As all attention was focused on the lady's chamber, I took the opportunity to descend through the house by the main staircase. This led me to an even more opulent first-floor hall.

I peeked through the double door opposite the staircase and found a high-ceilinged drawing room full of well-cushioned furnishings, a table in the center bearing an arrangement of peacock feathers in a vase, velvet draperies covering the floor-to-ceiling windows, and paintings of beautiful landscapes adorning the walls. I was not expert enough to know if these were paintings by great artists or simply purchased for their pleasing colors, but there were many of them.

I withdrew and continued to the ground floor, where the

well-groomed footman who'd simply stared at us through the etched-glass front door turned to me with a haughty frown.

"All settled," I said brightly. "I lost the way to the back stairs, love. Just point them out, will you? There's a good lad."

The footman, sneer in place, marched past me down the hall and wrenched opened the baize-lined door. I sent him an indulgent smile as I scuttled through and down the stairs. He slammed the door behind me.

"All done, Mrs. McAdam?" the cook asked as I breezed into the kitchen.

I started at the name before I recalled that I'd told it to her. "Yes, indeed. Quite a lot of shopping for one day, wasn't it? I imagine she's going to a ball or something of that sort."

Mrs. Gibbons rolled her eyes. "Not that one. She buys things day after day. Can't wear the same gown more than once, can she? Born with a silver spoon in her mouth, I hear. Husband overindulged her, and now that he's gone, she has Mr. Kearny to spoil her like a lapdog. Suppose *we* were to behave that way, eh, Mrs. McAdam? We'd never live it down."

"No, Mrs. Gibbons, we should remember who we are." I did not simply mean our place in the social world, but who we were deep inside, regardless of what strata we'd been born into. "I'd rather work hard and earn an honest crust than live off a man's whims."

"Well, she's got him wrapped around her fingers, no doubt." Mrs. Gibbons moved to the table with the vegetables and lifted a paring knife. "It was good of you to help, Mrs. McAdam. You have a fine afternoon."

She wanted me gone, and I did not blame her. I wondered if she was expected to prepare an elaborate supper for the lady and whatever guests she entertained tonight.

"And you, Mrs. Gibbons." I paused on the threshold of the

outer door. "If you save the juices of the roast hen, add some broth and pieces of all those vegetables, they'll go together into a savory pie. A nice treat for you and the maids when the work's done."

Mrs. Gibbons brightened as she gazed at the vast array of vegetables strewn before her. "An excellent suggestion. Thank you. You pop by any day you're free, love. It's nice to have someone to chat to."

I made a vague promise to and climbed the stairs to the street.

I strolled a little way along Wilton Crescent, ignoring Daniel and Lewis, as though I truly had come to saunter through the elegant area on my day out. I heard the hansom slowly following. Once I turned onto Wilton Place, I waited for Lewis to reach me, then Daniel stretched out an arm and assisted me into the cab.

"I know where all the embezzled money has gone," I said as soon as I was seated and Lewis drove on. I described the house and Mrs. Wheeler in a few strokes, then my anger bubbled over. "The blasted man. Mr. Kearny made me like him by defending Sam. And all the while, he is a cheat and a fraud. He will not get away with it."

Daniel's mouth set in a grim line. "No, he will not."

"Then let us find him and haul him to the police."

"I will do that," Daniel said in the tone that told me Mr. Kearny would have no quarter. "I'll hunt up Inspector Mc-Gregor and have him and his boys lie in wait for Mr. Kearny. They'll get him. You go to your daughter while you can."

The afternoon had slipped by, and my time with Grace would soon be at an end. Pain bit my heart, but I sat up straight.

"We will go to Mr. Kearny *now*," I declared. "I do not want Sam to spend another night in that awful place. Joanna and his children need him at home." Grace, I thought, would not only understand my choice to pursue Mr. Kearny instead of coming to her, she would also approve.

Daniel studied my determined expression, then he turned and called out to Lewis. "Take us to Daalman's. Double your fare if you're there before it closes for the day."

Lewis shot a nod at Daniel, flicked his whip, and sent the bay horse lurching forward in a swift trot.

23

We crossed the metropolis in a remarkably short time. Lewis knew not only how to encourage his horse to move quickly but also how to maneuver the cab through and around carts, carriages, omnibuses, and pedestrians with deft precision.

He charged through Cheapside and the short way along Poultry and through Cornhill to Leadenhall Street. Moments later, he halted the cab in the tiny lane before the discreet house that was Daalman's Bank, the horse barely breathing hard from his exertion.

Daniel descended first and handed me out, and it was a mercy he helped me down. I was so angry I barely knew what I was about. I clung to his steady hand as we made our way to the bank's front door.

The doorman observed us frostily when he answered Daniel's ring of the bell. Whether he recognized me from when I'd accompanied Lady Cynthia, he made no indication.

"The bank is closed, sir." He pronounced the *sir* dubiously, raking his gaze over Daniel's working clothes.

"That's all right," Daniel answered cheerfully. "We're only waiting for Mr. Kearny. He's still about, is he? It hasn't gone six yet."

"The employees are working, but the bank is closed to visitors after four. Even then, you must have an appointment to enter."

Daniel shifted his weight from foot to foot, peering past the doorman into the dim interior. "We could wait for him to come out, I suppose. No one will notice us lurking, will they?"

"You will *not* lurk," the doorman stated. "Or I'll send for the police. Clear off."

Before the doorman could retreat, I stepped in front of Daniel. "Please inform Mr. Kearny that Mrs. Holloway wishes to speak to him," I said in my frostiest tones. "It is of vast importance."

The doorman took me in, a woman in a neat frock and coat and carefully kept hat. At the moment, I was far more presentable than the scruffy Daniel.

I was prepared to bring out Lady Cynthia's name to make him admit me, but he heaved a sigh and retreated into the shadows of the foyer. "I will inquire."

He closed the door heavily, leaving us outside.

I was about to give the bell a long and indignant push, when the door creaked open again. The youthful doorman's assistant in his red uniform peeked out, glanced behind him, then beckoned us to quickly enter.

Daniel and I stepped into the unnatural hush of the front hall. A whisper of voices echoed down from above, unintelligible by the time they reached us. The doorman, who must have gone to deliver the message himself, was nowhere in sight.

Daniel murmured something to the doorman's assistant I did not catch, because I had started marching toward the stairs. I would not tamely wait for anyone in Daalman's to deign to admit me.

I ascended without impediment to the first floor, the whispers seeming to recede as I did, which was most unnerving. My plan was to walk to the room I'd looked into on my last visit to see if Mr. Kearny was in it or demand anyone there to tell me where he was.

What I'd say to him, I had no idea. The fact that Mr. Kearny had pretended to befriend Sam, then blithely let him take the blame for his embezzlement filled me with incandescent rage. Sam, the man my best friend loved with all her heart, was having his reputation tarnished and his body endangered because of Mr. Kearny's perfidy. Fraudsters were good liars, I should have remembered.

The door to Mr. Zachary's office opened abruptly, and three people emerged. I halted in the middle of the corridor, unable to hide but unwilling to run.

One of those who strode toward me was the doorman, his bearing filled with annoyance that I hadn't remained outside like the uninvited guest I was. The other two were the willowy Miss Swann and Mr. Kearny himself.

"Mrs. Holloway?" Mr. Kearny's voice was welcoming, ingratiating. "How can I help you? Is Mrs. Millburn all right?"

His use of Joanna's name wiped away any eloquent speeches I could have made. I waited for him to reach me in silent anger, my fists balled.

The doorman, his duty fulfilled, moved past me with a huff of disapproval and pattered down the stairs, probably to make certain the unkempt Daniel hadn't followed me inside.

Mr. Kearny halted before me, his demeanor only that of a

concerned friend. Miss Swann, more puzzled than worried, peered at me as though trying to understand why I was standing in the upstairs corridor.

I recalled watching Miss Swann's sister in drab gray leading their elderly relative down the equally gray street to take the air. I could feel sorry for Miss Swann, I supposed, who had to return home each day to the unsmiling women I'd seen. Her salary must pay for the house and the care of her relations.

At the moment, however, my attention was all for Mr. Kearny. No accusatory words leapt to my lips, though I longed to lecture him long and hard and then have the doorman's assistant run for the police. I hoped Daniel was attending to that detail.

I could only gaze at the man, my wrath at the thought of Sam sitting so dejectedly in that room in Newgate consuming me. Sam's desperate attempt to maintain his politeness when I visited, his flickering hopes when Mr. Thanos and he went through the papers, and his obvious dejection at being apart from Joanna broke my heart. As did the memory of Joanna clinging to me and weeping, believing she'd never see her beloved husband again.

I thought of my own terrible fears that Grace would have to be turned out of the house she'd grown up in, that I'd have to send her far away to keep her safe. That I wouldn't be able to afford a decent place for her to live.

This man, with his selfish fecklessness, had nearly taken all that away from us.

"Mrs. Holloway?" Mr. Kearny prompted, likely thinking I'd taken leave of my senses.

"Mr. Kearny." I fixed him with the gaze I reserved for a footman who dropped a crown rib roast with all the trimmings I'd labored over for a day to shatter on the floor. "I am so very disappointed in you."

Mr. Kearny continued to stare for a moment. Then a flush crept over his face, visible even in the hallway's dim light, his lips parting.

"It's—I—It isn't—" He spluttered and floundered, while Miss Swann regarded him, her brows raised.

"It isn't what it seems?" I asked in a hard voice. "Is that what you wish to say, Mr. Kearny? That I am mistaken that you have bled money from Daalman's for years and years? That you stood by while Sam Millburn took the blame, watching while he was hauled away by the police. That you destroyed a man you called a friend, destroyed his *family*. And then sat in Joanna's parlor bleating about how concerned you were, how you wished to help her. What about that poor woman sitting in Wilton Crescent who believes you love her? Does she have any idea you're nothing but a petty thief?"

Miss Swann at first gaped as my accusations poured out, then as my voice rose in volume, she closed her mouth and became brisk. "Perhaps we should discuss this in private," she said to me.

"Why?" I demanded, seeing no reason to be quiet. "Are you afraid that everyone in this bank will realize what a deceitful swindler Mr. Kearny is?"

"Follow me, Mrs. Holloway," Miss Swann ordered. "And you, Mr. Kearny." She did not touch the quivering Mr. Kearny, but at her stern gaze, he turned around and hastened toward the office at the end, Miss Swann marching before him.

I had no choice but to follow. I did not want to risk Mr. Kearny rushing down a back staircase or leaping out a window to get away. I hurried after them, sweeping into Mr. Zachary's office just behind Mr. Kearny.

Miss Swann shut the door and moved to stand behind Mr. Zachary's desk. Mr. Zachary himself was absent, but I could only vaguely wonder where he was.

Miss Swann bent her severe gaze on me. "What evidence do you have that made you force your way inside and begin accusing one of our bankers at the top of your voice?" Her tone told me she thought me common trash.

"There is plenty of evidence," I stated. "Beginning with the false contracts and moving on to the papers directing money into accounts that he withdraws from all over London. I'm certain that an inquiry in these banks will reveal people who recognize Mr. Kearny when he comes in for his funds. There is the evidence of a house in Belgravia, leased by Mr. Kearny to stuff his ladybird into. A ladybird of very expensive tastes, I must say."

"I never meant to take anything," Mr. Kearny broke in, sweat beading on his forehead. "It just happened, Mrs. Holloway. I swear to you. And then kept happening." He began to rock back and forth, as though he couldn't help himself. "Miss Swann . . ."

Miss Swann listened to his breathless confession, her expression becoming more and more frozen. When he appealed to her, she took a step back, anger glittering in her eyes. Not only, I thought, because Mr. Kearny had stolen from Daalman's, but because he was breaking down and admitting it.

I knew even as I spoke that the evidence was not solid. Mr. Kearny might be paying for his lady with an extravagant allowance from his parents in Harrow. We had not yet proved that the handwriting on any of the papers was his. Nor that he was the owner of the many suspected accounts or had taken any money from them. However, Mr. Kearny's shame was rendering the thinness of the evidence immaterial.

"I'm sorry." Tears rasped in Mr. Kearny's voice. He wasn't apologizing to me, I realized as he pivoted and sent a beseeching look at Miss Swann. He was apologizing to *her*, to Daalman's.

"I am sorry too, Mr. Kearny." Miss Swann was tight-lipped. "You'd better go, hadn't you?"

"But—"

"You have robbed them for years," I snapped at Mr. Kearny. "And you shoved the blame onto a man you called your *friend*. If Sam hadn't been here to be your scapegoat, you would have chosen someone else. You cannot expect any mercy."

"Sam *is* my friend," Mr. Kearny tried. "Truly. I liked him right away, helped him find a place here. I never meant for all this to land on him."

"Yet, you said nothing," I repeated. "You stood by and let Sam be taken, perhaps to hang. What about Mr. Stockley? Why did you kill him? Had he come too close to revealing your crime?"

Mr. Kearny looked confused a moment, then his eyes widened until they bulged. "Are you accusing me of killing Stockley? I never did. I swear to Providence, I never touched the man. I took the money, yes—it was there for the taking, and so very easy. It just needed some clever tweaking so no one would notice it going. But I'm not a *murderer*. Good Lord, I'd never do *that*."

He gazed at me with a mix of so much indignation and abject terror that I began to believe him.

"Go," Miss Swann repeated to Mr. Kearny in her icy voice. *"Now."*

Mr. Kearny gulped. He faced the two of us women, me condemning, Miss Swann infuriated—a forbidding goddess protective of her temple.

Then he bolted.

I snatched at his coat, but Mr. Kearny was too fast for me. He slammed open the door and sprinted into the hall, the door banging shut again from his momentum.

I knew I'd never catch him. I was hampered by skirts even if I could run as swiftly as a man in fine condition. I raced to the window instead, fumbling with the curtains and tugging at the window sash.

The window stuck fast, but I saw I did not need to shout down a warning. Daniel was already hard on Mr. Kearny's heels as that man barreled into the lane below me. Daniel emitted a series of sharp whistles worthy of Mr. Grimes, and I saw movement at the end of the lane. Someone would catch him.

I turned to find Miss Swann directly behind me, her face hard with determination.

"You will say nothing," she instructed.

I sent her an incredulous look. "I will not report an embezzler so your precious bank won't be slandered? It is too late to cover things up now, in any case, Miss Swann. Mr. Kearny will be caught and taken to the police."

"Mr. Kearny will never come to trial. I will make certain of it."

"You would let Sam Millburn rot in prison, instead? Or be hanged for a crime he did not do?"

"Mr. Millburn does not matter," Miss Swann answered, tight-lipped. "Daalman's existed long before he was born, and it will continue long after he is dead."

"What do you mean, he does not matter?" I stepped to her in outrage. "Sam has a wife and children. He matters to *them*. They cannot get along without him. Think of what would happen to your sister, and your—your grandmother—if you were in prison in his place."

Miss Swann's face lost all color. I wasn't certain if the elderly woman was her grandmother or any relation at all, but my argument clearly enraged her.

"How dare you?" she demanded. "What can you even know of my family? I am a Daalman, the only one of them who works in this building day in and day out. I protect their name, their history. *I* do." Miss Swann tapped a long finger to her chest. "Who are *you*?"

"I am a cook," I said with all my dignity. "And I know a woman who's lost all sense of right and wrong when I see her."

"A cook," Miss Swann sneered. "How can you possibly understand? This bank would be nothing without me."

"Mr. Zachary runs it," I pointed out. "And the board."

"Mr. Zachary." Miss Swann's lip curled. "He does what I tell him. He understands his place."

"And gives you whatever keys you ask for." My words slowed as I abruptly understood who had killed Mr. Stockley and why.

"He does not need to give me anything," Miss Swann snapped.

I glanced at a wall panel behind the desk that was slightly out of skew with the others. Mr. Kearny had indicated Mr. Zachary kept all the keys in a locked cabinet behind such a panel. I guessed it would be easy for Miss Swann to take the key to *that*—Mr. Zachary might leave it carelessly about, but even if he did not, I didn't doubt she was sharp enough to lift it from him.

If Miss Swann copied the cabinet's key, then she could gradually make copies of all the keys within it, which opened every door in the building. The board might not have entrusted the keys to her, but that had not stopped the resourceful Miss Swann.

"You can unlock any door you wish," I continued. "You do not let the fact that two different keys must be used stop you from entering a strong room."

"No, I—" Miss Swann broke off, as though realizing she was about to say too much. "Enough of this."

She followed the words with a swing of her arm. Too late, I realized she'd lifted a small marble vase from one of the tables while I'd been at the window.

The heavy vase still held flowers, and water poured down as the marble crashed to my forehead and sent me to the floor.

When I opened my eyes, my first thought was that I was happy to be alive.

The second was that there was very little light. The third, that the room I'd woken in was cold. My head hurt in a way it hadn't since I'd lived with Joe, and any movement sent it throbbing.

I sat up gingerly, suppressing a groan, and supported my back on whatever was behind me. The fact that I knew how to be gentle with myself after being beaten down was sad testimony about my married life.

Crisp footsteps tapped toward me, and I looked up into the cold face of Miss Swann.

Oh dear.

24

As Miss Swann regarded me icily, I winced and put a hand to my head.

A glance at the large object I leaned against showed me a tall cabinet with many drawers, all shut, all fitted with keyholes. The rest of the room held many such cabinets. There was one window, very high in the wall, that let in the fading afternoon light.

A strong room, I presumed. The little-used one, perhaps where Mr. Stockley had died.

"How did you carry me up here?" I asked, rubbing my aching temple. "I am not a small woman."

"I had assistance," Miss Swann said coldly.

I wondered by who, but I knew she would not tell me. The thin but strong doorman? One of the other bankers or clerks in her thrall? "How did you lure Mr. Stockley here? Did he offer to show you evidence of the embezzlement? Or the extent of it? Something like that could not get about to your share-holders. Can't have a panicked run on Daalman's, can you?"

"Stockley was an arrogant idiot who also did as he was told."

"Why not give Mr. Kearny to the police?" I asked her, want-ing to keep her talking. "He is clearly guilty."

"He'd never still his tongue," Miss Swann said. "He's too weak, and he knows too many secrets. Mr. Millburn knows nothing, so he can give nothing away. The thieving will stop now, in any case, and we can go on."

Her priority wasn't the money, I realized. Mr. Kearny might want the riches for what they could buy him, but for Miss Swann, the only important thing was reputation—of her family and of the bank.

"Mr. Kearny is too high up in the hierarchy, isn't he?" I said in understanding. "If there are other irregularities, he'd talk about them to save his own skin. Such as how Daalman's sur-vived the panic of '73, when so many other investment and joint stock banks were going under. Were you here then, Miss Swann?"

"Of course I was. I have always been here. And yes, I did what I had to in order to save us. You would not understand it, so I will not explain to you."

I likely wouldn't understand at all—the chicanery banking institutions went through to keep afloat was beyond my com-prehension. But an investigation by financial experts would certainly reveal the fraud.

"Mr. Millburn was expendable," I went on. "Is that why you encouraged Mr. Zachary to hire him?"

Miss Swann made an almost imperceptible shrug. "He had a good mind. I thought he might be useful one day."

Her casual dismissal of Sam made my blood boil. "Please

do not speak of him in the past tense. Mr. Millburn still has a very good mind, and a good heart. When he began to bring what he'd found to Mr. Stockley, you grew worried. Mr. Stockley, whom you call an arrogant idiot, was likely honest enough to want the embezzler stopped and, yes, arrogant enough to think he could take matters into his own hands. You brought him up here to find out what he knew, then when you couldn't make him agree to shut up, you struck him down. Like you struck me." I rubbed my forehead again and laughed feebly. "I suppose I have a harder head than Mr. Stockley did."

"I did not mean to kill him, not then," Miss Swann said. "But you have the right of it. Mr. Stockley was more frail than I anticipated."

Her words, *not then*, chilled me. I suppose she meant she'd planned to kill him later, in a more secret place, and now had decided to do the same to me. I could only hope that Daniel, finishing the chase for Mr. Kearny, would return to find me.

"If you killed him, why did you then ask Mr. Kearny to help you unlock the door, knowing Mr. Stockley would be found?" I asked.

"I hadn't wanted that to happen either," Miss Swann answered. Her irritation at those who thwarted her plans was unnerving. "Mr. Stockley was missed, and Mr. Millburn so helpfully said he was on this floor, where the two of them had been meeting privately. I assumed Mr. Millburn knew all about me. So, instead of having Mr. Stockley transported to the river and disposed of, I decided Mr. Millburn should be taken for killing him. That way, his meddling would be finished, Mr. Kearny would obey me, and all would be well."

"All would be well for everyone except Mr. Stockley and Mr. Millburn," I corrected her. "What will you do about Mr. Kearny? He will be arrested today."

"No, he will not. I recruited help, in the form of a ruffian I'd seen wandering nearby—ironically, he was looking for Mr. Millburn. They are dangerous, these street men. Violent, even."

I went cold. She must mean Mr. Jarrett, who'd pretended to want to help Sam. I had to concede that Miss Swann seized opportunities well.

I regarded her with a complacency I hoped confused her. "I am only a cook, as I told you," I said. "But you have no idea what powerful friends I have. They are good friends, honest ones, and they don't give two straws about the fate of Daalman's Bank."

"They ought to. We control much of the wealth of this nation."

I recalled Mr. Monaghan warning Daniel away from deeply investigating the bank. "Perhaps you should look to see where all the wealth of this nation is actually going."

Miss Swann regarded me with narrowed eyes. She had no faith in my declarations, but I could see that some part of her wondered what I meant. I closed my mouth and tried to look wise.

Miss Swann firmed her lips and backed away, finished with the discussion.

I scrambled to my feet as she turned, trying to fling myself at her. But my head hurt, I was clumsy, and I stumbled. Miss Swann deftly let herself out the door before I could reach it, and she shut it in my face.

I grabbed for the handle. Too late. I heard one key turn in the lock, then another in the second lock. I banged on the door but got no reply but Miss Swann's footsteps as she marched away.

"I want to go to my daughter, you bloody woman." I hammered on the door until my hands hurt, then I turned my back to it and slid to the floor, my head aching so much I wanted to be sick.

"Panicking and raging will accomplish nothing," I told myself. "Daniel will come for me."

It might be a long time, however, before Daniel realized I was not with Grace or back home in Mount Street. He'd return to the last place he'd seen me, in the window of Daalman's, and he'd find me. Hopefully before Miss Swann returned with Mr. Jarrett to kill me and dump me in the river.

This would never do.

Miss Swann's mistake was underestimating people. She had a high sense of her own importance and a low sense of others'. Kindhearted Sam was dispensable. A cook was nothing more than a woman who sweated in a kitchen all day and only knew how to slap chops and potatoes onto a plate.

This cook had been a charwoman's daughter and had run through the streets of London fending for herself. She'd also had a husband she'd learned to hide things from, and she'd discovered how to survive.

"Shall I wait for Daniel to rescue me?" I asked the air in a quiet voice. "I think I shall not."

The sky had gone dark while Miss Swann lectured me, the winter afternoon over, but the gas lamp below the high window leaked some of its light upward. It was enough, once I'd sat still awhile and let my eyes adjust, to make out shapes in the darkness.

I climbed to my feet and felt my way about, finding row upon row of cabinets, storing who knew what records in their recesses. A person could read the history of Britain, I thought, going through these drawers.

The strong room was tidy, as I'd expected it to be. Miss Swann would never let a scrap of paper be out of place. The fact that Sam had smuggled out some of the records showed how resourceful he truly was.

I found open shelves and ran my hands along them, coming upon locked boxes that likely contained more papers. I reached up the shelves as far as I could, fearing to climb up on them. I was dizzy from the blow Miss Swann had dealt me, and I'd more than likely fall.

I'd worked my way around the room, beginning to despair of discovering anything but locked cabinets and boxes, when I happened upon a loose shelf. Its back corner tilted, one of the supports having worked itself loose.

My heart beating faster, I removed the few boxes from the shelf and pulled it all the way out. It was held in place not by wooden pegs or metal brackets, but by a thick wire fitted into a slot in the wood. The wire had worked free on one end, which had made the shelf rock.

Much tugging and twisting on my part freed the second end. I pulled out the wire with glee and only hoped it would not be too thick.

My mother would have been appalled if she'd realized one of my childhood friends had taught me to pick a lock, even more if she'd known it was Joanna. Neither Joanna nor I had much use for the skill these days, and I prayed that I remembered it.

The locks on this door could be turned with a key on either side. At first, I feared there'd be no keyhole on the inside, but this was a large room full of confidential papers. If someone needed to research, they might want to lock themselves in and not be disturbed. Of course, with their two-key system, a second person would have to let them in and out.

I bent the wire until it was pliable. I needed two tools for the locks, one for tension and the other for picking, but I'd have to make do.

I folded one end of the wire fairly tightly and slid the bent side into the bottom of the first keyhole. I fiddled a bit until I could feel the bolt move slightly. Trying not to become too optimistic, I held that steady and slid the other end of the wire into the hole with it.

Pushing the second half of the wire high into the lock, I wriggled it firmly but gently, wanting to move the bolt without breaking the wire or jamming the lock. The procedure is simple to explain, but sweat broke out on my forehead as I worked, despite the cool temperature of the room. Another reason I wanted to escape is I had no intention of succumbing to the cold in there.

The lock was very stiff, probably because it hadn't been used in a while, and the lock was old. It had been kept in working order, obviously, but not oiled very recently.

At long last, I felt the bolt lift high from its seating. Carefully, I moved my tension wire and, to my relief, heard and felt the bolt slide back.

Letting out a breath, I eased the wires from the keyhole and went to work on the next one.

The second was even stiffer than the first. I calculated that twenty frustrating minutes had passed before the bolt finally withdrew.

I folded up the wire and thrust it into my coat pocket before turning the door handle and cautiously and quietly opening the door a crack. The hall without was empty. No sounds came to me from downstairs, no voices, no footsteps.

The bank had closed, the employees gone home, I realized. That meant it was past six, the time I was due to be home myself.

Miss Swann had robbed me of my last hour with Grace, and that I would never forgive.

The hall was very dark as I left the strong room. I made my way carefully toward the stairs, my hand on the wall to guide me. I wondered if Miss Swann had remained behind or had gone back to Marylebone to be with her sister and grandmother, deciding to deal with me tomorrow. Or perhaps she waited in the lower rooms to admit Mr. Jarrett to kill me and rid her of my body.

The last thought poured fear through me. I halted, took a deep breath, and glided down the stairs, as silent as a ghost.

No one assailed me as I went, and no sound filtered through the building. Not even the rumble of traffic on Leadenhall Street, which would still be thick at this time of the evening, could be heard.

When I reached the first floor, I hesitated. I was almost free, but if I ran to the nearest police station or all the way to Scotland Yard to find Inspector McGregor, how could I prove that Miss Swann was responsible for what she'd done? Mr. Kearny would babble all if he were caught, but Miss Swann could easily contradict him.

I wondered if Miss Swann had her own office, or if she simply wandered about the building giving orders. I recalled that when Cynthia and I had sat in Mr. Zachary's chamber, Miss Swann and the maid had entered through a small door in the back wall. I'd assumed it led to a servants' staircase, but now I decided the door was worth investigating.

After a long listen, I hastened down the hall toward the front of the building, trying to make my footsteps as quiet as possible. The hall seemed to have grown longer, and it was certainly spookier in the near darkness.

But it had an empty feeling, as did the rooms I'd passed. Miss Swann must have departed as usual, in order to not draw attention to herself. I did not even hear the doorman, though they must employ a night watchman of some sort. I decided that if I encountered a watchman, I'd simply tell him I'd been locked inside the building and convey relief that he'd found me.

No one moved in this corridor—on this entire floor—but me. I reached Mr. Zachary's office, which I found unlocked. I entered very, very quietly, half expecting Miss Swann to be standing behind the door with another vase.

The office too was empty. It was a showpiece, I realized, furnished to impress the investors who came to see how their money was doing. Mr. Zachary, and Miss Swann with the tea trolley, were poised to give them a show, ensuring their visitors of the bank's efficiency and exclusiveness.

The door behind Mr. Zachary's desk was locked. I sank to my knees and used my wire to open it. This lock was much easier, as it was a small, standard lock, not the more solid ones of the strong room. I had it open in less than a minute.

It was too dark to see what the chamber within contained. I found a desk by bumping into it, then groped over its contents until my hands closed around a matchbox. This building had gaslights, I recalled, and a small room would have a sconce. I located this by feeling my way around the wall and encountered one above the desk.

Taking a chance no one would see this light, I struck a match. My hands shook so that it took several tries, but by the match's light, I turned up the gas and lit the sconce.

The dim glow showed me a small, windowless office. The trolley that had borne tea for Lady Cynthia and me had been shoved against the back wall, a narrow door next to it likely the one leading to the back stairs. The maid would carry the tea up, put it on the trolley, and wheel it out as she had for our visit.

The desk was small, an elegant lady's desk, and beside it was a bookcase that held books and boxes for papers like the ones Sam had used. The desk's single drawer was locked, but the key was in the keyhole. Presumably, Miss Swann did not believe anyone would violate the sanctity of this room nor ever dream of opening her desk.

I unlocked the drawer and went through its contents and soon came upon a ring containing many keys. I simply looked at them without lifting them, but several resembled the key Mr. Kearny had shown Joanna and me that he said opened the strong room door. There were too many here for Miss Swann to carry without her pockets clanking, but I assumed she took what she needed when she needed them, and left the rest behind.

I also found, shoved all the way into the back, a paperweight that glimmered in the lamplight. A smear of something black marred one side.

Letting out a breath, I closed and locked the drawer, sliding its key into my pocket.

I turned out the lamp and left the room, then took the time to pick the lock closed. I wanted no one in here but Miss Swann and the police.

I hurried across the muffling carpet of Mr. Zachary's office and out into the hall. It was then that I heard the footsteps on the stairs, ascending toward me.

They were bootsteps, hard and hobnailed. They did not move with the deliberate pace of a watchman checking every corner, but with determination, up and up. With them came the sharp click-click of a woman's heels.

I shrank back into the shadows beside the door. The two people reached the first-floor landing, then they continued on up the stairs, heading for a higher floor. A man's voice rumbled down.

"Just give me the keys, missus, and wait outside."

"Of course I am not going to give you the keys," Miss Swann answered. "You finish your business and then I will lock up after you again . . ."

Her matter-of-factness chilled me most of all. Miss Swann was prepared to let Mr. Jarrett—I'd recognized his voice—kill me in cold blood and carry me off, upon which she'd lock the doors as though nothing had happened. After all, she could not let Jarrett possibly steal old records from the strong room.

Once they'd reached the upper floors, I dashed down the hall as quickly and quietly as I could and started down the stairs.

Not quietly enough. The footsteps halted, and Jarrett let out a curse. Then he charged after me.

He moved fast. I ran recklessly downward, barely reaching the ground floor before he was on the landing above me. I sprinted for the front door, praying that it hadn't been locked, the key gone from the keyhole. I'd never have time to pick it open.

The door had been bolted. Presumably, Mr. Jarrett had done that, or Miss Swann, making certain their prey did not escape.

There was a lock as well, but a key glistened in it. I wrestled with both bolt and key as Jarrett barreled down the hall at me. Once he caught me, I had no doubt he'd simply break my neck.

The bolt squealed backward. The moment I turned the key in the lock, Jarrett's hand landed on my shoulder. I spun around and kicked him, hard, and as I expected, he closed his other hand around my throat.

At the same time, the door behind me burst inward. Jarrett grunted, his hold slipping. I wrenched myself from him and hurled myself out of the building, straight into the arms of Daniel McAdam.

Streaming around him were police constables in blue uniforms, and behind them came Inspector McGregor.

I staggered from Daniel, who was trying to hold me upright, reached into my pocket, and thrust the desk key at Inspector McGregor.

"That opens a drawer in Miss Swann's office behind Mr. Zachary's on the first floor," I babbled. "You'll find the paperweight she used to kill Mr. Stockley, along with evidence she could access any room in this building."

Inspector McGregor stared at the key and from it to me. Then his scowl settled in place, and he snatched up the key and dashed into the building, bellowing orders to his sergeant.

"Kat." Daniel's voice sounded far away. "Kat, love. Bloody hell, what did he do to you?"

"Catch her," I told Daniel. "She'll know all the ways out. There are some back stairs that should come out in about the middle of each hall. Probably go all the way down to the coal cellar."

Daniel wanted to stand here and hold me—and probably question me about my discovery of Miss Swann as the killer—but he understood what I meant. If Miss Swann escaped the police tonight, she'd find every way to prove she hadn't done any of the things I'd accused her of, including locking me in the strong room and fetching Mr. Jarrett to kill me.

Daniel gently handed me to someone else—it was James, my blurred vision saw—and started inside.

"Please thump Mr. Jarrett for me," I said, my voice waning. "He gave me such a fright."

Daniel sent me a grim smile and ran in, calling to Inspector McGregor.

My legs gave way, and I found myself sitting on the step

under the demure plaque that read *Daalman's*, James cradling me.

"You're all right, Mrs. H." His voice had deepened, and he sounded so much like Daniel, I wanted to cry. "It's all right. We've got you."

25

My hopes that Sam would be set free instantly did not come to fruition. While the constables had dragged off Mr. Jarrett to the nearest nick, and Daniel and Inspector McGregor had stopped Miss Swann as she very coolly exited through the cellar door and climbed the stairs to the small passage behind the bank, both had to be charged, and a judge had to decide that the case against Sam was to be dismissed.

I was not to know all this until the next morning, however, because after I'd collapsed on the steps of Daalman's, I lost all coherence.

James, the dear boy, got me into Lewis's cab, and Lewis knew exactly where to take me. Both Lewis and James half carried me down Clover Lane, me by turns thanking them and insisting I'd be perfectly fine walking on my own, and into Joanna's house.

I'd had no idea how bruised and battered I was until I

glimpsed myself in the small mirror on the hall tree and cried out in dismay. The left half of my face was purple and red, and a gash opened above my eyebrow. My hat had been torn, and its brim drooped over my right ear. Blood had seeped from the cut to stain my lips and chin, down into the collar of my frock. With my hair frazzled from the wind and my flight, I looked as though I'd been caught in a very bad hailstorm.

As I dazedly touched my face and hair, Joanna descended upon me, exclaiming her concern. Then Grace was there, and I couldn't see anything else.

They put me to bed, Joanna and Grace fussing over me, the other children falling over themselves to bring me tea and cakes, or to change the water from the washbasin while Joanna doctored my wounds.

Grace stayed by my side, holding my hand and looking very worried. I tried to say something about James and Lewis, but Joanna shushed me, assuring me they'd been given a large meal and tea in the kitchen before they'd both departed.

I croaked out the story to Joanna, whose eyes widened at the tale. I hadn't wanted Grace to hear the more frightening parts, but for some reason I couldn't seem to release her hand. Grace hugged me hard when I got to the part about Mr. Jarrett assaulting me, and she called Mr. Jarrett a very bad name I wasn't aware she knew.

After that I slept hard. A voice in the back of my mind told me I should be getting on with preparing supper, but my fright and exhaustion overcame me, and I fell into a profound sleep.

I woke in the morning sore and aching, my mouth parched. Joanna brought me breakfast on a tray as though I were a great lady.

I wedged myself up against the pillows, then groaned as I realized what waking in Joanna's bed meant.

"I'll be sacked," I said mournfully. "My agency will not like that. I'll have to scrub floors for the rest of my life."

"Nonsense." Joanna sounded more her usual self, though I saw uncertainty about Sam in her eyes. "I sent word to your Lady Cynthia that you'd been injured. She returned a note that said you were on no account to be moved, and she'd settle things with her aunt."

Some relief washed over me, but I'd not be easy until I was back in my kitchen. Tess could not handle so much on her own for too long.

Joanna curled her hands in her lap as her tears threatened to fall. "Kat, what you have done for me. Oh, my dear, you might have been killed."

"I am made of stern stuff," I reminded her. "And you helped too. If you'd not taught me to pick locks when we were seven years of age, I'd have been for it."

Joanna tried to laugh. "I taught you, but you were always better at it than I was."

"Don't tell my mum." I echoed the words I'd given to her when we'd been children.

Joanna's smile was shaky. "My friend, what would I do without you?"

"What would I do without *you*?" I countered. "You and Sam have given me a wonderful gift, looking after Grace for me. There's nothing I wouldn't do for you." I clasped Joanna's hands. "We will bring him home, Joanna. I promise you."

I made myself enjoy being looked after for the morning, but later that day, I insisted on rising and going home. Grace did not want me to, and I did not want to be parted from her, but I knew I had no choice. I hugged her and promised her a fine outing on Thursday. Grace bravely nodded, trying to conceal her unhappiness.

I expected I'd walk home, or perhaps Lewis would be lingering in his cab, but the carriage I found waiting for me in Cheapside belonged to Miss Townsend. It was driven by her coachman, Dunstan, and waiting next to it was Daniel.

He assisted me inside, and we rolled away, snug on the seat together, just the two of us. Presumably Miss Townsend had lent Daniel the coach, but I was too tired to ask why.

Daniel told me then that Miss Swann and Mr. Jarrett had both been arrested, a magistrate already making short work of Jarrett. He was on his way to Newgate, but by Daniel's intervention, would not be housed in the same room as Sam.

Miss Swann had immediately consulted a wily solicitor who was even now concocting reasons she should not be detained or charged.

"The Daalman family no doubt will come to her rescue," I said, tasting bitterness.

"Or turn their backs on her," Daniel countered. "They are as adamant about the bank's good name as she is. Time will tell."

I sank into his embrace, at this moment having no reluctance to show him how grateful I was for his presence in my life.

"By the way," Daniel said after he'd kissed my lips, being careful of my bruises. "I did thump Jarrett. Thumped him hard. Mr. Grimes helped."

"Good," I said, and leaned into him once more.

A t home, Tess exclaimed over my bruises, and Lady Cynthia tried to tell me to go to bed and stay there.

"I am perfectly all right after my rest," I assured her. "Sore, but no longer frail. I'd rather cook, if you don't mind, instead of lying in bed fretting."

Cynthia, who also preferred action to idleness, understood.

When I praised Tess for keeping things running as well as she had, Tess threw her arms around me in an impulsive hug.

"As long as you don't leave me on me own too long again," she said. "I was that scared you weren't coming back, Mrs. H. When Lady Cynthia said you were hurt, I imagined all sorts."

Mrs. Bywater entered the kitchen with her decided stride at that moment, and Tess abruptly released me. She wiped her eyes before she went back to chopping herbs for my white wine sauce.

Mrs. Bywater was followed by Mr. Davis, who, to my surprise, set a small valise near the coatrack at the back door.

Mrs. Bywater studied my battered face before letting out a *hmph*. "You don't look as injured as Cynthia led me to believe. But accidents are what comes of having days out. You'd be much safer if you stayed at home."

I was not going to resume the ongoing argument about my days out with Mrs. Bywater at the moment. "It ended well, Mrs. Bywater. I will serve a syllabub for the sweet tonight, if you approve."

Mrs. Bywater loved syllabub, probably because it contained a large quantity of sherry. She softened a modicum.

"That will do nicely, Mrs. Holloway. I have come to tell you that you and Mrs. Redfern will have to assume some of Mr. Davis's duties, because he has decided to take *three* days out, at the same time." Her tone registered displeasure at this extravagance.

Mr. Davis avoided my gaze as he addressed Mrs. Bywater at

his haughty best. "My train does not depart until well after service tonight, madam. I will be at table, as usual, and leave Mrs. Holloway thorough instructions as to the wines to be served while I am absent."

Mrs. Bywater sniffed, unappeased by his assurances. "See that you do," she said, and then swept from the room.

"Where are you going, Mr. Davis?" Tess asked with her disarming frankness.

"Bury St. Edmunds," Mr. Davis replied. He finally looked at me directly. "To a funeral."

"Oh, hard luck." Tess sent him a sympathetic glance, then dropped her focus again to the herbs. "Well, most funerals feed you well afterward."

Mr. Davis raised his brows, but I sent him an understanding smile. "My condolences, Mr. Davis."

Mr. Davis continued to regard me steadily, then he gave me a nod. "Thank you, Mrs. Holloway."

S am was not released until the following Monday. That he gained his freedom at all was in large part due to Sir Rupert Shepherd arguing long and hard with the judge assigned to Sam's trial that there was too much doubt about his case to continue. Another suspect for the murder had been arrested, and a witness—Mr. Kearny—was insisting that this suspect had been threatening him and was sure to have killed Mr. Stockley.

Though Miss Swann was fighting valiantly to keep from being tried, we heard from Sir Rupert, via Miss Townsend and Cynthia, that as Daniel had speculated, the Daalman family had decided to turn against her. The reputation of the bank was more important to them than a family tie. They blamed the whole of the troubles on her and Mr. Kearny, and then worked to suppress the scandal.

I couldn't help but feel sorry for Miss Swann's sister and elderly relation, dependent on her wages, but as they were also part of the Daalman family and hopefully innocent of Miss Swann's misdeeds, perhaps they'd be looked after. I would make certain to inquire about them.

Sir Rupert at last won his point. The judge relented and signed the order that released Samuel Millburn and exonerated him of the crimes he'd been accused of.

I stood with Joanna and family in the street outside the blank wall of Newgate Monday afternoon, waiting for a side gate to open and discharge any prisoners set free that day. Other families waited as well—wives, children, husbands, mothers—huddling together or rubbing their hands against the cold.

I'd thought Joanna would want to meet Sam alone, but she insisted we accompany her. A large party, she'd said, to parade Sam triumphantly home. Daniel had arrived at Joanna's to let her know the time of his release and to escort us to Newgate himself.

When the gate opened, excitement stirred. The first man out was not Sam. A middle-aged gent blinked at the glare, then ran to the woman I assumed was his wife and threw his arms around her. The couple embraced joyously, then stumbled away down the street, entwined in each other.

My gaze lingered on them hurrying off so happily, until I heard Joanna's sob.

Turning, I saw Sam had emerged. He paused to shrug his coat higher on his shoulders, his form a bit thinner than it had been before his arrest. Joanna had her fingers to her lips, her eyes alight with joy.

Sam glanced about at the other prisoners reuniting with their families as though worried no one had come to greet him. Joanna, unable to remain still, dashed to him across the slick street, her skirts flying.

Mark leapt into the air, shouting, "Dad!" the girls jumping with him. Even Matthew, calmer than the others, bounced on his toes, ready to run to his father.

Grace put herself in front of them. "Wait. Let Aunt Joanna be first."

As the four children quieted down, my pride rose in my girl, who understood things with wisdom beyond her years.

Sam spied Joanna running to him and stilled, as though not believing it was truly her. A moment later, he caught Joanna in his arms and hauled her tightly against him.

They remained like that for a long time, the pair locked in an embrace, unmoving except to sway a little. The hug went on and on until passersby, including grim-countenanced laboring men, stopped to watch, their faces softening at the loving reunion.

I wiped my eyes. "Goodness, this wind is sharp," I murmured.

Grace smiled at me, not fooled, her own eyes wet. Daniel coughed, leaning closer to me.

At long last, Joanna and Sam parted. Sam spied his children, fell to one knee, and opened his arms.

As one, they rushed to him, tumbling over one another to find their father's embrace. Grace quivered next to me, until I sent her after them as well. Sam scooped her in as heartily as he had his own brood, Joanna's broad smile warming my heart.

The children helped Sam to his feet, pulling him toward Daniel and me, Sam laughing, his eyes alight with happiness.

Sam shook Daniel's hand and embraced me, then he wound

his arm around Joanna, took his youngest daughter by the hand, and announced they were going home. Joanna turned to us as they started off.

"Thank you," she said to me, then to Daniel. "Thank you, my dearest friends."

She swung around again to let her husband lead her away, their children scampering alongside them.

Grace's hand slipped into mine, and I impulsively leaned down and kissed her.

"It is good to see him again," Grace said wholeheartedly.

"It is," Daniel agreed, his eyes suspiciously moist. "Does me good to know that Sam has his family again."

I squeezed Grace's hand and wound my arm through Daniel's. "As I have mine," I said quietly.

Daniel started, but he quickly pulled me to his side and bathed me in his smile as we followed in the Millburns' wake.

The winter wind held new iciness as we strolled along, but I was warm as could be, surrounded by the ones I loved.

Photo by Silvio Portrait Design

Jennifer Ashley is the *New York Times* bestselling author of more than one hundred novels and novellas in mystery, romance, and historical fiction. Jennifer's books have been translated into more than a dozen languages and have earned starred reviews in *Publishers Weekly* and *Booklist*. When she is not writing, Jennifer enjoys playing music (guitar, piano, flute), reading, hiking, knitting, gardening, and building dollhouse miniatures.